WINDY CITY SERIES

REWIND
it BACK

WINDY CITY SERIES

REWIND *it* BACK

LIZ TOMFORDE

Entangled Publishing, LLC
644 Shrewsbury Commons Ave., STE 181
Shrewsbury, PA 17361
rights@entangledpublishing.com

Amara is an imprint of Entangled Publishing, LLC.

Visit our website at www.entangledpublishing.com.

Edited by Erica Russikoff
Cover and edge design by LJ Anderson
Cover images by benedek/Gettyimages, Africa Studio/Shutterstock
Interior design by Britt Marczak

Deluxe ISBN 978-1-64937-922-1
Standard ISBN 978-1-64937-923-8

Printed by GV Group

First Edition May 2025

10 9 8 7 6 5 4 3 2 1

ALSO BY LIZ TOMFORDE

Here's to the 10 characters, 5 couples, 3 teams, 2 sets of siblings, and 1 amazing friend group that changed my life.

This one is dedicated to you, the readers.
Thank you for hanging out in Chicago with me.

Scan QR code for Content Warnings

Playlist

Are You Even Real - Teddy Swims & GIVĒON ♥ 2:27
Nights Like This - Kehlani feat. Ty Dolla $ign ♥ 3:21
Asking For Too Much - Aaron Page feat. Tone Stith ♥ 2:56
My Boo - Alicia Keys & USHER ♥ 3:43
Hate That I Love You - Rihanna feat. Ne-Yo ♥ 3:38
Second Chances. - Kiana Ledé feat. 6LACK ♥ 3:12
Hold On - H.E.R. ♥ 3:23
Change - Arin Ray & Kehlani ♥ 3:12
hillside - Gabriel Jacoby ♥ 2:52
Nobody Gets Me - SZA ♥ 3:00
Reason - Blxst ♥ 2:59
A New Thing - Madison Ryann Ward ♥ 3:37
Favorite Girl - Marques Houston ♥ 3:33
One Of These - Ella Mai ♥ 3:44
Anyone - Justin Bieber ♥ 3:10
ICU - Coco Jones ♥ 4:01
Brown Eyed Lover - Allen Stone ♥ 3:57
BIRDS OF A FEATHER - Billie Eilish ♥ 3:30
Run Through Fire - Pink Sweat$ ♥ 3:04
Easy (Unplugged) - DaniLeigh ♥ 3:59
This Is - Ella Mai ♥ 3:26
4 Ever - Lil' Mo feat. Fabolous ♥ 3:42

Rio

"I prefer an emerald cut."

With my fork and knife in hand, I slice my steak. "I don't know. This porterhouse cut is cooked to perfection."

"Diamonds, Rio." Chelsea's tone holds no patience. "Not meat."

No shit, she's referring to diamonds, but I'm trying my best to play dumb because preferred ring style is the last thing I want to talk about on a second date. I'd like to know if she's a kind person. If she and her mom are close. If she enjoys traveling. Shit, I don't even know if she has any allergies.

"I'm lactose intolerant."

Her face morphs into confusion at my sudden change in subject. "What?"

"Dairy." I take another bite of my steak. "It fucks me right up. Sometimes I take a pill beforehand and sometimes I just raw-dog it and deal with the consequences."

"Did you just say you raw-dog it when referring to your dairy intake?"

"Yeah. If there's ice cream and I don't have a pill on me, I'm not going to *not* eat it, you know? Are you one of the lucky ones with a stomach that can handle dairy?"

"I was asking what kind of rings the wives from the team have." She swerves the conversation right back to where I don't want it to be, but I keep eating and refuse to answer. "Do any of them have to work?" she tries instead. "Probably not."

"Some of them work, yeah. One of my closest friends is married to my teammate and she works for a senior dog rescue."

Chelsea's nose scrunches up before she schools it and forces a smile back on her face. "Well, that's nice. I guess."

"What do you do for work?"

A quick moment of worry passes through me that maybe she's already told me before and I'd forgotten.

We had gone to dinner shortly before I left for the summer, but it had been so long ago, I couldn't remember anything bad about the date. So when she asked if I was interested in going out again, I figured why not give it another go?

Well, it wasn't exactly an ask. The text read, *"When are you taking me out again? I'm free on Friday."* But same thing, I suppose.

"I create content," she answers without missing a beat. "Influencer-type stuff. Mostly fashion and lifestyle."

"Very cool. So you work for yourself. Do you like it?"

She shrugs before polishing off her glass of chardonnay and waving it in the air to silently ask our server for another one, lifted brow and expectant stare included.

Don't like that, I think to myself.

Maybe she doesn't realize it's rude, I try to justify.

"I like the perks of it," she continues. "I make my own schedule. I'm given free products. That kind of thing."

I almost expect her to ask what I do for work, but she knew before we ever went on our first date.

"Do you have any pets?" I ask.

"No. Too much responsibility."

"Are you close with your family?"

"Not particularly."

Are you close with your family, Rio? Why yes, I am. I just got back from three months in Boston, spending quality time with my ma during the off-season. Thank you so much for asking.

Her chardonnay is set on the table before our server clears our now empty plates and I'm that much closer to this being over.

I scold myself for feeling that way.

For *always* feeling that way.

I can't remember the last time I even made it to a second date, so I should focus on that small victory I suppose. But this is what tends to happen. I'm eager to meet someone, desperate, you could say. We go on a first date, I don't feel that spark, and that's where the connection dies.

Try harder.

"What do you do for fun?" I continue.

"I'm almost always out with my friends. I get invited to a lot of events, so that keeps me busy. I enjoy working out. I like trying new restaurants—"

"I love trying new restaurants!" I sit up, way too stoked about finally finding some common ground.

Chelsea eyes me, thoroughly unimpressed by my excitement. "Cool."

Shit.

"Do you like music?" I try again.

"Doesn't everyone?"

"We should pick a song." Pulling out my phone, I begin to scroll through my music library.

"Pick a song?"

"Yeah, you know, since it's our second date. We should pick a song to remember it by. That way, when we hear it, it'll remind us…" My words die when I see her face.

Her eyes go wide, practically screaming how fucking weird she finds me, and when she opens her mouth to respond, it quickly closes without anything to say.

Because she's not *her*. No one else has been.

"Or not," I decide.

3

That forced smile is back. "Let's not."

Chelsea looks around the restaurant, for the exit I would presume, and I don't blame her.

"Do you want to get dessert?" I ask.

It takes a moment for her to decide until eventually she surprises me by leaning over the table and slipping her hand over mine. "Actually." Her tone has gone all soft. "I was thinking we could do dessert back at your place."

Oh.

That is...not what I was expecting.

"I just got back today from spending the summer in Boston, so unfortunately, I don't have any groceries right now."

She smirks seductively. "That's not the dessert I'm referring to."

Yeah, it's perfectly clear that's not the dessert she's referring to, but I was hoping for a "he's fucking clueless and has no game, so never mind" kind of outcome.

But it's once again one of those situations where it doesn't matter if I say all the wrong things, or hell, if I don't say anything at all. At the end of the day, I'm a professional hockey player and that alone gets me more first dates and overnight invites than I let anyone know about.

But I know what I'm looking for and this connection isn't it.

"Chelsea, I'm—"

"It'll be fun."

I chuckle. "Chelsea."

"You're really going to say no?" She smiles knowingly. "Rio."

She says "Rio" in a tone that may as well mean "you're out of your goddamn mind to turn me down," and I've gotten that tone from more women than I'd like to admit.

There's no denying she's a beautiful girl, and if I were the type to bring someone home without seeing a future, maybe I would.

But I'm not.

I discreetly pay the bill when it's set on the table before saying,

"Thank you for coming to dinner tonight."

It's then she realizes I'm serious about this date ending here. Her eyes slightly roll, but I don't let that change my mind, and when she pulls out her phone, she types away at the screen without answering me.

"Should we get going?"

She doesn't look up from her phone. "No need. I'm going to meet up with friends at a party around the corner."

"Oh, okay. I picked you up, so I thought the least I could do would be to—"

Her smile turns pitying as she stands and slips her arms through her coat. "I made backup plans but have a good night alone, Rio. Thanks for dinner." She waggles her fingers in a careless wave before slipping out of the exit she was eyeing earlier and leaving me alone.

Maybe I should feel shocked or offended, but it's not the first time I've been left at a table by myself after deciding not to continue the night back at my place, and I'm sure it won't be the last.

But fuck it, this glass of red wine I've been nursing all night is delicious and I'm not embarrassed enough to let it go to waste. So instead, I sit back in my chair at my solo table and enjoy it while fishing out my phone, only to find it flooded with texts.

Zanders: *Rio, did you make it back?*

Indy: *Please say yes! I miss you!*

Stevie: *Taylor asked where Uncle Rio was every Sunday dinner this summer. It was very sad. You should never leave again.*

Kai: *Welcome back, man!*

Miller: *Girls' nights were not the same without you!*

Kennedy: *Is this the first Sunday dinner we're all going to be at since May? Looking forward to seeing everyone.*

Isaiah: *But is Rio back? He's not answering.*

Zanders: *He better be back. We have our first practice of the season tomorrow.*

Me: *I will not answer until every single person has asked about my well-being and I'm waiting on one...*

Zanders: **laughing emoji**

Kai: *Some things never change.*

Indy: *Baby, that's your cue.*

Ryan: *I'm not doing this.*

Miller: *He could be hurt or lost or stranded without food and water and we would never know because you won't ask a simple question, Ryan.*

Isaiah: *I didn't know the group adopted a puppy.*

Stevie: *He's* our *puppy.*

Kennedy: *Our sweet little puppy that just wants to know if Ryan cares about him.*

Me: *...*

Ryan: *Fine. Rio, you back or what?*

Me: *Your care and concern for me hold no bounds. Honey, I'm home!*

Ryan: *I hate this.*

Me: *I know. The distance was hard for me too, Ryan.*

Ryan: *I'm leaving this group chat.*

He does for only a split second before his wife adds him back.

Indy: *See you all at our place on Sunday!*

Regret churns in my gut that one of their houses wasn't my first stop when I got back to town. Instead, I was home only long enough to drop my bags before picking Chelsea up for our date.

Part of me thinks I should stop trying. I've looked nonstop for years, ever since I moved to Chicago, and I'm starting to believe the real thing doesn't exist anymore.

Then there's the reminder that I got to watch eight of my friends find it over the years, so I know, firsthand, that it's still out there.

I finish off my glass of wine before texting Indy separately.

Me: *I'm stopping by on my way home.*

Indy: *Yes, please! Missed you. Don't leave home for so long again.*

"I take it the date didn't go well?" Indy surmises as we sit on her couch in the living room.

Ryan comes back from checking on their sleeping two-year-olds before joining us for my debrief.

"Do they ever?" I ask in return.

"Where did you take her?"

"Sullivan's on Eighth."

Ryan stiffens in his seat and a playful smile tilts on Indy's mouth. "Oh, I love that place. I've been there on a da—"

"Watch it, Blue," he says gruffly, pulling her onto his lap.

They grin at each other as if they're sharing a secret and maybe I'd find the whole thing a little too sickeningly sweet if I didn't want it so badly.

But also, there really is no secret. We're all aware that before the two of them were together, Ryan pulled Indy out of a date from the same restaurant I was at tonight.

Indy was a flight attendant for my hockey team years ago and she's been my best friend since. She met her now-husband when Ryan's sister offered Indy his spare room to live in, and the rest is history. Ryan is the captain of Chicago's basketball team and even though I've been a massive fan of his for years, he's also become a good friend of mine.

"What was the issue?" Indy asks me.

"She…" I hesitate. "Wasn't into it. Not interested. You know me. I either friend zone myself or scare them away."

Not a complete lie. She wasn't interested in what I'm looking for.

But I don't fill my friends in on how often I *don't* scare them away. I don't tell them just how often I try to friend zone myself and that doesn't work. I let them believe that I'm some hopeless idiot with absolutely no game because that seems easier to explain than the fact that I'm twenty-seven years old and have never once hooked up with someone that I didn't have a deep connection with.

I'm a slow burner. Always have been. Shit, I didn't lose my virginity until I was nineteen and even then, it was to a girl who I had known since I was twelve.

"Sorry, man," Ryan says. "It'll happen."

"Yeah, maybe." I stand and stretch. "Well, I'm heading out. Just wanted to pop in and say hi. Love you guys."

"Love you, Rio."

"Did you hear that, Ryan?" I ask from the front door. "Did you hear how easily she said that?"

He shakes his head at me. "Never going to happen."

"Never say never, Shay!"

It's late by the time I pull into my driveway, but my neighbor's new front yard lights illuminate the house next door plenty for me to see it's not the same house I lived next to three months ago.

"Has your house always looked that much better than mine?" I ask, getting out of my car.

Wren laughs from her mailbox, looking over her shoulder at her place. "No. I spent the summer having it renovated, but for a poor grad student, I do have a much prettier house than the pro hockey player living next door, don't you think?"

We meet on the sidewalk, halfway between our houses, and I bend to give her a hug.

"Good summer?" I ask.

"As good as I could've asked for my last summer before graduation to be, which means I lived in a classroom, never saw the sun, and spent my weekends studying in a construction zone. Yours?"

"It was good. Nice to spend some time with my family. Nice to spend a few months in Boston, too."

She gets a knowing look on her face. "How much are you

hating the idea of leaving another Northeastern fall behind?"

"Let's not talk about it."

She gestures to my house. "I left your mail on the kitchen island. Opened the windows a couple of times a week to keep it from getting stuffy inside. Your one and only plant is thriving, so you're welcome for that."

"It's a succulent, Wren. All you have to do is leave it alone."

She nods approvingly, clearly proud of herself. "Well, I did a great job of that."

Wren has been my neighbor for years. Her brother bought the house directly next to mine so she had a place to live while in school, and we've been good friends since.

"Good friends" as in we talk shit about our other neighbors over a beer every once in a while, or offer a cup of sugar if the other is out. Or in this case, we look after the other's property if one of us is traveling out of town.

Her brothers are professional athletes, so she's never once batted an eye at me or my teammates who come over, and I always liked that about her.

We're the only two who live alone on the street, all the other homes filled with families. Which makes a lot of sense, seeing as all the houses are massive and sporting four or five bedrooms. There's a university nearby, so a few houses rent rooms to graduate students, but they're so busy studying I never see them.

Wren's older brother, Cruz Wilder, is a big-name basketball player who bought the place next to mine so his sister could live rent-free during school. They always had a plan that they would customize the builder-grade house and sell it for a profit when she graduated. He calls it an investment, but I've met Cruz. He simply didn't want his sister stressing about finding a good living situation while in school.

I also like to tell myself I too was making an investment when I purchased this new-construction home at twenty-one years old and not because I was a fucking idiot. My rookie year, not a single guy on the team lived outside of the city. They all had apartments. Some of the guys with smaller contracts roomed together, but they were a quick drive, walk, or rideshare to the arena.

But my dumbass thought it was a great idea to buy a four-bedroom house twenty minutes outside of town. As if I thought I would be settling down with a family and not a still single twenty-seven-year-old all these years later.

At least I have a bit of space, a nice yard with a hot tub, and I will say, my house has become the go-to place for the team to hang, mostly because it actually fits everyone.

And who knows? Maybe my *investment* will end up paying off next year.

I point to Wren's house again. "So, you redecorated? Like you got the walls painted?"

"Something like that. You want to see?" She checks the time on her phone. "I have exactly five minutes left on my study break."

"We'll make it a quick tour." I follow behind her. "Next time you have a study break, dinner is on me. I'll get takeout from that Greek place you like, and you can fill me in on all the neighborhood gossip I missed out on."

Over her shoulder, she lifts a brow.

"The next two times?" I try again.

"I did watch your house for three months and you're filthy rich."

"Fine. Three nights of takeout and I'll take your trash out to the curb every week for the next month."

"And this is why you're my favorite neighbor."

That's all we've ever been to one another—platonic neighbors. Don't get me wrong, Wren is great, but I've never looked at her as more than a friend, and I know she feels the same way about me. I have a lot of friends who are women and she's one of them.

She opens the front door—the freshly painted front door. It's a deep brown that contrasts nicely against the new sage-green siding and crisp white trim.

Her flooring is the first thing I see. Brand-new hardwood in a light but warm shade. Accented walls, some covered in modern wallpaper, others painted in subtle yet inviting colors. Her stairs sport a new banister, the kitchen cabinets got a fresh coat of paint, and the countertops have been upgraded to something that feels a bit more custom. Even her light fixtures are shiny and new and seem to pull the whole space together.

"Jesus," I exhale, spinning in a slow circle and taking it all in. "I hardly recognize the place."

"She did an incredible job."

"And who is *she*?"

Typically, I ask my friends that question in a way that silently adds: *Is she single? Is she nice? Would she be interested in someone like me?*

But right now, I'm more so wondering who the hell turned this plain house into a magazine-worthy home and if she's available to do the same to mine.

It's a far cry from the builder-grade box Wren's brother originally bought, and if I end up putting my place up for sale at the same time as him next summer, I'm going to be fucked. No one is going to take a second glance at my house when his looks like this.

Wren gives me a tour of the second story. The loft is now configured to be a game room or a potential playroom, depending on the buyer. The upstairs bedrooms all have their own unique designs that breathe that same luxury and custom feel as the rest of the house.

But as she walks me down the hallway, I stop when I find a bed in one of her spare rooms. The upstairs rooms have always been empty, unlike the guest room downstairs where her brothers crash when they're in town.

I point to the bare mattress sitting on a bed frame. "Are you getting a roommate or something, Wilder?"

"Actually, I am. Once her current lease is up in October."

That's surprising to hear because for years now it's been the two of us living alone in our stupidly big houses. Though, the reasons for our empty homes could not be more different.

Wren studies too much and never wanted roommates, and her brother is loaded enough to make that happen for her. While I'm the sad fucking sap that was waiting for someone who never came along.

"Why?" is all I can think to ask.

"Why am I now getting a roommate? Because she needed an affordable place to live, and we get along well. She's actually the lead designer on the house. She was here every day this summer and we became friends. Plus, she works all the time and will only really be here to sleep." She nods down the hallway. "Come on. I'll show you the rest."

The bathrooms are redone with fresh tile and modern fixtures. There are fancy picture lights hanging over framed photos along the hall. Even the fucking laundry room is cool and dark and moody.

"Well, I'm screwed," I state plainly. "My place is never going to sell when it's competing against this."

"Cruz wasn't messing around when he said he wanted a return on his investment." She swats me on the shoulder. "You could do the exact same thing, you know. Hire a designer. Upgrade that hockey frat house of yours if you're serious about selling."

Am I serious about selling? I'm not sure yet, but I didn't sign my early contract extension with the Raptors last season for a reason. I wasn't sure I was ready to sign six more years of my life away from Boston. Away from my hometown. Away from my family.

This is probably the last big contract of my career and I'm at a crossroads that I need to decide if I want to spend the entirety of my hockey years playing for Chicago or if I want to try to test free agency and fulfill my childhood dream of playing for the Boston Bobcats.

My mom sure as fuck wants me back home and if it were up to her, I'd be selling my house and moving the day this season and my current contract ends.

Wren is my only friend who knows about the possibility of me selling because as soon as she graduates in the spring, she's doing the same damn thing. Moving home to be close to family.

"How'd you find her?" I ask. "The designer, I mean."

"Have you ever heard of Tyler Braden? He's a famous interior designer. Local to Chicago."

I shoot her a deadpan glare.

"Well, I don't know. He's got a line in Target and his own show on HGTV. You have a mother and about a thousand friends who are women. I thought maybe you have."

"That's who you hired? Cruz threw down that much cash for a flip?"

"Well, I wanted to because I'm obsessed with Tyler Braden and that would be a dream, but the budget my brother gave me was definitely *not* a Tyler Braden budget. However, it was enough for me to hire one of his interns and as it turns out, she's amazing at her job and now my new friend who I will absolutely bribe into taking me to the Tyler Braden Interiors holiday party this year. So, it's a win-win."

I chuckle. "And how do *I* go about hiring her?"

"I'll send you the design firm's contact." She pulls out her phone to text me. "Shit. Study break is over."

"I'll let you get back to it. Good to see you, Wren. Thanks for taking care of my place all summer."

"Of course. So, are you going to do it? Hire the same designer?"

"I just might."

There are two outcomes here. I'm putting my house on the market next summer or I'm planting long-term roots. Either way, the house isn't ready to sell and if I happen to meet someone serious, it sure as hell doesn't look like the kind of place I want to bring a woman home to.

"Oh, hey!" Wren smacks my arm. "How'd the date go?"

And then there's that. The reminder that I've been in Chicago for six years, and there's a good chance my person isn't here.

Hallie 2

"And you remember where the laundry room is?"

"Wren." I chuckle. "I only stopped working on your house a couple of months ago. Of course, I know where the laundry room is."

"You're right. I don't know why I'm being so weird. It's just that I haven't lived with someone else in a long time and I want to make sure you're comfortable."

If she saw the state of the apartment I'm moving out of, she wouldn't be worried about my comfort. Before it was renovated, this house would've been a major step up from my previous living situation, and now that it's had a makeover...well, now it's far nicer than what Wren's brother is charging me for rent.

"And are *you* comfortable?" I ask, setting my duffle bag on my new bed. "I know you don't need or probably want a roommate, so if this is making you—"

"I'm happy you're here. Truly. It'll be fun."

I offer her a grateful smile as I unpack my clothes. "I think it will be too. And shoot, if we end up hating each other by the end of it, at least it's only temporary. You can forget I ever existed come May."

She laughs. "I don't think that'll be an issue. And besides, I need a Tyler Braden introduction, so if worse comes to worst, I'll just fake as if I like you."

"Works for me. I have a feeling you're going to be the best fake friend and roommate I've ever had."

The truth is there's nothing about Wren that's fake. She's a sincerely nice and thoughtful person. She always provided coffee and homemade desserts to the contractors who were working at the house this summer. She'd offer me rides when my car was acting up, which was initially embarrassing, seeing as I work for a luxury interior design brand, and my vehicle doesn't exactly scream "extravagance and style." And when she learned about my second job and the hours I was pulling just to make ends meet, she offered me a room to rent in a price range that was much more manageable than what I was paying to live downtown.

Over the months, we learned that we both have brothers—her three to my one. We bonded over the fact that we're both transplants to the area—her from the West Coast and me from the East Coast and a different part of the Midwest, depending how you look at it. And we quickly learned that we're both so busy between her school and my work, that living with each other will probably feel a whole lot like living alone.

So no, there's nothing fake about our friendship. And it's been a bit of a confidence boost knowing that as a twenty-five-year-old, I was able to make a new friend in a new city. I was quick to make friends when I was younger, but that's not always easy to do as an adult.

Even though Wren is moving back to her hometown after graduation, Chicago is where I'm planning to stay long-term, and I'm hopeful that she's simply the first in a long line of new friendships I make here.

"Hey, did my neighbor ever reach out to the firm about hiring you?" she asks.

"He did! Thank you so much for the referral. I need one more big project before my internship is done, and living so close now, this will be perfect."

"Glad to hear it. His bachelor pad needs an upgrade. When do you start?"

"Soon, I hope. I'll get the project overview during our staff meeting on Monday."

She gestures to the bag on my bed. "Can I help you with anything?"

"I'll be okay. I still need to grab the last of my boxes from the apartment when I'm downtown tonight."

"Oh, are you working at the bar?"

"No, unfortunately. I tried to pick up a shift, but my manager denied the request. Said I'd have too many overtime hours if I worked tonight. But I do have a date and we're meeting at the office downtown, so I'll grab the last of the things from the apartment afterward."

Wren perks up, leaning off the doorway. "A date? Hallie Hart, way to bury the lead."

"Don't get all excited."

"Who is he?"

"A new client of Tyler's. He recently bought a condo that Tyler is designing for him, and we crossed paths at the office a couple of weeks ago."

"Well, don't you sound overjoyed that a wealthy guy with great taste is taking you out on a date."

I chuckle. "I don't know. I'm flattered, but I've been out of the dating game for quite a while and frankly, I'd rather catch up on sleep. But Tyler asked me to go and I'm trying to kiss his ass so he hires me full-time when my internship is over next spring."

"Seems like sound reasoning to me. Worst-case scenario, you meet someone new and get a free dinner out of the whole thing. Where are you guys going?"

"I'm not sure where he made reservations, but he told me to dress warm."

"Weird." She pushes off the doorway again, this time to leave. "Well, let me know if that shitty car of yours breaks down and you need a ride home. I'm happy to come pick you up."

"Hey, don't hate on my car. She's doing just fine, thank you very much, and I don't need her to hear you talking shit about her."

"Hallie, I can practically smell the oil leak from here. Promise me when you get that full-time position, the first thing you'll do is buy yourself a new car."

I parked my "shitty" car in the farthest spot in the employee parking garage, hoping no one will notice it. Wren wasn't entirely wrong. It's run-down and definitely has an oil leak.

It has an *everything* leak, if I'm being honest.

I told Brian I'd meet him at the restaurant, but he was adamant about this being a one-car parking situation. He offered to pick me up at home, but this is a first date, and I don't know the man, so there's not a chance in hell I was going to give him my address.

The design firm is common ground.

He seems normal. He's a handsome guy, a bit shy and nervous, but that's okay, I think.

Truthfully, I don't really know what my type is or if I even have one. It's been so long since I've even been interested in someone, that it almost seems like I'm starting from scratch and figuring out what I like. I've been a bit too preoccupied the last few years to think about dating.

But if I want to get all honest with myself, the idea of trying to get to know someone again sounds terrifying, and maybe that's partly why I've busied myself so much over the years—as an excuse to avoid it.

So, this shy and nervous thing Brian has going for him seems safe to me.

"Are you moving here to Chicago?" I finally break the silence while he drives. "Tyler said you bought a condo here."

"I won't be living here full-time, no. I've got a place in South Florida and a house in Arizona, but I'm planning to be here every few months."

"That's a lot of properties to manage."

He chuckles to himself, some of his nerves dissipating. "I have someone who takes care of them when I'm away."

I pause. "And who is that someone?"

He doesn't answer and my attention immediately darts to his left hand, looking for a wedding ring indent or a change in skin tone from the lack of sun. There's neither, but my woman's intuition is on high alert.

This is what I hate about dating, trying to learn as much as possible by not only listening to what they say, but reading between the lines. It's a whole lot easier when you grow up with the person and innately know their character inside and out.

Brian takes a right onto another block, and it's the same route I use when going from the design offices to the bar I work at.

"Where are we going to dinner?" I ask.

"It's a surprise." His eyes flit to me, a mischievous grin on his lips as he leans back, driving his too-expensive car with one hand. "You look nice tonight, by the way."

That shy façade is quickly slipping into charming territory.

I return my attention to the passenger window. "Thank you. So do you."

"Do you like sports?"

"Playing or watching?"

"In this case, watching."

"Sometimes." I glance back at him suspiciously. "Why do you ask?"

His smile turns proud, not an ounce of shyness to be found. "Just curious."

Brian's speed slows as we edge into a line of traffic, and I watch as the sidewalks fill with pedestrians all moving in the same direction we're headed. Restaurants and bars along the block are packed with patrons, the excited energy palpable even from inside the car.

Music is blasting from down the street, buildings are illuminated with red-colored lights, Chicago team flags are hung in their windows, and up ahead, there are traffic monitors ushering cars into certain lanes and parking lots.

Anxiety prickles my skin. That intuition I was referring to is now buzzing with alarm.

"Brian, why did you ask me to dress warm?"

He chuckles but doesn't answer. Instead, he rolls down his window to talk to a traffic monitor, and this time when I watch out the passenger side and take a closer look, I realize all those people outside are wearing red, black, and white.

And they're all headed to the United Center on the next street over.

No. No, no, no. We can't go there.

"Are we going to the United Center?" I ask, the nerves now evident in *my* voice.

Once again, he doesn't answer me, smiling smugly as if he expects me to be thoroughly impressed. But I'm not. I'm terrified.

All I can do is pray that tonight is a Devil's game. Basketball… basketball would be fine.

"My buddy has season tickets and couldn't make it tonight," he explains. "Hope you like hockey."

Fuck my life.

I take a closer look at the crowd swarming the arena. Most are wearing Raptors jerseys. *His* jersey.

My mouth goes dry. "We could've walked from the office."

And I could've run in the opposite direction as soon as I realized where we were going.

"I wanted to give you an opportunity to ride in this car." Brian turns into a private parking lot. "It's pretty sweet, isn't it?"

That shy front is long gone. He's fully smug now.

Brian is speaking to me as we go through the private security and scan our tickets, but I'm not listening. I'd blame it on the rowdy crowd in the halls as soon as we enter the arena, but if I'm being honest, the only thing I can hear is the ringing in my ears.

My entire body is intensely aware of my surroundings because I shouldn't be here. I've avoided this building since moving to Chicago six months ago. I wouldn't even dare walk the same street, and now here I am, inside.

Brian leads the way to find our section and I follow behind, eyes nervously tracking the area around me. This arena is huge. It's got to sit, what? Twenty thousand? He's never going to see me in the crowd of this many people.

But they're not just people. They're *fans*...wearing his jersey.

We round a corner, and my heart drops, halting me in place when I come face to face with *him*.

Well, a twenty-foot version of him, printed onto a sign and hung from the rafters for all his fans to see. There's another on the wall in a different pose. A life-size cutout version that kids are taking pictures with down the hall.

I can hear my blood pumping in my ears as I look at that face. Those green eyes. That sneaky smile.

I've seen it too many times to count.

"Hallie." My name brings me out of my daze to find Brian waiting by an older gentleman, holding out his phone to show him our tickets. "Let's go. We don't want to miss puck drop."

Yes, I do. Truthfully, I'd like to miss the whole game.

A large velvet curtain blocks the walkway from the seats. "Have fun," the older man says as he holds it open for us to enter.

The ice is blinding white. The music is blaring. The chill is sudden.

Brian puts his hand on my lower back, ushering me to walk ahead of him. So I do just that, holding on to the stair railing and climbing up—away from the ice.

He laughs, nodding in the opposite direction. "Our seats are down there, Hallie."

Of fucking course they are.

Head down, I don't look at the ice as I follow him. I watch the back of Brian's feet, willing him to turn into an aisle soon, but he doesn't. He keeps climbing down, closer to the rink.

I feel eyes on us as we pass loyal fans. Neither of us is wearing team colors or jerseys yet we're closing in on the seats by the ice.

I'd give them my seat if I could.

The air is noticeably colder the farther down we go. It's too close. *Way* too close, and still, Brian doesn't stop walking.

"Are you sure we didn't pass the row yet?"

"Positive."

I risk a glance up at the rink and God, it feels like I'm practically on it. No players are currently skating on the ice, so I allow myself a moment to take it in.

He's *everywhere.*

From the player intros on the jumbo screen to the jerseys surrounding me. It's a different number than he used to wear, but I knew he changed it when he got drafted into the league.

"This is us," Brian says, edging his way through the fans that have their hands and noses pressed to the glass, hoping for a closeup glimpse of one of their favorite players when they skate out.

Because that's where we're sitting. On the glass. Row one.

"Chicago defends twice on this side," he continues as if it's the best thing in the world that we get to sit behind their goalie for two of the three periods.

But *he* plays defense.

I need to get out of here. Fake sick. Lie about an emergency, but if my heart keeps pounding at the rate it is, I might not have to fake much.

"Thank you for coming out with me tonight," Brian says, palm meeting my knee. "I was so happy when Tyler told me you said yes."

God, I'm the worst. This guy is trying to impress me and I'm over here having an existential crisis.

Before I can decide if I should stay or leave, the lights drop low and the music hums. The in-arena announcer riles up the crowd while everyone finds their seats just as the team flies out of the locker room and onto the ice, red jerseys zooming past our seats.

I don't dare look for him. I keep my eyes down on my lap.

It's been so long.

He's got a game to play. His focus will be on the ice. It's not like he's going to come out here and scan the crowd. Plus, my hair is so much shorter than it used to be, so even if he did take the time to look, there's no chance he'd recognize me.

He'll never know I'm here.

This is fine.

"Thank you for inviting me," I say to Brian. "Sorry if I'm a little off. It's been a while since I've dated."

"Don't worry about it. It's been a while for me too." His smile is kind before he nods towards the ice. "So, hockey is made up of three periods. Offense is split into four lines. You'll see them swap out by the bench and it'll look like chaos."

He continues on about the rules and I turn to face him, nodding along as if I don't already know these things from attending a certain player's games too many times to count.

Brian's phone dings in his pocket, but he ignores it and resumes. "Zanders is their captain now. Number eleven. He's a defenseman. Cocky son of a bitch, but insanely good. His blue-line mate is DeLuca. He's—"

"Water!" someone yells right next to my ear. "Ice-cold water!"

The concessions guy continues to shout, and it thankfully drowns out everything Brian was saying about the player I know more about than any random stat line he could spit out.

After the anthem and customary puck drop, the game starts, but I barely watch. I keep my attention on my lap, on the crowd, on literally anything other than the ice in front of me.

The first period drags on for too long. I hear his name cheered too many times. I know he's on this end of the rink, and all I can do is pray for the second period, so he'll finally switch sides.

Would it be rude if I cut out after two periods? Maybe I can convince Brian that I'm not feeling well, and we should reschedule.

His phone pings again, but he ignores it.

"I can't believe you haven't watched a second of this!" he shouts from next to me.

"I'm not feeling great."

That's it. Lay the groundwork.

He doesn't hear me, just like he doesn't hear his phone that won't stop going off with back-to-back text messages.

The Raptors are on defense, causing the crowd around me to ramp up their cheers.

It's loud, but I still hear Brian's phone go off again.

"Your phone is blowing up right now." I raise my voice this time so he can hear me.

He keeps his eyes on the game, the action happening right in front of us, as he pulls out his phone to mute it, but that's when I see the screen. There are endless texts from the same person. I don't know what they say, but whoever it is, their contact name is only an emoji. The diamond ring emoji.

Brian glances down at the screen and immediately tries to hide the phone away in his pocket, but it's too late.

I saw it.

"I thought you said you haven't dated in a while." My tone is accusatory.

He won't look at me. "I haven't."

"Are you married?"

He does that annoying thing again where he doesn't answer me, and now I realize that shy, nervous energy from earlier was because he was out here going on a date with someone who isn't his wife.

My disbelieving laugh is a bit manic, but that's how I feel right now. "I'm leaving."

I stand to do so, but the game is still in play, so I quickly sit back down and wait for a whistle.

"Hallie, it's not what you're thinking. We're in an open relationship. It's just that it's newly opened, so I haven't dated in a while."

"And you don't think you should've told me that you're *married*? Come on. Get so fucked right now."

An impossibly loud bang rattles the glass in front of me, stealing my attention to find a player from Tampa pinned against the boards after an excruciatingly painful hit. The player slumps to the ice, giving me a perfect view of the man who delivered the blow, only to find *him*.

Rio DeLuca.

Number thirty-eight glares down at his opponent as the crowd bangs their fists against the barrier, shaking the glass to celebrate the big hit.

He moves to skate away, but as he shifts his weight on his blades, his eyes flit upward.

To me.

He freezes in place, and I watch as both recognition and disbelief dawn on him. His lips slightly part, those green eyes tracking every inch of my face, and I try to look away, but I can't. I'm too locked in, too focused on the man in front of me who is hardly recognizable from the boy I once knew.

He's so close. Only a piece of plexiglass separates us, and I want to run away. He blinks quickly, dark brows cinching in confusion before his attention ticks to the guy I'm next to for hardly a breath before refocusing on me. Cataloging me. Studying me.

The arena has emptied out.

It's completely silent, only him and me.

I remember the first time I ever saw him. He was playing hockey that day too, but so much has changed between then and now.

Now, he's the one person I've actively worked to avoid since moving here. The one person who almost kept me from taking the internship in the first place, simply because I knew he lived in this city.

My heart flutters like it used to before I remember everything that happened.

Because I may have loved Rio DeLuca once, but I don't anymore.

Rio

"Y ou need to keep working on your balance," my dad says, helping me up from yet another fall. He makes sure I'm steady on rollerblades before letting go of my arms.

"My coach said—" The wheels of my skates fly out from under me before I can finish my sentence.

I fall right on my elbow, but my dad made me put on my pads before coming out to practice so the impact doesn't hurt that bad, and I try to get up as quickly as possible so I can keep practicing with him. He works a lot but will help me practice a couple of times a week and I do my best to impress him each time.

With my hands on his arm, he helps me wheel from the driveway to the grass where I drop onto my butt to sit.

"My coach said the dance classes I'm taking are helping with my coordination."

He chuckles. "I bet they are. Hey, I got to go help your mom with dinner, so let's call it a night for the skates." He bends to make himself eye level with me as he unclips my rollerblades. "Are you still enjoying hockey? Because if you're not having fun, we can try football or baseball or even soccer. There are a lot of other sports where you wouldn't have to skate, you know."

"No, I like it. I think I'm getting better. I want to keep playing."

He unhooks my helmet, tossing it to the grass. "Okay. Then we'll keep playing. Be inside and washed up for dinner soon, yeah?"

My dad ruffles my messy hair before jogging into the house to help my mom.

He's always helping her. He's always kissing her or dancing with her in the kitchen. It's pretty gross, but all my friends say I have the best parents, and I totally agree with them. They met when they were my age, which is so weird to think about.

Pulling my feet out of my rollerblades, I unfasten my elbow and knee pads. I grab my hockey stick and gather my pucks in a pile in the middle of my driveway. The net is centered in front of our garage where I always practice. The garage door is peppered with plenty of dings and dents from my missed shots, but I'm getting a little better at making them in the net.

With my socks on, I shoot, but it goes wide, bouncing off the hanging light on the front of the house.

Thankfully, it doesn't break. My mom would be pissed. She's already upset that the garage door got dented, but she also didn't tell me to *stop* practicing either.

I wish I had a friend on my street who I could play defense against, or they could play goalie while I shoot, but there are no other kids around here.

Everyone on our block has lived here forever. That's just how it works in this part of Boston. Our house is the same house my nonna grew up in. She raised my mom here, and now I live here. I've had the same neighbors my whole life. Some have kids in high school and others are having babies now, but no one is my age.

Last night at dinner I asked my parents if our new neighbors had kids, and my mom said she wasn't ready to think about someone moving into Cecilia's house yet, so the conversation ended there.

Cecilia was my nonna's best friend and had always lived in the house right next to mine, but she died a couple of months ago and her family didn't want to live there, so they sold it.

I didn't bring it up again at dinner, but when I went to bed last night, I prayed that my new neighbors would have a kid my age.

I work on the stickhandling drill we learned at practice this week, moving the puck back and forth along my driveway before shooting it at the net.

I miss again, and when I turn back for a new puck, I watch a car pull into Cecilia's driveway and park in front of the house.

It's a normal car like my dad has, but this one is dark green and looks new.

Standing in my driveway, I watch as a lady gets out, looks up at the red brick exterior of the house attached to mine before rounding the trunk to lift out a small moving box, carrying it into the house Cecilia used to live in. The lady has dark hair and looks around my mom's age.

A man gets out next and carries in a bigger box behind her. Then the back door of the car opens and a blond boy steps out. He's holding a lacrosse stick and he's my same height.

He looks up at his new house before noticing me standing next door.

I wave. "Hey."

He waves back. "Hey. Do you live here?"

"Yeah."

He walks in my direction, gesturing to Cecilia's house. "I'm moving in there."

"That's cool. I'm Rio."

"I'm Luke." His eyes are trained on my hockey stick. "You play hockey?"

"Yeah, but I'm not very good."

He holds up his lacrosse stick. "I play lacrosse, and I'm really good."

"That's cool. How old are you?"

"Twelve."

"Me too."

He smiles. "Cool."

My attention returns to the car to watch a girl climb out of the back seat too. She's shorter than me and Luke but her hair is dark brown and wavy like mine. She's wearing jeans that flare out at the bottom and a pink sweatshirt with a big yellow smiley face on the front.

She doesn't look over in our direction. Instead, her eyes are locked on her new house. She's got headphones over her ears and a cassette player in her hand.

"That's my sister," Luke says. "You don't have to be friends with her since she's a girl."

"I have a lot of friends who are girls. And they're all really smart and funny. I take a dance class and there are only girls there."

"You take a dance class?"

"Yeah. It's helping me skate better."

"That's weird."

Luke's sister is still staring up at the house next to mine. Her eyes follow the roof line, watching where her roof connects to mine until finally, she looks down and her attention lands on me and her brother.

"Hallie!" Luke shouts, waving her over.

She holds up a finger, silently telling him to wait before refocusing on her house.

Luke shakes his head. "She's so annoying sometimes."

I don't have a sister, but a lot of my friends think their sisters are annoying, so I guess that's a common thing. But I'd love to have a sister. Or a brother. I don't care. It's lonely being an only child.

Finally, Hallie pulls off her headphones, draping them around her neck, and joins us on my driveway.

She looks exactly like the woman who walked into the house earlier, but a younger version.

"Hi." She grins at me. "I'm Hallie Hart."

Luke groans. "You don't have to tell everyone your first and last name."

She simply shrugs, completely unbothered. "I like it."

Luke rolls his eyes at his sister.

"I'm Rio DeLuca," I say, giving her my last name too.

She smiles bigger.

"Luke!" their dad calls from the front porch. "Come help your mom get the dishes unpacked."

Their dad waves at me and I lift my hand to wave back. He seems nice.

"You don't have to help too?" I ask Hallie.

"Nope. I packed them. Luke has to unpack them. How old are you?"

"Twelve."

"I'm eleven. Today."

"It's your birthday?"

"Yep. March eighth. When is your birthday?"

"August third."

Her brows turn in, her head tilting to the side. "So, you don't get to have a birthday at school?"

"No. It's always right before school starts."

"I usually get to have a birthday at school, but not this year. We drove here today from Minnesota."

"That's pretty far away, right?"

"It's so far away. My friends are all there. But my mom said I get to paint my new room any color I want, so it's okay, I guess."

"That's awesome. My room is just white."

"I think I'll do yellow. Do you like yellow?"

I shrug. "I guess so."

"Yeah, I think it'll be yellow." She points up to a window facing my house. "That one is my room. Luke got to choose first and he picked the bigger room."

I point to the window on my house that faces hers and shares a roof. "That one is my room."

"You can watch me paint my room from your room!"

"Okay. That sounds cool."

31

"Do you want to be friends?"

Well, that was easy. Just last night I was praying for a new friend, and here she is. "Sure!"

"My brother will probably tell you not to be my friend."

"I don't care. I'm friends with a lot of people. I can be his friend and your friend. Or we can be secret friends."

Her smile grows. "Okay." She looks down at my feet. "Where are your shoes?"

"I was practicing my skating, but I had to take them off because my dad went inside, and I fall too much. But I'm getting better at skating."

"Do you like music?"

"Yeah."

"Me too. I love music." She presses the rewind button on her cassette player.

"CDs are way better than tapes," I tell her. "You should start buying CDs."

"I like tapes. CDs scratch too much when you rewind them and then they don't work right."

"What are you listening to?"

"I don't know the name. I just picked a song to remember the moment."

Huh?

She must realize how confused I am because she adds, "I pick a song when something cool or important happens so I can remember it. Then when I want to relive a moment, I rewind it back and start the song from the beginning."

That's kind of weird but I don't tell her that. I also don't think it'd bother her if I called her weird. I think she'd keep doing what she's doing.

And that makes her pretty cool.

"Are you trying to remember moving?" I ask.

"Yeah. And meeting a new friend. You should try it sometime."

"Okay. Maybe I will."

Her smile turns proud.

"Rio!" my mom calls from the front door. "Dinnertime, *Tesoro*."

She glances at Hallie quickly before peeking out the front door to look for our new neighbors. My mom gives her that signature kind smile she always wears and goes back inside.

"I have to go," I tell my new friend.

"Okay. See you later." She waves as she skips back to her house.

I stop on the front step of my porch as she does the same, looking over at me. "Happy birthday, Hallie."

Her smile is so big I can see all her teeth. "Thanks, Rio."

4

Rio

Was that her?

It had to be her. I'd recognize that face anywhere. Those hazel eyes. That wavy hair which is so much shorter than it used to be. It may have been six years since I last saw her, but I'd never forget.

I've thought about Hallie Hart more times over the last six years than I'll ever admit, and yeah, there's been a few instances where I let myself believe I saw her. Where I mistook someone else for her, as if my imagination was playing tricks on me.

Tonight though, I'm *positive* that was her.

At least I was positive in the moment, but then Zee yelled my name loud enough that it finally broke me out of my daze and forced my focus back on the game. I stayed on the ice for the rest of my shift, but as soon as I was back on the bench, my attention went to find her again…only for that seat to be empty and to remain that way for the rest of the game.

So, I'm a bit less confident that I wasn't hallucinating her.

Pulling into my driveway at home, I cut the engine and sit. It's late, close to midnight at this point, and my body is exhausted and ready for bed thanks to the overtime win. But I don't get out of the car. I sit and replay every detail of seeing her.

God, she looked good. She always looked good, though, so that wasn't much of a surprise.

I still remember the first time I ever saw Hallie Hart, with that unbothered smile on her face, completely confident in who she was. But she wasn't wearing that smile tonight.

Fuck, was that her? The further I get from that fleeting moment, the more I second-guess myself.

I just need to go inside and sleep it off, get my mind off whoever it is I saw tonight. But before I can get myself out of my car, my attention is drawn out the passenger window to watch as someone pulls into Wren's driveway.

And once again, I'm asking myself if I'm hallucinating.

A dark green Nissan Altima parks in front of my neighbor's house. It's the exact same car that parked in front of my neighbor's house the day the Harts moved next door to my family home in Boston. Same make. Same model. Same year.

A woman gets out and rounds the car to lift a box out of the trunk.

Goddamn. What is wrong with me? I'm having the worst case of déjà vu right now picturing Mrs. Hart carrying the first moving box into their new house. The one that had all the dishes that Luke had to unpack. It feels like yesterday and a lifetime ago all at the same time. But it's also happening right now.

This time there's no Mr. Hart following behind. There's no blond boy with a lacrosse stick or a hazel-eyed girl with her headphones covering her ears, sitting in the back seat.

I open my car door, not tearing my focus away from her because that's *not* Mrs. Hart. Yes, her hair is shorter now, but besides that, she's the spitting image of her mom.

And then I hear myself say a name I haven't spoken in six years. Because this time, I know for sure I'm not hallucinating.

"Hallie?"

Box in hand, she whips her head in my direction, eyes going

wide as she assesses me, her gaze halting me in place. When I was a teenager, I remember feeling like I'd kill to have her eyes on me, but I don't let myself want that anymore.

Slowly, I cross the lawn in her direction, her gravitational pull on me as strong as it's always been.

"Rio." She swallows. "Hi."

Oh, it's her all right because I'll never forget the way my heart used to skip a beat when she'd say my name. It takes everything in me to keep my arms at my side instead of wrapping them around her shoulders and pulling her into my chest like I used to, just to make sure she's real.

Chocolate hair, with shimmers of lighter brown painted throughout, cuts bluntly below her chin. She used to keep it long, but it suits her this way. Now, it shows off that stunning face of hers. Soft freckles dot along the bridge of her nose. Her eyes that I remember being bright and kind now watch me with unease. Her mouth that used to beam with a smile no matter the situation, is now turned down in the opposite direction.

Regardless, she's somehow even more beautiful than the last time I saw her, and that pisses me off. Because first off, how is that possible? And secondly, she fucked me over. Shouldn't karma come into play here and give me a win?

She sets the box on Wren's front step before facing me again, arms crossed at her middle as if she were using them as a shield against me.

But she's not the one who needs a shield. *I* am. It may have been six years ago, but I haven't forgotten what happened.

"What are you doing here?" There are no pleasantries, no softness in my tone.

Her brows furrow in confusion as if she's asking herself what *I'm* doing here.

I throw my thumb over my shoulder, pointing at my house. "I live here, Hallie. So again, what are you doing here?"

Her eyes go impossibly wide as she takes a step back. "But I live here."

"No, you don't? Wren doesn't—"

Her new roommate.

You've got to be fucking kidding me.

I take a step closer, panic taking over. "Did you know I live next door? Is that why you're here?"

She scoffs, arms unfolding, hands anchoring at her hips. "Are you joking? I've tried to avoid you since I moved to Chicago. You think I'd purposefully move next door? To what? Be close to you? Relive our childhood? No thanks, Rio. I'm good off that."

There she is. I remember that ferocity.

Since I moved to Chicago.

"*When* did you move to Chicago?" I say it as if I have every right to know the answer, and a part of me feels like I do. She knew I lived here. She should've warned me.

Her chin tilts up defiantly. "April."

She's been here for six months?

"And you didn't think you should tell me?"

"And say what?" She exhales a laugh. "'Hey, remember me? That girl you hate. Yeah, I moved to Chicago! Let's get drinks!' It's been six years, Rio. You don't own this city, and I don't owe you a phone call. And besides, even if I did, I lost your number years ago."

That feels like a fucking punch to the gut and hurts more than I want to admit. No, we haven't spoken since I left Boston, but there were a few times in my first year here that I may have tried to call Hallie, but her line was disconnected.

I hadn't allowed myself to try again since.

Tension lingers between us, neither of us knowing what to say.

"You can't live here," is what I finally decide on.

"I don't have much of a choice."

"The city is fucking huge. There are other options rather than the house ten feet away from mine, Hallie."

Her lips purse in anger, her jaw setting in place. Oh, she's fuming now.

"I don't have *other* options. Not all of us get to make millions of dollars a year playing a game, Rio. Some of us are just trying to survive paycheck to paycheck. So yes, I will be living next door and trust me, it's not because I want to be anywhere close to you. I'll be here until May when Wren's brother sells the house, and if that's going to be an issue for you, you can go ahead and take some of those millions of dollars you have and buy yourself a new place to live."

She wants me to buy a new place? That's my plan. That's exactly why I hired—

Wait.

No, she can't be.

Everything clicks. The roommate. The designer. Hallie always wanted to be an interior designer. She was going to school for it the last time we saw one another.

"Are you the one who renovated Wren's house?" I ask, accusatorily.

Her face balls in confusion and I watch as the realization dawns on her the same way it did me. Head falling back, exposing that pretty throat, she squeezes her eyes closed. "And you're the neighbor."

Fuck.

"Well, that's not going to work," she decides.

"Yeah. No shit, that's not going to work."

She jolts back slightly, as if my words hurt her. We were always careful with each other until we weren't. Hallie is a soft soul with a tough shell, and that exterior seems harder than it used to be.

Regardless of our history, I never wanted to see her hurting.

She hurt you.

"You know that wouldn't work, Hal."

"Don't call me that."

I hold my hands up in surrender. "Hallie. We both know it wouldn't work for you to be at my house every day. I cannot hire you."

A beat passes between us.

"I know." Her tone is defeated.

The silence is thick again, every part of this interaction feeling fucking surreal. I never thought I'd be standing in front of her again.

She's so goddamn beautiful. So hardheaded still. For a moment, I let myself remember how overwhelming it felt to be near here. She used to steal all my thoughts. She used to occupy my entire existence.

I almost forgot what that felt like.

I've spent six years subconsciously comparing every date to her. Comparing their laugh to hers. Their kindness to hers. Their confidence to hers. Their taste in music to hers.

I haven't spoken Hallie's name in six years, but she has been living rent free in my mind while I try to replicate what we had before everything went to shit.

I need to walk away. Go pack a bag and move in with Ryan and Indy until May.

"Let's just stay out of each other's way," she says, breaking the silence. "You'll hardly even know I'm here."

"No chance of that happening," I mutter under my breath.

"What was that?"

"Nothing."

My eyes find hers, unspoken words passing between us. There's too much history between me and the girl next door, and there's something else that my friends don't know.

That thing I've been looking for since I moved to Chicago? That connection? That one person some search their entire lives to find? I had already found her when I was twelve years old.

At least I thought I had.

I know what I'm looking for because I had it once, and now the only girl I've ever loved is moving into the house next to mine.

Again.

I turn back, headed straight for my place, needing to put a

fucking door, wall, *anything* between us. I'm halfway across my lawn when a visual of her at my game tonight pops into my mind. I didn't miss that she was there with someone.

"The guy you were with tonight." I slowly shift back to face her. "Who was he?"

The set in her jaw is evident even from here. "Not your job to worry about."

Nodding, I turn back to my house, hands casually tucked in my pockets as I continue to walk. With my back to her, I make sure my words are loud enough for her to hear them.

"Lose him."

Hallie

5

L *ose him.*

Lose him?

Where the hell did he find the audacity to say that to me after six years without seeing each other? Without *speaking* to each other?

Rio DeLuca can go ahead and fuck himself.

I mean, I did lose Brian, but not because I was told to. As soon as I could, I ran out of the arena and got a rideshare back to my car. Then I gave Tyler an earful this morning about doing his research before thinking of setting me up again.

But Rio believing he has any right to tell me who I can and can't date? It's clear now that sometime during the last six years he lost his goddamn mind.

He lives next door…again. What the hell did I do to earn this kind of bad luck? I've been overextending myself, trying to make ends meet financially, and now that I've finally found a place I can afford enough to keep from falling further into debt, *he* ends up being the neighbor.

Yesterday was spent paranoid, periodically watching out my new bedroom window to make sure I wasn't coming or going at the same time as him.

And I have to do that until May. How the hell am I going to avoid him until May?

"Hallie," my name rings somewhere around me. "Did you hear me?"

I blink out of my daze to find the entire design team staring at me from their seats around the conference table.

"I'm sorry." I sit up, adjusting in my chair. "What did you say?"

Tina shoots me a look from the front of the room, notepad in hand. She's Tyler's right-hand woman. She's not a designer, by any means. There's not a creative bone in her body and she'd tell you that herself, but she's the organization and business brain behind Tyler Braden Interiors.

Even though I've been zoned out and not listening to a word of the meeting she's facilitating, I like her.

"I was congratulating you on your next project," she says. "A full house renovation and the client requested you specifically. Said he loved what you did to his neighbor's home and put a deposit down on his project the same day as his inquiry."

The entire team claps for me and I'm certain I can't turn a deeper shade of red. My eye catches Tyler's, sitting at the head of the table in his three-piece suit, beaming a proud smile and clapping for me along with the rest of my peers.

Well, they aren't my peers per se. They're mostly full-time designers who make a shit ton of money working for Tyler Braden. Then there's me and the three other newbies who started working here this spring with the promise of a one-year internship. Tyler doesn't always hire his interns full-time, but from what my coworkers have told me, if he's impressed by my work, he most likely will.

Unfortunately for me, he's not going to be very impressed when I tell him this project fell through.

"With how large this renovation is," Tina continues, "it should take up the rest of your internship. Two full home renovations in your first year is impressive, Hallie."

My attention falls on Silas, another one of the interns. He couldn't look more annoyed with me, and I completely get it. He hasn't had a solo project yet, and instead, spends most of his days fetching coffee, shredding documents, and cleaning up after client meetings. If I didn't have Wren's house to work on this summer, I would've been there right along with him.

"This week, I'll go over the client profile with you, and next week, you can meet with him face to face," Tina says. "He's a professional athlete, so he travels quite a bit. I know you can't work evenings, but you may need to be flexible with your schedule on this project."

I can't work evenings because I'm already working...at my second job that no one here knows about.

"Oh, a professional athlete." One of the designers whistles. "Which sport?"

Tina looks down at her notepad. "Hockey."

"Hot."

"Jealous."

"I'll be your second assistant on the project," all echo around me.

Swallowing, I keep my eyes on the pen in my hand that I can't stop tapping against the table. "Actually, that project fell through. For me, at least. There's a..." I hesitate, still unable to look at anyone, namely Tyler. "Conflict of interest. I'm sure he'll be calling soon to get someone else on the renovation."

The room is silent around me, tension and judgment swirling around. It lingers that way for at least ten seconds, though it feels more like an hour, when I finally risk a glance in Tyler's direction. Disappointment is written all over his face.

"That's a shame to hear," he finally says. Breaking eye contact with me, Tyler redirects his attention. "Tina, make sure we don't lose that project, even if that requires me to be the lead designer on it instead. Find out who he's comfortable working with, but we aren't losing this client."

"Of course."

Shit.

I can feel the disappointment suffocating the room. I truly think if the entire design team started screaming at me about how much I suck at this job, things would feel less awkward than they do now.

I'm equally disappointed, but it's out of my hands. This felt like my shot, my big opportunity to show Tyler what I've got, but I couldn't have planned for Rio, of all people, to be the homeowner. What am I supposed to do?

I just need to find another renovation to finish out my internship, but when I glance up and catch Silas's smug little smirk, it acts as a reminder that projects like these don't come around often. And like him, I'll be sitting around, twiddling my thumbs, and fetching coffee instead of stretching my design muscles if I don't land another one.

The meeting goes on, but I'm only half listening. I'm too busy wracking my brain for any contacts I might have that could potentially hire me. The stylist who cut my hair this summer said she's going to open a new salon location. Maybe she needs a designer, or maybe she has a client who is in search of a new home office. Maybe I'll get lucky and overhear somebody at the bar say something about building a new home they need help with. I need to get out of here and start hustling.

"Great meeting, everyone." Tyler stands from his seat. "Let's get some good work done this week and remember, I'm always here to bounce ideas off of."

The rest of the team stands from their seats, chatting with each other as they exit the conference room. I get a couple sympathetic smiles on their way out, an encouraging squeeze on my shoulder.

None of it helps.

Tyler, fashionable motherfucker that he is, takes a seat on the conference table in front of me, long legs still firmly planted on the floor. "I don't love that you just lost a major project."

I shrug, attempting to act unaffected. "And I don't love that you set me up with a married man this weekend, but here we are."

Tyler narrows his eyes, staying silent for a beat. "Touché. I take full responsibility for that one." The tension dissipates a bit. "Hallie, you've done such a good job so far and I'd love for you to be part of this team permanently, but I can't hire you based on one renovation. I need to see more."

"I know."

He knocks the table with his knuckles before standing. "Find another project. I believe in you."

Alone in the room, I lean back in my chair, eyes on the ceiling.

I need to fix this. I need to find another project because as much as I want to be a part of this design team, the facts are, I *need* to be. I need the salary that comes with it.

"Hallie," Tina says, startling me.

I find her standing next to me as I sit.

"Tyler might have said you need to find another project, but what he really meant is that you need to find a way to get back on *this* one. I know you've already had one this summer, but an entire home renovation isn't a common job, especially for an intern. Tyler wants to hire you, it's obvious, and one way to ensure that happens is by getting yourself back on board as lead designer for this project. If Mr. DeLuca contacts me, I'll stall on replacing you until the end of the week, but that's the best I can do for you. Whatever it is, fix it, okay?"

Easier said than done.

I nod in agreement. "I'll do my best. Thanks, Tina."

Her sneaky smile lifts. "So, what's the issue? Are you and his sister mortal enemies? Did you sleep with his best friend and never return a text?" She gasps. "Did you sleep with *him,* and it was so bad you can't look him in the eye again?"

"He doesn't have a sister and I'm pretty sure all his best friends are married."

Her head sways from side to side. "Well, from what I hear, you have a thing for married men."

I narrow my eyes. "I blame you as much as Tyler for that one. You're a woman. You don't set someone up before a full FBI-level social media stalking session."

She laughs. "So, it's the last one, then."

Definitely not the last one.

"It's a bit more complicated than that," is all I say.

Parked in the back of the employee lot, I sit in my car, eating the homemade PB&J I made for lunch.

I stay out of sight during lunch hour because I don't want to give my coworkers the chance to, once again, offer that I get in on their lunch delivery order. Mostly because I don't have it in me to sit there, eating my borderline stale sandwich and say no, yet again, because I can't afford it. My self-control dwindles every time I see one of my coworkers with a poke bowl or twenty-dollar salad at their desk.

And right on time, as I'm thinking of things I can't afford, my alarm goes off, reminding me it's the due date for one of my loan payments. I log on and pay fifty dollars over the minimum payment because that's all I can afford this month, then I check my banking app to see what little money I had in my checking account dwindle down to almost nothing.

I have a different loan payment due next week and rent is due the week after that.

Yes, I make money at the design firm, but it's nothing compared to what the full-time designers make. I'm in a learning program, and that paycheck has an end date to it if I don't get hired onto the team. And sure, I have five shifts at the bar this week. That should cover my next two big bills. But then my phone bill is due, and it's right on to worrying about how I'm going to cover the next month's payments.

The cycle is never-ending. It feels like I'm drowning, even with my decreased rent, but there seems to be one clear way to keep my head above water.

As much as I don't want to, I know what I have to do, and I'm not in a position where I can be above begging.

Back on my phone, I look up the Chicago Raptors game schedule for this season, needing to know what time I should plan to wait for him on his front porch steps tonight where I'm going to do my best pleading.

A quick Google search tells me they have a game in Columbus tomorrow, followed by two more games on the road. From what I remember him telling me years ago, the teams typically fly out the day before, and if the flight is short enough, they try to squeeze in a practice at home beforehand.

It's a bit alarming how easy it is to find where their practice arena is—two blocks from here—and another quick search lets me know that the practices are open to the public. There's no practice schedule online, but my desperation is reminding me I've got nothing to lose.

What else am I going to do? I have until the end of the week to rectify this, and it's not like I have his number anymore.

So, I finish off my PB&J and start my walk to the rink.

It's a crisp fall day and the walk is nice. Chicago is a bustling city. It's not New York City busy, but its own version. Yes, the buildings are tall, and the streets are littered with people, but the lake is right there. There are beaches within walking distance of skyscrapers. A river flows through the center of it all, and I love it.

I enjoyed my years in Boston. Minneapolis too. But Chicago feels *right*.

Now, I need to figure out a way to stay.

When I get to the rink, the lot is full of cars, which seems like a positive sign. I should maybe take a moment to look for his truck before I head inside, but my nerves don't allow me to slow down. A man exits as I approach the main entry door. He holds it open for me, but the crowd inside continues to file out, so I open the other door instead, going the opposite direction from the main flow of traffic.

I earn a few confused glances as I walk straight inside the emptying rink with faux confidence, but that mask slips when I immediately spot the black and red practice jerseys contrasted against the white of the ice.

The team is huddled around their coaches, and it takes everything not to go running back to work as fast as I can. But I've got nothing to lose and everything to gain, so I follow the curve of the rink around to the side the players will exit the ice before going to the locker room.

On the side that's clearly not meant for the general public, I wait while their team meeting finishes, sitting awkwardly by myself on a cold metal bench next to a random boombox.

The team begins to file off the rink, shooting the shit with each other as they pass. I earn more confused glances from them, but no one asks what I'm doing in an area that I shouldn't be in.

One of the players passes by the bench I'm sitting on, eyes assessing me before bouncing to the boombox at my side. "Rio!" he shouts, and my stomach instantly drops. "Don't forget your shitty boombox!"

"It's not shitty," I hear Rio say as he takes a step off the ice. "It's well-loved. Big diff—"

His attention immediately lands on me, halting him in place, standing steady on the blades of his skates. His eyes don't leave me for even a moment as he removes his helmet and lets it hang at his side.

Sweat trickles from his forehead, rolling over those dark brown waves. You'd think his hair was black unless you've been close enough to run your fingers through it.

I clearly didn't give myself the chance to really look at him the other night. It was too dark out. I was in shock, too stunned by seeing him in person after all these years to really *see* him.

Yes, I may have looked him up online a few times over the years. So what? I was curious. It's human nature to be curious. But those two-dimensional photos were nothing compared to the real thing.

Dark hair. Olive undertone to his skin. Height that was genetically gifted and ridges of muscles that were hard-earned.

I've always been attracted to Rio DeLuca, and it pisses me off that nothing has changed. Even during those awkward early years when everyone else saw him as a friend, I always saw him as more. Then he had himself a glow-up in the middle of high school, shot up about six inches, and finally those other girls saw what I always did.

But this version of him—twenty-seven years old and bulked up from the NHL—feels cruel to have to witness. He's fucking gorgeous, but it doesn't change that I still want to hate him.

"Don't give him shit for his boombox," another player says as he steps off the ice. He has the number eleven on his practice jersey, and I remember the name "Zanders" was written across the back from the game on Saturday. "He's the only reason we have decent music in the locker room."

"That piece of shit doesn't even have Bluetooth!" someone else adds.

Rio doesn't look away from me the entire time. He doesn't engage in the conversation around him. His teammates have to move around his frozen form to get to the locker room, and it only draws more attention to us.

Zanders pauses next to him, following Rio's line of sight until he finds me. His attention goes right back to his teammate, and he continues that back and forth a few more times.

The silence is screaming that there's a story here and Zanders picks up on it when he asks, "And who is this?" in a far too amused tone.

"No one," I say at the same time Rio says, "Hallie."

His tone is gentle when he says my name, and for a moment I

think maybe he forgot about the jaded history between us.

The silence lingers again.

"My neighbor," he finishes after blinking his way out of his stare. "She moved in with Wren."

That doesn't even begin to explain who he and I have been to each other over the years, but it's enough that Zanders doesn't press the issue. He simply removes his glove and reaches his hand out to shake mine while introducing himself.

"Well, I'm going to leave you two to whatever the hell is making this moment so awkward," Zanders finishes while joining the rest of the team headed to the locker room. "Nice to meet you, Hallie."

I offer a wave to his back. "You too."

"What are you doing here?" Rio must remember that we're more enemies than friends these days, judging by the sharp bite to his question.

That's the moment I decide to stand, as if anything could make up the height between us. He's a solid 6'3" barefoot, and now with his skates, he's got to be around 6'7".

I'm more than a foot shorter than that, and with the heavy bulk his pads add to his frame, I couldn't feel smaller.

But I can't. I need to be big. I need to find my assertiveness. I need to figure out a way to get us both what we want, while reminding him that what he wants is *me*.

As a designer, I mean. I was the designer he requested to work on his house until he realized our history.

"I need you to let me do your home renovation."

Rio scoffs a laugh and walks right past me, not even bothering to spare me a "no."

I grab his arm to stop him, and I wish I hadn't. Even through his jersey and undershirt, I can feel the muscle he's added to his forearms in the years since I've last seen him.

He stops, staring down at my hand that's holding him, so I quickly remove it.

"Sorry."

I've rarely felt embarrassed around Rio in the past, but that certainly changed between this interaction and the last.

His glare hardens, and for a moment I wonder if it's odd for him to despise me so much. Hatred was never a natural inclination for the lovable boy I grew up with.

"Please." My tone is soft, but the desperation is clear. "I need this."

Those green eyes soften, searching mine, and I swear I see him. The person I was most comfortable with. The one who knew what I needed without me having to ask. The person who knew *me* better than I sometimes knew myself.

But then he reminds me that we aren't those people anymore when he simply says, "Not a chance."

"Rio, I'm begging you."

"Well, stop begging then, Hallie. It's not going to work. There's not a dollar amount in the world you can bribe me with to allow you to spend every day of the next six months in my house."

Ouch.

I nod my head once. "Well, I guess it's good that I don't have a dollar to spare for that bribe, even if I wanted to."

"What do you mean by that?"

"It means that I need this job, Rio. I *desperately* need this job. Do you really think I'd allow myself to come begging to you if I didn't?"

His eyes once again search my face for the answer. "Why?"

I can't give him the detailed explanation—that I need this salary to pay off my debt—because there's not a chance in hell I'm going to explain *why* I'm in that kind of debt. And I know him. I know that will be his next question.

But it's clear I need to give him something.

"I've got a shot at my dream job here."

"Okay. How about you find a dream job in a different city then?"

I don't let that response linger. "I'm interning for this big-time firm, and I could get hired on as a full-time designer at the end of it, but I need another project to showcase what I've got."

"Find a different project then," he says simply. "Preferably in a different city."

"Can you get over that already? I'm here and I'm not going anywhere, so deal with it."

His jaw hardens.

"As far as the project goes," I continue, "it's not that easy to find a new one. Not for an intern, at least. I got lucky with Wren's house and even luckier when you accidentally asked for me."

At that moment, a few of Rio's coaches skate off the ice.

"Leaving for the airport in ten, DeLuca," one of them says as they pass by us.

"Yes, sir." He nods. "I'm on my way."

The coaches all slip into the locker room.

Rio's defenses seem to fall a bit once it's truly only us again, like he's tired of all of this. "I don't want to hire you, Hal."

As much as I want to, I don't correct the nickname he used to call me by.

"I know."

"I don't want you in my house. I don't want to have to see you every day." He runs a hand through his hair, and I watch the way his fingers flex around his texture. "Fuck, Hallie, before Saturday, I thought I'd never see you again."

The words come out with a painful edge, and I'd be lying if I said they didn't slip past my armor and land a hit. Most of me never thought I'd see him again either.

"I know."

Just when I think he may change his mind and tell me he'll let me do the project, he grabs his boombox off the bench and exhales. "I have to go. We're leaving on a road trip for the week."

Every part of me wants to ask him if he's already called the firm and requested my replacement or if he's planning to call later. But he seems overwhelmed just from my being here, so I don't.

Instead, I stop him by asking, "What's up with the ancient boombox?"

He rears back playfully. "Watch yourself, Hart. I believe the term you're looking for is *classic*."

I try not to let the smile tick up on my lips, but it finds its way there for a brief moment. "What's up with the *classic* boombox?"

He shrugs. "It still works. Why replace what's not broken? And the guys can give me shit for it all they want, but I'm the only one on the team with good taste in music."

"You're welcome for that."

He laughs, deep and full, and I feel it through every nerve in my body.

It's been a long time since I've heard that sound, and I missed it.

"Bullshit," he says through his laughter. "You're welcome for *your* taste in music."

"What kind of delusional state are you living in, DeLuca?"

Those dimples sink into his cheeks, that glimpse of my old Rio coming back to life. "There was a solid year when you *only* listened to boy bands. And when we were together, you wouldn't let me listen to anything else either."

"Exactly! It's called taste. Look it up."

"You once told me the wrong band's name when we were listening to a mixtape you made me because you genuinely didn't know the difference between them. They all sounded the exact same."

I laugh and it feels nice. Light and nostalgic. "God, how do you remember that? That was forever ago."

"Hard to forget the years you had shit taste in music, Hal. It's been burned into my memory and not in a good way." His attention drifts back to the locker room as if he wants to leave the playful shit-talking before it gets too comfortable. "I really do have to go. I've got a flight to catch."

I nod in understanding, letting that easy moment between us pass. "Okay."

He doesn't turn away immediately, but eventually he does, pausing in the entryway of the locker room. He speaks to me without looking back in my direction. "I'm sorry, but I can't give you an answer on the renovation right now."

"I get it."

He breathes a laugh to himself. "Do you, though?" Those pleading green eyes look at me over his shoulder. "Five minutes and it feels like that again, like nothing happened. Imagine six months. I don't want it to be like that again. After everything, it can't."

Because I didn't tell him the truth all those years ago. He doesn't want to forgive me for it.

Well, I don't want to forgive him either.

"I do get it." Entirely defeated, I simply nod. "Have a good road trip, Rio."

With that, I don't spare him another glance. I leave, walking back to the job I'll only have for another six months.

6

Rio

"**A**re you eating enough?"

I laugh into the phone. "Yes, Ma. I'd be eating right now if you let me get off the phone."

"Hey, now. I labored with you for thirty-four hours. I can keep you on the phone for as long as I'd like. Don't forget that."

"That was twenty-seven years ago. It's time you stop holding that over my head and let it go."

"I'm your mother. Your *Italian* mother, at that. It's my job to guilt trip you," she says. "So, you miss me, or what?"

"Jesus," I chuckle. "Of course I miss you. How was Sunday dinner? And why are you still cooking?"

I can tell she has me on speakerphone because the sound of a wooden spoon scraping against a metal pot is crystal clear through the line. Sunday dinner may as well be called Sunday lunch, so there's no reason she should still be cooking at this time of night.

"The Morenos' grandson is visiting for the week, and they brought him over today. He said he loved my Bolognese sauce, so I figured I should make them a batch. You know, in case he gets hungry while he's visiting his grandparents. Carla has never been one for the kitchen."

"Ma," I scold.

"Don't 'Ma' me. You know how good my Bolognese is. Best in the neighborhood."

I shake my head at her but also salivate at the mere thought. She's in no way wrong.

As much as I love our family dinners in Chicago with all my friends, nothing quite compares to the Sunday feast my mom would prepare growing up. Our Sundays almost always included the entire neighborhood coming over for dinner. It was one of my favorite things about growing up where I did. Everyone was, in a sense, family.

In the years since I moved away from home, my only real concern has been her. The guilt from living far away sits heavy on me. I'm an only child after all, and that's how I was raised. Children take care of their parents once they reach a certain age.

A Sunday check-in is a must for her, but we call and text randomly throughout the week too. She's the best woman I know, always cheered me on, and she's been through the ringer over the years. She handled it the best she could, but as her only son, I want to protect her.

And yes, I'm a self-proclaimed mama's boy and completely unashamed about it.

"Who came over today?" I ask her.

"The usual neighborhood suspects, a few of the ladies from my bingo night, and your uncle Mikey."

My dad's brother has been going to every Sunday dinner this last year, and my mom's neighborhood friends have been coming to my childhood home since I was a kid.

The neighborhood consisted of ten staple families, with previous generations living in those same homes long before I was alive. So, when the Harts moved to town, they didn't just shake up my world, but everyone on the block took an interest in the new family.

"I made semifreddo for dessert," she continues.

"Ma! What the hell? That's my favorite."

"Well, move home and you might get some. Any word from Boston?"

I close the door to Indy's office, making sure my friends can't hear me. "You know there won't be anything concrete until the season is over."

She sighs into the phone. "I just want you home, *Tesoro*."

"I know. I'm working on it."

There's a beat of silence on the phone. Yes, I'd love to play for my childhood team. I'd love to live closer to my family. But that's not without the guilty notion that it's what I feel I *should* do for her.

The truth is, even though I didn't sign my early extension with Chicago, I haven't made up my mind that I want to leave. I love it here. My friends are here. In a way, I grew from a boy to a man here, and I'm not sure I'm ready to walk away from this place yet.

"Tell me about your week," she says. "Then I'll let you go."

Without hesitation, my thoughts go to Hallie.

The image of finding her waiting for me outside of practice last Monday, much in the way she used to when we were in high school.

How it felt to see her again. The lack of sleep I've gotten from knowing she's sleeping in the house next to mine. How right it felt to banter with her for a moment. How fucking good she looked by the rink, wearing that blue and white checkered skirt that hugged her hips and thighs. It was topped with a vintage Harley Davidson sweatshirt that was cropped to show a sliver of her stomach, and she was layered in both gold and silver jewelry. She once told me that style didn't have rules, and she's lived by that motto ever since.

Hallie has always been stylish, whether that be in her fashion or interior design. She had the confidence to wear whatever she wanted to, and that confidence made any style of clothing work for her. Even pieces that might seem wacky or loud, that others were afraid to experiment with, Hallie found a way to make them cool.

She once went through this phase where she painted each of

her nails a different color, simply because she couldn't choose one, and even that little quirk started a trend among the girls in our school.

Seeing her again now, seeing the renovation she did on Wren's house, it's clear that creative expression hasn't gone anywhere.

But I don't tell my mom any of that. I don't tell her that I've thought about my childhood neighbor every day since seeing her again, and I certainly don't tell her that Hallie is living in Chicago now. It would only further her case that it's time for me to move home.

Instead, I debrief my games and travel from the week. She tells me about how much money she won at bingo night. We make tentative plans for when I'm in Boston for work next, and she finally lets me go after I promise to get her and Indy on a video call soon so she can teach my best friend how to make her famous Bolognese sauce for one of our family dinners—as if I didn't grow up watching her cook, and already know exactly how to do it myself.

"Sorry," I say, exiting Indy's office to find my friends already around the Shays' dining room table. "Did I miss anything?"

"Nope. Just got the kids to sleep upstairs," Stevie says.

Stevie is married to my teammate, Evan Zanders or Zee as we call him, but I originally met both Stevie and Indy years ago when they were flight attendants for our team's private plane. She and Zee got together that first year we all met and the rest of our crew kind of formed from there.

Indy went on to marry Stevie's brother and then four more friends came into the fold when the Rhodes brothers, who play or have played for Chicago's MLB team, started coming around more. Kai Rhodes met his wife, Miller, when she spent the summer nannying for his young son, and Isaiah Rhodes met his wife, Kennedy, when she joined his team's medical staff. The four members of the Rhodes family started coming to Sunday dinners here at the Shay house and thus formed our little Chicago found family of nine.

Yes, *nine*. Because everyone is paired up except for me.

Miller takes a seat at the table next to her husband. "I swear Max gets so excited about seeing his friends every week, that by the time it's bedtime, he's so exhausted that he sleeps better here than at home."

Indy smiles from across the table. "I love how much the kids all love each other."

Kids now refers to all five of them. What was once just Max here sleeping upstairs during family dinner, has turned into a whole slew of little ones.

Zee and Stevie have one. Ryan and Indy have two, as do Kai and Miller. Isaiah and Kennedy are too focused on their careers to think about having kids, and I...well, I'm single as fuck, so there's that.

We all dig into the pizzas in the center of the table, and I make sure to take a few slices from the one with dairy-free cheese. They're homemade and fresh out of the Shays' new brick oven outside.

I'm adding a helping of salad to my plate when Ryan asks, "Miller, how's the new location going?" referring to Miller's second patisserie she opened downtown earlier this year.

"Great. The team is on top of it, so I've been able to be somewhat hands-off now that it's up and running. I hired a new general manager for that location. Her name is Beth, she recently moved here from Oregon, and she's great. Smart. Organized. Single." Miller drags out the last word.

I take a mouth full of salad as all eight of my friends shift their attention my way.

"What?" I ask slowly, eyes bouncing to everyone around me.

Isaiah cocks his head in confusion. "Are you feeling okay?"

"I'm fine. Why?"

"Something is clearly wrong," Zee says.

"What the hell are you talking about?"

Stevie's blue-green eyes narrow. "Miller's new general manager. New to town. Single."

"I know. I heard. I'm glad she has someone solid running the patisserie."

"That's it. He's sick," Kennedy interjects. "I'm a doctor. I would know."

"That's your cue." Indy nudges her shoulder into mine. "It's *always* your cue."

Oh.

"I think you'd like her," Kai says to me. "I met her. Nice girl."

"Okay," Miller huffs. "She's not *that* nice."

Kai's knowing smile spreads. "Jealous."

She playfully rolls her eyes. "Always."

He wraps an arm over her shoulders, pulling her into him where he places a kiss on the top of her dark hair. Miller knows as well as the rest of us that she's not actually jealous, nor does she need to be. Kai has never looked at another woman the way he does her.

"What I was trying to say," Kai continues, "is that she might be a nice girl for *Rio*."

Indy sits up with excitement. "I couldn't agree more."

My brows cinch in confusion. "You haven't even met her."

"And when has that ever stopped *you* from being interested?"

"I just…" I hesitate. "I think I'm going to hit pause on the whole dating thing for a while."

From the other side of Indy, Ryan chokes on his food.

"Shit." Kennedy's eyes go wide, her mouth slightly agape. "He's sicker than I thought."

"It's not that big of a deal." I return my attention to my plate. "I'm tired of doing the same small talk on every first date. I just need a little break from trying."

Stevie's smile turns knowing. "And this has nothing to do with a certain someone who was waiting for you outside of practice last week?"

I immediately turn to Zanders. "You're a fucking gossip."

His laugh is loud. "You really thought I wasn't going to tell her? I tell her everything. Especially when our friend is looking at someone in a way I've never seen before."

"Her name is Hallie," Stevie supplies.

"And how exactly was he looking at *Hallie*?" Isaiah asks Zee.

"A lot like you when you got to marry Kennedy. He looked like a love-sick idiot. And I'm not talking about infatuation. There was history there."

Every pair of eyes swings my way once again.

I shake my head. "You don't know what you're talking about."

Miller's mouth lifts into a smile. "We're not denying the history part, I see."

"Can we talk about something else?" I ask, taking a bite of my pizza to avoid any conversation surrounding Hallie.

"Sure," Ryan says. "When is the house renovation starting?"

Jesus. I can't get away from the subject.

It's all too much to explain. Who Hallie is, regarding both our history and present predicament with the house. Why the renovation hasn't begun. Why I may have been caught looking at her like a love-sick idiot when I've never looked at someone else that way before.

Because none of them know that there was a time that I *was* love-sick for her.

No one here knows I've been in love before. No one knows that though I had a front-row seat to watch them all find their person over the years, I had found mine long before any of them.

At least, I thought I did.

I'm still so fucking confused on what I should do about the house, still in shock from seeing Hallie again, that I don't have it in me to explain.

"I'm going to grab another bottle of wine for the table." Standing from my seat, I take the empty bottle of red with me. "Anyone need anything from the kitchen?"

The group stays silent, and I can feel every pair of eyes on me as I leave the dining room to hide away in the kitchen. I toss the empty glass bottle in the recycling before bracing my hands on the counter in front of me to take a deep breath.

I've only known about Hallie being in Chicago for a week and already, it feels like things are getting too muddled. I've kept our history a secret from my closest friends all this time, as if leaving everything between us in Boston and not speaking of her would help me pretend as if it never happened.

It didn't do shit for me. I simply spent the last six years living in a delusional state of denial, telling myself I wasn't hurt over it all, while subconsciously comparing everyone to our relationship because that's what I was looking for.

"So, who is she?" Indy asks, reaching around me to grab a fresh bottle of wine off the counter.

Exhaling, I turn to face her, leaning back against the kitchen counter with my arms crossed over my chest. "She's the designer assigned to my house project."

Indy raises a single eyebrow as she uncorks the bottle. "You know what I'm asking, Rio."

Stevie joins us in the kitchen. "Oh, don't mind me, I'm..." She looks around for something to do, a reason she'd need to be in the kitchen right now. "Helping with the wine."

"And I'm doing dishes," Kennedy says, carrying a single plate to the sink. A single *clean* plate.

"I'll be honest here. I'm being nosey." Miller hops onto the kitchen counter, taking a seat. "Spill it. Who's the girl?"

That pulls a laugh out of me.

There's something about my friendships with women, especially *these* women, that I value in a way that's different from my male friendships. Sometimes, with the guys, we tend to shoot the shit and laugh off the hard stuff too quickly. But when I need to discuss a tough topic, I tend to find that I get a more empathetic and understanding approach from the women in my life.

So, if there's anyone I'd be willing to open up about Hallie with, it's these four.

With half as many eyes on me as there were in the dining room, I finally admit, "We grew up together in Boston. She was the girl next door."

Too many knowing smiles reflect back at me in the kitchen.

"We have...a *sordid* history and I unknowingly hired her to renovate the house. I didn't know she was living here until last week, but once I realized it was her, I made it clear that someone else needed to be on the project."

"That's what happened outside of practice?" Stevie asks.

"She was there to ask me to reconsider. Said she was desperate to work on the house. Needed to show her boss what she could do so she could get hired full-time or something like that. I think she's in an internship program but wants a permanent position."

Kennedy's smile turns sympathetic. "When was the last time you saw her?"

The images of those last days in Boston flood my mind. It was the worst time of my life, and I've tried my hardest over the last six years to block it out.

"Shortly after I had gotten drafted, before I moved here permanently."

"What happened between you two?" Miller asks.

An odd surge of protectiveness coats my chest like a piece of armor. Though Hallie and I have a sordid history, it's still *our* history, and everything in me wants to keep it that way. Regardless that I got hurt, I don't want my friends to have that first impression of her. I don't want anything to skew their opinion of her.

"I'd rather keep that between her and me."

Every single one of the girls' shoulders drop, heads tilting with big sad eyes as if they're playing out some kind of rom-com version of a destined reconnection.

"You four can stop looking at me like that."

Miller's smile slips into a smirk. "Like what?"

"Like you think this is it. As if she were the one who got away, and this is our second chance. It's not going to happen, so get that out of your minds. Trust me, too much bad happened between us in the past for there to be any good between us now."

Indy is the one I'm most reluctant to look at, because when I finally do, I see the realization all over her face. Without me saying anything, she knows. Maybe not all the details of Hallie and me, but I can tell she knows I loved the girl and got my heart broken over it.

Then she does the most Indy thing possible and finds the positive.

"Honestly, who better to design your house?" she asks. "She knows you."

She has no idea how accurate that statement is.

"Whatever happened between you two," she continues, "and I don't know the details, but is there really no part of you left that wants to help her? If she's coming to you like this, she must really need the job, and I can't imagine you being okay with *not* helping her."

Fucking Indy.

My molars grind together, jaw ticking because once again, she doesn't realize how true *that* statement is either.

I've had a soft spot for Hallie Hart since the day I met her, and as my resolve slips away, I realize that softness hasn't changed one bit in the years since I last saw her.

Indy smiles proudly. "Just a thought," she says before she and the other girls leave me in the kitchen.

Little shit.

My phone feels heavy in my pocket, begging me to pull it out and get ahold of her. I take my time finding Hallie's new number in my contacts—the one I may have asked Wren for earlier this week—before shooting her a text.

Me: *You start tomorrow.*

7

Hallie

(AGE 13)

"Happy birthday, Hallie girl." Mrs. DeLuca places a cake on the table in front of me with thirteen candles lit and ready for me to wish on.

My smile is beaming as I look around to find my dad with his arms wrapped around the front of my mom's shoulders, holding her to him. I watch as Mr. DeLuca slips his hand into his wife's while they all sing for my birthday. Luke and Rio sit across the table from me, and then a blush creeps across my chest when my eye catches with Rio's, finding him singing louder than anyone else.

I don't have it in me to look his way again while the song finishes, and I certainly don't make eye contact as I blow out my candles.

My wish is the same as it's been all year. It's the same thing I wish for every time I pluck a dandelion from some grass, see a falling star in the sky, or notice when it's 11:11 on the clock.

Our parents are busy chatting and laughing with each other when Luke sits forward, elbows on the table in front of us and asks, "So, what'd you wish for?"

"I'm not telling you."

"Oh, come on. What is it? You got some big stupid crush that you don't want to tell us about? Did you wish that he'd like you back or something?"

My eyes flick to Rio sitting next to my brother, my cheeks flaming with heat. "Shut up, Luke. No, I—"

"She can't tell us," Rio cuts in. "Otherwise, it won't come true."

He smiles at me, dimples sinking into his cheeks, and it makes me smile right back.

"Whatever." Luke wipes his finger across the white icing before sticking it into his mouth. "It probably won't come true anyway."

"Lucas William Hart," our mom scolds. "Get your dirty fingers away from your sister's cake. That's going to be your piece, if Hallie even decides to give you any now." She grabs the cake from the table. "Come on. I'll slice and you serve."

Luke rolls his eyes, standing from his seat to help our mom in the kitchen.

Rio leans across the table, speaking quietly to me. "Don't listen to him. Your wish will come true."

Those kind green eyes sparkle under the dining room light, his dark hair falling messily into his face. He's so cute and has no idea. It makes my stomach somersault.

"Thanks."

His grin tilts up on one side, soft and genuine, just like him. "Happy birthday, Hal."

Okay, if I could scream without causing our families to stare at me, I totally would. I love when he calls me Hal. It's like a secret only he and I have.

It's been exactly two years since we moved to Boston and in that time, Rio and Luke have both turned fourteen and become best friends. And Rio and I...well, we're friends too, but it's different than his friendship with Luke. They play sports together and talk about girls. They're in eighth grade while I'm still in seventh. When Rio has sleepovers at my house, it's in Luke's room and my brother doesn't ever let me hang out with them.

But Rio is always nice to me, whether Luke is around or not, and though my brother doesn't know that Rio and I are friends, we definitely are. I'm sure of it. Just look at the gifts he got me for my birthday this year. I know his mom didn't pick them out for him.

Only Rio knows that I want to be an interior designer when I grow up and he gifted me a notebook filled with grid paper. I love drawing houses from a bird's-eye view, designing layouts, and I was doing it on lined paper before, but the grid version is going to be so much better.

From his window, he's watched as I painted my room three times since we moved in and rearranged the furniture more times than I can count. When he asked me why I kept changing it, I told him how I was practicing to become an interior designer.

He also got me a new cassette tape for my birthday, and if it were anyone else, they would've bought me a CD because they're way more popular now, but I still think tapes are better. That's how I know Rio picked out my presents himself.

Luke sets a slice of cake in front of me before passing plates out to both our family and the DeLucas.

"Thank you for making this, Mrs. DeLuca," I say before my first bite. The devil's food cake melts in my mouth as soon as it hits my tongue.

Both Luke and Mr. DeLuca had this cake for their birthdays this year, and it was so good both times, I knew it was the right flavor to request for mine.

Rio's mom squeezes me in a hug from behind. "Anything for you, sweet girl."

My attention darts up to find Rio, once again, smiling at me.

"Mia, I'm going to need this recipe," my mom says. "Both my kids love it, and they never agree on anything."

"Already wrote it down for you, Steph." Mrs. DeLuca gestures to the kitchen and the two of them disappear out of view.

Not only are Luke and Rio best friends, but so are our moms. They do everything together. Plan birthdays, arrange carpools, and more times than I can count, I've caught them up late on the back porch sharing a bottle of wine. It works out well that we live ten feet away.

I guess you could say our dads are best friends too, but I'm not sure if dads have best friends. They've never called each other that, but they spend every Sunday either watching football together or working on Mr. DeLuca's old car in his garage.

Our parents even planned a family vacation for all of us this summer to Florida. It's the best, living so close to the DeLucas, but sometimes it feels like I'm the odd one out. Sometimes I feel like I'm trying to tag along with my older brother and his friend, and Luke usually gives me a hard time for it. Then our moms invite me to join them, but it's not as fun.

"Happy birthday, baby girl." My dad smacks a kiss to the top of my head. "I cannot believe how much you're growing up. You're the spitting image of your mom."

"Happy birthday, Miss Hallie," Mr. DeLuca adds.

"Thank you."

They finish their slices of cake before slowly making their way to the garage, leaving me with only the boys in the dining room.

"I got the new Mario Kart game," Luke says to Rio. "Want to go play it?"

"Definitely."

They stand to leave, and Luke is already at the front door when Rio pauses halfway there, turning back to me. "Want to come play, Hallie?"

"No," Luke whines. "She doesn't know how to."

I give Rio a smile. "That's okay. Thanks though."

His attention goes from me to my brother, then back to me, before he returns to the table, taking his seat once again. "It's your birthday. What do you want to do?"

"You should go play."

"Rio, let's go," my brother begs from the front door.

"You go ahead. I'm going to stay here."

"That's so dumb. She's fine."

"I'll catch up with you later."

Rio turns back to me and doesn't even flinch when Luke closes the front door a little too hard and a little too loudly.

"What do you want to do?" he asks again.

I shrug, looking for something interesting enough that he'll want to stay here and not go with my brother instead.

"Luke got you a friendship bracelet kit," he says. "Do you want to make those?"

I chuckle. "You don't want to do that."

He smiles at my laughter. "I do! But you need to teach me how."

"Really?"

"Absolutely. I'll make you one for your birthday."

"Okay." My cheeks hurt from the splitting grin on my face as I grab the kit from the other side of the table where my opened presents are. As I do, my eye snags on the new boombox the DeLucas got me. "Can we listen to music while we make them?"

"We better," Rio says. "Do you want to listen to the new cassette I got you?"

I'm not sure I can light up more than I am now. "Yeah, that sounds good."

The new boombox plays CDs too, and as cassettes are becoming harder to find, I'm sure that'll come in handy when I'm forced to switch. But for now, I click my new tape into place.

"Which song are you playing first?" he asks.

I take my time choosing a song from the track list because I know this is a moment I'll want to remember, and whichever song I choose is going to be one I put on next year's mixtape because I'll want to rewind it back and play it on repeat for a long time to come.

I write the number thirteen on my finished mixtape, signing it with an "H" and a heart. You know, for Hallie Hart. Heart like Hart. Anyway, it's my new signature and I love it.

I've been working on finishing this mixtape for hours so when I finally look up from my desk, I find that the sky is pitch black, with only the glow of the moon for light.

Outside my window, there's a person sitting on the roof that connects the DeLucas' house to ours. The same roof that connects Rio's room to mine.

I'd maybe be scared if I didn't already know it was him. I've woken up in the middle of the night a couple of times and spotted him out there, lying on his back and staring up at the moon. I've never asked what he's doing out there, never asked why he was still awake. I think maybe because I didn't want him to know that I can see him. Which, I guess, doesn't really make sense. We wave to each other from our rooms all the time, so of course he knows I can see him. I guess I didn't want him to feel like I caught him doing something he's not supposed to. I didn't want him to stop sitting out there on the roof between our rooms.

It's late, and checking the clock on my nightstand, I see there's only twenty minutes left of my birthday. If it were a school night, my mom would've already checked to make sure I was asleep, but it's Saturday and after Rio volunteered to hang out with me all day, maybe he'd be okay if I caught him.

I crack my window open and the cold spring air hits me in an instant. I whisper, but I'm loud enough for him to hear me. "What are you doing?"

When he whips in my direction, his face is etched in panic, like he's about to be in trouble, but when he finds it's only me, his mouth tilts into a smile. "Can't sleep. What are you still doing up?"

"Enjoying my birthday."

"Want to enjoy it out here?"

Oh my God. I'm holding my lips closed to keep me from squealing. I swear that birthday wish was so much stronger than all the other wishes this year.

"I um...don't you think we'll get in trouble for being on the roof?"

He shrugs. "I haven't gotten caught by anyone yet. Well, besides you. You don't have to though."

I want to though.

I push my window open further, eyeing the ledge. It's only about a foot drop and this part of the roof is completely flat. Before I lose my nerve, I swing one leg over the ledge before sitting on the windowsill and bringing my other leg out as well.

Thankfully, we've had an unseasonably warm week, so I'm not worried about snow or ice. It's all melted at this point, but still, I crawl on my hands and knees to meet him in the middle of the roof between our houses.

He chuckles as I take a cautious seat, and it's then I realize though it's not snowing, it's still freezing out here and I didn't think to throw a sweatshirt on over my sleep shirt. But I also don't want to crawl back to my room and risk missing out on this.

I hold my knees close to my chest to keep as much warmth in as I can.

He nudges his shoulder into mine. "Did you have a good birthday?"

"Yeah."

"What was your favorite part?"

This.

"Um, maybe going to get my nails done with your mom this morning?"

I hold my hands out to show him.

"Ten different colors?" he asks with a laugh. "Couldn't decide?"

I shake my head no.

"Kind of like your room." He nods towards my window where I recently painted my bedroom walls...again.

This go around, I decided to do each of the four walls a different color shade of green. I like it. For now.

"My mom loves you," he says. "I'm pretty sure she wishes you were *her* daughter."

I giggle, but my teeth chatter as I do.

"Are you cold?"

I quickly shake my head. I don't want him to tell me to go back to my room. "No. I'm fine."

He unzips his hoodie, slipping his arms out. I catch sight of the friendship bracelet I made tied around his wrist. He was trying to make one for me too, but he had a hard time figuring out the knots and only got a couple of inches finished.

He holds out his hoodie for me to take.

"Aren't you going to be cold?" I ask.

"I play hockey. I'm used to the cold. I'm warm enough."

I keep my lips pressed together to hold in any excited noises that want to escape.

His sweatshirt is warm from his body heat when I slip my arms through the holes, and it smells so much like him, I think his scent might be embedded in the fibers. I try to cover my deep inhale as I hide my hands in the pockets, realizing I was too excited to get out here that I still have my birthday mixtape in my grasp.

There's a silence between us, both of us just sitting on the roof and looking at the moon. I search for something, anything to say, wanting to extend the moment for as long as possible.

"How was hockey practice?" I ask.

Rio shrugs. "It was a scrimmage. I didn't get to play much."

"Maybe you'll get to play more next week."

"Probably not." He sighs. "The other guys are so much better than me."

I don't know what to say to that because he's not entirely wrong. I've been to a lot of his games and when he does get to play, it's kind of obvious that he's not as good as his teammates. He's become a better skater, but he's not great at the stick and puck handling aspect. Though, he's usually excited to just be out there.

"I think I'm going to quit."

"What?" I jolt back and he reaches out to steady me as if he thinks I'm going to fall. He quickly takes his hand off my leg when he realizes I'm safe. "Why would you quit?"

He lifts a brow as if to say, *do I really have to explain it?*

"I'm not going to make the high school team next year, so what's the point? Maybe I should try lacrosse with Luke. At least I wouldn't look like an idiot on skates."

The defeat in his voice makes me sad. He's always so positive about things, even not being the best at hockey.

"Do you even like lacrosse?" I ask.

"I don't know. Maybe."

No, he doesn't.

"I don't think you should quit."

He huffs a white plume of cold air, and I know he's freezing right now. "Why not?"

"Because it's your dream to play for the NHL. For the Boston Bobcats. Your favorite team."

"That's never going to happen, Hallie. I'm not good."

"You don't know that. You'll be in high school next year and your coaches will be even better. You'll get better too. And I like going to your games to watch you, even if you don't get to play."

He stays quiet and that feels like I said too much, so I fidget with my hands to keep the silence from turning too uncomfortable.

Rio looks at my lap out of the corner of his eye.

"What's that?" he asks, nodding towards the pockets of his sweatshirt I'm wearing where there's an obvious rectangular outline.

"Oh, it's um…" I pull it out. "A mixtape."

He eyes the label. "Thirteen? Thirteen songs?"

"Thirteen, like how old I am."

"And what's that?" he asks, his forefinger running over the H and the heart.

"Me. Hallie Hart. H and a heart."

The heart has a little extra tail that I accidentally drew, not stopping it where the two ends were supposed to connect.

Rio covers it with his finger to hide the imperfection. "That's cool. H heart. Hallie Hart."

My cheeks hurt from holding back my smile.

"What songs?" he asks.

"All my songs from this year. My important-moment songs."

"You put them all together? On one tape?"

"Yeah. This is my third year doing it, so I have three of them now."

He nods approvingly. "That's so cool, Hal."

Eyes on my lap, I turn a little shy. "Thanks."

"Can I listen to it?"

That grabs my attention. "You want to listen to it?"

"Yeah, and I want you to tell me what happened to make them important songs to you."

Oh.

"Well...I...I don't know. Some of the songs aren't good songs. They're just songs I was listening to when something important happened, you know? You probably won't like the music."

"I still want to listen to it."

"I...but..."

"Please?" he asks gently.

It washes away any nerves I have.

"Okay." I hold it out to him. "You can have this one to listen to. I can make another."

His green eyes sparkle. "Really?"

"Yeah, if you want it."

"Absolutely, I want it. I just... I don't have a way to listen to it. I don't have anything that plays cassettes."

"You could use my new boombox if you want."

"Do you want to listen to it now?"

"Now?" My eyes go wide. "It's midnight and...and..."

He cocks a brow, and I instantly feel silly. He's older. Probably doesn't have a curfew as early as mine. He and the other eighth graders probably stay up past midnight all the time.

"I'm not tired yet," he says. "We could listen to it in your room. We'll keep the volume down."

What? He's never been in my room before. He's always in Luke's room when he comes over, but no part of me is tired now either.

This is cool. Listening to music in my room after midnight.

"Okay," I agree. "Just be quiet so we don't wake up Luke or my parents. Or do you want me to wake up Luke? He can come to my room too if you want."

"You don't have to if you don't want to. We can listen just us two."

This can't be happening. This is the best birthday ever.

Quietly, Rio follows me back through my window. While I set up the boombox on my nightstand, he takes a tour.

"I like your room," he whispers. "Even cooler up close than it is when I wave to you from my window."

He checks out some of my drawings I've pinned to the wall, looks carefully over my trophies from swimming and soccer. He plops into my bean bag chair and doesn't tease me for my baby blanket that I still have the way my brother does.

I sit on my bed, still wearing his hoodie, and Rio stretches out to lie down on the floor next to the mattress, lacing his hands behind his back.

"What happened during the first song?" he asks.

Oh, wow. Okay this is happening, and this is going to be so much more embarrassing than I thought.

"I um...well, don't tease me, but this boy told me he liked me right before spring break last year."

He sits up quickly and with only the moonlight, I can still see his brows pinched together. "Who?"

"Kevin Gross."

Rio's face contorts in disgust. "Kevin Gross? Hallie, eww. His last name is Gross for a reason. That guy collects bugs between class periods and keeps them in his pocket."

"It happened almost a year ago!" I whisper-yell. "And I don't know. It was the first time anyone had ever liked me, so yeah. I wanted to remember it. I was listening to this song right before he told me."

Rio lies back down with a huff. "Play it."

I do, pressing the play button as "Waterfalls" begins to filter quietly through the speakers.

He shakes his head. "You wasted a TLC song on Kevin Gross? Wow."

I laugh, lying back on my bed to mirror his position.

We listen to the whole song in silence and during the long pause before the second song begins to play, Rio quietly says, "Hallie?" from the floor.

I whisper right back. "Yeah?"

"Did you like Kevin back?"

"No. Not like that."

There's another long pause.

"Well, maybe that was the first time you were told, but I know for a fact it wasn't the first time someone liked you."

My eyes feel like they're going to pop out of my head with how quickly they widen. Does he mean himself or someone else? My heart is thundering in my chest and if I were braver, I'd ask him what he means. But I'm not. I don't ask for clarification and instead, decide to overthink that single sentence for the rest of my life.

The next song begins to play, and completely casually, like he didn't just drop a potential bomb on me, he asks, "Why is the second song important to you?"

8

Rio

"And you're sure that's all it is?" Hallie asks into the phone. "Because I can take work off if I need to. I can drive out there."

She's pacing, retracing her same three or four steps in the corner of the design firm's conference room, phone held tightly to her ear.

We were starting our first design consultation when her phone rang, so I'm currently sitting at the conference table when she hesitantly checks over her shoulder to see if I'm eavesdropping.

Of fucking course I'm eavesdropping.

Every tense muscle in her shoulders and back screams that she's distraught and something is wrong. And as if on instinct, my own body is bunched in anticipation, waiting to see what she needs, even though every fiber of my being would like to believe I don't give a shit.

"Promise me, Luke," she continues, turning back to face the wall. "You'll call me if it gets any worse." Her brother says something on the other line that causes her shoulders to drop an inch. "Thank you. Okay. Love you too. Bye."

I wait for her to tell me what's wrong, but she doesn't explain.

Instead, she ends the call and gives herself a moment to collect herself in the corner before returning to the table.

She's got this phony grin on her lips as she opens her laptop, attempting to resume our meeting. "Sorry about that."

"What's wrong?"

She shakes her head, extending that forced smile across her mouth as if I, of all people, wouldn't be able to tell it's fake.

"Is everything okay with your brother?" I ask.

"Everything is fine."

She won't make eye contact with me.

"Hallie, something is clearly wrong."

"Rio, please. We both know you don't actually care if something is upsetting me."

If only that were true. It'd make my life a whole lot easier if I could care less about this girl.

"Right?" Hallie's attention finally meets mine, testing me to answer her.

But I can't focus on the answer when she's looking at me like that, her eyes big and curious and hazel.

So *fucking* hazel.

I almost forgot how pretty they are, how they lean more green than brown depending on the light. How they'd screw shut if we were watching a scary movie together. How they'd softly close when I'd kiss her mouth. How they'd turn dark, her pupils blowing out when I'd kiss the rest of her.

She's staring right back at me, and when her lips slightly part, my attention drifts down to them instead.

Fuck, I missed those.

I still remember the first time we kissed.

I remember the last time too, and that memory snaps me out of the stupid little spell that naturally lives between us.

What the hell am I doing?

This is why, even all these years later, it's a bad idea for me to be alone in the same room as Hallie Hart. The pull between us is still there and I hate that.

"Yeah." I clear my throat. "If you're done taking phone calls, maybe we can get back to our meeting."

Those hazel eyes flash with hurt and I hate *that* almost as much as I want to hate *her*.

Too mean.

"How is um..." I rub my palm against the back of my neck. "How is Luke, by the way?"

She looks up at me with confusion, thanks to my mental whiplash, but her face quickly morphs into a scowl. Asking about her brother was clearly the wrong thing to say. I haven't spoken to my old friend in as many years since I last spoke to his sister.

Hallie's attention is back on her computer screen. "He's fine."

"Is he still in Boston?"

"South of Minneapolis, actually."

"He moved back to Minnesota? I had no idea."

Her jaw tics, as if she were grinding her molars together. "And how would you? It's not like you've spoken to either of us since you left Boston, and Luke didn't even do anything wrong for you to cut him out of your life like that."

She's right.

Luke didn't do anything wrong, but I was young and hurt and took all my pain out on anyone in close proximity to the situation.

Luke was a good friend growing up. Sure, he was a dick to his sister when we were younger, but he grew out of that and became the quintessential protective older sibling. For the entirety of my teen years, Luke was practically my brother, but when I moved away, I deleted his contact from my phone simply to keep myself from giving into the temptation of calling him to check on Hallie.

Yes, Luke was important to me, but that relationship didn't hold a candle to the importance his sister would hold in my life.

Hallie turns her wrist over, checking the time on her watch, before shifting her attention back to her laptop. "Let's just focus on the meeting," she says. "It's getting late."

It's only four o'clock.

"Somewhere more important to be?" I ask.

She doesn't answer me. Instead, she concentrates on filling out a client profile form on her computer without having to check with me for any of the answers. My full name, age, birthday.

Regardless of my attempts to keep our connection at a distance, there's this weird warmth in my chest that I haven't felt in a long time. I've been on so many first dates, been asked so many fucking times what my favorite color is, that this feels nice. Being known, even if it is just the basics, feels *nice*.

But it can't feel nice with her, so instead, when I catch her checking the time again, I push.

"Do you have other plans or something? I may be mistaken, but weren't you the one begging me for this job?"

"Yes." It comes out with a bite. "But our meeting was set for two o'clock, not four. I have another...*commitment* I need to be at by five."

The image of that fucking guy pops into my head. Him sitting next to her at *my* game. I'm not one to be violent off the ice, but everything in me was wishing the glass that was separating us would've magically disappeared, so I could've reached out and grabbed him by the goddamn neck.

Okay, that's dramatic as fuck, but I didn't expect the blind possessiveness I'd feel after not only seeing Hallie again but seeing her with someone else. Someone who wasn't *me*.

"A date?" I can't help but ask.

She's working away at the computer, filling out information she already knows. "Not exactly your concern, now, is it?"

So that's a yes.

I was only late to our meeting because I got stuck at work. They gave me extra film to watch before our game tomorrow night against Dallas, and then I needed more time in the training room to work on my right calf because it's been uncharacteristically tight lately. The medical staff wouldn't let me leave until I got treatment. I didn't mean to be late. In fact, I called the design firm and apologized for running behind, but now, I'm wishing I took even more time getting over here. I wish I had an excuse to keep her here even longer.

Leaning back in the chair, I lace my fingers, resting my hands on my stomach. "We should make sure this meeting is as thorough as possible."

"Really? That's how this is going to go?"

"This is my home, after all, Hallie. My safe space. My respite from the outside world. It's going to take time and deserves your full attention."

She rolls her eyes. "You can give it a rest, Rio. I get it. You're going to make sure I'm late."

I'm going to make sure she doesn't go at all.

In the chair next to me, Hallie crosses one leg over the other before pulling out her phone to type a text, presumably to whoever *he* is, letting him know she's not coming.

It doesn't feel natural to be a dick, especially to her, so the guilt settles in quickly. Part of me wants to tell her never mind, she should go, but most of me would rather stomach the guilt than having to live with the knowledge she's on a date with someone else.

It was one thing when she didn't live here. I got pretty good at lying to myself, tricking myself into believing she didn't exist and therefore not having to think about her dating. But it's entirely different having to witness it with my own two eyes.

So, I let her finish the text to tell whatever his name is know she's not coming.

She's in all black today. Black jeans, ripped apart at the knees. Black boots with a heel that does insane things to her legs and ass. A black satin shirt, unbuttoned at the top, allowing the layers of silver and gold necklaces to tease as they fall and disappear behind it.

Fucking beautiful.

She always has been though.

But beyond that, I remember my other favorite things about her. She's strong yet caring. Determined yet kind. There was a time when my absolute favorite thing in the world was to simply be with her. If I would allow myself to admit it, I missed Hallie Hart.

As she texts, I watch as she slips her short dark hair behind one of her ears, giving me a perfect view of her face and neck. The soft angle of her jaw. The cute slope of her nose. Her full brows and light freckles.

"I love your hair like this."

Fuck me. Did I say that out loud?

That's confirmed when her attention whips in my direction, those dark brows furrowed, once again confused.

That makes two of us.

If only she could see inside my brain, she'd realize it's a fucking mess right now. The back and forth, not knowing how to treat her, unable to find a safe middle ground. We haven't spent time together since everything turned to shit, and clearly, I have no idea how to act around her now.

"What did you just say?" she asks.

"Your haircut. It looks good on you. Shows you off. When did you cut it?"

A warmth creeps up her cheeks, allowing them to turn a shade of pink and I visibly watch as the wall she's built up, drops a bit along with her tense shoulders. "About six years ago. I've kept it short since."

After I left is what she meant.

More tension lingers between us.

I wait for her to meet my eyes again. "You look good, Hal."

Too nice.

What am I doing? Either I want to hate her or I don't. I swear, I'm going to need someone else to start sitting in on these meetings to keep me from slipping up and saying stupid, honest shit.

Hallie's attention slices back to her computer. "We should

talk about the house. Your hopes for the renovation. Your overall goals."

I clear my throat. "Yeah. Yeah, that's a good idea."

Reaching between us, I find the leg of her chair and pull, bringing her seat flush to mine.

"What are you doing?"

Hell if I know.

"I...uh...couldn't see the computer."

Her brows are cinched before she eventually exhales a laugh. "You're as charming as ever, DeLuca."

"Thanks, b—" I stop myself, *thank God*. "...Hallie."

That was almost a slip of the fucking tongue if I've ever heard one.

Thankfully, she doesn't seem phased, which means she has no idea that I almost just referred to her as "baby" like I used to when we were younger. Sometimes I'd use it in normal, everyday conversation. Sometimes through text. Always when our clothes were off.

Professional. Working. Relationship, I remind myself.

But clearly, I have no clue how to do that. Not with her.

When I look at Hallie, all I see is the girl from my past, my literal favorite person. But then I remember that she's not her anymore, I'm no longer that same guy, and that pisses me off. I'm either too comfortable with her or too mean, when all I need is to be professional.

"What are your goals for your home?" she asks. "What are your plans for it?"

I get my mind focused back on the task at hand. "It's in a good neighborhood. In a good school district. I bought it with the intention of building a family there."

Hallie's fingers halt, hovering over the keys.

Just when I thought this meeting couldn't get any more difficult.

It only grows more tense when she asks, "And do you still see that for yourself? Having a family in that house?"

She braves a look at me, her eyes asking a whole lot more questions than only that one.

"I'm not sure," I tell her honestly. "But if I sell, I'd imagine a family would be the buyer, so it seems practical to gear the renovation towards that. Either my family's home or someone else's."

Having this meeting with her, of all people, is a special kind of fucked up.

Hallie types again, filling the answers in on the form, but then her fingers abruptly halt once more. She closes the laptop, turning her entire body towards me.

"You're really thinking of selling?" she asks. "To buy something newer?"

No one in Chicago, other than Wren, has heard me say this. But it's Hallie. She used to be the first person I talked to about anything.

"To move back to Boston, actually."

"Oh."

"If I were to wait until free agency and see if they make an offer next off-season, I mean."

"You'd leave?"

"I'm not sure. I haven't made any final decisions, but it's a possibility. My mom wants me home."

She smiles softly. "I bet she misses having you close by."

Then, somehow, even more tension settles in because my family is not a safe subject for us to discuss.

"But yeah, that makes sense," Hallie shifts the conversation. "Playing for Boston was always the dream, right?"

One of them.

"No one else really knows, so that needs to stay between us," I add. "Well, Wren has an idea. That's why I wanted to hire you in the first place. I'm not sure that I'm leaving, but I want the house to be ready to sell in case I do. Wren's brother will be putting his house on the market around the same time I might. I want to make sure I get the biggest return on my investment if I go that route."

She nods in understanding. "Update the house without breaking the bank on a renovation you might not get to enjoy long-term. Makes sense."

"Exactly."

She opens her computer and types more notes. "Your friends don't know you're thinking of leaving?"

"No. I mean, my closest friends are either professional athletes or married to one, so I think they probably understand what it means that I didn't sign my early contract extension. But I haven't explicitly said anything, so if you can keep that between us, I'd appreciate it."

She breathes a soft laugh. "Who am I going to tell? I don't know your friends."

"But you'll probably meet them. You're about to spend a lot of time in my house. They come over quite a bit. It feels inevitable that your paths will eventually cross."

She hesitates for a moment before asking, "Is there anything else that you'd like me to keep between us? If I do meet them, I mean."

My eyes search hers and I know exactly what she's asking.

"They know your name. I think they've all picked up on the fact that there's history between us, but they don't know the details. The way I see it, they don't need to."

"You're telling me you never once vented and talked shit about me?" she asks with a laugh.

"No." My tone is even. "Never once, Hal."

Her laughter dies.

More silence lingers.

"Did you ever talk shit about me?" I ask, a hint of humor in my tone.

"Only to Luke."

"What about your dad? God, he probably fucking hates me now, huh?"

Her body tenses and the air shifts around us, going cold once again.

I have no idea how to do this. How to stop bringing *us* up.

"The house," I redirect. "Let's focus on the house."

She shakes her head, trying to shake off the constant whiplash of this meeting. "Yeah, tell me more."

"It...uh...it needs...something. I bought it brand new from the builder, so it's essentially a plain white box."

I wait to see if that connects any dots for her, but it doesn't.

"At least we won't have to undo anything," she says. "We have a blank slate to work with. That's my favorite. This is going to be fun." There's a genuine smile currently lifting on Hallie's lips as she grabs a notebook and pen.

It hits me then. She's doing it. This dream she had that we talked about for years, working for a big-name designer in a big city. Hallie is doing it.

Pride swells when the realization hits me.

And that pride feels conflicting too because I shouldn't care anymore, but all I can see is the girl next door, the one I'd watch from my window as she redid her childhood bedroom more times than I could count. All to get here.

"Let's talk about your likes and dislikes." Hallie draws a line down the middle of the notebook, putting an X on one side and a heart on the other.

That fucking heart. It makes my own skip a beat, seeing her draw one again.

It's Hallie's version of a heart where one side overlaps and extends past where it's meant to stop, giving it a little extra flick at the end.

I don't know what comes over me. Probably the same form of insanity that caused me to pull her chair close to mine and almost call her "baby." But whatever it is, it makes me reach out and cover the imperfection of the heart with the tip of my forefinger.

I swear all the oxygen leaves the room.

She stares at my finger and in that moment, I know that every birthday she had from ages thirteen to nineteen are currently running through her mind.

Too nice. Too comfortable. Too nostalgic.

For a second, it feels like the old us sitting next to each other. But then I remember it can't feel that good again, so I pull my hand away from the heart.

"Why would you do that?" she asks, her voice quiet.

I push down the natural inclination to comfort her and instead say, "I'm surprised you even remember."

Her brows are furrowed when she looks at me. "What?"

"I'm surprised you remember anything about us, really. You didn't seem to give a shit about our history the last time we saw each other."

The words taste horrible as they come off my tongue.

Too mean, I quickly realize.

We sit in silence, and just when I think she's grabbing her notebook to continue our meeting, she instead puts it in her bag, followed by her laptop.

"What are you doing?"

She stands, slinging her tote bag over her shoulder. "Leaving."

Hallie is already at the door by the time I realize what's happening.

"Wait. Why?" I stand too.

"Why?" She laughs condescendingly, turning back to face me. "Why do you think, Rio? I thought I could do this, work together, but there's no way. Not with you."

"Hal—"

"One minute you're being the old you, and the next you're being a jerk. Then you keep bringing up the past. Pick a lane, Rio! The back-and-forth is exhausting. I'm just trying to do my job and have a working relationship with you, but you're not letting me. At this point, I'd rather lose out on this opportunity than spend the next six months getting mental whiplash from being around you."

Fuck. I clearly swung the pendulum way too far in the mean direction.

She exhales a calming breath, facing the door and not me. "You used to be my best friend, and yeah, we haven't seen each other since then, but I'd rather hold on to the memory of the sweet neighbor boy I loved than replace it with this version of you."

Without looking back at me, she leaves.

9

It's close to two a.m. by the time I pull up to Wren's house. *My* house. The house I'm living in right now.

I don't know how best to refer to it. It's temporary, so it doesn't feel right to call it home, but it's also the place I'm sleeping and where all my belongings currently reside.

I pull my car close to the curb, parking on the street instead of the driveway. The only time I've parked in the driveway was the night I moved in and had boxes to unload. I know the car has some kind of leak and after all the work we did on the house to make it ready to put it on the market soon, I'm not going to decrease its value by leaving oil stains on the concrete from my shitty car.

Cutting the engine, I sit, unable to find the willpower to get myself inside the house. The soles of my feet feel like they have their own heartbeats, thanks to a long night behind the bar, and the idea of getting back on them to walk inside feels impossible.

Tonight's shift was rough. I got stiffed more times than I could count, someone walked out on their tab without paying, and I had a drink spilled down my shirt. And that all happened *after* that scary phone call from Luke regarding my dad and the shit show of a meeting with Rio.

Initially, I texted my boss and told him I was going to be late, but when the design meeting became too much, I hightailed my way to the bar. I made shit money tonight, but it's more than I started the day with, so it's something, I guess.

The two a.m. silence is nice. Calming and welcomed after a long shift in a loud bar followed by an equally loud drive thanks to my rattling engine. I don't want to move. I want to sleep right here, wearing my beer-scented clothes and god-awful non-slip shoes.

I lay my head back, about to close my eyes, when a figure catches my attention out of my periphery. It's the middle of the night so I should probably have some sense of fear, but I'm not scared in the slightest. I'd recognize him anywhere.

Rio is sitting on his front steps, elbows leaning on his knees and hands laced together when he looks up and over in my direction. It's not a quick glance, but a lingering stare, letting me know that the reason he's on his front steps is because he's waiting for me.

My stomach instantly fills with dread. I thought I'd have more time until I had to face him. I'm not ready to do this again, especially at two in the morning.

Sure, me running out of our meeting was a tad dramatic, but it was the compilation of everything. Seeing him again. Living next door. Him asking about my brother and telling me I look good.

Seriously, what the fuck was that?

Then immediately, he tried to be a jerk as if he realized he was being too kind.

Don't get me wrong, Rio could've said a lot worse, but the guy doesn't have a naturally mean bone in his body. So, I guess it was the realization that he feels he *has* to be shitty towards me, as if that's what I deserve from him now, that hurts the worst.

I'm trying to move forward, attempt some sort of working relationship, but he kept bringing up the past—a past in which he obliterated my heart and left me to figure out life without him.

My attention finds him again when Rio pushes off the steps, and with his hands tucked into the pocket of his sweatpants, he starts in my direction, crossing the lawn that connects our two houses.

It's chilly out, but he looks obnoxiously comfortable in those black sweatpants and his team-issued hoodie. His curls are a bit frizzy, as if he took a shower and didn't put any product in his hair after, but his eyes look heavy with the need for sleep.

I'm not surprised that he's awake at this hour, though. I remember him being a ball of energy at times and that's *without* drinking caffeine, but his brain doesn't always understand when it's time to wind down. Rio has never been a great sleeper. I found him in the middle of the night, sitting on the roof between our childhood bedrooms enough times to prove that.

Well, that is until my thirteenth birthday when he fell asleep on my bedroom floor as we listened to music, and he realized he could sleep just fine there. I started keeping my window unlocked after that, and he started sneaking in to sleep on the ground by my bed when he couldn't find rest on his own.

God, the nostalgia is making me sick. Today's meeting only made me miss him. The old him. But he made it perfectly clear that version no longer exists.

Before Rio fully crosses the lawn to me, I stuff my serving apron in my tote bag, including my cash tips before finding the strength to get out of the car and meet him on the driveway.

"Hey," he says, his voice tired, and I'm not sure if it's because of the late hour or if he's been stressed about how our meeting ended.

I stop about two feet away from him, arms crossed around my middle. "Hey."

His eyes trail up and down my body, looking at my clothes and clearly trying to figure out where I've been. I'm not stupid. I know he assumed I had a date tonight, but I'm also not going to correct him. The man is a professional hockey player, loves his mom, and looks like *that*. I'm not naïve enough to think other women don't see what I always did, nor am I going to try to convince myself that he's not actively dating. So even though I'm not, he doesn't need that clarification.

"Are you okay?" His tone is gentle.

I nod. "Are you?"

"Yeah. No." He hesitates. "I don't know. We need to talk about earlier—"

"I don't want to argue right now, Rio." I take a step by him, heading for the front door. "It's been a long day. I'm exhausted."

"I'm not here to argue." He wraps a hand around my bicep to stop me, but it's gentle, light enough that it wouldn't actually hold me back if I wanted to keep going. "I'm here to apologize."

I follow his hand, up to his face, to find green eyes pleading for me to hear him out.

"I'm sorry about today. I...I have no idea how to be around you anymore, Hallie." He rubs that same hand against the back of his neck. "I know I made things weird, asking about Luke. The thing with the heart. I've only ever been one way with you, and now I'm having to constantly remind myself that we aren't those people anymore."

It's strange. I've known that for a long time now. I've known that any kind of cordial, working relationship we might be able to form, any kind of tolerance for one another, will never come close to the way we used to be together. But still, it doesn't feel great to hear that confirmed from the other party involved.

He's quiet for a moment before he admits, "I don't know how to treat you anymore."

"I don't either."

"So much has happened between us and when I'm around you, I can't help but bring it up. I haven't once mentioned you or anything about us growing up in Boston together since moving here, and suddenly you're in my life again and it's the only thing on my mind."

Well...*ouch*.

He must notice me wince.

"Fuck, not like that." He takes a step towards me, hands held out before he, once again, slips them into his pockets. "Well, no. It's exactly like that, I guess." His expression is apologetic. "What I'm saying is that for so long, I tried to pretend as if *we* didn't happen because it hurt to think about you. It hurt to talk about you. And now, I can't stop thinking or talking about the past because you're here and it feels nostalgic." He closes his eyes briefly, pausing his rambling for a second. "I'm still mad at you, Hallie, but I also don't want to spend the next however many months trying to be a dick to you. It doesn't feel right."

That, surprisingly, makes my lips twitch with a grin.

He narrows his gaze at me, but I watch the smile start to stretch on his own mouth. "Don't laugh at me, Hal."

"I knew you were trying your hardest to be mean." I chuckle. "It needs some work, by the way. You trying to be a dick. Lacks consistency."

That boyish smile turns up on the corners of his lips. "I know."

It feels like it's my turn to be honest.

"I'm not used to being around you and us not getting along," I tell him. "It's throwing me off balance, trying to figure out how this is going to work."

"I don't think it *is* going to work."

Shit.

Sure, in the heat of the moment this afternoon I thought about calling it quits, but that doesn't help me stomach the fact that Rio is *firing* me.

"If we continue like this, I mean. I don't think it's going to work if we continue like this."

"You want to replace me on the project."

Rio's head rears back. "What? No. No, I don't want to replace you. I want to start over."

"Start over?"

Those green eyes meet the ground with a bit of shyness. "If you want."

"But you hate me, remember?"

His attention immediately meets mine, glare hard. "I don't hate you. Hurt, yes. But I could never hate you, Hallie."

My lips part to say something, but then close when I can't find words.

There's that heaviness settling in again, the way it so often does between us now, but I decide to not allow it. We used to have fun together without all this tension living between us.

I hold my hand out to shake his, and his eyes trail it suspiciously. "Hi. I'm Hallie Hart."

There's this moment of déjà vu from the first time we ever met, when I was eleven and he was twelve, and he was just happy to have kids his age living next door.

I can tell he feels it too when he's staring at my hand with confusion, but then realization dawns and a knowing grin slides across his lips. "You don't have to tell everyone your first and last name," he says, the same way my brother did all those years ago.

"I like it."

He slips his hand into mine and the electrifying slide of his palm against my own acts as a reminder that we haven't intentionally touched in years. Nothing about it feels friendly or professional, especially when the pad of his thumb slides across my knuckle in a gentle stroke.

"I like it too," he says.

My hand is still in his when he runs that same thumb over the soft skin of the inside of my wrist before letting it go.

Something strange happens in my stomach at that. Good God, are those butterflies? No, no they're not because there's no way I could feel any sort of excitement around this man again. I'm simply mistaken because it's been so long since I've felt butterflies. Six years to be exact.

He stretches his hand out again for me to shake. "So, what do you say? For the sake of my house and your job, should we try to be friends?"

Friends. I could laugh. Seems an impossible stretch from where we are now.

This time it's me eyeing his outstretched hand. Slowly, I put my palm in his again, and contrary to the last, this handshake is quick and friendly.

"Friends," I agree.

Feels wrong. Tastes like a lie.

"So, what's next for us?" he asks.

What's next for us?

"With the house, I mean."

Oh.

"Well, we do need to retry that meeting from today. I had some important things I needed to go over with you. And"—I look towards his place—"I'll need to do a walk-through of the house soon."

He quickly nods. "You want to see the house. My house."

I chuckle. "That is how this works, after all."

"I don't have a game on Wednesday or Thursday night, so one of those evenings would work."

Tina's reminder rings in my mind about me having to be flexible for this particular client. The problem is, I don't have the consistent income to be flexible. I need to work.

"Actually, evenings aren't great for me. Keeping our meetings between business hours would be best."

He eyes me curiously, and I can sense he's trying to figure out what it is I'm doing with my nights, but he doesn't pry. Because we are trying to be friends. Professional, non-overstepping friends.

"Friday then," he offers. "After my morning skate and before my game. Let's say three o'clock. My place."

"Friday at three it is. Don't be late this time."

He chuckles. "I'll do my best."

A moment lingers between us, neither knowing what to say when Rio finally gestures towards my house. "It's late. You should get some sleep."

I make the same motion towards his place. "So should you."

"Yeah, well, you won't be surprised to learn that not much has changed in that department. I'm lucky if I can get a few hours a night."

Like an instinct, it's on the tip of my tongue before I remember that we aren't kids anymore. We can't sneak to each other's houses to sleep and pretend it doesn't mean anything.

So instead, I offer him a weak, tired smile and leave for my door. Once I reach it, and before I go inside, I look back over my shoulder at him. "Good night, *friend*."

He grimaces. "Yep. Don't love that."

I chuckle, unlocking the front door. "Good night, Rio."

He stays there, hands in his pockets, watching me go inside. "Night, Hal."

Wren left the entryway light on for me, as well as the one on the porch. When I close the front door behind me, I lock it at the same time, but before I turn off the porch light, I look for him one last time through the peephole.

Rio is still standing there, hands in his pockets, wide stance as he faces my door, looking at it as if he can see me through it.

But he can't, so I indulge in checking him out without the consequences of getting caught.

I understand that technically he's the same man I've always known, but so much of him has changed. I thought he was the cutest boy I'd ever met back when he was shorter, had acne, wore braces, and didn't have a natural athletic bone in his body. But now? *Good God.* If I allowed myself to look at him in that way again and wasn't jaded from the past six years, I'd be in trouble.

After one final glance, I turn off the porch light and it's only then Rio finally walks back home.

10

Hallie

I hold my hand up to knock on Rio's front door, but instead, decide to let it drop to my side.

Theoretically, I knew it might be strange working on his house, but I didn't give myself the opportunity to really let it sink in just how uncomfortable this could be. I didn't give this first walk-through a second thought until the anxiety kept me up for most of the night, tossing and turning in my bed.

We've seen each other a couple of times in passing this week. He was mowing his lawn one morning when I left for work and was then grabbing his mail around the time I made it home from my shift at the bar. I didn't want to question why he might be getting his mail at two in the morning, so I let myself chalk it up to poor sleep.

There haven't been any more words exchanged. Only small acknowledgments that the other exists—a casual wave or tip of the chin. Because we're *friends*.

I could laugh at the thought.

We're not friends. We're just trying not to kill each other. And personally, I'm trying not to rip off his clothes.

The clock on my phone switches to three p.m., so I, once

again, raise my hand to knock, but before I can, the front door swings open.

Rio is standing there, beanie pulled down over his ears, joggers cinching at his ankles, right above his bare feet. But that's not what has my mouth hanging open. It's the fully unbuttoned flannel cuffed around his elbows that he's wearing without another shirt underneath.

Like a hot lumberjack.

There's enough dark hair on his chest to remind me that we really were young the last time we saw each other, and when my eyes trail down to his abdomen, I find myself questioning what happened to all the junk food we consumed when we were kids. Trailing further south, that dark hair starts again, just under his belly button, creating a visual path to a part of him I've thought about far too often over the years.

"Hallie."

My attention pulls up to meet his. "What?"

"I asked if you were going to put your hand down."

Yeah. I'm standing here like an idiot with my hand still held up, ready to knock on the door and gawking at the guy like I've never seen a shirtless man before. Like I've never seen a shirtless *him* before.

He's your client.

I quickly wrap my airborne hand around the books I have held tightly to my chest.

"That was creepy," I say, turning it back on him. "I was about to knock on the door."

He gestures to the doorbell camera, crossing his arms and leaning a shoulder against the doorframe. "Not as creepy as it was for me to watch you standing and staring at my door for multiple minutes. Figured I'd come check to see if you were coming to our meeting."

"Well..." I stumble. "Are you sure *you're* ready for this meeting? Do you want to, I don't know, put a shirt on?"

His playful smirk lifts way too fast. "Nothing you haven't seen before, Hart."

"Please stop talking."

"You were the one looking."

I straighten my spine. "Can we get to work now, *friend*?"

That knowing smile grows. "Sure. Come on in, *friend*."

As he pushes off the door, letting me past him, his flannel shirt opens, allowing me to catch a peek of black ink sprawling over part of the left side of his chest and ribs.

Now, there's something I haven't seen before.

"Dining table is straight ahead," he says as he holds the door open for me. "You can set your things down there."

My eyes are glued on his new ink, attempting to catch more of it as I pass him, but also attempting to be subtle. I'm clearly *not* because once I set my things on the table and turn back to the entryway, Rio is busy buttoning his shirt.

He's finishing the last button by the time he meets me at the table. "Can I get you something to drink before we start? I have water, tea, coffee—"

"You have coffee here?"

"Yeah." He motions to a small part of his kitchen counter that's occupied by multiple machines. "I have an espresso machine and regular drip coffee, so whatever you want."

"But you don't drink coffee."

This soft smile tilts on his lips, like he likes that I remembered that.

"It's not for me. It's for when I have guests over."

"Oh."

"Oh no," he quickly corrects. "Not those kinds of guests."

"You don't need to explain." I busy myself with organizing the design books I brought over, opening them and spreading them across his table. "It's not my business anyway."

But the image puts a bad taste in my mouth. Not that I'm naïve to think he hasn't been with anyone else in all these years, but as his first, I don't want to know anything about the women who followed.

"My teammates, Hallie. They spend a lot of time here, so it's for them. And my best friend is kind of addicted to iced coffee. A few years ago, she was staying here for a couple of days, and her now husband gave me so much shit for not making her coffee correctly that I had to step up my game. That's all I meant by *guests*." He points to one of the books on the table, the one filled with a crisp palette of whites and grays. "And put that one away. I fucking hate that one."

I chuckle because just as he used to, Rio knows how to soothe any discomfort.

I close that book and slip it onto a chair so it's out of view. "Can you make a latte?"

"You still like yours with vanilla?"

"Please."

Rio makes his way over to the small coffee bar he's created on the far corner of his kitchen counter, measuring out the espresso beans and pulling a shot. From the fridge, he grabs a carton of almond milk, but I can see that he has oat and regular dairy milk in there too.

To an outsider, this might seem odd, him having a coffee bar when he doesn't drink caffeine or having dairy milk in his fridge when he's lactose intolerant. But the thing is, Rio has always been good to his friends, has always had this innate way of loving and taking care of those important to him. One of his best characteristics is making those around him comfortable and welcomed, so a fully stocked coffee station for friends who are visiting, makes perfect sense to me.

He froths the almond milk before adding it to the mug, then attempts his best at a design with the foam. But even from my view, I can tell the art looks like shit.

His eyes are locked on the mug, adding the last of the heated milk and doing some overexaggerated thing with this wrist as if that's going to make the design look any better.

"I know you're over there trying not to laugh at me."

That does make me laugh. "I'm not."

"Your lying hasn't really improved since I last saw you, Hal."

Rio realizes what he said the same time I do, and the awkward tension settles in around us like it has so easily since seeing each other again.

He clears his throat, crossing through the kitchen and holding the mug out to me. "Almond milk, if I remember correctly."

I take it from him, grateful for the swift attempt of moving forward.

"Perfect. Thank you."

I don't tell him that I don't like almond milk. I only ordered it when we were younger because I knew he'd ask for a sip of my latte since he couldn't handle the amount of caffeine if he ordered his own, and I didn't want the dairy to bother him.

"And the latte art?" he asks. "That's perfect too, huh?"

There's literally no art. It's just a couple of white blobs of foam randomly scattered across the top.

"What exactly is it?"

He scoffs. "It's a swan, Hal. Obviously."

"Oh, yes. I see it now. It's very...intricate. Very...abstract."

He bursts a laugh, and I take a sip to hide my smile from hearing the sound. I'm not sure if it's his laughter or the latte, but every inch of me goes warm.

"Thanks for protecting my ego."

I playfully roll my eyes. This man has never had an ego needing protection. He's a goofball who has no problem making a fool out of himself to allow those around him to let down their guards.

I take another sip of my latte because holy shit, this is good, and as someone who loves a luxury espresso drink but can't afford to splurge, this is *everything* right now.

"Feel free to practice that latte art on me anytime you want. This is delicious. Thank you."

He leans a hip on the kitchen counter across from me, watching me drink. "You're welcome."

Taking another sip, this time a bit of foam sticks to my upper lip. I don't think twice about cleaning it off with a slow slide of my tongue until I look up to find him watching the whole thing.

His green eyes are hooded and focused on my mouth.

"It's good."

He hums, his attention lasered in. "Good."

Friends.

"Do you want to try it?" *Good Lord*, why does my voice sound like that? It's all breathy and soft.

He wets his own lips as his phone rings, breaking the moment. With a quick clear of his throat, he checks the screen where his dad's name is large enough for both of us to see.

The energy changes once again when Rio's glare hardens, looking at the screen then up to me. "I have to take this, but I'll make it quick," he says, slipping into a room down the hall before closing the door behind him.

I don't give myself a moment to wonder what his relationship with his dad is like these days.

Because we're friends. Professional, working friends.

Friends who stare at each other's mouths, but friends, nonetheless.

And since I'm here doing my job, I take myself on a self-guided tour of the first floor.

Rio's walls are all white, like he said. It doesn't seem like anything has been done since the day he bought the house. Builder-grade gray carpet lines the living room, dining room, and hallway. The floor in the kitchen is a square tile with swirls of gray and beige, and the backsplash is a stark-white subway tile. The countertops are a black and tan granite with heavy contrast, and the cabinets are a dark faux wood.

There's nothing innately wrong with this house. It's still considered new when you think of the lifespan of a home, but it also doesn't have much personality. And for this home to be Rio's, the man who has more personality in his little finger than most people have in their whole being, feels wrong.

It's also screaming *frat house* thanks to the empty liquor bottles lining the top of the cabinets and the Xbox in the living room, that's been transformed into a home theater, with more controls than I've ever seen attached to a single console. The furniture is mismatched, as if he just needed enough seating for everyone and couldn't care less about the aesthetics of it all.

If there's one thing this little tour of mine confirms for me, it's that his friends and teammates spend a lot of their time off here, and space for them is a priority to him.

I'd write that down in my notebook if I felt like I needed the reminder, but him making others a priority is an ingrained part of him that I've known about since I was eleven.

The door to the first-floor bedroom opens, but Rio's attention is glued to his phone as he ends the call with his dad. His jaw is tight, his nostrils flaring a bit on his way back to meet me.

I should ask if everything is okay, but us broaching the topic of either of our families right now would only blur that professional and friendly line we're attempting to tow.

"Should we talk about design concepts?" I ask instead. "I brought some color palette examples so I could get an idea of what speaks to you."

He glances at his phone one more time before he focuses back on me with a quick nod of his head. "I have no idea what that means, but yeah."

I chuckle, taking a seat at the table while he chooses the one directly next to me, regardless that there are about six other options that'd give us some distance.

I allow him a moment to scan the books out on the table, some showcasing light and airy aesthetics, others a bit darker and moodier. Some have character in every inch of their designs and others are more simplistic and modern.

"Do any of these draw your eye? Do you see anything that you'd like to wake up to every morning?"

Waiting for his response, I pull my attention from the books to him.

Only to find him already looking at me.

"Do you still listen to music?" he asks out of nowhere.

"What?"

"When something big happens. Do you still attach a song to it so you can remember it when you relisten? The first day of a new house project, for example."

Nostalgia floods me. All those nights on the roof between our houses. All the mixtapes and CDs I gave him over the years.

But there hasn't been much good that's worth remembering as of late.

I shake my head, quickly averting my attention back to the design books. "I don't do that anymore."

Out of my periphery, I watch him grab his phone, tapping away on the screen before suddenly, a smooth and steady rhythm begins to play over the surround-sound speakers in his house. The song is soft and melodic before a keyboard filters in, accompanying the beat.

I recognize it as a popular song we used to listen to growing up, but it never made one of the yearly playlists. He mentioned a few times that he felt it should've.

I turn his way, but now he's fully fixated on the design books sprawled across his dining table.

"Focus, Hart." He doesn't look at me as he says it.

"Have I told you that you're infuriating, DeLuca?"

"Not today." A smile tugs at the corner of his lip. "I'm not sure what I want. Regarding the house."

"What catches your eye?"

He hunches over the table, roaming the different aesthetics, unable to land on one.

Green eyes look back at me. "If this were your house, what would you do?"

The answer sticks in my throat.

Because there was a time I thought I *would be* designing our house.

"I um..." I hesitate, finally pointing to a few of my favorite design books. "I like a mix, personally. Some traditional, and a combination of mid-century modern and organic modern. If it were my home, I'd add color and dimension to the walls with moldings and wallpapers and give each space its own story while also making it cohesive and functional, so that it's livable but interesting." I pause my rambling because this is something I've thought far too much about. "But this is your home, so it's about what you like."

He checks the different books I referenced. "I like that idea."

"Which idea?"

"All of them."

"Well, you have time to think it over. You don't need to make a decision today."

He shakes his head. "You've always had good taste, Hallie. I like your vision. I trust you."

That last sentence feels big and heavy and meaningful. Maybe not to anyone else in any other situation, but for him to say that to me after everything, even if it's simply regarding his home décor, it feels important somehow.

My confidence builds. "I think there are some cool things we could do to make the home unique to you. Interesting things we can do with art and your favorite music. That is, if you decide to keep the home instead of selling."

"Could we look at both options? Designs that would be good for selling and ones that would be if I stayed?"

"Of course. That's a smart idea."

"Great." His smile is eager and one I haven't seen directed at me in a long time.

Look at us working together.

"Would it be okay if I took some before pictures of the house?"

I ask. "For my social media."

"But you don't have social media."

The statement is out of his mouth before he can think better of saying it, and the panic written on his face is screaming that he wishes he could take it back.

I can't hold back my knowing grin. "How would you know? Have you looked for me or something?"

He scoffs. "No."

My smile grows.

"Well...yeah, maybe I have. Maybe I was curious." There's a long pause before he adds, "More than once."

That armor I try to wear around him chips away a bit, because for so long, I was convinced he left Boston and forgot I existed.

"I looked you up a few times too," I admit.

"Yeah?"

"Of course, Rio. But you weren't hard to find. Famous hockey player that you are now and all."

His face scrunches up in disgust at the word *famous* and he can try to deny it all he wants, but Rio was the talk of the neighborhood once he got drafted. And not having to hear the town fawn over him while I was heartbroken was the best part of moving back to Minnesota.

I motion towards the stairs. "Will you show me the second story?"

"About that." He rubs the back of his neck. "Well, there's not much to it, and I didn't make the bed, so don't judge me."

I exhale a laugh but it's simply to cover the nerves. There's no part of me that wants to think about why his bed might be disheveled or who helped him get it to that state, yet here I am, fixating on that question.

Leaving my latte behind, Rio leads me up the stairs, showing me the two other empty bedrooms and the spare hall bathroom, then to the double doors at the end of the hallway. He opens them and stands aside to let me enter first.

White walls. Gray carpet. Tan duvet cover. Absolutely no personality in his own bedroom.

It's nothing like the room he grew up in that had bits of him in every corner. Trophies on shelves, photos of his family and friends, posters of his favorite musical artists and sports teams. Endless Boston Bobcats memorabilia.

Any nerves I felt dissipate. There are no signs of another person being in here, at least not last night. His king-sized bed is unmade on one side, while the opposite is tightly tucked and unslept in. The nightstand closest to his side of the mattress is cluttered with reading glasses, a water bottle, and Tylenol while the opposite is completely bare.

"It's…" I search for the words. "Clean."

"It's boring, Hal."

"It is boring."

"I just…" He scrubs a hand down his face. "I'm going to say this to you as an interior designer and not as my…" He drifts off, not finishing that sentence. "But if I stay here, my hope is that one day, this room won't be only mine."

He wants me to design the room that he and his future wife might share. Where they'll sleep next to each other. Where they'll sleep *with* each other. Fucking lovely.

This will get me my dream job, I try to remind myself.

"Okay." It's the only thing I know to say that doesn't expand on how much I hate the thought of me designing his future wife's bedroom. I quickly cross the room, needing to get this over with so I can get out of here. "Two closets?" I ask, reaching out to grab the doorknob of one.

He rushes to meet me, holding his palm firmly against the closet door to keep it closed.

"What are you doing?" I ask.

"We can leave this closet as is."

"Can I at least look at it?"

"Nope."

I eye him suspiciously. "Why are you being weird? If you remember, I was the one who found that *Playboy* magazine under your mattress when you were fifteen. It really can't get much more embarrassing than that for you, Rio. Show me the closet."

"Okay, as I told you a hundred times, that was Luke's magazine. He was hiding it from your mom in my room."

"Sure thing." I reach for the knob again, but this time, Rio places his entire body in front of the door to block me.

I can't help but laugh in disbelief. "What are you hiding?"

He simply smiles down at me, his eyes light and bright.

This time, when I try to reach past him, he takes my wrist and in a swift move, has me turned around with my back to his front and both my wrists trapped in a single one of his hands.

His laughter vibrates my whole body and I can't help but mirror it with my own.

"So nosey, Hal," he teases, walking us back to the center of the room.

But when we get there, he doesn't let go and I don't try to squirm away. My muscles don't bunch in alarm. They loosen against him.

It feels like a drug, being this close to him, one that I used to be highly addicted to.

God, I missed him.

My throat works through a swallow. "I prefer the term 'curious,'" I say in response, but the teasing has morphed into something different. Something heated.

His grip around my wrists loosens, but he doesn't step away. His thumb swipes over my hand in a languid stroke, his breath dusting my ear, his chest pounding against my back.

This is decidedly outside of *friends* territory.

I spot a duffle bag on the floor in the corner of the room with this jersey number on it. "For example, I'm curious why you changed that." I nod in the bag's direction. "Your number."

That's what makes him step away. In fact, he creates distance as soon as the question is out of my mouth, his palm gliding over my hip bone as he does. "I don't remember. It was a long time ago."

Turning to face him, I open my mouth to tell him I don't believe him when we both hear the front door unlock and open downstairs.

"Hi, honey!" a woman calls out from inside his house.

What the hell?

"Rio, are you home?" she continues. "I used the key you made me to get in."

What the actual fuck?

My wide eyes shoot to Rio, but he's just smirking down at me.

"Don't worry," he says. "It's just my friend, Indy."

"I'm not worrying."

"Tell your face that, Hal."

"Where are you?" Indy calls from downstairs.

"Coming!" he shouts back. "Come on, Jealous." Rio puts his hand on my lower back, leading me back to the stairs. "I'll introduce you."

"I'm not jealous," I mutter under my breath.

When we make it back downstairs, it's not only Indy waiting for him. There are a total of four women hanging out in his kitchen. And sure, maybe I could admit that a bit of jealousy sparks, seeing them so comfortable in his home when I feel like a newbie here. But that jealousy quickly dies when I notice all four of them are wearing wedding bands on their ring fingers.

"Oh, it's the whole crew," Rio says, leading us into the kitchen to join them. "What are you all doing here?"

Every pair of eyes is locked on me and yeah, maybe that'd be intimidating if they weren't all smiling at me a little too excitedly.

"Hello?" he asks, but they're all looking right past him to me. "Okay, well fuck me, I guess. Hallie, this is Stevie, Indy, Miller, and Kennedy." He gestures to each one as he says their names. "Everyone, this is Hallie. But I have a feeling you all already know that and she's exactly why you're here."

I'm a bit envious of the community he has here in Chicago. He and I always had large circles of friends when we were younger, but the last few years have felt isolated from taking care of my dad. It's one of the many reasons why I couldn't have been more thrilled when Wren and I hit it off, but I'd love to expand my circle of friends in this city. Especially girlfriends.

I attempt to commit their names to memory.

Stevie with the curly hair and worn-in Nikes on her feet.

Indy with her blonde braid and Converse.

Miller with her tattoos and overalls.

Kennedy with the Vans and striking red hair.

"Hi," I offer with a small wave.

"It is *so* great to meet you, Hallie." Indy steps up, pulling me into an unexpected hug.

She holds on even tighter and with my bulging eyes, I catch the other three girls laughing over her shoulder.

"Ind," Kennedy chuckles. "Not everyone is a hugger."

"Well..." She releases me, still holding me at arm's length. "Everyone should be."

I smile at her. "I'm a hugger."

Indy rejoins her girlfriends. "See? I like her already."

"Hal," Rio says. "You met Stevie's husband, Zanders, last week after practice."

I'm about to say something when Miller and Indy look at each other, hands over their hearts, crooning, "*Hal*," as if that's the most precious thing they've ever heard.

"Okay," Rio cuts in. "I'm going to need my key back if you're going to make things weird."

"Definitely not making it weird." Miller mimics zipping her lips, but then adds, "But first, can I ask, did Rio always bring the boombox everywhere? Like, all the time? And by all the time, yes, I'm referring to *all the time*." She adds a wink for dramatic effect, her voice laced with insinuation.

"Miller Rhodes!" Kennedy smacks Miller's shoulder with laughter.

"He didn't need to bring it," I tell her. "I had my own that he could use. Great taste in music even then. A lot of R&B during those times, if I remember correctly. And by those times, yes, I'm referring to *those times*."

Miller smiles devilishly at my quick response. "Oh, I like you."

Rio shakes his head, but he's got this soft, thankful smile on his lips that absolutely *does not* make my stomach flip.

I've always had this innate need to protect him. Growing up, he was an easy target because he made himself the butt of the joke most of the time, but I didn't play into that. He could be a joke to everyone else, but he was never a joke to me.

"So, what's up?" Rio asks again. "What are you all doing here?"

"Just swinging by before the game," Stevie says. "We wanted to say hi."

He eyes them suspiciously. "You *swung* by? Twenty minutes out of your way."

"Yep!" Indy chimes in. "There's a babysitter watching all the kids at our place, we're meeting up the guys at the arena, and we knew you two were meeting here so we came to see if Hallie wants to join us in our box at your game tonight."

"Indy," Rio scolds quietly.

"What?"

"She can't come. She's busy."

Ouch.

That doesn't feel good to hear, but at the same time, it acts as an instant reminder to not let myself get too comfortable here. With him. In his house. With his friends. We're simply working together right now. I'm not part of his everyday life anymore.

"Okay, rude," Miller cuts in. "Love you so much, but we were asking her."

"He's right. I can't make it," I tell them. "But thank you for the invite."

Rio could not look more guilty. "Or if you're not busy, you could go," he amends, tentatively looking in my direction. "If you wanted to."

"Yes!" Kennedy encourages.

It sounds fun. Sitting in a box suite. Going to his game, just like I used to. Hanging out with these girls who seem to genuinely enjoy each other's company and who care for Rio. But unfortunately, I don't have the luxury of affording a Friday night off work, even if there was any part of him that actually wanted me to go to his game and wasn't offering out of guilt.

I keep my focus on the girls. "I can't tonight. I have plans."

"You have plans?" Rio repeats in a question.

A shift at the job he doesn't know about, but yes. *Plans.*

"You should cancel those plans and come hang out with us," Stevie suggests.

"Great idea, Vee," Indy cuts in. "This is why you're my favorite sister-in-law."

"Yeah," Rio agrees. "You should cancel those plans and hang with the girls."

If we weren't in front of his friends, I'd call him out for not wanting me around when he thought I didn't have something better to do, but now that he knows I already made plans, he's telling me to bail.

"I wish I could, but I can't cancel." Heading to the dining table, I gather my design books. "But thank you for the invite. Maybe next time." I check my phone for the time. "I should get going. It's almost end of the workday, but it was so nice to meet you all."

I give them all my best smile before bolting for the door.

I can hear Rio's bare feet chase after me. "The end of the workday, huh?"

"Yes, and I need to be downtown by five."

He meets me at the front door. "For your plans. On a Friday night."

There's a tic in his jaw that tells me he believes I'm going on a date.

I don't correct him.

"Yep. I'll email you with notes from today and let you know

the next steps in the design process."

He doesn't even try to dance around it when he asks, "What are you doing tonight?"

I laugh in disbelief as I leave his house.

"Hallie."

"You were the one who was quick to tell them I couldn't join. You were right. I *am* busy."

He closes his eyes in frustration, collecting himself. "That was just a reaction. The wrong reaction. I didn't mean that you couldn't join them. They'd love to have you."

"It was the right reaction. Best not to get too comfortable while doing this job." I cross the lawn to my house before calling back, "Good luck in your game."

11

"Have you ever been here before?" Zanders asks as we cross the street to the bar.

"Never even heard of it," I tell him. "But I don't really go out when we're home anymore, so it's not all that surprising, I guess."

He pauses in front of the bar. "Are we getting old?"

"Yes, you are," his wife chimes in.

Zanders wraps an arm over her shoulders, pulling her to kiss her temple. "Thanks for that, Stevie girl. How's Tay?"

"Indy and Ryan are back home." Stevie holds out her phone to show us the picture Indy texted of Taylor sleeping between her two cousins. "She was so excited to have a sleepover."

"And I'm excited to have a parents' night out, if you know what I mean." Zee pumps his brows a couple of times before Stevie playfully smacks him in the stomach.

"Yes, we all know what you mean," I deadpan. "It's so fun being the only single one left."

Zanders opens the door, letting Stevie in first, then me.

As soon as we're inside, we don't even attempt to continue the conversation because this downtown Chicago bar is packed and way too fucking loud. I've been in the league so long now, that going out post-win has lost its appeal, but our rookie scored his first NHL goal tonight, so all the boys agreed to take him out to his bar of choosing to celebrate.

While Zee figures out where our team is, I check my phone again. It's only about the tenth time I've looked to see if Hallie texted me back after my desperate attempt to get her attention right before my game started.

Me: *Hey.*

It's still unanswered.

I don't know what I was thinking, telling her she couldn't join my friends at my game tonight. It was a dick move, but it was also one of those instinctual moments of trying to protect myself. She came to every game of mine until I left for college, and it caught me off guard to think of her coming to one of my pro games now.

Hallie is still new in town, and I know how much she values having and making friends and I'm over here stopping that from happening. I also know that she would love those girls.

And on top of all of that, I'm fairly certain she's on a date tonight, and if I would've just shut my goddamn mouth, she could've been at my game instead.

A fucking date. Again.

What else would she be doing so late on a Friday night? And all week, I've caught her coming home after two in the morning. Is she seeing someone? Is it that same guy I saw her with at my game?

"Rio! Zee!" one of my teammates calls out, waving us over to join the rest of my team in the private corner of the bar.

With my text still unanswered, I slip my phone back into my pocket.

This side of the bar is a bit quieter but still packed because most of my teammates brought someone with them. I say hello to everyone before finding the last two empty chairs at the table. I offer one to Stevie, but she takes Zee's lap, leaving the last seat for me.

"DeLuca." One of my teammates, Thompson, pats me on the back as I sit. "The girl I'm seeing brought a friend for you. They're in the bathroom, but they'll be out soon."

"Oh. That's okay." I quickly shake my head. "I'm not really trying to meet someone right now."

Thompson throws his head back in laughter. "Rio, you're always trying to meet someone."

I look to Stevie and Zanders, and the panic must be obvious because Zee cuts in for me. "Thompson, he's not into it tonight."

"Well, he needs to be." Thompson bends down to speak to me quietly. "I'm trying to...you know...finally close the deal. And her friend is always hanging around. I need you to do me a solid tonight and keep her occupied."

"Yeah. Abso-fucking-lutely not."

"Rio, c'mon."

"He's not interested," Stevie adds defensively. "Leave him alone."

"There they are!" Thompson says far too enthusiastically, throwing his arm over his girl's shoulders when the two of them approach. "Kylie, this is my buddy I was telling you about. Rio, this is Kylie."

"I already know who you are," Kylie says. "I was hoping I would get to meet you."

One of my teammates leaves his chair, so Thompson grabs it.

"And look!" he says, shoving it next to me. "There happens to be an empty seat for you."

He's pulling his date to the far end of the very loud, very rowdy table before Kylie has even sat down.

No, I'm not interested in her in that way, but she's still a human being that just got pawned off by her so-called friend and I innately feel sorry for her.

"Uh..." I stumble. "Hey."

"Hey." Kylie's attention bounces between me and Zanders as she sits down. "This is wild. I'm such a big fan of yours. Both of you."

Great.

"Are you having a good time?"

"Well, it definitely just got better, but I could use a drink."

"Yeah," I exhale. "I could use one too."

The rookie who scored his first goal tonight is making his rounds, already buzzing with alcohol when he throws an arm over Zee's shoulders. "There's my captain! What a goal, huh?"

"Yeah, Big Shot. Hell of a goal. How do we get drinks around here? Do we go up to the bar or do they come here?"

"Oh, they'll come to the table." He holds up his empty beer bottle. "I need another. And man." He smacks Zee in the chest. "One of the bartenders here, she's a smoke show. That's why I come here all the time. I think tonight is the night I ask for her number. What do you think?"

Zee, Stevie, and I laugh at our too-excitable teammate. He reminds me of how I acted while I was trying to meet any and everyone in hopes of proving something to myself. Trying to prove that love did in fact still exist, even after Hallie and I broke up. Even after watching my parents' divorce. I was convinced it was out there somewhere. I just had to find it.

"I say you go for it," I chime in. "Use that first-goal confidence to your benefit."

"Yeah." He nods quickly, switching from having his arm slung around Zanders' shoulders to mine. "Yeah, Rio, you're right. Isn't he so right?" He shifts his attention to Kylie. "You are so lucky, you know that? This guy, he's the best!"

Our rookie squeezes into the space on the other side of her, sharing a seat with another of our teammates, before stealing his beer.

Kylie leans into me.

Fuck it. I can't do this tonight. I can't even *pretend* to do this tonight. I just want to go home and see if Hallie might be home too.

I stand from my seat.

"You okay?" Stevie asks.

"I'm going to call it a night. See you both at family dinner on Sunday?"

"You're leaving?" Kylie asks.

"I am. I..."

"He doesn't feel well," Zee adds for me.

I don't love lying to the girl, but he's not far off. I've been frustrated over Hallie ignoring my text all night, been sick thinking of her out with someone else. Been mad at myself for being so fucking rude about her going to my game with my friends.

"I hope you have a good night," I say to finish.

Part of me wants to ask Zee to make sure she makes it home safely since her friend just bailed on her, but I also don't want her to get the impression that I'm interested in more than that.

"Oh, the bartender is coming!" our rookie shouts before turning back to me and Zee. "Do you think I should shoot my shot now, or wait until the end of the night?"

I'm not staying to watch this possible train wreck go down. Instead, I grab my car keys from my pocket and take out my phone again, just to see if Hallie has responded yet.

Spoiler alert: she hasn't.

"Oh, shit," Zanders mutters under his breath from next to me.

"Does anyone need another?" a woman asks while I'm focused on my phone screen, but the voice is one I'd recognize anywhere.

When I shift my attention up, it locks on her, but she's not looking at me. She's busy taking my teammates' orders on the other end of the table.

Hallie is standing there, a bright smile on her lips as she repeats orders back when they're thrown in her direction, committing them to memory.

I fall back into my seat.

What the hell is she doing here?

Her short, wavy hair is half up in a cute, messy way. Her little button nose, and the freckles across it, scrunch up each time she smiles at one of my teammates. She's wearing jeans that show off the curve of her hips, an apron tied around the small of her waist, and a simple black tee that may as well be painted on her body.

"I'll take another, please!" our rookie holds up an empty beer bottle to show her and that's what finally brings her attention to our end of the table.

To me.

Then to the girl sitting at my side.

Then over to Zee and Stevie before her focus falls on me again and stays.

That smile has dropped into parted lips. Those shiny hazel eyes are now laced with panic.

Kylie decides that's the moment she's going to put her hand on my forearm. "Are you staying after all?" she asks.

Hell yes, I'm staying.

Hallie immediately looks away.

"It's Hallie, right?" Zanders asks.

"Yes," Hallie says to my friend. "Hey, Stevie. Good to see you again. What can I get you?"

"Hey!" Stevie smiles back at her. "I didn't know you worked here."

Stevie looks at me as if silently asking, *did you know?*

"Second job." Hallie shifts on her feet, clearly uncomfortable. "So, what can I get for you?"

There's a heavy pause as the awkwardness settles in. I sure as fuck don't want Hallie waiting on me and I don't think my friends do either.

"I'll take a vodka cran," Kylie says at my side, her entire body turned in my direction. But I'm not looking at her. I'm staring straight ahead at the girl next door and trying to figure out what the hell she's doing here.

Hallie's eyes bounce between me and the stranger I'm sitting next to, and because I can read her like a fucking book, I know she thinks we're here together.

"You got it." Hallie turns to Zanders and Stevie. "And for you two?"

"Um…" Zee hesitates, nodding in the direction of another bartender working behind the bar. "We'll go up and grab a round ourselves. It's busy. You're busy, so don't worry about it."

"No need." Hallie's smile is forced now. "There's an open tab for your party already. It'll make it easier if you order through me."

There's a long pause because no one wants her waiting on us. She should be hanging out *with* us.

"I'll take…" Stevie begins. "Something on draft. An IPA if you have one."

"Same," Zanders adds.

Kylie scoots in closer. "What are you going to get?"

Hallie finally looks in my direction and I watch her jaw tense as she waits for my order.

I shake my head. "Nothing for me, Hal."

Hallie immediately turns back to the bar, quickly weaving through bodies and I lose her in the crowd before I can even register what just happened.

"You two seem to have some history," Kylie observes.

"You could say that. Look, Kylie, you seem like a nice girl, but I'm not in the position to meet anyone right now. My head is somewhere else at the moment."

With someone else at the moment.

A smile tilts on her lips. "Don't worry about it, but you should probably go tell her we aren't here together."

"Did you know she worked here?" Zee asks.

"Not a fucking clue."

I'm immediately out of my seat to follow Hallie, and at the same time, our rookie stands from his seat too.

For a moment, I want to ask him what the hell he's thinking, trying to ask her out. Doesn't he remember she was waiting outside our practice for *me*? But then I recall that he was sick that day and has no idea that his favorite bartender and I have history.

"I'm going to do it!" His tipsy grin is way too big. "I'm going to go ask for her number."

"Hey, Rook?"

He looks my way, so stupidly excited. "Yeah?"

"Sit the fuck down."

"Yep."

He does just that, and as I leave the table to go find Hallie, I hear Kylie turn and introduce herself to him.

There are so many people packed up against the bar, trying to order. There's another woman working the well, and a guy taking orders from waiting patrons, while Hallie is busy getting our table's drinks made.

I push my way past waiting customers to get as close to her as I can.

"Hey, watch it!" someone yells with a shove to my chest that does absolutely nothing to move me.

I simply lift a brow at his attempt.

"Holy hell. You're Rio DeLuca. Man, I'm a huge fan. Didn't mean to shove you." He opens his arms, giving me a path to the bar. "Go for it. Or can I get you a drink? Let me get you a drink."

"Not drinking tonight, but thanks."

"Hey!" he yells at Hallie. "Hey, barkeep! I need to order."

I step in front of him, blocking his view of her. "Do not fucking talk to her like that. Wait your turn. She's busy."

He holds his hands up. "I'm trying to get you a drink, man. Chill."

Turning my back on him and collecting myself, I face Hallie and raise my voice over the rowdy bar. "What are you doing here?"

"What does it look like I'm doing?" she asks while also pouring a beer on draft. "I'm working."

"Why?"

"Because I work here."

"You know what I'm asking."

"Rio, leave me alone and let me do my job. I'll be over in a minute with your friends' drinks."

"Do you need money or something?"

Shit. That came out wrong.

She pauses, turning off the tap to keep it from spilling over. "Fuck you."

"If you need money, I can—"

"You can what? Give me some? Help me out? Jesus," she laughs in disbelief. "We haven't seen each other in six years, Rio. You think I'm going to just take your money? You have literally no idea what I've been through since we last saw each other."

That gives me pause. She's angry and she's right. I have no idea what these last six years looked like for her. And I haven't taken the time to ask.

"Tell me then."

Her voice is sharp as she continues to pour drinks. "Go back to your table."

"Is this where you've been every night this week? Is this why you're getting home after two in the morning? You're working days at the design firm and nights here. Why?"

"Oh my God, Rio. Because I'm broke! Is that what you need to hear? Have I embarrassed myself enough that you'll leave me alone now?"

Shit.

"Hallie, nothing about that is embarrassing."

She scoffs a disbelieving laugh. "Yeah, it's not at all embarrassing to bartend for you and your teammates. Go back to your date."

"I'm not—"

"Rio, go back to your table and I'll be right over to *serve* you."

She says it as if trying to point out the imbalance between us now. Initially, I didn't see it, didn't even think of it. I only ever felt hurt and anger over what she kept from me all those years ago. But for the first time since she's come back into my life, from Hallie's point of view, I can understand why she'd be angry with *me*.

I left and clearly, our lives took two very different paths when I promised her we'd always be on the same one.

"Is everything okay here?" Another bartender steps up, some blond muscular dude, sliding his hand around Hallie's lower back and leaving it to rest there. "Do you need me to take care of this guy for you, Hal?"

All I see is red.

"What did you call her?"

"Rio, don't."

I keep my focus on him. "No. What the fuck did you call her?"

Hallie steps away and out of his touch, but the guy extends his arm, keeping his palm pressed to her lower back.

"Get your hands off her."

He doesn't listen to me. This time, he slides his hand over her hip, and I swear to God, if there wasn't a bar top in my way and if I wouldn't end up on the news for it, I'd punch him square in the face for thinking he could touch her like that.

"Do we have a problem here?" he continues. "Should I call the cops?"

"Oh, get so fucked right now."

"You're not calling the cops, Carson." Hallie jerks out of his grasp. "You." She focuses on me, her hazel eyes wide with anger as she points to the door. "Outside. Now."

She says something to a different coworker, something about the drink orders she's working on, before storming through the crowd and out the front door, expecting me to follow.

Which of course I do.

The chilly Chicago breeze hits me as soon as we're outside. Hallie crosses her bare arms over her chest and like instinct, I peel off my flannel and hold it out to her.

"I don't want your shirt."

"It's freezing out. Take it or we're going right back inside so I can punch Ken Doll straight in the face for calling you Hal."

She rolls her eyes. "Why are all you men so goddamn dramatic?"

Taking my shirt, she slips her arms through it before cuffing the sleeves enough so that her hands peek through. "There. Happy?"

"What are you doing here?"

She exhales, collecting herself. "I can't keep having this conversation. I'm working."

"If you need—"

She holds out her hands to stop me. "I swear to God, if you say what I think you're about to say, I'm leaving."

"If you need help," I repeat. "I can talk to Wren's brother about your rent. He doesn't even need the money. He would be happy for you to live there rent free."

"God, you have no idea, Rio."

"Of course I have no idea!" I hold my arms out wide. "Because you won't tell me what's going on!"

Her jaw hardens. "What's going on is that we're two completely different people now. I work five shifts a week here, after my full days at the design firm, because that's what I have to do to make ends meet. I'm sleeping in someone else's spare room, because that's what I can manage, and I can barely afford to feed myself. Does that make you happy to hear?"

"Jesus. Of course not, Hal."

"If I can get hired full-time at the design firm, then things will change, but for now, this is my reality and it's very different from yours. I know that. Now you know that. And I swear to God, Rio, if you try to give me some kind of handout right now, I'm going to lose my shit. I've made it this far without your help, and I'll be just fine going forward."

Of course, she doesn't tell me *why* things are as tight as they are financially, but I also know not to push it further. She's upset that I found out about her second job, and I think she's also a bit embarrassed. But Hallie is a hard worker. She grinds when she needs to. She used to pick up babysitting hours and miss out on big social events when we were younger, simply because she wanted to save up so she could afford to put herself through design school.

So, her hustling isn't what's so confusing. It's *why* she needs to hustle in the first place that I still can't make out.

"Okay," I say in defeat.

"Okay."

"You didn't text me back."

"You didn't give me anything to text back to. Hey?" she asks, mimicking my text. "You're better than that, Rio." Hallie nods towards the entrance of the door, the tension diffused. "I have to get back to work."

She walks past me, but before she can get to the door, I reach across her body, grabbing the handle, and keeping it closed. Keeping us alone outside.

She slowly lifts her gaze to look at me, our faces mere inches from one another.

"Don't let him call you that," I say quietly. "He doesn't fucking know you."

She lifts a brow. "And you think you still do?"

"Yeah, Hal. I still know you. And you still know me. Better than anyone."

I watch her throat move through a swallow. "He's never called me that before. I think he thought you were some random guy so he was pretending to mark his territory."

"Yeah, well you're not his, so tell him to keep his hands to himself too."

Her eyes drop to my mouth. "I'm not yours either."

We'll see.

It's the first thought that runs through my head, when I'm so used to that anger towards her being the inclination.

I wet my lips, leaning in awfully close. "You sure look good in my shirt for not being mine."

"Get fucked, DeLuca."

I smile as I open the door. "Would love to. You just let me

know when and where, Hart."

She enters the loud bar, throwing a middle finger over her shoulder for me to see.

But all it does is make my smile grow because Hallie can pretend to be unaffected by me, by us, by our history, but she's still wearing my shirt when she gets back to work and looks damn good in it.

The last of my teammates left in rideshares by the time the bar closed. I hung out with them inside, drinking water and making sure there was a generous tip attached to our bill until we got kicked out.

I didn't bother Hallie the rest of the night but I sure as fuck kept my eye on her.

And just as she always has been, she was personable and kind, even when people turned into drunken assholes. Behind the bar, she would listen intently when someone decided she was the one they wanted to spill every detail of their lives to. She was nonstop on her feet, pouring drinks, and cleaning up broken glass.

And that was *after* a whole day working at the design firm and my house.

Once we all got kicked out for closing time, I pulled my truck into the same lot, behind her car and waited.

Ken Doll walks out with her, laughing at something she says, and as much as I hate that her smile isn't directed at me, the guy is kind of massive and I don't hate the idea of knowing he walks her out each night.

Surprisingly, the grin on her face doesn't fade when she spots me getting out of my truck. Her expression doesn't waver, as if she knew I'd be waiting for her after her shift.

But when he spots me, Ken takes off towards his car after giving Hallie a quick wave.

And she's still wearing my shirt.

"I want to hate that guy," I tell her, meeting her at her car, but keeping my eye on his retreating back. "Do you work with him every night?"

"Most nights. If I'm not working with him, I'm working with his boyfriend."

That earns my attention and when I whip in her direction, she's got this shit-eating grin on her face.

"You couldn't have told me that earlier?"

"Must have slipped my mind." She unlocks her car. Manually. With the actual key because that's how old this thing is. "Your girlfriend left with your buddy. The young one who comes in here all the time."

"Good for them. She's not my girlfriend, but I did feel bad that her friend bailed on her."

Her smile is soft, as if she already knew all that. "You didn't need to wait for me. I'm exhausted. I'm heading home."

"I wanted to make sure you got to your car safely." I open her car door for her and wait until she gets behind the wheel. "See you at home."

She playfully shakes her head. "See you at home."

I close the door for her and get back into my truck, turning on the engine and waiting for her to start her car so I can follow her home.

I can tell she tries to start it because her taillights flash for a moment, but then they go dark again. Cracking my door open, I listen as she tries again, only for a whirring sound to come from the engine.

Her eyes find mine through her side mirror and I gesture for her to get in my truck.

It's late, she's tired, and we can deal with this tomorrow.

What I want to tell her is that she needs to get a different car. One that's reliable and not leaking things all over the place, but tonight is not the night for that conversation. Not after she told me how much she's struggling financially and definitely not after she got embarrassed when I found out she was going to be bartending for me and my friends.

Instead, I get out and open the passenger side door of my truck for her.

"Sorry." It's said sheepishly under her breath as she climbs in.

"Don't be."

"I'll get it looked at tomorrow."

"Okay."

I close her in my truck before rounding the hood and getting in myself. I start the engine, cranking up the heat for her, before pulling out of the lot to drive back to our places.

We don't speak. In fact, it's almost uncomfortably silent for the first five minutes of the drive. Hallie is stiff in the seat beside me, sitting up straight with her hands tucked between her thighs as she watches the city go by out the window.

I don't know what to say other than something stupid about how much I missed her, or how I might not be as mad as I thought I was, or how the bedroom she's going to be designing, I had only ever pictured sharing it with her.

So, I make sure not to talk. Instead, I do the one thing that's always acted as our communication.

I turn on some music.

Out of my periphery, I see Hallie glance in my direction with a little smile on her lips as the tune fills the cab. It's only a minute before she's more comfortable in the seat, leaning her head back and closing her eyes.

Eventually, she rests her arm on the console between us and holy hell, the nostalgia from that image alone is strong, remembering the first time I had the courage to hold her hand while driving her home much in the way I am now.

We don't talk for the entirety of the drive, but I note when her breathing turns slow and steady. The ride is lulling her to sleep, which isn't surprising when I think about the hours she pulls on a daily basis. I think if I worked as hard as Hallie does, maybe even *I'd* be able to sleep.

When I take our exit, I change my mind and get right back on the expressway. God knows I'm not going to get any sleep tonight anyway, so she may as well.

I take note of the song that's playing and keep on driving.

12

(AGE 16)

"**N**ice win," Coach says to end our postgame meeting. "Get some rest and I'll see you boys bright and early Monday morning for practice."

We do a quick huddle and cheer before my teammates and I skate across the ice to the opening of the rink that'll take us to our locker room.

I'm nearing the end of my sophomore year of high school and somehow, someway, I'm playing for our school's varsity hockey team. After barely making the freshman team last year, I worked my ass off, earned some muscle and thankfully some height. I skated extra hours, focused on my balance and speed, and now I'm here, playing varsity hockey as a sophomore and already getting looked at by college recruits.

I fall in line behind my teammates as they exit the ice, letting the juniors and seniors hit the showers first. Partly because I'm the youngest on the team and need to wait for my turn when the water is no longer hot, but mostly because I know Hallie is here somewhere, waiting for me and I'd much rather see her post-game than anything else.

As I step off the ice, I find her standing with a huddle of her friends but looking at me, wearing a big smile and my away jersey over one of my stolen hoodies.

I think it's my favorite part of game days, knowing she'll be waiting for me afterward. Hallie has yet to miss one of my high school games, home or away. And sure, I see her plenty with our families being so close and her living next door, but there's something different about game days. I view them as a chance to impress her.

She peels away from her friends, headed towards me. "Nice game, eighty-three."

I nod towards her shirt. "Nice jersey, birthday girl."

Hallie steps into me, and with my helmet and stick in hand, I wrap my arms around her shoulders, placing a quick kiss to the top of her head. I tower over her now with my new height and added inches from the skates.

Arms around my middle, she rests her chin on my chest and looks up at me. "You're sweaty."

I chuckle. "Sorry."

"I don't mind."

Her eyes are all sparkly as she looks up at me, and I take it in. There's nothing I crave more than these moments when she has her attention on me.

Unsurprisingly, when Hallie got to high school this year, she was instantly well-liked. Yes, she's the prettiest girl I've ever seen and equal parts confident and outgoing. But more than anything, she's kind. To everyone. Popular or unpopular, she will become your friend if you let her. So yeah, plenty of other guys at school have their eye on her, which makes the times Hallie has her eye on *me* all that more satisfying.

"Nice win, DeLuca!" Luke hollers.

His voice has me and his sister instantly breaking away from each other and when I look up, I find him and all four of our parents headed down the bleachers in our direction.

Hallie creates more distance by stepping back.

"Thanks, man," I say. "I didn't think you were coming."

"Lacrosse practice got out early."

Their dad knocks his fist with me. "Heck of a game, Rio. You're looking strong. The way you were beating some of their guys to the puck?" He shakes his head. "You've gotten so fast on those skates."

"Thank you, sir."

I've always liked Mr. Hart. He's been like a second dad to me, and he and Hallie are really close. He's close with Luke too, of course, but Luke would rather go out with his friends than stay home with his family, whereas Hallie will cancel plans if her dad wants to spend time with her.

I meet my mom with a kiss on the cheek.

"Proud of you, *Tesoro*," she says.

"Thanks, Ma."

"That's my boy." My dad throws his arm over my shoulder, but he has to reach up to do it. I'm officially taller than him now, both on and off the skates.

"Great game, Rio," Hallie's mom says, standing next to her husband.

"Thank you, Mrs. Hart. You didn't all have to come."

"We wanted to come see you play." Mr. Hart tucks Hallie under his arm. "And it's what the birthday girl wanted to do for her special day."

Hallie's cheeks go a shade of pink.

"Hallie," her mom begins. "Are you sure you don't want to do a birthday dinner tonight? We can change our reservation from four people to seven."

"Wait," Luke cuts in, speaking to his sister. "I thought you already had plans tonight and that's why we couldn't do dinner. Because I made plans to...*study*."

That's a lie. He made plans to take Lacey Williams on a drive, so they park somewhere and make out all night.

"No dinner this year," Hallie says. "I'm babysitting the Holmes kids tonight."

Her dad squeezes her closer. "Saving up for school."

Her eyes flit to me and those freckled cheeks flame again.

None of our parents are particularly wealthy. Sure, we have a nice home that's been passed down for generations, and my parents got me a pickup truck that's the same age as me when I turned sixteen. But neither Hallie's parents nor mine will be able to pay for us to go to college. So, she's saving every penny she can from babysitting, and this summer, she's planning to become a lifeguard at our local pool. Luke and I are hoping for athletic scholarships. Him for lacrosse and me for hockey.

It doesn't surprise me that Hallie would rather babysit than celebrate her birthday. She's going to do whatever it takes to make her dream come true and I couldn't be prouder of her for it.

"Well, me, you, and your mom are having a girls' day on Saturday to make up for it," my mom adds. "We'll go get our nails done. Do a little shopping."

Hallie smiles at her. "I'd love that, Mrs. DeLuca."

My dad moves behind my mom, folding his arms around the front of her shoulders, holding her back to his front before he plants a quick kiss to her temple.

Yeah, it's a little embarrassing for them to be all lovey-dovey with each other at my school, but at the same time, I feel like I'm one of the lucky few whose parents still genuinely like being with each other.

I admire their relationship. They met each other when they were the same age that I met Hallie and have basically been together ever since. It's the kind of relationship I want to find one day, and if I'm being honest, I think I may have already.

I've never looked at a girl the way I look at Hallie. I've never had the kind of friendship we have with anyone else. I've never even considered dating someone who wasn't her.

I've gotten teased by my teammates for turning down other girls. I've had my sexuality questioned because I'm sixteen and haven't dated. But frankly, Hallie Hart is all I see.

No, we aren't boyfriend and girlfriend. We've never kissed or done anything like that. But it just feels...right. We haven't even told each other we like each other, though I'm pretty sure it's mutual.

I think.

I don't know for sure, but she hasn't really given anyone else the time of day, so maybe?

Regardless, her brother would kill me. Hallie being in high school with us was the first time that Luke realized his friends were interested in his sister, and he's become a little too protective of her. And on top of that, our families are so intertwined that it'd be a huge problem if we didn't work out.

So, yeah. I haven't said anything to her about how I feel, but she's my favorite person. The person I enjoy spending time with the most, and I can't ignore that it feels like the same thing my parents have.

"Luke, you'll take your sister to the Holmes house, right?" his mom asks.

"Um..." He hesitates. "No. I have to study. Can't you guys drop her off?"

"The restaurant is in the opposite direction. Drop your sister off then you can go study."

Luke opens his mouth to argue with his mother, but his dad gives him a sharp look, telling him not to.

"I can drop her off," I cut in. "I don't mind. It's on my way home."

My eyes flit to Hallie to find her biting back a small smile.

"If that's okay with you both," I add to her parents.

I've had my license since my birthday last August, but I've never driven with only Hallie in the car. It's always her and Luke or her and my mom.

Her parents look to each other before Mr. Hart says, "Be careful with my girl, Rio."

I nod. "Always, sir."

Our parents say their goodbyes to us before leaving the rink to go to dinner together.

"You have to study?" Hallie questions her brother. "Could you have not tried to come up with a more believable lie? We all know you're going to go meet up with your girlfriend."

He shrugs smugly. "It worked, didn't it? And Lacey is *not* my girlfriend. We're just talking."

"And hooking up," I add.

Hallie grimaces. "I didn't need to know that part."

A group of guys walks by but one of them stops and eyes Hallie up and down. "Hey, little Hart."

"Hey, Dylan." Hallie smiles shyly at the guy I recognize from Luke's lacrosse team.

My eyes bounce between them, because what the hell was that?

"What's a guy have to do to get you to wear his jersey the way you wear DeLuca's?"

"Get lost, Dylan," Luke cuts in, unimpressed.

Dylan holds his hands up. "I'm just being nice to your sister, Hart."

"She's off-limits."

Dylan looks at Hallie with a smug little smirk. "Got it. Good to see you, Hallie."

He leaves with his friends, but not before giving her one last look over his shoulder.

Luke refocuses on his sister. "You know you're not allowed to date any of my teammates, right?"

She rolls her eyes. "Yes, Luke."

"Or anyone in my class," he continues. "And especially not any of my friends."

"Mm-hmm," she mumbles. "So you've said. Plenty of times."

"I'm serious, Hallie. Guys my age are only after one thing, and I'm sure as hell not letting any of my friends near you when I know what's on their mind."

I'm not after only one thing from Hallie. I'm after everything with her, but still, it feels like he's reminding me to not go there, though Luke has no idea of my feelings for his sister.

"Speaking of guys your age being after only one thing," she says, head cocked. "Aren't you late for your *study session* with Lacey?"

Luke smiles knowingly. "Yes, I am. Happy birthday, sis." He gives Hallie a hug before turning to me. "Thanks for giving her a ride. I owe you one."

"Happy to."

Understatement of the year.

"Pick a song for the drive?" I ask Hallie as she sits on the passenger side of my truck.

She's wearing this excited smile before digging into the glove compartment where I've stashed a combination of tapes and CDs. The best part about this old truck is that it still has a cassette player that works.

"What do you have in here?" she asks.

"You'd know better than me. You're always leaving your music in there."

The truth is, I have no idea what's in my glove box because the only thing I listen to when I'm driving alone are Hallie's birthday mixtapes. But I was smart enough to hide those before she got in my car. She gave me one on her fourteenth birthday last year and remade the two from her previous birthdays, the ones she had made before she started sharing them with me. And tonight, I'll get a new one.

A few months after Hallie got that boombox for her thirteenth birthday, I asked for the same for mine, simply so I could listen to her yearly mixtapes in my room. And now, they play on repeat in the truck. Because yes, I have a huge freaking crush on the girl and want to know about all the songs that represent important moments in her life.

"Oh, I've been looking for this!" she says before clicking a tape into the cassette deck.

I groan as soon as the harmonized voices start playing through the speakers. "I thought I tossed that."

Hallie squirms excitedly in her seat as the music begins to play.

"Hal, I really need you to move on from your boy band phase. It has me questioning your taste."

She relaxes in her seat, resting back on the headrest with a smile.

It makes me smile too.

I continue to drive, keeping my speed right at the designated speed limit. I promised her dad I'd take care of her and the last thing I want to do is get a ticket while Hallie is in the car and never be allowed to drive her alone again.

"Luke is so annoying about me not talking to his friends," she says out of nowhere.

I quickly glance her way, trying to get a read on who or what she's referring to before refocusing on the road. "Why do you say that?"

"I don't know. I'm fifteen and he's only a year older than me. It wouldn't be all that crazy if I were interested in one of his friends."

Wait…what does that mean? Me? Or someone else?

Thumbs tapping the steering wheel, I swallow down my nerves. "Are you referring to that guy Dylan?"

"I didn't say that."

"Do you like one of Luke's friends or something?"

Hallie's voice is quiet. "I don't know. Maybe."

I reach out to turn the music down because it's too loud in this cab when all I want is to hear her say "yes." That yes, she does like one of her brother's friends. That the friend she's referring to is me.

My long sleeve falls down my forearm as I adjust the volume

and before I know what's happening, Hallie's fingers reach out, lightly tracing the friendship bracelet on my wrist.

"I can't believe you still wear this, and I can't believe it hasn't fallen off."

I drop my arm onto the bench seat between us, letting her continue to run her fingertips over the softened threads.

The music is quiet now, so the only thing I can hear is my pounding heart, thumping in my ears.

I keep driving with my left hand with my eyes on the road, leaving my right hand to rest on the seat between us.

Hallie's touch has become more languid, running over the old bracelet she made me until her fingertips take a different path, moving up and gently running over the back of my hand instead.

I can't fucking breathe.

She's tentative with her touch, as if she's not sure if I'm going to stop her, delicately exploring the back of my hand, until finally, she slips her fingers to glide against my palm.

Without overthinking it, I open my hand and intertwine my fingers with hers. She stills for a moment, before curling her fingers around mine, putting us palm to palm.

I'm too distracted, too focused on what's happening between us to concentrate on driving. Thankfully we're on a backroad and not the interstate, so I pull my truck off to the side of the road, coming to a full stop. But I don't put it in park because that would require the use of my right hand and it's currently occupied.

"What's wrong?" Hallie asks.

With my foot firmly on the brake, I'm finally able to fully look in her direction. "I promised your dad I'd be careful driving you, and I'm too distracted to be careful."

Her lips slightly part.

"Hal, Luke would kill me."

Her eyes flick down to our intertwined hands, resting on the bench seat between us. I can feel her grip soften in mine, as if she were about to pull away, so I tighten my hand around hers to keep it there in mine.

"So maybe let's not tell him," I add.

A tick of a smile twitches at the corner of her lips.

There's a moment where we just sit there, holding each other's hand. It feels like there's an evident shift happening before I gesture to the road ahead of us. "We're almost to the Holmes' house."

"Okay," she whispers. "I suppose you need your hand back then."

We let go of each other, slowly separating, and when we do, I click her seat belt to unfasten it. She looks up at me, confused, until I put my hand back in hers and pull inward, subsequently pulling her across the bench to sit directly next to me instead of leaving the middle seat unoccupied.

"Fasten your seat belt, Hal."

She's biting back a smile when she uses her right hand to wrap the seat belt over her lap and click it into place. I place my left hand on the top of the wheel while resting our intertwined hands on Hallie's leg. Then I drive the rest of the short distance as cautiously as possible and a few miles below the speed limit.

"Thanks for the ride," she says as I park in front of the Holmes' house.

"Anytime."

She gives my palm one last squeeze before sliding across the bench seat and opening the passenger door. "Meet you on the roof tonight?"

I smile softly at her. "See you there."

My mom falls onto the couch next to me as I'm finishing up my homework.

"You guys got home late," I say with a raised brow. "It's a school night, young lady."

"Nice try. It's Friday." She drops her head back on the couch behind her. "You know how it is when we get together with the Harts. We have too good of a time. That restaurant was delicious. You'll have to come with us next time. Then Steph found this adorable little wine bar, so we may have stopped in and split a bottle. Or two."

"Glad you guys had fun."

She pats my leg. "We missed you three. Did you get Hallie to her babysitting job okay?"

I refocus on my homework, nodding.

"You're a good friend to her, Rio."

"Yeah."

"And to Luke."

"Mm-hmm."

"But have you told him that you're in love with his sister?"

That earns my attention. "Ma!"

"What?" she asks behind a fit of laughter. "Well, it's true."

"No, it's not. It's not like that between me and Hallie."

It doesn't feel right to say, especially after that moment in my truck today. But my mom tells Hallie's mom everything and the last thing I need is for Luke to find out I'm crushing on his little sister.

"Oh, *Tesoro*." She exhales deeply to stop her laughter. "Yes, it is. I see the way you look at her. I'm just surprised Luke hasn't noticed it yet."

I'm focused on my homework again and my voice is less defensive when I say, "It's not like that."

"Okay. You're right. My bad for thinking that it was."

I cautiously look over at her to find her smiling at me knowingly.

"Luke would kill me," I say.

She nods. "He'd be upset. You guys are at that age where he'd take it personally, but he'd get over it eventually."

"And we're so close with their family."

"We are," she agrees. "Steph is my best friend, and I love

Hallie as if she were my own. But how is that a bad thing?"

"I don't know. You probably aren't aware of this, but Hallie and I are really close. Probably closer than me and Luke."

"Oh, I know." She waves me off dismissively. "Honey, when are you going to learn that I know everything?"

I roll my eyes. "What I'm trying to say is that I don't know if Hallie really feels the same way I do and I don't know that I'm ready to risk what we have to find out. Plus, I don't think I'm ready to admit that to Luke yet."

She nods in understanding. "I'm not saying you need to tell either of them about how you're feeling, but if you ever want to talk to *me* about it, I'll always be here to listen."

"Yeah. Thanks, Ma."

She ruffles my hair as she stands from the couch. "I'm headed to bed. Your dad is waiting for me so we can watch our show. Good night, honey."

"Night."

She's halfway up the stairs when I stop her. "Hey, Ma?"

"Yeah?"

"Am I really that obvious, or are you just saying that?"

She cackles. Wildly. Like a woman who downed two bottles of wine with her husband and best friends. "Rio, if you had 'I'm in love with Hallie Hart' tattooed across your forehead, it might be a little more subtle."

"Okay," I say with a rising inflection. "It's clearly past your bedtime, Mother."

She's laughing all the way upstairs and into her room.

I finish the last of my homework before going to my own room to brush my teeth and change into sweatpants, a hoodie, and a pair of sneakers.

It's a bit before midnight—right on time.

I look out my bedroom window to hers, where I can see her brand-new wall color—pink this time—and new furniture configuration. She only changed it up twice this year.

Hallie's not outside yet, so I grab my warmest blanket before walking to the centerline of the roof between our houses, taking a seat to wait for her. I checked the roof the other night, and it's only gotten warmer since, so thankfully, there's currently no snow or ice to stop us.

Yes, Hallie and I sneak out and meet up here quite often, but there's something about her birthday meet-ups that are always my favorite. Partly because there are a few winter months that we don't get to do this. It's too cold and there's too much ice on the roof, so we don't regularly meet up out here until after April. Yet, we're a little reckless and always risk it for Hallie's birthday in early March.

I mean, this part of the roof is flat, so it's not all that risky. We aren't completely out of our minds. But my other favorite thing about these meet-ups is that it signifies that soon enough, the sun will begin to melt the snow away for the season and we'll get to sneak out here whenever we want for the rest of the year until the next winter comes around.

Hallie's bedroom window slides open. "Have you been waiting long?" she asks as she steps out onto the roof.

"Just got here."

I lift the other half of my blanket for her to sit beside me. She does, scooting in close, before I cover her with it.

"The moon is so bright tonight," she says, looking up at it.

She's right. It's bright enough I can see the dusting of freckles over her nose and the upturn of her lips as she smiles at the sky.

"How was babysitting?"

"Well…" she sighs. "The oldest had a temper tantrum about bedtime and the youngest was teething. But they tipped me extra for working on my birthday, so I guess it was worth it."

"You'll have enough saved up for school in no time."

"Hopefully. It's expensive, so we'll see."

"Do you know where you want to go yet?"

"I'm not sure. Somewhere away from home, though. I'm

excited to have the whole college experience one day."

"Yeah," I agree. "Same here."

She sits up straighter. "I have two things for you. First." She places my folded jersey on my lap. "I need to return that to you. Thanks for letting me borrow it, but I need your home jersey for when you play on the road next weekend."

"I'll get it to you once it's out of the laundry."

Her eyes are glued on my jersey sitting in my lap. "I've never asked you why you picked that number in the first place. You've been number eighty-three for as long as I've known you."

I chuckle. "Well, I was ten years old when I got to choose my number for the first time, and I didn't know what to choose, so I picked my favorite day. I thought I was so cool picking my birthday. Eighty-three. August third. It's stuck ever since. Can't imagine having a different number now."

She hums. "Clever."

"And the second thing you have for me?"

She gives me an unimpressed look because we both know what it is.

Out of the front pocket of her hoodie, well *my* hoodie that she stole, Hallie pulls out a CD case with a single silver disk inside.

"Hallie Hart," I begin in disbelief as she hands it to me. "What the heck is this?"

"I know. I know. I hate to admit it, but it was time to switch. Half the songs I needed for this year's playlist weren't even on cassette tapes, so I had to burn a CD. And even CDs are becoming hard to find."

"Wow." I shake my head, looking at the disk in my hands. "It's the end of an era."

The CD is signed the same way all the previous tapes were, with an "H" and the outline of a heart for her last name, followed by the number fifteen. Her heart drawing is the same as it always is, with a little tail extending past where it's supposed to stop.

Like instinct, I reach out with my forefinger, covering that extra bit. The little imperfection that I find perfect every year I get to see it.

She playfully pushes my hand away and fully covers the signature with her palm. "You always do that. Every year. I know the way I draw hearts is weird."

I try to move her hand away so I can see it, but she doesn't budge.

"I don't think it's weird, Hal. I think it's my favorite part."

Her grip on the CD case loosens and this time, when I move her hand, she lets me. She lets me slip my fingers between hers. She lets me run the pad of my thumb over her knuckle.

I look up to find her already watching me with those sparkly eyes.

"No one else draws their hearts like this, so every time I see one, I know it's you. That's why I like them so much."

Her smile goes soft.

"Happy birthday, Hal."

"Thank you." It's hardly a whisper, so she clears her throat and nods towards the CD. "Should we go listen?"

"Only if you tell me why each one of these songs is important to you."

That smile grows. "I always do."

She stands first and I follow, tossing my blanket and jersey back through my window before crossing the roof to her room, closing her window after we're both inside.

Hallie is already in the closet, pulling out the extra blankets and pillow we stash for my sleepovers.

"You're staying over." She says it as a statement before adding, "Right?"

It's been months since I've been able to, thanks to the winter weather blocking my ability to sneak into her room, and I'm desperate for a good night of sleep.

"Is that okay?"

She shoots me a look, reminding me I don't have to ask. I typically *don't* ask. I usually just sneak over here and plant myself on the floor next to her bed on the nights I can't sleep. Been doing it for years at this point.

I make myself comfortable on the ground with my makeshift bed as Hallie gets the mix CD ready in the boombox.

"What happens if it scratches?" I ask, remembering that was her initial concern with switching over.

She holds up three more copies, all signed with the H, the heart, and the number fifteen. "I made backups."

I'm chuckling as she climbs into bed, lying on the side closest to me, but my laughter dies the instant the first song begins to play.

"You're kidding me," I state.

Now she's the one laughing.

"Are they all going to be boy band songs?"

"I don't want to ruin it for you. Just listen."

I groan. "I'm disappointed in you, Hal. New rule for next year. No more boy bands."

She's laughing again before she explains why this song is important to her. As she does every year, she describes what was happening when she listened to it that made her want to rewind it back and relive that moment. That continues for the entire CD, and no, I don't love the song choices, but I do love hearing about all the big, important moments she had this year.

We listen in the dark, somewhat lying next to each other—her on the bed and me on the floor—when the final song begins to play.

I recognize it instantly. It's hard not to when I just heard it today. It's the same song we listened to in my truck.

Hallie rolls over, lying on her stomach so she can look down at me. "This was a last-minute addition," she admits quietly.

"And what happened that was so important when you heard it?"

I already know the answer, but I want to hear her say it.

She smiles down at me softly. "It was the first time I realized that you may feel the same way about me as I've always felt about you."

It may be her birthday, but I swear, with that single sentence, she just made all *my* wishes come true.

13

Rio

Out my living room window, I watch as Frank parks Hallie's car on the street in front of the house next door. He manually locks the door, leaves her keys in her mailbox, and gets into the passenger side of another vehicle that followed him here.

I hold my hand up to him in a wave as they drive off.

Frank has been my mechanic since I moved to Chicago. Everyone should have a good mechanic on speed dial and Frank is the best. Not only because he's honest and fair, but because when I called him early this Saturday morning, he was happy to tow Hallie's car to his shop so he could take a look at it.

Yeah, she'll probably be pissed that I handled it myself, but fuck it. She can be mad all she wants, but she needs a working car.

Hallie was never all that prideful about money. That's a new development. When we were younger, we were both well aware there was going to be a pay disparity in our chosen careers. But I don't think her new view of money is due to some martyr mentality. I truly believe if anyone else offered her help, she might accept it.

But that offer coming from me? It's all anger.

Anger towards me, that her life has been harder than it was

supposed to be, harder than I told her it would be. Anger that she's working two jobs and brutal hours to make ends meet because I left and didn't take her with me when I promised I would.

Last night, I drove for another hour before getting Hallie home, and once I finally made it to my bed, I didn't sleep much. That's not a new development by any means, but the hours spent lying awake were also spent coming to some harsh realities. I've only ever focused on my own anger towards her, never once stopping to think why she could have that same sentiment towards me.

I'm not sure if she's home tonight. I'm not sure if she had a shift at the bar and if Wren drove her there. Most of me wanted to go next door and offer to give her a ride or hand her the keys to my truck if she wanted to drive herself, but there's still a piece of me hoping to keep some semblance of distance from her, to not let us get too messy or intertwined.

That part of me also knows it's playing a losing game.

Tired of thinking about the girl next door, I grab the remote off the coffee table, and as soon as I'm about to drop onto the couch for the rest of the night and binge-watch some TV, my doorbell rings. Which is weird because it's a Saturday night, most of my teammates are going out again, and my other eight friends are having a date night at the three-star Michelin restaurant downtown that's near impossible to get into without having a reservation booked a year out.

No, it wasn't the captain of our city's hockey team who got the exclusive reservation, or the best point guard in the NBA. It wasn't the newly retired ace pitcher of the Windy City Warriors or his stud shortstop of a brother. It was Miller who scored the table without a wait because the head chef there is begging her to collaborate on a new dessert menu and is using this reservation as a bribe.

With how stoked Miller is for this dinner, I'd say it's working.

Of course, I was invited to join when the night was being planned, but I didn't have it in me to play the ninth wheel yet again. It's different at family dinner, but a full-on date night where I'm the only one solo? I'm happy to sit this one out.

Apparently, I'm not fast enough to answer the door. By the time I'm nearing the entryway, it's already being unlocked and the handle is turning.

Way too many people are on my front porch once the door swings open.

Indy holds up my house key proudly before her, Ryan, Zee, Stevie, Kai, Miller, Isaiah, and Kennedy pile into my house with all their kids in tow. My friends are dressed to the nines. Their kids are wearing pajamas.

"I'm going to revoke those house key privileges," I tell Indy.

She waves me off as she walks by. "No, you won't. You love us."

"What's going on?" Closing the front door, I follow the group into my living room.

"Babysitter canceled," Miller explains, which in fact, doesn't explain anything at all.

Taylor Zanders ambles over to me and I pick her up, slinging her onto my hip. "Still wondering why you're here. Shouldn't you all be downtown for dinner?"

The other kids—Iverson Shay and his sister, Navy, along with Max Rhodes, climb onto my couch, making themselves comfortable in front of my television. Kai keeps his sleeping baby girl, Emmy, held tightly to his chest.

Indy's smile screams that she's about to guilt trip me. "Remember how you're my best friend and you're in love with my husband and would do anything for him and I'm totally cool with your one-sided man-crush?"

"It's definitely two-sided," I scoff, glancing at Ryan. "And I don't know. He's starting to lose his appeal."

Ryan chuckles. "We need you to watch the kids, Rio."

"Did they make you ask because they thought you'd have the best chance at getting me to agree?"

He shrugs, not disagreeing, which only tells me I'm correct.

"Wait." My brows shoot up. "You need me to watch all five of them? At once?"

"Not Emmy," Miller adds. "We can take her with us."

I like to think I'm good with kids, especially these ones. But babysitting four at one time? Not a chance in hell I'm that good.

I look around at my friends to confirm this is some kind of joke they're trying to pull on me, but it's clearly not.

Miller is begging me with big, pleading eyes, trying to remind me how hard this reservation is to land.

Kai nods in her direction while looking at me, as if to say, *please don't disappoint my wife, man.*

Before I continue down the line, knowing I'll get even more guilted into this, I shake my head. "This feels like child endangerment. There's no way."

Stevie cuts in. "They'll be asleep in an hour, they're already in their pajamas, and we'll be back by nine. All you need to do is throw on a movie and hang out until we're back."

Kai furthers the campaign to get his wife to this dinner. "They wanted to hang out at Uncle Rio's one more time before your house becomes a full-blown construction zone. Isn't that right, Bug?"

I look to Max. "You have *Spider-Man*?" he asks from the couch.

I shake my head. "Sorry, Maxie. I have nothing fun here. Only vegetables and boring TV that adults like. No toys. No snacks. No fun."

He giggles manically because he's spent his whole life around grown-ups and can already understand sarcasm at four years old. "No. We see *Spider-Man*!"

Isaiah stands behind Kennedy, wrapping his arms around the front of her shoulders, holding her back to his chest. "We believe in you, Rio. You can do this."

I narrow my eyes at them. "You two don't even have kids. You're both filthy rich and can do whatever you want, *whenever* you want. Why are you joining in on the guilt trip?"

Isaiah shrugs. "I didn't want to feel left out."

Kennedy chuckles at him. "And this dinner means a lot to Miller."

"Tay," Zanders says to his daughter on my hip. "What do you think? Do you think Uncle Rio can do this?"

Taylor nods enthusiastically before resting her head on my shoulder, snuggling close, and wrapping her arms around my neck.

I immediately close my eyes in defeat.

Goddammit, these kids.

When I reopen them, I spot the shit-eating grins plastered on all my friends' faces because they know she got me. They know I'd do anything for these kids and their parents, and they know I'm about to spend my Saturday night off work watching Bluey or some shit while eating my body weight in Goldfish crackers.

"Fine," I finally agree. "But I'm going to pump them so full of sugar before you all pick them up that none of you are getting a wink of sleep tonight. And Miller, you owe me so many homemade desserts, it's not even funny. In fact, I want one of your menu items named after me. Something that everyone likes and looks good on the plate. An Italian dessert, obviously."

"Obviously." Her excited grin grows. "Thank you! Thank you!"

The eight of them move quickly, trying to get out the door before I change my mind.

Stevie plops a bag on my kitchen island, quickly explaining all the shit she brought in case the kids need it. Some books. Some stuffies. Some snacks, including little crustless PB&Js that I'm for sure going to eat myself.

They all kiss their kids goodbye, and Zanders gets a movie started on my television.

Kai stops at the door, turning back. "Max, you're the oldest. You're in charge. Keep an eye on Uncle Rio for us."

Max giggles at his dad from the couch, while I secretly throw

Kai the middle finger.

"On a real note, Rio, thank you for watching them," he says. "Mills has been working her ass off between the two patisseries and she's been looking forward to tonight all month. I would've hated for her to miss it."

I shake him off. "Don't mention it. You guys know I'd do anything for you."

"And we'd all do the same for you." He lightly knocks on the doorframe as he leaves.

Indy is the last out, with Ryan waiting on my porch for her, but I stop her before she reaches the door.

"Indy, honestly, do you think this is a good idea?"

"Good?" She tosses her head from side to side in contemplation.

"See! Child endangerment. I've only got two hands."

"Are you really that worried about it? You've watched my two before, and we wouldn't leave our kids with you if *we* were worried. You'll be great. They all love you."

"Four, Indy. There's four of them."

This knowing grin spreads on her lips. "You could always…" She shrugs. "I don't know, call for backup? Word on the street is you've got a new neighbor. Any chance she's good with kids?"

14

"**L**ook at you!" I whistle as Wren joins me in the kitchen, cute outfit on, hair and makeup done. It's a stark contrast from the too-busy student I typically find in the house. "Going on a hot date tonight?"

"Gross. No, I'm meeting up with my brother. His team is in town to play against the Devils tomorrow, so we're grabbing dinner with one of his teammates tonight."

She eyes the bowl in my hands. "I made pasta last night, you know. You're welcome to eat the leftovers."

Sitting at the kitchen island, I hold my bowl of cereal up, spoon and all. "I'm good."

"Hallie, you ran out of milk yesterday and you're eating that dry. Not to mention, it's dinnertime. Please eat some of my food so I don't have to watch you try to swallow down that dry-ass cereal."

I do just that, attempting to swallow a sawdust-like bite. "I just need to run to the store for groceries."

Once I can pay to have my car fixed, I remind myself.

She slips her phone into her purse. "Has anyone ever told you that you're stubborn, Hallie Hart?"

"I prefer the term 'determined.'"

I've gotten through so much worse over the last few years, all on my own, that this financial rough patch seems like nothing in comparison.

Wren huffs a laugh. "Yeah, I'm sure you do prefer the term 'determined,' but those leftovers are going to go to waste, so please eat them. You're my friend. What's mine is yours."

The idea of warm, buttery pasta has my mouth watering, which is kind of needed because she wasn't wrong about this cereal being dry as hell. Plus, Wren's help feels less pitying than the financial handout Rio offered last night.

She leans her elbows on the kitchen island, facing me. "I feel like I haven't seen you in weeks. How are you? How's Rio's house project going?"

"It's going. I'm working on the overall design concepts, so once those are approved, construction will begin."

"Can I just say that I *cannot* believe that you two have so much history? The stay-at-home moms who live on our street would go nuts with that kind of information. They all love Rio."

I roll my eyes, muttering, "Yeah. I bet they do."

"Jealous," she teases.

"Not jealous in the slightest. We're...*friends*."

She bursts out a laugh. "You think you can be friends with that man? I woke up in the middle of the night to get water and caught him dropping you off. I saw the way he was looking at you. Friends, my ass."

I refocus on my cereal. "Well, you have no idea what you're talking about."

She hums knowingly.

"What about you, Wilder?" I ask, pivoting. "Are you seeing anyone?"

"Nah." She waves me off. "No point when I'm moving soon."

"Have you ever dated while living in Chicago?"

"A few dates here and there. A short-term situationship last year, but I don't think I ever let myself get invested in anyone because I always knew I'd be moving home eventually."

"And back home, is there anyone there?"

A tick of a smile begins to lift on her mouth, but she brings her water bottle up to her lips to hide it.

"There is!"

"No. No, it's not like that. I'm just looking forward to getting back home. Cruz got traded to our local NBA team this year, but so did his childhood best friend. So, yeah, I'm looking forward to going home."

Wren doesn't make eye contact with me as she says it, but I still see that little sparkle when she brings up Cruz's friend.

"And this new teammate of his...is this the same teammate that's going to dinner with you tonight?"

She shoots me a look. "If you want to keep talking about my brother's best friend, I'm going to keep pressing you about our neighbor."

"So that's a yes. No wonder you look so good. Does Cruz know you have a thing for his friend?"

"It's not like that. We haven't seen each other in a long time with him playing on a different team than Cruz and my going away to school. We hardly know each other as adults."

"Hmm," I hum. "Interesting."

"Nothing is interesting. Forget I said anything. I'm going to be late." She moves frantically, grabbing her purse and car keys. "I'll see you after dinner!"

She's out the front door before I can ask any more pressing questions.

My rumbling stomach has me quick to find the leftover pasta in the fridge, and once it's warmed from the microwave, I make myself comfortable on the couch with a blanket over my legs and my dinner in my lap.

My phone rings as soon as I take my first bite.

The overwhelming hunger disappears when my stomach pitches, watching my dad's name scroll along the top of my phone screen.

It's that typical spike of anxiety I get whenever I see him

calling. Every worst-case scenario runs through my head in an instant. I'm so used to getting bad news when it comes to him that it's my nature now to assume the worst.

I'm sure that would seem overdramatic to someone else, but to me, the person who's taken care of him for the past six years, who has been with him on his worst days, it's my way to mentally prepare myself. I've been caught off guard too many times, that I've learned to brace myself anytime I see him, Luke, or the doctors calling me.

"What's wrong?" is the first thing I ask when I answer the phone.

"Can't a father call to say hello to his favorite daughter?"

I exhale an audible breath, my shoulders dropping from where they're hiked up to my ears, and the anxiety begins to settle.

"Hi, Dad." I close my eyes in relief, bringing myself back to center. "What are you up to?"

"Eating dinner."

"Same here. Do you want to eat together?"

"I'd love to."

I pull the phone from my ear and video call him instead. As soon as his face overtakes the screen, I take the opportunity to assess him.

His coloring looks good. His face seems far more filled out than I've seen it in the past. Overall, he looks...*healthy.*

He's currently smiling at me so big that I can't help but smile back.

"What are you having tonight?" I ask as I prop my phone on the coffee table, using my water bottle to keep it standing.

He's sitting in his well-loved leather recliner. "Grilled chicken and green beans." Bringing the phone closer to his face, he checks out the Tupperware I've got in my lap. "But I want whatever you're having."

"Buttered noodles covered in parmesan."

He audibly groans, throwing his head back.

I chuckle. "Did Sarah cook tonight?"

My dad looks around the room then keeps his voice quiet. "Oh yeah, she did. Love the girl, but I swear, if she keeps refusing to salt my food, I'm going to have to bribe my grandson to do it."

Sarah is Luke's wife. She's sweet, a great mom to my nephew, and a wonderful partner for my brother. She's also a big reason why Luke offered to move back to Minnesota and take over care for my dad last year.

A few years after my dad's diagnosis, I begged for Luke's help. At the time, he refused, wanting to focus his time and finances on his new family.

As alone as it made me feel, I understood. He had a new wife, they were expecting their first child, and he had moved on. Whenever we got bad news about my dad, it affected him differently. He had his own family and support system to lean on emotionally when he needed it.

Envy had started to bloom, wishing I could have the same. I had grown borderline resentful towards him until Sarah called me about a year ago and told me she convinced Luke to move back to Minnesota to help. She wanted her son to know her grandpa and she wanted me to have the opportunity to chase my own dreams and live my own life.

That's why, after all this time, I'm in a city where *I* want to live, pursuing a career *I* want to have. They moved back to our home state and bought a place with an in-law suite for my dad. I wouldn't have the chance to do what I want to do right now if it weren't for Sarah and Luke stepping up.

"How have you been feeling?" I ask.

"Good. Really good. Don't worry about me, honey. That's not your job anymore."

"It's always going to be my job, Dad."

He smiles softly and I can see the apology in it. "And how are you doing, Hallie girl?"

I simply nod. Because telling him that "I'm surviving but not thriving" would only cause him to worry.

"How's the design firm? Is that fancy designer paying you enough?"

I chuckle, not giving him the full truth. "Yes, Dad. He pays well."

My family doesn't know that I have a second job. They believe I moved in with Wren simply because we hit it off this summer and not because she *also* offered me cheap rent. They have no idea how tight money is or that my car is currently out of commission. I don't like lying to them, but if they knew the truth, they'd ask *why* I'm struggling if Tyler Braden Interiors pays well, and there's no chance I'm giving them any details about my debt.

My dad and I continue to catch up while we eat together over video chat. It's exactly how I'd want to spend my Saturday night off work. Yes, I'm grateful that I have this opportunity to live my own life, but that doesn't mean I don't miss him. I was right by his side, every day for the past six years.

It's why I can't see myself moving farther than Chicago. Even though I'm away from him, at least it's a drivable distance.

I'm mid-bite when a text drops onto my screen.

Rio: *Any chance you're home and I can bribe you to come over?*

"What's that face for?" my dad asks.

I shake my head, fixing my expression. "Just got a text that took me by surprise."

"Anyone I know?"

"Yes," I draw out. "It was Rio."

"How's it going with him?"

"I don't know. We're trying to be friends."

"That's good to hear. You know, I never understood why you two had such a falling out."

"Dad." My tone is flat because he knows as well as I do why we had a "falling out." "You, of all people, know how hard those years were. He chose not to be around."

158

"Hallie, he didn't know."

That truth hangs heavy in the air when I don't have an argument to return.

It's silent for a beat before my dad continues. "I know I don't understand all the details of your relationship, since most of it was kept secret from us, but some big, heavy things were happening in your lives at the time. Things that you shouldn't have had to navigate at nineteen years old. I hate to think that other people's decisions are the reason you two lost contact."

"It wasn't only because of other people. It was because of us too."

"Well, you might not want to hear this, but I've always liked Rio and I'm glad you two found your way back to each other, even if it is just as friends."

Another text drops onto the screen, quickly followed by more.

Rio: *I'm trying to pick up my game and thought that was better than, "Hey." Open to any suggestions that'll earn me a response.*

Rio: *Maybe you're working tonight in which case, feel free to ignore me.*

Rio: *Actually, don't ignore me. I'm too needy for that.*

Rio: *If I'm coming off desperate for you to text me back, that's because I am.*

"And she's holding back a smile, people," my dad announces.

I roll my eyes. "I gotta go."

"Tell Rio I said hello. Love you, Hallie girl."

"Love you too, Dad."

Exiting the phone call, I find my text messages.

Me: *What kind of bribe are we talking about here?*

Rio: *Offering bribes will get a pretty girl to text me back. Noted.*

Me: *Stop flirting and tell me what you're offering, DeLuca.*

Rio: *Homemade lattes delivered to your doorstep for an entire week if you come over and help me babysit tonight.*

Me: *You're babysitting? As in you're the adult in the situation?*

Rio: *Right? Four kids, Hal. This seems dangerous. I need you.*

I don't let myself overthink that last sentence too much or recall all the intimate moments in which he had said that to me before.

Rio: *Please get over here. You have way more babysitting experience than me.*

Though my instincts are screaming at me to tell him to fend for himself, I can't.

I don't want to.

Me: *Make it a month of latte deliveries and you've got yourself a deal.*

Rio: *Done. Front door is unlocked. Let yourself in.*

Yes, I know this is a bad idea. I shouldn't want anything to do with him, yet for some reason I'm quick to stand from the couch and bolt out the front door before I can come to my senses, before I can overthink the fact that this is going to be our first time spending any real time together outside the parameters of work.

But as soon as I'm outside, I'm stopped in my tracks, frozen on the front porch, because parked right there on the street is a car.

My car.

I didn't deal with my car today because, frankly, I didn't know what I was going to do. I wanted a day to relax after a busy work week and pretend I didn't have responsibilities that needed to be taken care of. I had planned to figure it out tomorrow.

How the hell did someone get into it? I have the one and only key on my key ring.

I pull out my keys to confirm, only to find the ring sans the one for my car. And that's when I realize. Rio stole my car key while I was sleeping in his truck last night, didn't he?

Relieved is the initial reaction, but that's quickly followed by embarrassment because this situation only acts as a reminder that Rio has enough money to throw at any problem that may come up while I'm struggling to buy groceries.

Don't get me wrong, if this were anyone else, without all our history, I'd happily let them help. But with Rio, it just feels sad.

Like he left and I couldn't make it on my own, so he wants to help now because he feels bad.

Crossing the lawn, I rehearse exactly what I'm going to say, but as soon as I open his front door, that speech gets thrown out the window.

I'm greeted with a wail of a cry in conjunction with a squeal of laughter and the distinct sound of something running over the texture of a wall. Back and forth. Back and forth.

"It's okay, Navy," I hear Rio coo. "We won't watch that."

"Wow! I like that!" I hear a little boy yell in excitement. "Can I use that color?"

I cautiously step into the living room.

Rio is bouncing a little girl in his arms as she continues to cry onto his shoulder, but on the couch, a boy who seems to be around the same age, is peacefully passed out asleep. I glance to the corner of the room, then down to the ground to find two more little ones, a girl with curly hair and a boy with bright blue eyes, excitedly coloring all over the plain white wall with crayons.

"What's going on?"

Rio spins in my direction and as soon as his eyes meet mine, they close with relief. "Thank God, you're here. It was fine. We were doing good, but then Max started a movie, and it was too scary for Navy, so now she's crying, and then those two wanted to color but I didn't have any paper, so I figured you're about to repaint the walls anyway, right? So why not use those as a canvas? And somehow, Iverson has been passed out asleep through it all. Bless him."

I nod slowly. "I'm sure their parents are going to love that they learned to color on walls at your house."

"I'm the fun uncle, Hal. They knew what they were signing up for when they dropped them off here."

I chuckle and the little girl in his arms—Navy, I believe is her name—stops crying long enough to ask, "Who's that?"

"That's my friend, Hallie," Rio says.

I smile at her. "Hi. What's your name?"

The other girl with the curly hair and hazel eyes cuts in. "That's Navy. She's my cousin."

"Ahh. Well, it's nice to meet you, Navy." I shift my attention back. "And what's your name?"

"I'm Taylor. Baby Iverson is my cousin too. Max isn't my cousin, though. He's my best friend. I like your clothes. Do you live in this house too?"

I hold back my laughter. "It's not my house, but I do live next door."

"Taylor is Zee and Stevie's daughter," Rio explains. "She got her dad's outgoing personality, in case you couldn't tell." He sets Navy on the couch. "Hallie is going to hang out with us tonight. Is that okay?"

The two older ones, Taylor and Max, nod, but Navy just sits there on the couch until finally, she gives me a little smile.

"How about instead of coloring, we try a movie again," I suggest. "Do you like popcorn? I bet Uncle Rio has popcorn."

"*Spider-Man*!" Max shouts.

Navy starts crying again.

"Wow," Rio exhales. "Navy girl, you really are your mother's daughter. Max, no *Spider-Man*. It already scared her once."

"Ariel!" Taylor supplies as she and Max join the other two on the couch.

"Absolutely not, Tay." Rio's brows are pinched. "Spoiler alert, but she gives up her voice because she thought some random dude was hot. We're strong independent women here. The only princess movies we're going to watch are the ones where they realize they don't need a man."

This time I can't contain my laughter, which has Rio looking in my direction with a smile.

"*Moana*?" Max offers.

The girls don't disagree.

"*Moana* it is!" Rio is quick to find it on his television, getting the kids covered in blankets, and turning the lights off as the opening scene comes on. "We're going to go make popcorn. Please, for the love of God, be good."

He slips his hand into mine and pulls me into the kitchen. It feels natural to hold his hand again, but it shouldn't after it's been so long, so when we make it to the kitchen, I gently pull mine away.

Rio slips into the pantry and comes out with two bags of popcorn. I meet him in front of the microwave.

"My car is parked outside."

"Is it?" He doesn't look in my direction, unwrapping the popcorn bag.

"Rio, you can't—"

"I didn't pay for it, if that's what you're about to say. Frank, my mechanic, he's a big hockey fan. I told him the situation and gave him tickets for his whole family to our next home game in exchange for getting your car up and running. He left the key in your mailbox."

That makes me pause.

"But it's only a short-term fix. He said he doesn't think it has many miles left. You may want to look into getting something else soon."

I already knew that, so the confirmation doesn't take me by surprise or riddle me with panic. It's a shit situation, but it is what it is. I knew when I sold my car a few years ago for some quick cash and started driving my dad's old car instead, it would only be a matter of time before I had to replace it.

"Thank you," I say genuinely. "I didn't know what I was going to do, so thank you."

He looks up at me, his eyes and smile equally soft. "Anything for you, Hal."

I nod towards the kids. "So, how'd you end up watching four kids on a Saturday night?"

He explains who belongs to who from his friend group and how their moms are the same women I met at his house. He tells me about the reservation they had tonight and how their regular babysitter fell through.

"They didn't invite you to join?" I ask.

"They did. They always do. They're good about including me, but there are certain times, regardless of how much they involve me in their plans, that it's obvious I'm the odd one out."

"Do they give you a hard time about that?"

"No," he quickly answers with a shake of his head. "No, of course not. It's a me thing. Sometimes I just get tired of being the single friend. I don't need to join them on their romantic date night."

A spark of interest ignites, though I shouldn't care that he just admitted to me that he was single.

"So…" I attempt to keep my tone uninterested, disengaged, casual. "Have you been dating at all?"

And apparently, I'm a masochist because I'm *asking* him to hurt me by telling me all about the women who came after me.

Rio looks at me out of the corner of his eye as he starts the microwave, lifting a brow and silently calling out my interest. Or maybe he's asking if I'm positive I want to know the answer. But I can't exactly back down now without seeming sad and pathetic, the girl he moved on from who hasn't been able to do the same.

"Innocent question." I hold my hands up. "We're friends now, remember? Friends ask those kinds of questions."

He turns, fully facing me with his arms crossed over his chest, and it's then I realize how close we're standing. His knee bumps mine when he shifts his weight, his sock-covered toes slide against the arch of my foot.

"I've gone *on* dates, but I'm not dating anyone in particular," he explains. "I've gone on lots of dates, actually. But nothing long-term. Nothing serious since—"

Me.

Neither of us has to finish his sentence to know that's what he was about to say.

There's a heavy beat of silence that sits between us at the realization.

"Hallie, I'm not going to lie to you. I've spent most of the last six years trying to prove to myself that it exists. Love or soulmates or whatever it is that I used to believe in. But after watching everything go down between my parents and then"—he looks at me—"what happened with us…"

His green eyes search my face, hoping to make me understand. Sure, he may have been on a mission to prove to himself all these years that real love exists, but I've been doing the opposite. I haven't dated. I haven't even looked, and yes, most of that is due to being busy taking care of my dad, but there's also a part of me that knew I wouldn't be able to replicate what we had, so what would be the point in even trying?

"Sorry." He shakes his head, trying to shake us out of this moment. "I'm not trying to make this heavy."

"It was real," I quickly admit. "For me at least. It was real. That's how I know it exists."

I watch as the words settle into him. "Yeah," he breathes. "It was real for me too, Hal."

We don't break eye contact, and there are no more spoken words, only the unspoken ones.

He finally clears his throat. "And what about you? What have the last six years looked like for you?"

Well, I sure as hell am not going to admit that I haven't dated anyone in all these years. Not after his confession.

"Busy," I say simply.

We both know that's not what he's asking, so he takes the more direct route. "Are you seeing anyone right now? What about that guy from my game?"

The microwave beeps, and it feels like the perfect out of this conversation. I remove the bag of popcorn and empty it into a large bowl.

"Hallie?"

"Did you hear that?" I ask. "I think the kids need something."

I'm halfway out of the kitchen when he says, "I thought this is what friends do? Ask these kinds of questions."

I don't slow down.

"Hallie Hart!" he calls at my back.

"Shh." I hold a finger up to my lips. "There's a movie on."

"You're going to give me high blood pressure, woman. How long are going to make me dwell on that question before you finally give me the answer?"

I shrug, letting him stew over it. If Rio were thinking clearly, he'd realize I don't have enough time in my schedule to be seeing anyone, but I like how flustered he gets at the prospect that I could be.

I sit in the only empty space left on the couch between Navy and her sleeping brother before giving Taylor the bowl of popcorn. She holds it in her lap as the other two absentmindedly dip their hands in, all three of them keeping their eyes glued to the television.

A moment later, Navy reaches over and takes my hand, holding it with one of hers.

I chuckle to myself, remembering how Indy hugged me immediately when we met. Rio was right. Navy really is her mother's daughter.

Rio joins a few minutes later, with a second bowl of popcorn for us in one hand, holding out a mug for me in the other.

"It's the first of a month's worth of lattes that I owe you. I leave on Monday and will be traveling for most of the month, but I'll make it up to you when I get back."

I look down at the blob of foam on top and a grin hitches up on my lips. "Stunning latte art."

"It was the side profile of an Arctic wolf. Perfect proportions. Then I took a sip and ruined it, but it was flawless before that. Trust me."

I take my own sip, putting my lips right where I can tell his were. It's the same latte as the one he made me yesterday. Vanilla and almond milk. "Thank you."

"You already fell asleep on me once last night. I need to keep you awake to hang out with me this time."

He rests the bowl of popcorn on my legs before he picks up a sleeping Iverson from the couch next to me, readjusting him to lay on his lap so Rio can take the seat on the couch directly next to me.

There's enough room on his other side that he could move over a bit, but he doesn't. He stays close.

His thigh presses against mine. His shoulder is flush with my own.

That is until he lifts his arm and wraps it around the back of the couch where I'm sitting, essentially putting his arm around *me*.

"Rio—"

"Shh," he hushes me, eyes glued to the TV. "There's a movie on."

"You drive me insane, you know that?"

"Hmm," he hums. "That makes two of us, love."

The old term of endearment gives me pause, but it doesn't affect him one bit. He simply grabs a handful of popcorn and tosses it back, eyes locked on the movie.

It feels *good*. Comfortable and easy, the way it always used to.

"I'm glad you're here," he whispers a few moments later. "I'm sorry for stealing your Saturday night."

"No, you're not."

I peek at him out of the corner of my eye, and his smile turns so proud. "Yeah, you're right. I'm not sorry at all."

"Thanks, Hallie," Indy whispers as she peels a sleeping Iverson out from under Rio's arm. "We appreciate you helping him."

"Anytime." I keep my voice quiet to not wake the hockey player passed out asleep with his head partway on my thigh.

Indy is the last out of the house after everyone picked up their sleeping kids, but she stops at the door, turning back my way. "We're having family dinner at my house tomorrow night after Ryan's game and before Rio and Zanders hit the road for most of the month. You should come. Everyone will be there."

Everyone is referring to Zanders and the girls I've already met before, along with her husband, Ryan, and the Rhodes brothers who I met tonight.

I glance down at my lap, making sure Rio is still asleep and not listening in on this conversation. "I'm not sure he would want me going to something like that with all his closest friends but thank you for the invite."

"I don't care what he wants," Indy says with an edge of sass. "It's my house. I can invite anyone I want to invite."

I chuckle. "Thank you, but regardless, I have a shift at my second job. I work nights at a bar downtown."

Indy readjusts her sleeping son on her shoulder. "Oh, I heard about that! Service industry?" She blows out a breath. "Been there. Done that. You're a saint, Hallie. Killer tips, though, huh?"

Her response takes me by surprise. I guess I expected Rio's friends, who are all professional athletes or married to one, would judge me for being a bartender. It's a hard job, dealing with the general public, working late hours, and constantly being on your feet. It's nowhere near as glamorous as telling people I'm employed by a luxury interior design firm.

"Yeah. Exactly. Great tips."

"Next time we have a parents' night out, we'll have to come see you. And family dinner, whenever you're free on a Sunday, we'd love to have you."

I nod with a smile. "I'll keep that in mind."

"Thanks again!" She closes the front door behind her.

It's just after nine p.m. and Rio is sleeping perfectly fine. I try not to let myself overthink why that may be. We were crammed on the couch with so many bodies, so yeah, his head ended up partially on my thigh, where it still is now, but it was purely due to lack of space.

He looks so peaceful, so content, like his brain finally shut up and allowed him a moment of peace. His dark hair is falling over his forehead and covering his eyes, so without thinking, I use my fingertips to skim his curls out of the way.

He hums.

Sleeping like this, he looks exactly like the boy who I found asleep on my floor more nights than not. And spending time with him tonight felt exactly like it used to, with no anger or hostility between us.

It was nice, but the kids are gone now, so it's time for me to leave too.

I scoot out from under him, using my hand to cradle his head, and wedging a pillow below him in place of my thigh.

He stirs for a moment, reaching out for me, but I'm far enough from the couch now that he doesn't find me and instead, slips his hand under the pillow and falls right back asleep. I quietly cover him with a blanket before leaving out the front door and softly closing it behind me.

Inhaling a deep breath, I let the crisp winter air fill my lungs and clear my head.

I missed him.

Plain and simple, I missed Rio DeLuca. All tonight did was continue to prove that to me. I missed driving with him in his truck. I missed listening to music with him. I missed those seemingly insignificant moments, the ones where I look back and realize how important they were to me. The way tonight felt. Laughing with him again. Smiling with him again.

I'm only halfway across the lawn when I hear his front door open.

"Hallie," he calls out.

Turning back, I find Rio jogging to me, meeting me in the center point between our houses, the way we always used to.

"Hey," he says, rubbing his eyes. "What happened?"

"The kids all got picked up, and you were asleep. I didn't want to wake you."

"When did I..." He looks around, clearly out of it. "When did I pass out?"

"About halfway through the movie."

"Wow." He inhales deeply, stretching out his back. "Sorry about that."

"Your friends are nice."

"Yeah. They're good people. I got lucky when I moved here, finding that group."

I give him a soft smile. "Well, goodnight. I hope you have a good road trip."

Turning back to my house, I only make it one step before he circles my bicep with his hand and swings me back in his direction, pulling me into his chest.

Rio wraps himself around me in a hug that's firm and comforting and desperate. His arms are crossed around the back of my neck, his face is buried into my hair.

It's the first time we've hugged since seeing each other again, and with my nose buried in his chest, I can't help but take a dragging inhale. He smells like him. The old him. Because this man is still that same boy I once loved.

Closing my eyes, I fall into him, wrapping my arms around his waist, and we just hold each other.

Outside, standing between our houses, we hold each other longer than friends should. We hold each other longer than two people who claim to still be hurt by each other should.

Rio takes a deep, centering breath. "I missed you, Hallie," he whispers into my hair.

I close my eyes even tighter, pressing my face further into his chest. It both aches and fills me with relief to hear those words. Because I feel the exact same way and it's been that way every day for the past six years.

Eventually, his arms uncross before his palms slide against my cheeks, simultaneously pulling my face away from his chest. Craning his neck, he rests his forehead against mine, his labored breaths blending with my own.

So close. He's so close. Our *lips* are so close.

We watch each other for a long moment before I use my tongue to wet my lips. I haven't kissed this man in six years, but it feels like that could change in an instant if Rio decides to shift forward and take what I know he wants.

When he nudges his nose against mine, his lips slightly brush my own, but he doesn't kiss me yet. He teases. He silently asks for permission.

"Hallie," he whispers against my mouth. It comes out pained yet urgent, as if there's more he wants to say but doesn't.

Like he's begging and apologizing all at the same time.

Still, he doesn't go in for the kiss. Instead, his thumbs stroke against my cheekbones as he waits for me to decide whether I'm going to close the remaining distance and meet his mouth with my own or stop this altogether.

But alarms are going off in my head. Alarms telling me to pull back and create distance. Alarms telling me that we wouldn't be able to come back from this. Alarms reminding me that though we're getting along again, I'm not ready to forgive or forget about the day he left or the painful years after. And I don't think he is either.

This kiss would only make my job ten times harder. This would only make my *life* ten times harder because this wouldn't just be a simple kiss for me. Not with him.

As much as every other part of me wants to lean up, my brain doesn't let me.

"I'm glad we're able to be friends," I whisper against him instead.

Rio's mouth instantly turns up in a smile and his chest slightly shakes against mine with a laugh. Those lips that were about to press against my own, move to my forehead, placing a kiss there instead.

"Night, Hallie." He tucks my hair behind my ears before hesitantly letting me go. "Sleep well."

I take slow steps away from him, telling myself that stopping us was the right thing to do.

I look back over my shoulder to find he hasn't moved at all.

I'm through my front door, but something doesn't feel right leaving things like that, so I take a step back outside.

"Hey, Rio?"

Hands in his pockets, he perks up. "Yeah?"

"I missed you too."

15

Rio

(AGE 17)

"**S**ince when are guys allowed at my little sister's birthday parties?" Luke asks, eyes locked on his living room as we stand in the entry to the kitchen.

"She's sixteen. Of course she's going to have guys here. *We're* here."

"We don't count. I'm her brother and you may as well be."

That makes me visibly grimace. I'll tell you one thing. Me and Hallie couldn't be further from *that*, even though neither of our families know for certain what's going on. Of course, my mom knows about my feelings for her, but she doesn't know the rest.

They have no idea how often we meet on the roof where she lays on my chest and I play with her hair while we simply talk. Or how I sleep in her room most nights—on the floor, but still. They have no idea that me saying I like her doesn't exactly encompass how I actually feel about the girl.

"I don't know why you're being weird about it," I say to Luke. "Our friend groups are completely intertwined at this point. Most of these people are your friends too."

He shakes his head. "That's my baby sister."

"Dude, you were sixteen like a year and a half ago."

"You don't get it, but you're lucky you don't have to deal with figuring out if your friends are actually your friends or if they're hanging around because they want to get with your sister." That statement hangs in the air before there's a loud crash somewhere down the hall. "What the hell?" he groans. "Everyone is sober. Why are they breaking stuff?"

He bolts in that direction, leaving me standing there and feeling like shit.

I want to tell him.

I've *tried* to tell him. I've started the conversation so many times this past year, but then I chicken out when he makes some remark about me being his best friend and knowing I'd never betray him by dating Hallie. I think our parents would be cool with it, but Luke... I don't see a day Luke would ever be cool with knowing I have feelings for his sister.

Hallie hasn't seemed too pressed about it, but she's made a few comments here and there about wishing she could hold my hand while at school or rest her head on my shoulder during lunch. Things we only do in the privacy of my truck when I'm driving her home after my games, or when we're alone on the roof.

But honestly, it's not like we've gone much further than that. Part of me is wanting to wait, to attempt to put my feelings on hold. Luke will be off at college in just over a year and maybe he'd care a whole lot less by then. But that means I'll be gone too, and there hasn't been a day that's passed that I haven't at least thought about kissing her.

I move slowly, I guess. And though I'm a year older than her, I'm equally as inexperienced. Sometimes I wonder if she's going to get over it. Over me. It's not like she can tell people that she's my girlfriend. Hell, I don't even know if she *is* my girlfriend. Is she going to get tired of waiting for me to make a move and decide she'd rather be out in the open with someone else?

Fuck, I've been so in my head lately, but her sixteenth birthday party isn't the place for me to be figuring it all out.

She looks so cute tonight, in her knit sweater and short skirt. Ten nails all painted in different colors. Long hair, sparkly hazel eyes, and a smile that lights me up whenever I see it.

Hallie is hugging her friend and saying thank you for a gift when she catches me staring at her from across the room.

She discreetly shoots me a little wink and though I know that's all I'll get of her today, I happily take it.

Though we always meet on the roof for her birthday, this year is going to be different. She's going to be busy being the center of attention at her sweet sixteen all night that we're going to have to meet another time.

The living room is crowded with our friends, a mix of people from her sophomore class and my junior. It makes it easy, stealing moments with her while at school because our friend group is big and we're always together.

Luke comes back holding up a broken lamp. "At least it was from my room," he says, throwing it in the trash and joining me to watch as Hallie opens all her presents. She gets a bunch of art supplies and some makeup. A few CDs which I know she's stoked about because they're becoming increasingly difficult to find.

She's almost done opening all her gifts when the front door opens and a group of guys from the senior class walk in.

I recognize them immediately. They're mostly football players—one is from the basketball team, and almost all of them are carrying a case or two of beer as they join the party.

The last person through the door is probably the most popular guy at our school—Grant Newcastle. He's the captain of the football team, senior class president, and I fucking hate him.

He and Hallie are both in the student council, and ever since they planned the winter dance together, he's been all over her.

"What the hell is he doing here?" I ask Luke, my tone sharp.

He looks at me suspiciously. "What happened to 'why are you being weird' and 'we're all friends?'"

"We're not friends with that guy."

Though, I do think Luke might give up a kidney if he could be.

"He asked Hallie to prom yesterday and she felt bad for saying no, so she invited him to her birthday party, I guess."

I swear my eyes almost explode out of my head. "Excuse me, what?"

"Not sure why you're yelling at me or what you're confused about."

I fully turn, facing him, but he's still got his attention on the newcomers. "He asked your sister to prom?"

"Yeah."

"And she said no?"

"Yep."

"Because you *told* her to say no or because she didn't want to go with him?"

Luke shrugs casually, and how he can be so casual about this, I have no fucking clue. "Probably because she assumed I wouldn't be okay with it and said no before I could. I don't know for sure."

"But...are you saying you'd be okay with it?"

"Yeah, I guess so."

What the actual fuck?

"I mean, it's Grant Newcastle," he continues. "Who wouldn't want to go to the senior prom with the guy? Hell, even I'd say yes if he asked me. I told her she should tell him she changed her mind, but she didn't want to."

Grant scans the room and when he spots my girl, he instantly starts in her direction, a cocky smile plastered on his lips. He taps on her shoulder, and when he gets her attention, she grins that gorgeous smile, but I can't tell if that's a typical Hallie smile because she's nice to everyone or if that one is reserved specifically for him.

Then he wraps her in a hug and holds on for way longer than he needs to.

I feel like I could throw up. Grant fucking Newcastle. How the hell am I supposed to compete with him? And why wouldn't she go for him? The guy is going to Boston College on a full ride next year to play football. He's got a perfect GPA. She wouldn't have to hide him from her brother, and he's staying close to town. Fucking great.

"Where's the hard stuff?" one of the seniors asks, the same one holding two cases of beer.

No one responds because there isn't any.

"Hart," Grant calls out to Luke.

Leaning on the wall next to me, he stands up straighter like a puppy who's finally about to get some attention.

"Do your parents have a liquor cabinet?"

"Oh, we aren't drinking," Hallie tells him.

Grant's smile turns mischievous. "Have a little fun, Hallie. It's your birthday after all. I need to take you to one of our senior parties soon. It's a little more...*lively* than this."

There's a collective laugh among the crowd, and people are hanging on every word that comes out of this guy's mouth like he's a fucking god. But he's not. He's just a douchebag who's genetically blessed.

Hallie eventually joins in and laughs too, but it's fake and forced and her smile is flat on her lips. She's embarrassed.

"We're not drinking, Grant," I say confidently. "We're having a good time without it."

"Or we could," Luke pipes up at my side. "I know where my parents keep it."

"Hell yeah, Hart!" Grant cheers, and for some reason his enthusiasm resounds around the entire room, and suddenly everyone is completely on board to start drinking.

I jog after Luke to stop him. "What are you doing?"

"Getting some alcohol. It's not a big deal, Rio. Grant's group is cool, and they want to kick it with us. What's the big deal?"

"The big deal is that you're being actively recruited, and I just signed my letter of intent to play for Michigan. If we get caught underage drinking, our scholarships are fucked."

Luke rolls his eyes, grabbing two bottles of clear liquor out of the back of a cabinet. "We're not going to get caught. We just need to keep quiet because our parents are right next door at your house."

When I follow him back to the dining room, Solo cups are being set out on the table and beer is being poured into them.

"Hallie, you're on my team," Grant says.

"Oh, no. That's okay. I'm not going to drink."

"I'll drink your share," Luke offers.

"Perfect. Thanks, Hart." Grant slings an arm over Hallie's shoulders. "It's settled then. You're on my team, birthday girl."

Her eyes dart to me for a moment, but it happens so quickly, I can't tell if she wants to play and she's apologizing to me, or if she wants an out. And soon enough the entire party migrates to the dining room to watch whatever drinking game is about to go down.

Someone turns on a speaker and the music starts bumping as the game begins. Hallie and Grant don't have much to drink because, annoyingly enough, they make a good team. But whatever alcohol his sister is supposed to drink, Luke does it for her.

They keep playing round after round because they can't lose. Luke stays close to Hallie, but that's mostly because Grant is close to her and my buddy is clearly obsessed with the guy.

Which only makes me feel like shit. Luke would be cool with Hallie dating him, and I'm over here too scared to tell him about my feelings in fear he'd end our friendship over it.

But she's genuinely having a good time, laughing and dancing to the music with all her friends, with the most popular guy in school giving her all his attention.

I'm glad she's having fun. I am. I just wish that guy next to her was me.

Music is blasting through my headphones as I lie in my bed with my eyes closed, trying my hardest to find sleep. The headphones aren't comfortable by any means, but I needed to drown out Hallie's and my parents' laughter filtering in my room from downstairs, and the music coming from her house.

I actively focus on shutting off my brain because that's the only way I'm successful at falling asleep. That, or I work my body so hard at practice or the gym that I'm too tired to stay awake. Or alternatively, I crash in Hallie's room.

With the last two options off the table for tonight, I concentrate on the first. But it feels hopeless knowing she's next door with someone else.

A familiar song starts playing from my iPod that's sitting on my nightstand, and I hope that's enough to lull me to sleep, but then the beat is interrupted by an unfamiliar *tap, tap, tap*. It's strange and off tempo, and it happens again, this time in a different part of the chorus.

Tap, tap, tap.

Tap, tap, tap.

Only then do I realize it's not my music at all.

Opening my eyes, I see Hallie on the other side of my bedroom window, knocking on the glass.

What the hell?

I throw my headphones and blankets off with urgency, jogging to the window and cracking it open.

"What are you doing?"

Her lower lip is shivering from the cold and her nose is pink. "Are you not coming?"

I push the window open fully, reach out, and wrap my arms around her middle to pull her into my room. She's absolutely freezing. I'm not wearing a shirt, only a pair of sweatpants, so I can feel how cold her skin is against mine.

"How long have you been out there, Hal?" Setting her on her feet, I grab a blanket from my bed to wrap it around her.

"Maybe twenty minutes." Her hazel eyes are so fucking sad. "Did you forget?"

"Of course not." I push her hair away from her face. "I'd never forget, but you were busy. Shouldn't you still be at your birthday party?"

"I left because you left, and I wanted to see you. I thought you were headed to the roof. That's my favorite part of today."

God, I suck.

I left because I was too busy to enjoy her birthday, occupied instead with having myself a pity party.

Picking her up, still wrapped in that blanket, I carry her to my bed and set her on my lap while I sit on my mattress.

"It's my favorite part too, Hallie. I'm sorry. I didn't think you were planning to meet me out there tonight with your party still happening."

"But we always meet. It's like our unspoken thing."

My forehead falls to her shoulder. "We could go out there now, if you'd like."

She shakes her head, slipping her arms out from under the blanket to touch my bare stomach. Her fingers feel like icicles, but her body starts to relax, and the shivering begins to subside when my body heat begins to warm her up.

She looks up at me, keeping herself close. Her mouth is right there. Her eyes fall to my lips, but because I'm such a fucking coward, I still don't lean in and kiss her.

Hallie sighs but tries to cover it by saying, "I have something for you." She grabs the CD case that's resting on her lap. "Year sixteen."

"I do love getting presents on your birthday."

She laughs to herself when she hands it over.

Another to add to my collection. Over the clear plastic case, I run my thumb over the "H," the heart, and the number sixteen. Then I use my index finger to cover the tail she always adds to her hand-drawn hearts.

Her head falls to my shoulder as I hold her.

"Are we going to listen to it together?" I ask quietly.

"Of course we are."

"Good." I place a soft kiss on her forehead. "Happy birthday, Hal."

We sit there for a while, her warming up and me holding her on my lap. She plays with the old friendship bracelet on my wrist while I work up the courage to say, "I didn't know Grant asked you to go to senior prom."

"It just happened yesterday, and there wasn't much to tell you about. Obviously, I said no."

"You didn't want to go?"

She bursts a laugh. "Rio, I'm your girlfriend. Why would I go to prom with someone else?"

Wait...*what?*

When I don't say anything, she lifts her head to look at me.

"Oh my God," she breathes, jumping off my lap, letting the blanket fall to the floor as she does. "Oh my God! Am I not? I thought it was another one of those unspoken things."

Both her hands fly to her mouth to cover it, but I can see the panic so clearly in her eyes.

"Hallie," I soothe, circling her forearms to pull her hands away. "I wasn't sure if you wanted to be, but yeah. Yes. Please. I want you to be my girlfriend. You have no idea how badly I want you to be my girlfriend."

She closes her eyes. "Why did I do that? I should've let you ask me instead of assuming that's what we were."

I pull her to stand between my open legs as I sit on my bed. "Well, we both know I move slow and sometimes need a little push, so this is a good thing."

She chuckles, a little defeated as her hands play with the hair at my temples. "You're perfect the way you are. I don't mind moving slow with you."

I want to kiss her. God, do I want to kiss her. I've never wanted anything more, but what if I'm bad at it? What if I fuck up and hit her teeth or something? What if I ruin her first kiss? She'd never be able to get a do-over.

While I'm reeling and nervous and entirely in my head, Hallie leans forward and presses her lips to mine.

Well, sort of. She kind of misses and barely connects with the corner of my mouth, but it's enough to tell me she wants this too.

Standing straight again, she swallows hard. "Just in case you need a little push with that too. This sixteen and never been kissed thing is feeling a little cliché."

My heart is racing. My skin is on fire. But also, I couldn't be more relieved.

Fuck it. I can do this.

"Put a song on," I tell her, nodding to my nightstand where both my boombox and iPod sit. I wait for her to do so, running the palms of my hands along the backs of her thighs, keeping her standing between my legs.

If I'm not listening to Hallie's yearly playlists, I typically use my iPod and headphones to listen to music. But Hallie doesn't reach for that. Instead, she flips through my old CD case quickly before picking one and skipping to the track she wants.

"Why do I need to pick a song?" she asks.

It starts playing through the boombox speakers and I can't help but laugh at the lack of subtlety in her song choice.

"Because I'm going to kiss you and when we listen to next year's playlist, I want this song to be on there so we can rewind it back however many times we want to and remember this."

Her smile blooms, and her arms wrap around my neck. "I was hoping you were going to say that."

I slip my hand into her long hair, pull her down to meet me, and press my own smiling lips to hers.

It's messy and mistimed, and yeah, I think I hit her teeth at one point, but it's also so fucking perfect. And eventually, with a little practice, we figure it out together.

16

Rio

"As of this week, you and Evan Zanders are officially the longest-running defensive duo ever in the NHL," a reporter says in our postgame press conference. "What do you think has contributed to your successful partnership?"

I sit forward, bringing my mouth closer to the microphone, running my hand through my wet hair, fresh out of the shower. "Uh...we're friends," I say simply.

There's a small laugh among the media, but that's clearly not enough of an answer because no one jumps in to ask the next question.

I'm not totally used to being called on to do interviews. I don't wear the captain's patch, and as a defenseman, I'm not the high scorer on the team. My contribution is rarely noticed on stat sheets. It's with defensive plays, big hits, and experience, so I hardly get called on for postgame media.

But of course, the one game we're home, the one *night* we're home, in an almost three-week span of road games, I'm called in for an interview.

My short responses aren't getting me out of here any quicker, so I try again. "I think the reason we're so successful on the ice is because we've built our chemistry *off* the ice. He's one of my best friends outside of the rink. We talk nearly every day. Add that to many, many years of sharing the blue line, and it's become almost automatic to know what the other is going to do in any given play."

More hands are raised by reporters, but thankfully our media manager cuts in. "Thanks, everyone. That's all the time Rio has for tonight."

I'm up and out of my seat, grabbing my water off the table and hightailing it out of the media room as quickly as possible. Don't get me wrong, I typically don't mind when reporters call on me and want my take on the game, but tonight is the *one* night I'm home.

Tonight is the *one* night I have any hope of seeing Hallie.

It's been five days since our almost-kiss, and I haven't been able to get her off my mind. Haven't really been able to get her off my mind in about fifteen years, but it's been all-consuming the past few weeks. Her living in Chicago is like a bad drug, knowing in my head I should stay away, but needing that hit of seeing her. The more time I spend with her, the more time I need.

Back in the locker room, I find it completely empty. With only one night in town, the guys were quick to get home to their friends or families while I was finishing up postgame interviews.

Typically, when we're playing in Chicago, I leave the arena in comfortable clothes, knowing I'm headed straight home. Tonight though, I change back into my pregame suit, grab my wallet and keys from my locker stall, and practically jog to my truck.

The bar is only a few blocks away and when I get there, I surprisingly find an empty space left in the lot. Hallie's shitty Nissan Altima isn't here, but that doesn't necessarily mean she's not working.

We've been texting here and there since I left on Monday. If she was getting ahold of me, it was with house-related things. If I was reaching out first, it was because I was wondering how her day was going or what she was doing.

On Tuesday, while I was in Tampa, the first snow had fallen in

Chicago, and she casually mentioned that she took a rideshare into the city for work, in case her car decided to give her issues again. She very well could have done the same thing tonight, and if not, and she's at home, I'll go there instead.

Because I want to see her.

As much as I shouldn't, as much as I want to write her off and hold on to old grudges, the truth is, I just want to see her. Now that I've admitted to both of us how much I've missed her, there's no use in pretending that I don't.

The bar is crowded for a Thursday, but it's not nearly as busy as it was the last time I was here. There are plenty of Raptors' jerseys, with fans grabbing a drink after the game. On my way to the bar, I get stopped more than I'd like, so I sign a couple autographs, smile for a few pictures, all while trying to get a glimpse past the crowd to see who's working tonight.

I haven't spotted her yet, so I weave my way through the bodies and high-top tables, finally making it to an empty stool tucked under the far corner of the bar top.

Ken Doll is taking orders, and another girl is working the well. There's no Hallie, though.

I'm standing from my seat to go find her at home when the side door swings open. Hallie steps through, arms full of multiple different bottles of liquor from what must be the storage space.

My chest does this annoying tightening thing that it's only done when I was a teenager, and the nerves instantly ramp up. They're excited nerves though, not the uncomfortable or scared ones.

It's no secret that I haven't exactly been smooth in my attempts to try to meet someone else in hopes of convincing myself that Hallie *wasn't* my person. I'm shit at talking to most women outside of the safety of the friend zone.

But I've never been anyone but myself with Hallie. Smooth, awkward, it didn't matter. That's part of the beauty of us growing up together, I guess. We've always known exactly who the other is.

There was no need to try to be someone we weren't.

Hallie doesn't see me immediately. Her eyes are locked on the labels of the bottles, organizing the new ones behind the already opened ones, lining them up to be used next. She's concentrating on the final whiskey bottle when someone shouts my name loud enough for the entire bar to hear me.

"Rio DeLuca!" some big, drunk dude hollers, stomping over and throwing his arm around me. "Huge fan!"

Hallie whips around, quickly scanning the bar before her eyes finally land on me.

I wear my most innocent smile when she finds me.

I've got this giant guy hanging on me, telling me how big of a fan he is, but I've got all my attention locked on her.

"Do you come here a lot?" he asks me.

I'm still looking right at her. "I have a feeling I'll be here quite a bit going forward."

She rolls her eyes, shakes her head, and looks away, but I see that smile fighting to break through.

"Man," the big dude says. "I've got to get a picture. My buddies aren't going to believe I saw you." He holds out his phone and takes a selfie of us before I can agree or disagree. "Okay, I'm going to leave you alone and make sure no one bothers you for the rest of the night."

He moves a couple of feet away, at the same time pushing a few other patrons too, leaving me with my own private corner of the bar.

My focus is still lasered in on Hallie's back as she gets back to organizing the bottles. Painted-on black jeans stretch over her ass before flaring out over her thighs, stopping just above the ankle where a shiny gold anklet lays. She's got this funky, brightly colored sweater on, and her short hair is half pulled up in a bun.

"Are you ignoring me?" I ask.

"I'm working."

Reaching up on her toes, she slides a new bottle behind a

partially used one. Her sweater rides up, giving me a full view of her heart-shaped ass before the denim cuts in around the waist.

"That's fine. Lovely view from this angle."

She looks over her shoulder and I let her catch me checking her out.

Turning, she comes down from her toes, pulling her sweater to cover her stomach, but all that does is draw my attention to the dip of the neckline where a black lace bralette peeks out.

Yes, I know what a bralette is, thanks to the girls' nights I've been a part of over the years. I've learned some crazy shit from those get-togethers.

I lean my elbows on the bar top, pushing myself forward, towards her. "Crazy seeing you here."

She crosses her arms on the bar, mirroring my position. "What can I get you to drink?"

"Water."

She lifts a brow.

"I'm not exactly here for the booze." My eyes drop down to her lips. "What time are you off?"

She tries to hide it, but I catch her attention flicking to my own mouth as I speak, and it takes everything in me not to ask if she changed her mind about that kiss.

She pushes herself off the bar, simultaneously pulling her attention away from my mouth to scan the room.

"I'm not sure yet. Depends on when things start slowing down." Hallie scoops ice into a cup and tops it with water from the soda gun. "Nice game tonight, thirty-eight," she says as she sets the glass on a coaster in front of me before nodding to the TV in the corner playing our local sports network. "You looked good out there."

That thing happens in my chest again, and suddenly I feel like a kid, knowing she watched me play, hoping I impressed her.

"No jersey?" I ask, nodding towards her colorful sweater.

"Not until you tell me why you changed your number." She

lets that statement hang to see if I take the bait, but I don't. "And besides, you've got plenty of other people wearing your jersey in here."

I hold eye contact. "Kind of only care about one."

A laugh bubbles out of her. "When did you become such a smooth flirt?"

"Smooth? That part pretty much only happens with you. The flirting part of that question really hasn't done much for me over the years."

She shrugs. "Always worked on me."

Those lips tilt into a knowing smile and fuck me if I don't want to lean right over this bar and kiss them. Kiss her.

"All right." She wipes down the work area around her before tucking that towel into the back pocket of her jeans. "I've got to get back to work."

"Okay. I'll be here." I lean back in my chair, bringing my glass to my mouth.

"Wait. You're just going to sit there while I work?"

I nod.

"Why?" She seems genuinely confused with those brows pinched together and her nose scrunched.

And that makes two of us because only a couple of months ago I thought I'd never see her again, and now, I don't want to let her out of my sight.

I shrug casually as if the answer were obvious. "I already told you, Hal. I missed you."

17

Hallie

It's after midnight when I slip out the back door of the bar to find Rio leaning against his truck, hands slipped in his suit pants pockets, one leg crossed over the other, and waiting for me.

He looked sinfully delicious when I found him at the bar, wearing that deep maroon suit and white button-down shirt, freshly showered straight from the rink. He looks even more edible now since removing the jacket and rolling his shirt sleeves to reveal those stupidly cut forearms. He's also added a dark gray beanie pulled down over his ears since coming outside. He's been waiting for me out here since I told him I was going to get tipped out and head home for the night.

He was quite the distraction, sitting there at the corner of the bar, drinking glass after glass of water and watching me work. I felt his eyes on me the whole time. Felt myself glow under the attention, regardless that technically, I'm not supposed to want it.

When the bar slowed down for one of us to get cut for the night, I volunteered, knowing I was too distracted to be much help anyway and that Rio wasn't going to leave until *I* did.

I didn't tell him I was working tonight, didn't tell him I didn't bring my car downtown, but he seems pretty satisfied with himself that he figured that all out on his own, wearing that boyish grin on his lips that I missed and leaning against his truck.

He's making it awfully difficult to remember why I didn't kiss him the other night.

"Any chance you need a ride home?" he asks.

"As a matter of fact, I do."

His smile turns proud.

Together, we round the hood of his car. Rio opens the passenger side door for me and right there, sitting on the seat is a folded blanket and a small pillow.

I spin on my heel to face him, and I don't think it's simply the chilly Chicago air that's making his olive-toned skin flushed.

"In case you wanted to get some sleep again."

Once again, I don't have words.

He rubs the back of his neck, that same nervous tic he's always had. "I can throw it in the back."

I'm really, really trying to remember why I didn't kiss him the other night. Something about heartbreak and working together and friendship. Things that seem wholly unimportant to me now.

I only realize I didn't respond when Rio makes a move to clear the seat off, but I'm quick to reach out and cover his hand with my own, stopping him.

"Please don't." My voice is soft. "Thank you."

This is thoughtful in a way that's overwhelming. Thoughtful in a way that's almost uncomfortable because it's been so long that someone's thought of me and my needs that I'm out of practice with being looked after.

I have this strange urge to cry because it feels so foreign, yet at the same time, simple, having someone else look out for you. To care about the things that you might need, including an extra twenty minutes of sleep.

All other words are stuck in my throat and the silence is thick before Rio offers me a placating smile, slowly pulling his hand out from under mine. He rounds the truck to his side, but I watch him close his eyes momentarily, like he's trying to swallow back a bit of embarrassment while simultaneously hoping to disappear.

Rio would have had to put these in here before leaving for his game, before he knew he would be driving me home. It's exactly what the boy I was in love with would've done.

He turns on his truck as I work my hardest to swallow down the emotions. I unfold the blanket, draping it over my legs before tucking it under my thighs, really making a show of it so he can see I'm grateful that he thought of me because I'm having a hard time with the words. Angling my body towards him slightly, I wedge the pillow under my head on the side of the seat that's closest to the middle, making myself comfortable.

That satisfied smile lifts on his lips again, his dimples sinking into his cheeks, and I don't think I've seen anything more lovely.

Rio pulls out of the parking lot, and I don't waste time, reaching for the truck's screen display and finding his music app. Because for the first time in God knows how many years, this is a moment I want to remember. I want to listen to music and allow it to give me hope. I want to associate a song with a memory.

"What are we listening to?" I ask.

That prideful smile turns soft, maybe even sentimental. "Whatever you want, Hal. I'm good with anything."

I pick something random, and we drive for the next twenty minutes without saying a word, just listening to music together.

Exactly like we used to.

All too soon, we near our exit on the expressway, and Rio merges to the right lane, getting ready to take it.

I work up the nerve and ask what I've been thinking about the entire drive. "I know it's your only night home and you just waited for me for hours, but is there any chance you'd want to keep driving?"

I don't dare look over at him. I know what I'm asking is selfish, but for the first time in a long time, things feel good between us, and I want to live in it for a bit longer. He's about to leave for two weeks. Who knows if he'll come to his senses in that time? Who knows if I will?

The car is silent between songs and without Rio's response, until finally, after what feels like forever, the sound of his blinker begins to click.

I look up to find him leaning his head back on the headrest, wearing a soft smile, and merging back onto the expressway.

He's really showing off that forearm with his rolled-up sleeve and one hand on the wheel as he drives past the city limits. Past anywhere I've ever been. He just drives, going nowhere in particular.

"Do you remember this song?" Rio asks when an old TLC song starts playing through the speakers.

"Of course, I remember this song. I specifically remember us listening to it in my bedroom one night and telling you it was playing the first time some boy told me he liked me."

"Kevin Gross," Rio mumbles under his breath. "I hated that guy, by the way."

"Why?" I burst a laugh. "He was a nice kid. Incredibly strange, but nice."

"He got to tell you he liked you before I could. That song should have been dedicated to me."

I'm still chuckling because this is ridiculous and petty and was almost thirteen years ago. "Well, if it makes you feel any better, the only memory I have of that song being on my yearly playlist is listening to it with you."

Rio is biting back his smile. "I guess that helps a little."

When the song ends, I actively choose the next one.

His head falls back in laughter as soon it begins to play. "I still remember how relieved I felt when you put this song on right before I kissed you for the first time."

I turn it up and let "Kiss Me" by Sixpence None the Richer blast through the speakers.

"It was subliminal messaging."

"There was no secret meaning in the song choice, Hallie. It was the least subtle thing you've ever done, and I was so fucking thankful for that."

We drive for another two hours, laughing at stupid memories we have as kids, playing old songs we used to be obsessed with. He takes a few back roads, cruising down unlit lanes until eventually, he pulls into a gas station, needing to refill the tank.

It's nearing three in the morning when he gets back into the cab and restarts the truck.

"Should we get home?" I ask.

He pulls back onto the road. "If you're ready, we can."

"It's almost three in the morning. What are you going to do? Keep driving me around until it's time for you to head to the airport for your trip?"

"I wouldn't mind."

I chuckle. "I should get some sleep. I've got to work in a few hours."

This time when Rio is driving down the expressway, he gets off at our exit. The turns he takes to get into our neighborhood are done slowly, about five miles under the speed limit, drawing this drive out for as long as possible. And though I know I'm going to be dead tired on my feet tomorrow, I also don't want this to end.

He parks in his driveway and kills the engine, but it takes a while for either of us to move. I'm the first one to, refolding the blanket and stacking both it and the pillow on his dashboard.

"Thank you," I tell him. "That..."

"Felt exactly how it's supposed to," he finishes.

I don't ask him to elaborate if that sentence should end with "between us" because we truly do have so much good history when we ignore the bad, or if he means in general. That it felt exactly how it's supposed to with "your person."

Then there's that voice in my head, the one who used to be in love with him, that's wondering if there's any difference between the two.

"That was the most fun I've had in a long time," I add, not agreeing or disagreeing with his statement.

I expect it to get a little bit awkward once we're out of the car and he walks to his house while I cross the lawn to mine. But surprisingly enough, Rio doesn't head up the front porch stairs to his house. He instead, rounds the hood of his truck and starts walking to mine.

"What are you doing?" I ask, still frozen next to his truck.

"What do you think I'm doing, Hart?" He turns to face me, walking backwards. "I'm walking you home. You coming?"

All those reasons I had floating around my head as to why I couldn't kiss him last weekend, right here in this very spot, are suddenly nowhere to be found.

I catch up to him, and we take the steps up to my front porch slowly, but only when I reach the front door do I realize that he stopped on the second stair from the top.

We both know he's trying to keep a safe distance, but I'm over here wanting to be reckless.

"What happened to you walking me home?" I tease, key in the lock. "You going to finish the job or what, DeLuca?"

He chuckles under his breath before he takes slow, hesitant steps up the stairs and across the porch to meet me at the door. Leaning one shoulder on the doorframe, he nods towards the unturned key.

"You should go inside, Hallie."

It's almost testing in the way he says it with his voice all gruff paired with a slight flex of his jaw. His hands are once again tucked in his pockets, like a physical manifestation of the restraint he's trying to possess.

I look down to the lock then up to him, and it feels like a representation of my own internal battle. I could go inside to keep things friendly and professional because I'm not fully over him leaving all those years ago when I needed him most. Not to mention, he doesn't know the whole story. Or I could lean up and press my mouth against his because he's the only person I've ever loved and he's standing in front of me all these years later.

The classic battle of the head versus the heart.

Today, the non-logical heart wins when I wrap a fist around the front of his shirt to pull him down, at the same time lifting to my toes, pressing a quick kiss to the corner of his mouth. It's a bit unpolished and almost a miss, my lips barely brushing against his.

Reminiscent of our very first kiss, I suppose. Just enough to tell him that I want this.

Pulling back, I catch his eyes and they're dark and hungry and hooded.

His attention moves back to my mouth, once again asking the question, "You single, Hal?"

I finally give him the long-awaited answer, nodding to tell him yes.

"Good." He takes a slow predatorial step towards me, tone sharp and leaving no room for question. "Because we aren't fucking friends."

With that declaration, he grips the side of my neck and slams his mouth onto mine.

Startling, the only sensation is warmth. Warmth from his mouth on mine. Warmth from the overwhelming presence of his body and the desperation in which he's kissing me. Because it is desperate. It's needy and it's wanting. It feels like there are *six years* of wanting wrapped into this kiss.

He gives me a moment to catch onto what's happening, for me to part my lips and ask for more. And when I do, when I give into him, it becomes all-consuming, every one of my senses ramping up to ten.

He smells incredible. He smells like *him*.

He tastes delicious. Just as I remember.

He feels strong and in control, with firm but measured pressure on my throat.

I can't see him with my eyes closed, but I can imagine how

fucking good he looks, towering over me and taking what he wants.

And as far as he sounds... God, the pleading noises coming from this man's throat right now alone could cause me to come undone.

Rio's other hand finally slips free from his pocket, and all that restraint to keep from touching me flies out the window. Both hands palm the sides of my face, pushing me flush against the front door. He moves me where he wants me, taking over and slipping his tongue past my parted lips.

The pads of his fingers grip my hair, his big thigh slips between my own, pressing us closer.

An unpermitted moan crawls up my throat as his tongue slides against mine, as I rock my seeking hips against him.

His responding groan vibrates against my body and God, it just feels *right*. No awkwardness, no figuring it out tentatively because I've been kissing this boy since I was sixteen. We were the ones who taught each other how to do it. It's second nature at this point.

His mouth is warm and soft yet unyielding. Firm in the way he knows what he wants. A little messy. A little untethered. A little unhinged. And there's a whole lot of eagerness from both our sides.

I circle his forearms, tracing the hills and valleys of muscle there, following the lines of veins bulging under the skin.

Slowly pulling away from my mouth, he rests his forehead against mine.

"*Fuck*," he breathes out against my lips. "I missed this, Hal."

He opens his eyes to watch as I run my hands up his ribs, right against his racing heart and chest, feeling every shallow yet hard-earned breath.

"Please don't stop," he says, but it almost comes out as a whimper. "Fuck, I missed the way you touch me."

I take my time touching him, feeling him, really exploring him for the first time since he's grown into this new body. My fingertips toy with the fabric of his shirt, pressing it flush against the skin by his chest and ribs. The white material is so thin, I can almost make out the black ink below it.

Too soon, Rio circles my forearms, moving my hands to run up his chest and neck, for my fingers to slide into the waves that are flipped out under the nape of his beanie. He closes his eyes again, when, of my own accord, I move my hands to bracket his face and pull his mouth back down to meet my own.

He hums this satisfying sound and God if that's not the hottest thing I've heard.

Rio's hands move, one gliding around my neck, fully surrounding it, his thumb stroking the pulse point there. The other slides between me and the door, his palm cradling my ass as he pulls me into him.

In all the times we've kissed before, he's never kissed me like *this*. Like it's the first time he's come up for air in years. It's frantic. It's full of longing. But he has no idea how much *I've* longed for this. How I spent most of the past six years wanting exactly this.

Wanting him.

Wanting him to change his mind and find me so I could explain everything and hope to make him understand. Hope to make him forgive me. Hope that he'd want *us* again.

And just like that, I remember I'm kissing the man I'm still heartbroken over.

He must sense a change in me because he slows things down, or maybe I do, I don't know. The kiss becomes softer and more tender, almost a bit apologetic. He gently runs his hand over my hair, down my neck, and over my rib cage as if he were committing it to memory. Then that same hand moves around behind me before I feel him slip something into the back pocket of my jeans.

"Please don't say anything right now," he whispers against me, seemingly knowing I was about to put a stop to all of this. "Just let us have this moment."

Words are stuck in my throat anyway, so I simply nod against him.

Behind me, he opens the door to my house and it's only then I realized he unlocked it and slipped the key in my pocket.

He pulls back, puffy lips, heavy eyes, flushed cheeks. His expression is sweet and full of longing as he takes in every inch of me.

"Let's not overthink this," he pleads, seemingly to be giving himself that same advice. He strokes his thumb over my cheekbone, finishing with one more gentle kiss to my lips. "I'll see you in a couple of weeks."

Then he leaves me speechless in the doorway of my house before crossing the lawn to his.

18

Hallie

"Tyler's renovation show starts filming its new season in two weeks from Monday," Tina says during our weekly design meeting. "So, if we're not in the office, it's because we're on set. But of course, I'll have my phone on me at all times." She checks the clipboard in her hand. "And the last thing on the agenda for today is project check-ins. Hallie, how's the DeLuca project coming along?"

Every person sitting around the conference table turns in my direction.

"It's...coming along."

Clearly, that's not enough of an answer, because Tina stares at me to continue.

I fiddle with the yellow note in my hands. "The initial concepts will be finalized this week, and once Mr. DeLuca signs off on them, the crew can start the demo."

The name "Mr. DeLuca" feels strange on my tongue, but referring to him as Rio in front of my colleagues also feels too informal.

Tyler sits forward in his fancy fitted suit, elbows on the table. "Hallie, get me those final designs that Mr. DeLuca approves of before I start filming. I want to see them in the next two weeks, just to get another set of eyes on them."

"Of course. I'll get them over to you as soon as I can."

It's common practice for Tyler to check over the interns' designs. It's the same process I went through when I worked on Wren's house, and I appreciate the second set of eyes. Especially his eyes. He's seasoned in the field and beyond talented. I'm happy to take note of the things he would adjust and why. I'm happy to learn from him in any way I can.

The rest of the designers go around the table, debriefing their projects. I only listen halfheartedly, too occupied with unfolding and refolding the small yellow note in my hands.

I unfold it to read it for what feels like the hundredth time since Rio left it on my doorstep this morning. It was stuck to the top of a to-go cup of coffee, accompanied by both a spare key to his house and car.

> *Thanks for letting me keep you up last night.*
> *You should've seen the latte art today. It was my best*
> *one yet until I took a sip.*
> *Drive my truck while I'm gone, please.*
>
> *-R*

I bite back my smile, recalling finding it all on my front step this morning just as Rio was climbing into Zanders' car, headed for the airport. That armor I've worn to protect myself from him has been growing weaker every day, and this, combined with that kiss last night, isn't helping the cause.

Our weekly meeting ends, and I file out with my coworkers, finding my way back to my cubicle. On my computer, I pull up Rio's project files—the aesthetic collage I've been drooling over, the color palettes I've dreamed of, and the 3D mockup of his home that I can't wait to see come to life once I implement my ideas.

It helps that someone from our team stopped by there to get accurate pictures, videos, and measurements when he first hired the firm, so I have all the information I need to work with.

It's only been about a week of thinking over his home design, but I've had fun with it. So much so that on Sunday, my day off from this job, I pulled out my work computer to get started. Spending time with him lately has been a helpful reminder that he's still the same person I knew growing up. The same man I know better than anyone else.

It makes this project all the more freeing, giving me the ability to flow creatively instead of second-guessing the clients' taste with each and every decision. The things that I love in home design, Rio will too. I know this because I used to explain in detail what I envisioned our future home to look like and he agreed with every part of it.

Essentially, what this project is, is the opportunity to design the house I've always dreamed of us sharing. Only now, that home I'm designing isn't ours. It's *his*. Which is a hell of a reality check, if I do say so myself.

Tyler's timeline is rattling around in my brain, reminding me to get to work, so I grab my phone to keep Rio in the loop.

Me: *Hi. I need to chat with you about a few work-related things. Do you have time?*

Rio: *We're about to land. I'll call you as soon as we do.*

Me: *That's okay. We can text.*

Rio: *Okay. How's your day going?*

Rio: *Also, I want to kiss you again.*

Straight to the point, I see. Chuckling to myself, I lean back in my chair with my phone in my hands.

Me: *I meant we could text about work-related things.*

Rio: *Right. So, about that kiss...*

I can picture the shit-eating grin on his face as he types, but I don't let him veer me off track.

Me: *I'm finishing up your initial design concepts this week. There are a few things I need you to choose between in the next two weeks. Layout, wall colors, that kind of thing.*

Rio: *I'm not home for two weeks.*

Me: *That's okay. I'll email everything over. Concepts, samples, etc. It shouldn't take long. I just wanted you to be aware to keep an eye on your inbox.*

Rio: *No can do. I want all the decisions to be made in person.*
Rio: *With you.*

That is…not what I was expecting for him to say. In fact, when I started this project, it was with the belief that Rio would make sure most of our communication was done over email to avoid being in the same room as me.

My thumbs are frozen over the keyboard, unsure of how to respond.
Me: *Rio.*

Rio: *Hallie.*

Me: *Don't be needy. I have to get my job done.*

Rio: *Needy is literally my number one personality trait.*

Me: *Well, in person is not going to work. I need to turn these concepts in to my boss before you're home. It's a hard deadline.*

Rio: *No deal, Hart.*

I inhale a centering breath because the man is going to make me lose my mind.

Me: *You don't need me to be there for you to tell me what you like.*

Rio: *That's probably true. If I'm remembering correctly, you did always know exactly what I liked.*

His lack of subtlety has my mouth gaping open because we both know he's not referring to interior design. But again, I don't let him deter me. We're *friends* now, even though he kissed me senselessly and now I'm the only one trying to hold up the professional part of our working agreement.

Me: *Remember how you let me take on this project to hopefully land a full-time job at the firm? Missing a deadline is for sure going to make me look bad.*

Rio: *I never said you had to miss your deadline. Get on a plane and meet me.*

Me: *You're out of your mind.*

Rio: *Trust me, Hallie. For the first time in about six years, I'm thinking perfectly clearly.*

He's lost it. He's absolutely lost it if he thinks I have the funds or the time to jump on a plane to have a conversation that would be equally as productive as an email.

But maybe if I can explain it to Tyler, he'd understand. He said it himself. Rio's schedule is complicated because of his career. I just need a few extra days to turn in final approvals once the hockey team is back in town.

It's nearing the end of the workday, so I drop my phone on my desk and head straight for Tyler's office, hoping he's still here. Thankfully, he is, standing in the far corner of his office with a stunning view of the river behind him, staring at a few different wallpaper swatches tacked to a corkboard.

He doesn't look in my direction when I stop at his door, but somehow, he still knows it's me.

"Hallie, powder bath. Eclectic and moody vibes. Which one?"

"Who's the client?"

"Me."

"The one on the left, obviously." I walk into his office with that answer.

He smiles to himself, taking the sample off the corkboard and placing it on his desk. "I knew I liked you."

"Well, you might not like me after what I'm about to tell you. I need an extension on that deadline for the DeLuca project."

Tyler takes a seat behind his desk. "No can do. Filming starts soon and I'm going to be way too busy to do any project approvals."

"Well, the thing is, my client wants to make all the decisions in person, and he's on a two-week trip for work. So, he won't be able to make it back until—"

"Go meet him," Tyler says plainly.

"Excuse me?"

"Go meet him. We're a luxury brand here, Hallie, which means we provide luxury-level customer service. If he wants to make decisions in person, go meet him in person. Tina will book you a flight and hotel. Let her know where you need to go, where you want to stay, and what day."

I wait for him to tell me he's kidding, that this would be a waste of time and resources, and something that can be done via email, but he doesn't.

"I wouldn't need a hotel," I eventually say once I realize how serious he is. "I could go there and back. The meeting shouldn't take more than a few minutes."

Tyler shakes his head. "I don't want him to feel like he's being rushed. This is his home. These choices are personal."

This very well may *not* be Rio's home if he ends up selling, but I understand what Tyler is saying.

"If he has a night off from playing," Tyler continues, "take him out for dinner. Buy a nice bottle of wine to split while he makes his design decisions. The firm will cover it. Tina will send you with a company card."

I clearly didn't think this through. If I had thought that jumping on a plane was a conceivable option, I never would have brought this to Tyler's attention because now, I have to tell him why I can't go.

"Tyler, I..." I hesitate, looking away. "I can't do that. I have a second job. I work nights as a bartender, and I can't afford to miss a shift."

My eyes swing back to him cautiously, but I can't read any sort of reaction on his face.

"You can't afford to miss a shift because you'd get in trouble with your boss, or you can't afford to miss a shift financially?"

"Financially."

He nods his head silently, probably coming to the realization that though I may fit his brand with my design eye, I don't exactly live out the Tyler Braden brand aesthetic when it comes to my personal life.

Wait until he finds out I got my Bachelor of Science in Interior Design degree from taking night courses online.

Hands intertwined, Tyler steeples his fingers under his chin. "I'll pay you overtime for every hour you're gone."

My head rears back in surprise. "Wait. Really? Like even while I'm sleeping?"

He chuckles. "Yes. Even while you're sleeping."

I eye him suspiciously. "Are you still trying to make up for setting me up on a date with a married man?"

"Yes," he says dryly. "Is it working?"

"It's working great. Keep it up."

"Find out the travel details and let Tina know."

"Okay. Wow. Thanks, Tyler. I appreciate it."

"Hallie," he says, stopping me before I can make it out the door. "When I first started to try to break into this industry, I didn't have more than ten dollars to my name. I spent my nights delivering pizza just so I could pay my rent because that's how badly I wanted all of this." He sweeps his arms out, as if to say this office, this view, this brand. "You shouldn't be embarrassed to let people know how hard you're willing to work to get what you want."

He's right about that. I am willing to work hard. I've been willing to work hard since I decided to make sacrifices to help my dad. Since I had to drop out of school and figure out how to get an education from home.

I offer him an understanding smile. "Thanks, Tyler."

I've got a major pep in my step as I scurry back to my desk and grab my phone.

Me: *All right, you win. Let me know where and when I'm meeting you.*

My phone instantly buzzes in my hand, with Rio's name scrolling across the top.

"Are you being serious?" he asks.

"Were you not?"

205

"No! I mean, *yes*, I was being serious. Of course, I want you to come meet me on the road, but I was just being a needy asshole."

"You really were being a needy asshole, but I told my boss you wanted to meet in person, and he was fine to cover the travel expenses."

He hesitates. "And are you fine? With your work schedule? Please don't miss shifts on my account."

"Tyler is paying me overtime to hang out with you, which by the way, is the only reason I'm willing to do it."

"Damn. Keep me humble, Hal. I really was going to cave on the whole in-person thing, but I'm glad I didn't."

"Hey, Hallie!" someone yells into the phone.

"Sorry, that was Zee," Rio says.

"Wait. Are you still on the plane?"

"Yeah. Just landed. Sitting on the tarmac and waiting to park."

"Oh, I'll let you go."

"You don't have to," he says quietly.

That makes my heart skip in a way it most definitely shouldn't. But I also feel a bit weird being on the phone with him while he's with all his teammates. The same ones I serve when they come into the bar. Regardless of what Tyler said, that part still feels a little embarrassing.

"I need to get back to work. Text me when you figure out what day I should meet you and where. And Rio, just so you know, I'm going to be so annoyed with you if this whole thing ends up being the epitome of the phrase, 'it could've been an email.'"

"Well, then." His voice gains a gruff edge. "I'll be sure to make it worth your time."

19

Rio

I 'm the first one on the team bus after our afternoon game against New York. Even though our hotel is only ten blocks away, and the walk could potentially be shorter, it's team policy to take the bus back.

My knees are bouncing while I wait for the rest of my teammates to finish their showers and postgame interviews because all I want to do is get back to the hotel.

Tonight is the night Hallie flies in to meet me. It's been about a week and a half since we kissed, and I've been impatiently waiting to see her ever since. Wondering if she regrets that night or if like me, she hasn't been able to stop thinking about it.

I don't know what the hell happened or when it all shifted so dramatically. Maybe it was having her in my home for the first time, or when she helped watch my friends' kids. Or maybe it's the culmination of the time we've been spending together that's reminded me of how much I missed her. Missed *us*. But the things I was so angry about only a month or two ago now seem inconsequential and unimportant.

All I know is that I want to see her, to be around her.

I was tempted to tell her the best day to meet me was the day after I left because that's how impulsive I'm feeling with her, but I didn't want Hallie to miss a Friday or Saturday night shift at the bar, assuming those are the nights she makes the most in tips.

Plus, choosing today means we have the night off, and with multiple teams within driving distance, we're staying in the city for an entire week, instead of only a night or two like we do whenever we travel anywhere else.

I just had to be patient, which isn't always my strong suit.

As I wait for the rest of my teammates, my phone rings. I'm expecting to see Hallie's name on the screen, maybe calling to tell me she checked into the hotel, but it's not her. It's my mom.

I'll admit, I haven't been answering her calls as often as I usually do, and that's entirely due to the fact she doesn't know Hallie moved to Chicago. I don't want to tell her, but I'm also terrible at lying to the woman.

Hence the avoidance, but it's Sunday and I don't go a Sunday without speaking to her.

So, I answer the phone. "Hey, Ma."

"Hey, Ma?" she asks, outraged. "Hey, Ma? You avoid my calls all week and when you finally answer it's with a 'Hey, Ma'?"

I laugh. "Your accent gets thicker when you're pissed."

"Oh, you little shit. You're going to put me in an early grave. You know that?"

"I'm sorry. It's been a busy week."

"Good game today, *Tesoro*. I saw that assist, but I'm still annoyed with you that you didn't want me to come up to New York. It's a short flight."

"The airports are nuts this time of the year."

"I could've driven. Taken the train."

"Too much sitting. I'll be in Boston on my next road trip. You and the whole neighborhood are coming to the game, right?"

"Of course we are. I can't wait. I got these shirts made with your face on it and we're going to be so loud, you'll be able to hear us from the ice."

"I have no doubt about that. See? You didn't need to come today. You'll see me play soon."

She sighs. "At least next year you'll be living here again, and I can go to every one of your home games."

I try to keep my voice low because my teammates are starting to filter onto the bus. "Ma, I haven't signed with Boston yet. That's not a done deal."

"Oh, Rio. Come on. We both know it's going to happen. It's your childhood dream! Don't doubt yourself."

It's not my ability that I'm doubting.

I swiftly change the subject. "What's for Sunday dinner?"

"Lasagna and a roast chicken."

She mentions only two courses, but I know she's probably whipped up about five.

"Your uncle Mikey has been here all day helping," she adds.

"You let Uncle Mikey into your kitchen?"

"Oh God, no. But he did take out the trash, so that was nice. Changed a few lightbulbs that I couldn't reach and tightened that loose stair railing."

"Ma, I told you I would do all that when I got there."

"I know, but he offered, so I figured it'd keep you from doing chores for me on your one day in town."

I make a mental note to thank my dad's brother when I see him next. With my mom living alone, I get worried about her keeping up that old house all on her own and try to do as much handiwork as I can when I go back to visit.

It's not necessarily the appeal of fulfilling my childhood dream that has me considering free agency for Boston. It's my mom being alone in that house and having no one to help her as she's getting older.

Zee takes the row behind me, leaning forward and crossing his arms on the back of my seat. "Oh, is that—"

I slap a hand over his mouth before he can say Hallie's name, trying to silently communicate not to say shit about her. "It's my *mother*."

209

"Oooh," he draws out, understanding. "Hi, Mrs. D!"

"Hi, Zee!" Pulling my phone away from my ear, I put it on speaker. "Are you going to come see me when you're in town?"

"Absolutely. Stevie is bummed she won't get to see you, though."

"Oh, I miss her. I miss all of you. I need to plan a trip out to Chicago soon."

"We'd love that."

A text drops onto the screen and we both look down to see Hallie's name.

H (heart emoji): *Just checked into the hotel.*

I give Zanders that look again, silently begging him not to say anything while my mom is on the line.

"Rio, honey, I've got to get going," she says. "The neighborhood is starting to show up for dinner."

"Okay, Ma. Have a good time. Love you."

"Yeah. Okay. Love you too." She rushes me off the phone before her loud Italian voice excitedly calls out someone's name—whoever just walked through her door—before she hangs up the phone on me.

"Are you sure your mother even loves you?" Zee asks over my shoulder.

"Fuck off. Yes, she just loves the neighborhood ladies a little bit more than her only child."

The bus finally starts moving so I find my text thread with Hallie.

Me: *On our way. See you soon. Dinner reservation is at eight.*

"She's already got the red heart emoji in her contact name?" Zee whistles. "You got it bad, my guy."

"It's for her last name. Hart. H—Heart. It's a thing from when we were kids."

I definitely didn't consider my friends looking over my shoulder and reading my texts when I updated her contact to match the way she used to sign her mixtapes.

"You haven't told your mom that Hallie moved to town?" Zanders asks.

I shake my head to tell him no.

"She wouldn't be cool with you two spending time together again?"

My sigh is heavy. "Not even a little bit."

He's silent for a moment until he nudges me on the shoulder. "I know your relationship with your mom could not be more different than the nonexistent one I have with mine, so I might not seem like the best person to give this advice. But if anyone told me not to spend time with Stevie, I'd be quick to reevaluate that person's importance in my life. I know you love your mom, we all love your mom, but you're a grown-ass man now, Rio. At a certain point, our parents' opinions can't be more important than our own."

"Rio!" one of my teammates calls out from the back of the bus. "Play some music for the drive."

I grab my boombox, the same one I bring almost everywhere, and set it on the empty seat next to me. Starting it up, I let it play whatever is in there as I try not to think about my mom, Boston, or Hallie for the rest of the drive to the hotel.

My head has been reeling since that bus ride.

It's not only my parents' opinions that feel too important, but also my parents' mistakes.

The two people who shaped my entire belief system, who shaped the way I view love, who I mirrored my own relationship off of, divorced six years ago and haven't spoken since.

Childhood sweethearts. God, I could laugh.

I spent so much of the past six years chasing this fucked-up need to prove that love actually exists and I just had to try my hardest to find it. I blamed that need on Hallie when just as much of that blame, if not more, could be placed on my parents.

I completely zoned out during my shower and while I was getting dressed for dinner, moving on autopilot. The same could be said for the elevator ride down to the lobby, knowing the reason I'm so concerned about telling my mom that Hallie is back in my life is because I don't want to hear what she has to say.

I've spent so much time being angry because *she* was upset. I felt protective of her in that way, but I don't want to keep basing my decisions on her feelings. I want to move forward.

God, everything feels so fucking confusing. I tried to move on with my life, sold on the belief that Hallie was the enemy, but suddenly, that belief doesn't feel so solid these days. All I know is that I haven't felt so like myself as I have the past few weeks, seeing her again. Even when we're fighting, even when I think about all the shitty things from the past, being with her feels like...*home*.

There's this nagging part of me that's questioning whether the homesickness I've felt for years now has been for Boston or if it's actually been for her.

My head is still spinning, trying to organize itself when the elevator opens and she steps out. She doesn't see me—the hotel lobby is fairly crowded—but I see her.

And all that confusion, all that second-guessing is thrown out the window because I do know what I'm doing. I have only ever loved one person in my entire life and she's here and fuck it, I don't care about the rest. I want to know if this could be something. If we could ever forgive each other. If we could ever try again.

Unsurprisingly, she looks great tonight. Her hair is pin straight and cut sharply below her jaw. A black satin skirt and dark green peacoat dress her up, but the lace-up combat boots and graphic tee add the casual factor. Then you add all that mixed metal jewelry she loves to wear, and she looks...exactly like the girl I've spent most of my life dreaming about.

I stand from my seat, fix my suit, and that's when she finally spots me.

"Hi," she says with that signature Hallie smile, adjusting her bag over her shoulder.

"You look…" All I can do is nod.

"You look…too." She gives me a once-over. "Are you wearing a suit to dinner? Or is that from the game?"

I can feel my cheeks warm as I run my palm over the back of my neck. "It's a different suit than my game suit. My dinner suit, I guess you could say."

"Is this place fancy? Should I change?" She throws a thumb over her shoulder towards the elevator. "I didn't bring many other options."

"No. No, Hal. You look perfect."

I don't think that does much to ease her worry about how nice this restaurant potentially is, and I can't say one way or the other because I've never been there. I told Miller I had a work meeting with Hallie in the city tonight and needed a last-minute reservation. She asked me how professional I wanted to keep it, and once I told her I didn't want this to feel professional at all, she called up a chef she knows and got us a table.

Hallie can call this a work meeting all she wants, but I'll call it as it is. It's a date. A chance to see if this thing could be real again.

Hallie adjusts the big bag on her shoulder, and when she does, I spot the sample booklets, notebooks, and laptop inside.

I slide it off her arm to carry it myself.

"Are you sure?" she asks.

"I made up some bullshit excuse about needing to make decisions in person, just so I could take you to dinner without having to wait two weeks to see you. The least I can do is carry all the stuff I made you bring."

"I knew it." Shaking her head at me, she bites back her smile. "This isn't a date, you know."

"Oh God, no. It's a work meeting, Hallie. Focus, please."

Together we start towards the exit, but I stop short of the door.

A nice restaurant is exactly the kind of place I'd plan to have a first date with anyone else. But this isn't *our* first date and if I want it to feel like a date at all, it should replicate the ones we used to have. When neither of us had money and the only place we could spend time together privately was in each other's bedrooms.

I slip my hand in hers to stop her from getting any farther. "What do you say we forget about the reservation? We could change into sweatpants and order room service for dinner while we look at your design plans."

A smile ticks on her lips. "That sounds a little more up our alley."

My stomach flips at the casual use of *our*.

"You're in the city for only one night," I remind her. "Are you sure you're cool staying in?"

"Well, you are the client. Whatever you say goes. I'm here to give excellent customer service."

I lift an interested brow.

"Not that kind of service. Get your mind out of the gutter, DeLuca."

"You put it there." Keeping her hand in mine, I walk us back to the elevator, and I keep holding it even after I press the button and wait. "Try to remember that this is a work meeting, Hart. I don't need you ogling me in my sweatpants the way you're checking me out in this suit."

The elevator doors open and a few of my teammates spill out.

Hallie instantly slips her hand out of my grasp and takes a step back, partially hiding behind me.

"Hey, Rio," one of them says. "Are you coming out with us tonight?"

"Not tonight. I'm hanging out with—" I move out of the way, about to say Hallie's name when our rookie interrupts.

"Hey, it's the bartender!"

Huh?

"What are you doing here?" he continues.

Hallie's face has never been more flushed than it is right now.

Her smile is weak, and her eyes are downcast with embarrassment.

It's absolutely wild to me that these guys who I spend every day with only know this woman, the same one who has consumed all my brain space for the majority of my life, as the bartender who pours their drinks.

An overwhelming surge of protectiveness surfaces. "You do know she has a name, right?"

Zanders comes out of nowhere and smacks him on the back of the head for me. "What if people only referred to you by your job title? Show a little respect, Rookie."

He rubs his head. "You do call me by my job title."

"Well, maybe we should be a little more precise and start calling you the winger who can't win a face-off to save his life." Wrapping my arm around Hallie's lower back, I settle my hand on her hip, pulling her into me and not allowing her to hide. "This is Hallie. We grew up together back in Boston. She's renovating the house you guys spend all your time at, so you can thank her for that. And yes, she also happens to bartend."

"Hey, Hallie," Zanders says, stepping up to give her a hug. "You two headed to dinner?"

She hugs him back. "Staying in, actually."

"Wait," the rookie cuts in again. "You're the one redoing his house? Does that mean I can make a request?"

I roll my eyes. "No—"

"Because if we could have a few more TVs in the living room, that'd be great. Imagine a whole wall of screens! We would have the best Xbox setup. We would probably end up moving in there because we wouldn't want to leave."

"And that's exactly why she's not going to do that. The hockey frat house is growing up and going away. Maybe your place could be the new hangout spot, Rook."

His eyes go big and bright.

I press my hand against Hallie's lower back when the elevator opens and empties again. "We're going."

"What's your name?" Hallie asks our rookie as she steps into the elevator with me.

"Mason."

"Nice to officially meet you, Mason."

He smiles at her with fucking hearts in his eyes. "Bye, Hallie. See you at your work soon, okay?"

I'm shaking my head as the doors close. Hallie presses the button for her floor, and I realize it's the same as mine.

"See? There's no need to be embarrassed around my teammates. They're normal people. Well...sort of. If anything, *Rookie* should be the one embarrassed, thinking he has a shot in hell with you."

She's staring straight ahead, chin tipped up. "And who says he doesn't?"

I whip my head in her direction. "Hallie. That's not funny."

She shrugs and I can see the smile she's trying to hold back through the elevator's reflection.

My mouth is still gaping when we get off on our floor.

I follow her to her room, leaning against the wall as she uses her key card to open the door so she can change into something more comfortable.

"Do I need to remind you about that kiss we shared the last time we saw each other?"

She laughs. "I'm not sixteen anymore, Rio. Just because we kissed doesn't make me yours."

I lift a brow. "Is that a challenge?"

"You can take that however you'd like." She's got this teasing smile on her lips as she slips into her room, closes the door, and leaves me alone in the hallway.

20

Rio

"You're telling me this still works?" Hallie runs her hand over my boombox sitting on the dresser in my hotel room.

"Like a charm."

"How old is it?"

I don't say anything, waiting for her to put the pieces together.

"No way!" Her head whips in my direction. "Don't tell me this is the same one you got when you were like fifteen."

"The one and only."

"Wow." She joins me on the couch. "And you didn't want to upgrade at some point?"

New ones don't play cassette tapes or even CDs anymore.

But I don't tell her that.

"Why fix what's not broken?" is what I say instead.

Hallie relaxes back on the couch with me, crossing her legs under her and opening her laptop. "So, these are the two layouts I've been playing with. We can fully scrap both concepts, combine them, anything you want."

I lean into her to get a better look at her computer, with my legs kicked up on the coffee table in front of us. The same coffee table that's covered in our now empty dinner plates.

We both changed, me into a pair of sweatpants and a tee, and her into leggings and my team-issued hoodie that she stole, before ordering the entire room service menu. Mostly because Hallie couldn't decide what she wanted to eat, and I just wanted her to have a good time with me, so I panic-ordered the whole menu.

Whatever. It was delicious.

Hallie brings the first three-dimensional concept up on her computer and I feel my entire expression shift as I take it in.

"That's my house?" I ask in disbelief.

"It could be. If you like it."

I lean in closer to the computer, subsequently leaning more into her. "Like it? I love it. How the hell is that the same house I have now?"

She uses the mouse to give me a tour, taking me through each room.

"These don't need to be the final color concepts or anything. Just an idea of what I thought would look good together. This option has a few partial walls added whereas the other one is more of an open concept feel. But adding walls also means adding to the cost, which if you're going to sell, might not be the best choice."

Of course, I knew she was good at her job. I saw Wren's house, but watching it happen firsthand, seeing her take nothing and turn it into this? She's *so* talented. So impressive, and I could not be prouder of her. Watching her paint her own childhood room a thousand times to, this? How does she not spend every day talking about how creatively gifted she is?

"Hallie," I breathe out, taking in the images on the computer. "Your brain is so fucking cool. How did you think of this?"

I watch as she tries to bite back her proud smile before she pulls up the second concept she's created.

I can't distinctly pull out what's different about this one, only that it is. In the same way as the first option, there's color covering every square inch, the choices feel intentional, and I can't imagine someone coming over and *not* feeling welcomed. Which is the main thing I'd want from this house, whether I keep or sell it.

"Do you have a preference?" she asks. "Between the two."

She looks over at me and that's when I realize how close we're sitting. We're leaning into one another, our shoulders overlapping with hers resting on top of mine. And our lips, our lips are only a breath from touching with her turned back to look at me like this.

When she realizes, Hallie doesn't move away, which feels like a win.

Fuck. I want to kiss her again.

"What would you choose?" I ask and damn, my voice sounds raspy as hell.

"Well, it's up to you. If cost isn't an issue, the big difference is the open concept or the intentional rooms. One isn't necessarily better than the other. It's a matter of preference."

"And if this were your house, what would you choose?"

Her eyes bounce to my lips before she readjusts, sitting up to create a bit of distance between us. "It's *not* my house."

There's this tone to her voice that's final and decisive.

I don't listen to it.

I slide my hand over her thigh because I miss having her close already. "Pretend it is. I need your opinion."

She exhales, and it sounds heavy and tired and wary to imagine anything about my home being hers. "I like the idea of adding a few walls. Open concept is popular right now, but I don't think it's the right choice for everyone."

"And why would that not be the right choice for you?"

"Other than trying to keep an open concept home clean? Because adding walls means each room could have its own moment and tell its own story. In an open concept, you need everything to flow perfectly from one space to the next since you can see it all at once. If your tastes change often, the way mine do, instead of updating one room, now you're switching up the whole house."

I huff a laugh, thinking about all the times I watched Hallie change her room while growing up.

"Walls it is," I say definitively.

"I should clarify that adding walls will not only add to the cost but also to the project timeline."

"Great. Add the walls."

Her gaze narrows suspiciously. "All of them? Because we can take a few out if you don't like them."

"All of them."

"Okay," she drags out. "Why are you making this so easy?"

This project *should* be easy. She probably doesn't remember this, but she once told me everything she envisioned for our future home, and I loved each and every idea she had.

"Is there anything else we need to go over?" I ask, stroking my thumb over the fabric of her leggings, my fingertips hooked over her inner thigh.

"Yes." Hallie switches her laptop for a sample booklet from her bag. "This part doesn't need to be a final decision type thing, but I do need to present an overall design concept to my boss."

I move the plates from the coffee table, giving her room to lay out and open the booklet. It's filled with collages of different aesthetics she created. There are pictures of furniture, color palettes, and different printed patterns. Wallpaper, maybe.

Again, I don't really know what I'm looking at, but whatever it is, I like it.

"Is there a particular aesthetic that draws your eye?" she asks, both of us sitting forward off the couch.

"All of them."

She laughs under her breath. "Well, that's good. We can pick and choose for this too. If there're certain things you like from each concept, we can combine them to make it your own."

My eyes slowly trail to her again. "Which would you pick?"

She lifts a brow, silently telling me this is also about my preference, before her attention drops to my mouth that's awfully close to her own.

"If it were your home, I mean."

I watch that wariness settle in again, but she doesn't hesitate, pointing to her favorite. It's a mix of deep greens, creams, and natural wood tones with furniture that looks comfortable but cool. The type you'd actually sit in and not the fancy designer stuff that seems like it should be displayed in a museum.

"That's the one," I decide.

"Rio—"

"Hal, I don't really know what the hell I'm looking at here, but you do. And you know I've always loved your style, so this really isn't all that hard of a decision. If you want that one, then I do too."

"Rio," she sighs.

I prepare myself for her to tell me something to the effect of "stop designing your house with me in mind" or "stop trying to dig up old memories."

But what she says instead is, "This could've been an email."

There's an ease between us, and it feels light and fun, the way it used to. I missed this. This comfortability and compatibility. I missed her wearing my clothes. Missed us doing absolutely nothing together. I've never been known the way she knew me, and it's becoming evident that hasn't changed one bit.

"Can I ask you something?" Sitting back, she crosses her legs under her, facing me on the couch.

"Of course."

"Why'd you want me to come here? To meet you on the road."

"Truthfully?"

She nods, bottom lip slipping between her teeth.

I think of giving her the whole and complete answer but instead, settle with a partial but true one. "Because I wanted to see you. That's all."

"Okay."

She finds my hand on the couch between us, bringing it back to rest on her leg. She softly toys with my knuckles. She traces the roadmap of veins on the back before finally, she finds a bit of bravery to slide her fingers between mine.

Hallie stares at our intertwined hands for a long while as if she wanted the reminder of what it looked like, and that's when I see them.

Her nails.

How I didn't notice them before, when she was typing on the computer or scarfing down the room service, I have no clue.

I take her hand, positioning her fingernails in my direction. "Hallie Hart. Ten different colors?" My smile is stupid big. "Talk about a throwback."

"Stop." She laughs, pulling her hand away.

"When did you do that?"

"Yesterday."

"Why?"

"I don't know. Because I always used to, I guess, and I've been feeling more like myself again lately." She looks up at me. "For the first time in a long time."

I slip my hand into hers again, letting our fingers lace. "Yeah. I completely get what you mean."

21
Hallie

The time glaring back at me from the alarm clock on the nightstand reads 1:48 in the morning.

There's absolutely no reason for me to be awake. I didn't have to work a late shift, my travel day was easy, and this hotel bed is one of the most comfortable I've ever laid on.

The only reason I can assume that I'm still awake is the man down the hall I can't stop thinking about.

Is he asleep? Maybe. Did his inability to sleep rub off on me? Possibly.

I want to call him. This is my turn after all, to do the things *I* want to do. But this also feels reckless, when I should be protecting myself.

Screw it. Neither of us was all that eager to say goodbye earlier when I left his room, so I grab the landline off the nightstand and dial his number. Well, his room number.

He answers on the second ring. "Hello?"

"Are you asleep?"

"Well, if I was, I sure as hell wouldn't still be after this phone just started blaring next to my bed."

I chuckle under my breath. "Sorry about that."

"Don't be. Why are *you* awake?"

"I don't know."

He doesn't say anything, waiting for me to elaborate.

"Would you…" I stumble. "Would you maybe want to come to my room and sleep here?"

"Yeah," he exhales quickly. "Yeah, I would. I'll be right there."

There's a moment, right after I throw the comforter off, that I slightly panic. My room is a mess. Clothes are everywhere. I purposefully packed my least sexy sleepwear to keep myself from doing exactly what I just did, so I am by no means prepared to have a man sleep in my bed.

There's a part of me that wants to clean up my room, to shove everything in my suitcase, to jump in the shower and see if I can find something cuter to sleep in, but then I remember this is Rio that's coming over and every muscle in me begins to relax.

His knock is quiet, just a rap of his knuckles. I open the door, the light from the hallway illuminating the room with just enough for him to see where he's going before he closes the door behind him, blanketing us in darkness once again.

He's standing close by, I can feel him, and once my eyes adjust again, I can see him reach out, fingers toying with the hem of my sleep shorts. Once he finds me, he trails that hand up my side, along my ribs until he wraps an arm around my shoulders and pulls me into his chest for a hug.

"Hi, Hal," he whispers softly, before placing a kiss on the top of my head and leaving his lips to linger there. "Thanks for letting me get some sleep."

He says it as if I was dead asleep and woke up only long enough to realize that he was probably still awake. As if I took pity on him by allowing him to come get rest, when in reality, I was tossing and turning thinking of him.

"Am I taking the floor?" There's an edge of humor in his tone, but knowing him, if I told him yes, he'd happily create a makeshift bed on the floor.

"I'm pretty sure you stopped *taking the floor* when you were about seventeen."

He laughs lightly, and the sound vibrates through every inch of my body. Warm and comforting and familiar.

Letting me go, he takes the side of the bed that's unused, and while still wearing his hoodie from earlier, I slip back under the covers with him.

My knee knocks his and his foot brushes mine as we try to get comfortable. I scoot back to create a bit of distance, keeping myself entirely on my side of the bed. Lying on my back, I cross my hands over my middle, not allowing any part of me to touch any part of him.

I shouldn't let any part of me want him here either, yet I do.

I really do.

"Since when do you sleep like that?"

Turning to look at him, I find he's lying on his side, facing me, stupid knowing smirk on his lips.

"Since when do you sleep in a shirt?" I say in retort.

"Well, I didn't think we were having that kind of sleepover."

"We're not."

"And that's why I'm still dressed, love. There's not a world in which I get in a bed with you, even partially clothed, and all we do is sleep."

I swallow hard. "Well, maybe that's why I'm sleeping like this. Keeping a safe distance."

"I'm not going to bite, Hal. Well, unless you ask me to."

I reach out to smack his stomach with the back of my hand, but he catches my wrist before I can make contact.

"Come here," he whispers, pulling me into him.

I find myself going willingly, rolling towards the center of the bed to face him.

"I want to kiss you again," he says softly.

I slightly shake my head, but there's not much authority behind it.

He wets his lips. "Do you regret it?"

"No," I quickly say. "But you can't kiss me because I want you to, and that seems dangerous."

His hand runs down my rib cage, his fingertips drawing circles along my hip bone. "Wanting this again seems dangerous?"

I nod. "Most of what got me through the past six years was the belief that you were terrible, and I was better off without you. It's been quite terrifying to realize…well, to *remember,* that you aren't terrible at all."

He pushes my hair behind my ear, cradling my cheek and running the pad of his thumb over the bone there. "Hallie, I—"

"You left and forgot all about me, Rio. Yes, this feels good again. It feels frustratingly right. There's clearly something still here, but I can't get past the fact that you forgot I even existed."

I'm hit with a pang of guilt as soon as the words are out of my mouth because he came over to get some sleep, not to argue with me.

He scoffs but it's pained, like he's just trying to find enough oxygen to breathe after that hit. "God, Hallie." His fingers tighten in my hair. "You have no idea how untrue that is. I wanted to. I tried so fucking hard to forget about you, and I couldn't. I know that me simply saying that doesn't mean shit right now, but soon enough, I think you'll realize just how hard I've been holding on to you all these years later, even when I tried to let you go."

"How am I supposed to believe that?"

His eyes bounce between mine, begging me to. "Give me some time to get my bearings here, and I'll show you."

Silence lingers for a long while, but I feel my body move towards him, while he does the same, slowly inching his way towards me. His hand falls to my hip again before it glides down, skipping my ass and hitching my thigh over his waist, pulling us even closer. His calloused fingertips continue to run over my skin, as he ever so lightly traces my upper leg.

Tentatively, I reach out, toying with his shirt before I gain a little more bravery and slide my hand up his neck, running my fingers through his hair.

We must be sharing a single pillow at this point, with our noses touching and our lips dangerously close.

"Sorry," I whisper into the space between us. "You didn't come here to get into it with me. You just wanted some sleep."

"I'd happily stay up all night, getting into it with you, Hallie. And we both know this conversation needs to happen. I want us to move forward."

"And what does that mean to you? To move forward."

I drop my hand flush to his neck and feel him swallow against my palm. "Do you remember earlier when you asked why I wanted you to come here?"

I nod.

"I didn't give you the entire answer then. But if I were to give you the whole truth, I'd tell you that even though I may have gone six years without seeing you, the thought of going two weeks now feels impossible. And no, I don't have the answer for why that is, but I want a chance to figure it out."

Words stick in my throat, so he continues.

"Did you know that all my friends have gotten to have their people on the road with them at some point? Stevie used to travel with our team as a flight attendant. That's how she and Zee met. Indy and Ryan met up when their team travel schedules overlapped. Miller spent a whole summer traveling with Kai and Max. And Kennedy, well she's the doctor for Isaiah's team, so they're always together. After all this time, I just wanted my turn."

"But I'm not your person." My throat burns while saying it, and the words taste like a lie as soon as they're out of my mouth.

"Yeah," he chuckles without humor. "That's what I spent the past six years trying to convince myself of too. But I'm tired of lying, Hallie. Aren't you?"

"I don't want to want you."

"Yeah, baby." He nudges his nose against mine. "That makes two of us."

He doesn't wait any longer before he leans forward and presses his mouth to mine, stealing any retort I might have.

Rio tightens my leg over his hip before gliding his palm up my thigh and over my ass again. He squeezes it at the same time he hums this satisfied growl against my lips. Then he continues on, slipping his hand under his sweatshirt I'm wearing, smoothing over my spine.

He quickly realizes I'm not wearing anything under his hoodie when he pulls his mouth away from mine.

"Fuck," he drawls out, head tipped back, and Adam's apple exposed. "Goddammit, Hallie."

I chuckle, pushing my hips into his and rolling them once, but this time, it's me who's letting out a needy moan.

He slips his hand into my hair, cupping my face before he drops his forehead to mine. "Hal," he exhales, already short of breath. "I want this. I want to give this another try. You and me."

I don't have an answer for him because it's too soon. This is all happening too quickly, regardless of our years of history. There's so much that he doesn't know yet, so much of my heart that's still broken that I can't even think of putting myself in that position again.

But this, his body rocking against mine. I want this. I can *handle* this.

I kiss him again, harder and without patience, licking against his lower lip until his mouth parts and I find his tongue with my own.

Rio's resounding growl is feral and hungry before he grabs my ass in one hand and flips us, rolling me onto my back. My legs open on instinct, and he settles his hips into the cradle of mine. His fingers slip between my own, pushing my hand into the mattress as he holds most of his weight up with his other arm.

He's so big, so overwhelming. So much more deliciously wide than the last time he was on top of me. I lift my hips up while he grinds down and that has our mouths separating momentarily, the sensation almost blinding with how good it feels.

I throw my head back as he drops his to my chest and grinds himself on me again. His sweatpants slide against the seam of my shorts, causing this insane friction against my clit. It's maddening, like it's not quite enough, yet it's more than I've had in such a long time.

"Yes," I hiss. "More. Please."

The desperate, needy sound that works its way up my throat is mirrored with Rio's own noises. And he's hard. God, he's so fucking hard right now. I can feel every inch of him.

It's been so long, this should almost feel foreign, yet my body moves, remembering exactly what to do.

Hooking my leg over his, I urge him to do it again.

Rio pushes my knee up to the mattress, grinding himself over me, the sound of our building breaths mingling in the otherwise silent room. He moves from my mouth to my neck, working a warm path down my throat.

I run my hands through his hair, holding on to him as he kisses and nips.

"I missed you," I admit in a breathy whisper, close to his ear.

He drops his head to my chest, pausing his movements before he cups my face and leans up to kiss me again. Slowly. Deeply. Desperately.

"Say it again," he pleads.

My lips turn up in a smile against his. "I missed you."

He hums at the admission while I find the hem of his shirt, slipping a hand underneath. My palm connects with the hard planes of his stomach, my fingers graze the hair on his chest as I push his shirt up. Because I want it off. I want it *all* off.

"Wait," he breathes, chest moving rapidly against mine as he settles his hand on my wrist to stop me. "Wait, baby."

His eyes flick up to mine, this pleading, desperate expression on his face.

"Do you think that... I mean, could you ever see yourself giving us another shot?" he asks. "Without your brother around to hide it from, without our families in the way. Would you ever want to try again with me?"

My heart is physically cracking at his sweet words, at the soft way he says them.

At the knowledge that I don't have an answer that he'll want.

"I don't know how to answer that," I tell him honestly.

"Try, Hal. Please. Just tell me what you're thinking."

Swallowing hard, I run my hand through his hair. "We both made mistakes. I know that, but you left when I needed you to stay."

I watch as any hope fades from his expression.

"You broke my heart, Rio, and I know I broke yours."

"I was young, Hallie. *We* were young. We were fucking kids who made mistakes. I was twenty-one years old and just watched my entire life fall apart and—" He closes his eyes, trying to regain his composure. "I took it out on you."

"I know," I soothe, running a hand down his face. "I know. I'm just trying to be honest with you. There's still so much you don't know, and—"

"Tell me then."

I smile at him weakly. I'm not ready to trust him with that part of my life yet, and I don't know if I ever will.

He exhales a defeated sigh before gently taking my wrist and pressing a light kiss there—his silent way of accepting the state of things.

I notice he doesn't move from between my legs, doesn't roll over back to his side of the bed, so I lift my hips, hoping to restart what he paused.

"Rio," I whisper. "I might not be ready for that, but we could have this."

He laughs sardonically to himself and closes his eyes as if it causes him physical pain to say what he's about to say. "You know I don't work that way. I can't do one without the other."

Meaning he can't do sex without the commitment.

"Still?" And yes, that's complete and utter shock in my voice because this man has been in the NHL for years and I kind of assumed he would've started having casual sex along the way.

And he probably has. But I don't qualify, because he and I have never been casual.

He smiles at my surprise. "Yeah, Hal. Still."

Leaning down, he kisses me once more. Slowly. Tenderly. All while cautiously climbing off me to lay at my side.

He brushes my hair away from my face. "Thank you for coming to see me."

I want to complain, to whine about him stopping things, but I can't. Not when he gave me his boundaries while also asking me to want him again. It's not that I don't want him. I just don't want to get hurt.

"Goodnight, Rio." I lean forward and kiss his lips one last time before I turn over, finding my way back to my side.

All too soon, there's a heavy arm wrapping around my waist, hauling me towards him until my back hits his chest.

"Are you out of your mind? Just because I need you to be mine before I fuck you doesn't mean I don't want to cuddle." He tucks one arm under me, allowing me to use his bicep as a pillow, while the other one curls around my middle, his hand slipped under my sweatshirt and his palm pressed against my skin. "But I call little spoon next time."

Chuckling, I curl myself into him.

There's an obnoxiously big smile on my face as I close my eyes and try to find sleep. But I'm too focused on his thumb drawing languid circles on my stomach and the way his breathing seems calm and steady behind me.

"I understand why you're hesitant or uninterested," he whispers. "I'm not going to push you to want me. But I am going to be here, waiting, if you ever decide you want to try again. I'm not going anywhere this time."

22

Hallie

(AGE 17)

"**H**appy birthday, Hal," Rio says, kissing down my neck. Smiling, I run my fingers through his hair. "Thank you."

Hovering over me, he continues his path of kisses down my chest and stomach, over my shirt. His own shirt is long gone, discarded somewhere on my floor.

We're in my room, on my bed. Rio snuck over here after my birthday dinner with both of our families. I love my parents, my brother, and the DeLucas, but this is all I wanted to do today. To be with him.

I run my hands down his back, curving around his waist.

Rio sucks in a sharp breath, eyes locked on my exploring fingers, trailing over the smooth skin of his stomach, toying with the waistband of his pants.

"Rio, please."

He hesitates, for longer than he ever has. He usually shuts this conversation down fairly quickly. We've been fooling around for a year now, but we haven't had sex.

And that's one hundred percent due to the guilt he feels about hiding our relationship from my brother.

His eyes bounce between mine, rolling it over in his mind. "I want to, Hallie. God, I want to so badly—"

My locked door handle jiggles, cutting off his answer.

Both our wide eyes turn to look in that direction. Neither of us says a word, holding our breath while we stare at the shadow of two feet under the crack of my bedroom door.

"Hallie," Luke says with a knock. "Are you asleep already?"

Rio's attention whips back in my direction and his panic is so evident. He throws himself off me, frantically grabbing his shirt from the floor and slipping it over his head.

I'm trying my hardest not to laugh as he attempts to shove his feet back into his shoes, tripping himself up and nearly falling over.

Luke knocks again and Rio bolts to the window.

Okay, now I can't help it. I burst a laugh and slap my hand over my mouth in an attempt to keep quiet.

"Don't laugh at me, Hart," he whisper-shouts as he climbs out the window, but I watch as that playful smile lifts, trying to keep himself from laughing too. "Meet me out here when you can."

I want to tell Luke about us. I want to tell everyone about us. But even though Luke would eventually forgive me for keeping our relationship from him, it wouldn't be that simple regarding his friendship with Rio.

It's nearing the end of their senior year, and neither Rio nor I want to ruin these last few months for either of them.

Eventually though, we will tell him.

Keeping the bedroom light off, I crack the door open. "Hey, what's up?"

"Are you going to bed already?" Luke asks.

"I was planning to. Are you okay?"

"Yeah. Yeah, I just wanted to hang out. I'm not going to be home for your birthday next year, so this kind of feels like the last one I get to celebrate with you."

I tilt my head. "Aww. Luke, you're getting sappy on me."

"Shut up. I'm going to miss you is all."

"I'm going to miss you too, but we still have five months until you leave for college."

"I know, but maybe tomorrow we can hang out? We could go see a movie, just us. Well, we'll invite Rio obviously."

"Yeah. Yeah, that sounds great. But how about we go just the two of us? Like a brother-sister thing. We could grab dinner beforehand."

"Cool. That sounds fun. I'll let you get to sleep." He walks down the hall to his room before calling out, "Happy birthday, sis."

Closing my door, I lock it again before grabbing this year's mix CD off my desk and climbing out the window.

There's a thick blanket laid out in the middle of the roof where Rio is waiting for me, lying on his back with his hands behind his head.

"It's perfect out here tonight, Hal. Look how big and bright the moon is."

He's right. It is perfect. The weather. The view. *Him.*

My brother's words ring in my mind.

"Perfect night for our last birthday together."

He cranes to look in my direction. "What are you talking about?"

I pad over to the centerline of the roof, lying on the blanket next to him. "You'll be away at school next year for my birthday. We won't be able to meet on the roof."

"We'll have every birthday after college though. Every March eighth. It's not our last." He studies me cautiously. "Is everything okay?"

I nod, but don't say anything.

"Come here." Lifting his arm, he nudges me to lie on his chest. "What are you so worried about?"

"Things are going to change."

"They are."

"Doesn't that scare you?"

He runs his fingers through my long hair. "A little bit, but I'm not scared for us. I'm scared of how much I'm going to miss you, and I'm scared about trying to focus on hockey when I know I'm going to be thinking of home. But you and me, Hal? There's nothing to be scared about when it comes to us."

I want to believe him, and of course, I believe that's how he feels right now.

But that doesn't mean I'm not insecure thinking about him moving away and forgetting about me. He's going to be playing hockey at a D1 school eight hundred miles away. He's got himself a full-ride scholarship, which I'm so proud of him for, but the guy is going to receive a lot of attention. He already does, but he doesn't even realize how many girls at our school have their eye on him. All because they don't know he's mine.

It's not that I'm worried about him being unfaithful. Rio doesn't have an unfaithful bone in his body. But I'm human, so yeah, there's a part of me that's scared he'll get a taste of life outside of our little Boston neighborhood and realize he wants more.

"You don't think you'll forget about me?"

He bursts a laugh. "You truly have no idea how ingrained you are in here, huh?" He taps his chest. "You're basically living rent free, Hallie Hart."

I burrow into him even more.

"I wish you could see inside my head, Hal. You'd see the picture I've got painted of our future, and every part of it revolves around you, okay?" With his knuckle, he urges my chin up so I look at him. "It's you and me. I promise."

I offer him a smile. "Okay."

He leans down to kiss me. "Okay."

I place the mix CD on his stomach and that grin on his lips turns up even more.

"I was waiting for this."

I may cringe a bit when we listen to it together later and he realizes that every single song is from a moment with him, but that's okay. He was a part of all my best memories this year, just like he is most years. Any memories I wish I could rewind and relive, are all the ones he and I have had over the years, growing up together. Learning each other. Falling for each other.

He wraps his arm around me tighter, pulling me into him as his other hand traces over the number seventeen and the letter "H" written in permanent marker on the CD. This year, he lingers for a while, following the lines around the heart I draw to represent my last name. Then he, as always, covers the little extra tail with his forefinger.

I don't push his hand away. I don't give him a hard time for teasing me and my wonky drawn hearts. I simply stare at his fingers, trying to ingrain the image into my memory because I know we won't be on the roof this time next year.

It makes me want to cry, thinking about it. Thinking about all the change that's about to happen in our lives.

"Hallie, do you know why I'm not scared?" He holds up the mix CD. "It's because I know I've got a lifetime of getting these from you. We've got a lifetime of best moments ahead of us."

23

Rio

I took a hard hit during today's game that fucked up my back, so I try to align the tight area with one of the jets.

This hot tub is, hands-down, my favorite purchase I've made for the house. There's nothing like 103-degree water when it's winter outside in Chicago. Not to mention, it has a prime sightline to Hallie's bedroom window, and I've caught her checking me out a time or two from up there.

It's been a couple of weeks since we got home from New York. It's been a couple of weeks since I've gotten a decent night of sleep too. It's also been a couple of weeks since we kissed, but I've done exactly what I promised I'd do that night. I haven't pushed her to want more or pressured her into giving us another chance. But I sure as hell haven't gone away either.

If she's working at the bar, I stop in. Sometimes with my teammates. Sometimes by myself.

Always to drive her home.

And most of the time, those drives turn into longer ones, either because we're having fun listening to music together again, or she fell asleep and I'm not ready to wake her.

I leave a vanilla almond milk latte at her front door each

morning with the shittiest version of foam art and a note that tells her what the design was before I took a sip.

I drop by the design firm to say hi if I'm downtown after practice or before a game because, yeah, I want to see her. I just want to be around her. Everything quiets when she's around. These past few weeks have served as a reminder that we're still so good together. That we're the same two people who were in love once.

But no, I haven't pushed her or asked her to give us another try. I've simply been me, allowing her to remember who I am.

I check the time on my phone, knowing I need to get upstairs to pack for our flight tonight, and hoping to have enough time to stop next door to see if Hallie is home so I can say goodbye. The team plane leaves in a couple of hours for a game in Philadelphia before we head to Boston, so I'll be gone for almost a week.

I can't wait. I'm stoked to go home for a night and play in front of my family and friends. It's also an important one with free agency coming up in a handful of months. It's one thing to have a nice-looking stat sheet and a career of accomplishments under your belt, but it's another thing to play a solid sixty minutes of hockey live in front of a team you're hoping might offer you a massive paycheck soon.

So, with all that floating around in my head, I climb out of the hot tub, turn off the jets, and pull the cover back on. I grab my towel, run it through my hair, and jog back to the house to get out of the cold.

But before I make it all the way to my back-door slider, I look up and halt in my tracks. Because right there in my kitchen, Hallie is standing behind the island, watching me.

And she's not just watching me like she's wondering what I'm doing out here, but she's watching me as if she's cataloging every new muscle I've earned since she last saw me naked. She's not even trying to be subtle about it and I fucking love that.

Hallie liked me when I was a scrawny teenager without an

athletic bone in my body. She was always so good about building my confidence and never letting me worry that I might not be enough for her. So, I don't question if she finds me attractive. Now, I feel like I get to show off in front of her.

I take my time toweling off, but I'm sure to put my shirt on before I get too close to the door. Yes, it's been on my mind for a couple of weeks now that it's probably time to start letting Hallie know just how much I *haven't* forgotten about her in all these years, but that needs to be done slowly with baby steps.

"Sorry," she says as soon as I open the door.

I try to bite back my smile. "For which part? Breaking and entering or for eye-fucking me in my own house?"

"Mostly the breaking and entering. Though, I do have a key and used the front door, so I'm not sure if that qualifies. And as far as the eye-fucking…" She tosses her head from side to side in contemplation. "I was the first girl to ever see you naked. I figured that gave me a free pass to see what you're working with now."

Chuckling, I round the kitchen island to meet her, finding different tile samples and cabinet hardware laid out, expanding over the counter.

"What's all this?" I ask, my palm instinctually finding the small of her back.

"A few samples I wanted to see in the space now that the demo is all done on the first floor."

This entire week, a construction crew has been here, ripping out carpet, pulling off baseboards, and jackhammering tile. It's been loud and messy and I'm already eager for this renovation to be done.

But then another part of me isn't. Because if Hallie decides she doesn't see herself giving us another shot, I don't know how much I'm going to get to see her once my house is done. Especially once she moves out of Wren's place. Especially if I end up in Boston.

"I thought you'd already left for the airport," she says.

My thumb draws languid circles on her lower back. "Our flight leaves in a couple of hours. Typically, we go right after the game, but not tonight."

"Are you excited to go home?"

That question gives me pause, because for a moment, my first thought is that I *am* home. But then I realize she doesn't mean this version of home, with her in my house.

"Yeah, I am. I love that city, and I get to see my mom."

Hallie smiles weakly, and I can tell she's trying her best to be excited for me to go home. But I also know the mention of my mom could bring down the mood, so I swiftly change the subject.

"I need to finish packing but do your thing. If you want, you could come upstairs and hang out with me when you're done."

She shakes her head. "I'm here to work."

"Okay." I tuck her hair behind her ear because I can't keep my fucking hands off her, and even though Hallie says she's here to work, she still leans into my touch. "Don't leave without saying goodbye."

Leaving her in the kitchen, I head for the stairs and I'm halfway up when I pause.

Because there's music playing throughout my whole house.

Music that Hallie put on.

I feel the smile begin to lift on my lips because the first day Hallie came to work on my house, she said she didn't do that anymore. But clearly, things have changed since then.

24

Hallie

I know I shouldn't want to spend time with him. I want to be petty. I want to hold a grudge the way I so easily did for the past six years. But the more time I spend with him, the more the armor cracks.

The highlights of my days revolve around him lately. Him popping into my work or leaving a coffee for me on my doorstep. Little moments that tell me he's thinking of me.

But it's not him thinking of me now, with me living right next door, that has me wary of jumping back into things. It's how easily he forgot I existed in the years we were apart. How seemingly forgettable I was to him.

Especially when he never once left my mind.

But I should get his opinion on these backsplash options. It's his house after all, and sure, we're still weeks away from needing these types of decisions to be made, but why not get ahead of schedule? We can discuss as he packs for his trip. And if he decides quickly and I end up hanging out with him for a while longer, well, then it is what it is.

Taking two options with me, I head for the stairs.

His bedroom door is left open, so I slip inside, finding his partially packed suitcase on the bed. He's not in here, though. Both of his closets are left open, including the one he blocked me from going into last time I was up here.

It's like a beacon, calling me to it, so I take a step in that direction, only to stop myself before I can take a second look.

As much as I want to, I can't do that.

Then I'm completely distracted when a distant and breathy *"fuck"* echoes from his attached bathroom, instantly stealing all my attention. I whip in that direction, wanting to hear it again, and wondering if that was real.

I don't breathe. I don't move. I don't make a sound as I listen harder, trying to convince myself that my ears were deceiving me.

They weren't. That's confirmed by the sound of the shower water running and muffling a moan.

As my hand slaps across my mouth to keep myself from making a sound, my eyes go impossibly wide.

Is he...

"Yes," he hisses. *"Fuck."*

Holy shit, he is.

I gently set the tile samples on the bed, not wanting them to make any noise when I cautiously pad across the carpet, keeping light on my toes, to press my ear against the bathroom door.

It's left open slightly, but I don't dare look inside. I stay hidden, listening closely to hear the distinct sound of skin sliding against skin.

Rio groans and the sound instantly does something to me. Turns me on. Turns me reckless.

I shouldn't be here. I shouldn't be listening. But I've been busy doing things I shouldn't be doing lately, so what's one more?

The shower walls work as an amplifier when he says, "Goddammit, Hallie, *yes.*"

I'm frozen in place. Entirely fucking cemented right outside of his bathroom, listening to him get himself off while saying my name.

I want to see him. I want to watch him work his fist over himself. I want a front-row view to witness this man come undone.

Fuck it. If he's saying my name, I'm basically in the room already.

Just a quick glance.

I lean forward slightly, peeking through the cracked door. His shower is a glass surround, *thank God*, and the steam hasn't obstructed the view.

And what a view it is.

Palm flat to the tile wall, Rio uses his other hand to stroke himself. Water pummels over his back, dripping down his body as he works his fist over his cock, pulling and tugging.

And *moaning*.

God, the moaning alone is a soundtrack I could come to. He sounds so desperate, so turned on, coupled with the slick sound of quick pumps along his shaft.

His entire side profile is on display. Long, sculpted back, lean waist, perfect fucking ass, and ridiculously thick thighs. He really is huge now with all that added muscle, but my current favorite ones are those in his forearms, flexing and moving as he strokes himself.

He's thick...*everywhere*.

But of course, I already knew that.

His stomach tightens. His chest heaves. He pumps over and over, focusing on the head, and I can tell he's close. And as much as I want to watch him, to remember the look on his face when he comes, I know I shouldn't be here.

Pulling back, I hide behind the door once again.

"Hallie," he repeats, short of breath.

It has me closing my eyes and crossing my legs from hearing him say my name like that again. Like it's a pleading prayer moments before he finishes.

"Hallie." His voice is muffled from the water still, but it's projected for me to hear. "If you're going to stand out there and listen, you may as well come in and watch. It's nothing you haven't seen before."

Oh shit.

How'd he—

Panic takes over and mortification settles in, but he's the one getting off on ideas of me while I'm in his house, so if anyone is going to be embarrassed, it shouldn't be me.

I swallow hard, still hidden in his bedroom, spine flush to the wall. "How'd you know I was out here?"

He laughs, and I can hear that his hand hasn't slowed in pace one bit.

I fake composure. "You told me to come up to your room if I wanted to hang out."

"Perfect. You can hang out in here."

"Rio."

"Get in here, Hal."

I know I don't have to do what he says, but fuck it, I want to.

I take a centering breath, turn the corner, and slowly push the door open. He's in the same position, only showing me his right-side profile, but thankfully that's the hand he's using to pump himself, giving me that same unobstructed view.

I take a slow sweeping glance up his body, taking my time and not being shy in my perusal. And when I make it to his face, I find his eyes locked on me.

His dark hair is wet and slick to his forehead. His green eyes are heated and heavy. His lips, they're parted and panting, but he slips the bottom one between his teeth as he watches me.

I'm completely mesmerized by his movements, unable to look away. His hand never stops stroking, and my attention falls to the head, red and swollen, leaking precum onto the shower floor.

I swallow hard. "I thought sex was off the table?"

"It is. I'm not fucking you. I'm just fucking my fist thinking of you."

Jesus.

245

No, we don't tend to be shy with each other, but to hear him speak like this, so confidently, so directly... It's hot.

"Fuck, Hallie, keep looking at me like that."

I step fully into the bathroom, leaving the doorway. "Like what?"

His Adam's apple bobs in his throat. "Like you wish it was your mouth getting me off and not my hand."

I nod quickly, telling him that's exactly what I want to do.

Every muscle in his body fires at that, his head thrown back. "I'm going to come just thinking about it."

He keeps his attention on me and that heated look has my core clenching and my legs tightening.

Mirroring his confidence, I take another step towards him. "Does that feel good?"

He chuckles this disbelieving laugh. "You have no idea. And *fuck*, please keep talking. Hearing your voice is going to make me come."

Okay. This is wildly hot, talking him through it.

I take another step. "How often do you say my name while getting yourself off?"

"A disturbing amount."

Another step. "And what exactly do you think about?"

His jaw clenches, his stomach contracts. "Everything. How good it felt to be inside you. How well you used to suck me off. How pretty you looked on your knees with my cock down your throat."

I remember the first time. I didn't know what I was doing, but he taught me what he liked once he figured it out too. I was nervous, but he took it slow even though he was ready to come the moment I wrapped my mouth around him. It was fun learning together. Teaching each other.

My bottom lip slips between my teeth at the memory.

"Holy shit," he pants. "Biting your lip like that. You're thinking of it too."

I quickly nod. "I can tell you're close to coming. I remember exactly what you used to look like when you were close."

"I'm so fucking close, baby. Please keep talking. Please keep looking at me."

His strokes are short and quick, and his eyes never leave me. I step closer to the glass enclosure. "I really want you to come."

"Yeah?"

God, that one strained and breathy word sets me on fire. My entire body is lit up and I don't know if I've ever been more turned on in my life. Shifting on my feet, I confirm this when I feel how slick I am between my thighs.

"Are you still thinking about me?"

"I'm always thinking about you, Hallie."

An unpermitted whimper escapes my throat at that admission.

"Fuck me. Those noises." He moans the sexiest sound I've ever heard before giving himself one, long stroke. His stomach bunches, showing off each and every one of his abs. His head falls back, but his eyes stay on me for as long as they can before they're forced shut from his orgasm.

He paints the shower wall in front of him as he comes, jerking and trembling. The rumble in his throat pulses through my own body, and eventually his hand slows, pulling out every last drop while he rocks his hips, chasing the high until he finishes.

I'm mesmerized. Standing and staring as the water rolls off him and rinses the wall, washing it all down the drain.

I'm also very turned on.

It's nice to know that after all these years, I still have that effect on him. I can still make him come, and I didn't even touch him myself.

Arms crossed on the wall, Rio leans his forehead on them, catching his breath before he laughs to himself. "Fuck, Hal. That was hot."

I swallow, wetting my parched mouth. "You owe me one."

"Mmm." That smile lifts and that sinister tilt sends a pulse straight to my core. "I'll keep that in mind."

Rio stands tall under the shower spray, letting it clean him off. He really is all man now. Hair on his chest, his legs, and trimmed by his cock. His *still hard* cock that's jutting out proudly as he showers.

He lathers himself with soap, continuing as if I'm not standing here gawking at him and didn't just help him orgasm.

"You're welcome to join," he teases. "But you know the rules. Just keep your hands to yourself."

I roll my eyes. "You're not very fun."

"I don't know." He directs that grin at me. "Personally, I just had a blast."

I should go before I do something stupid like climb into that shower fully clothed and beg him for an orgasm.

Without giving him a second glance, I rush out of the bathroom, down the stairs, and back to the kitchen. And when I return to the samples on the island, I continue to work as if nothing out of the ordinary just happened.

I play with different combinations. A ceramic tile in a simple shape versus a handmade clay option with perfect imperfections. Aged brass hardware compared to a classic black. Countertops with heavy veining or a more minimalistic option.

And none of that does anything to keep my mind off what just happened.

Does he always think of me while getting himself off? Did he always sound like that? Because I swear to God, that whimper-moan combination is going to be playing in my head on a loop when I go home, lie on my bed, and slip my hand between my legs.

I couldn't care less about picking out finishes for his kitchen right now, and that becomes obvious when twenty minutes later, Rio finds me while wearing a perfectly fitted suit with his suitcase in tow, and I still haven't made one single decision.

He sets two tiles on the counter to join the others. The same ones I left upstairs on his bed. "Well, I feel better now, don't you?"

"Get fucked."

He chuckles, hand sliding against my lower back before he hides his face in the crook of my neck and plants a kiss there. "I just did. Thanks for the assist."

I playfully push him away. "You're mean."

"Why?" He scoops me by the waist, bringing my chest flush with his. "Did you get turned on watching me?"

"You know I did."

There's that sly smile again. "Like you said, I owe you one. Give me a call later if you need me to walk you through it."

"Your rules are all over the place. So, phone sex is on the table?"

"Oh, it's all on the table, Hart. All you have to do is give me a chance."

My previously melting body stiffens in his hold.

His playfulness morphs when he realizes. "I'm joking around."

"I know."

He searches my face. "Take your time, Hal. I was giving you shit."

"I know." I fall into his chest and let him hug me goodbye.

He wraps his arms around me tightly, resting his chin on my head. "I'm leaving my truck for you to drive. It's parked in the garage. Zee is picking me up."

"Thank you for that."

"I'm leaving my espresso maker for you too, if you feel like making yourself a latte."

"But my latte art will never be as good as yours."

"Well, at least you're self-aware."

I chuckle against him.

"And the rest of my house is yours while I'm gone too," he continues. "For work, or for...exploring."

Pulling back, I look up at him. He doesn't have to explain. We both know what he's referring to.

"See you when I'm back home?"

I nod. "See you then."

His eyes roam over my face and his thumb dusts over my cheekbone as if he were about to kiss me. I can see him contemplating, struggling with himself not to, but eventually, he decides against it.

Leaving me alone in his kitchen, he takes his suitcase with him.

Once he's gone, I try to get back to work, but it's no use when all I can concentrate on is that closet upstairs. I attempt to find an ounce of patience, but it's pointless. All I needed was his permission, and now that I have it, I can't wait any longer.

Leaving the samples on the kitchen island, I take off for the stairs, heading straight for his room. That closet door is wide open, left intentionally for me to see. But before I can take a step in that direction, my nerves slow me down.

I have no idea what I'm about to find.

What was so bad that he didn't want me to see a few weeks ago, but has no problem with me discovering now?

I can't even begin to guess, so while trying to brace myself for anything, I step inside.

I quickly learn this isn't his main closet. It's filled with backup hockey gear, extra luggage, and some old jerseys he's saved from over the years. I can tell they're old because they have a number eighty-three on the back, and he hasn't worn that number since college.

There doesn't seem to be anything out of the ordinary in here, and again, I don't know what I'm looking for. But when I push his old jerseys apart on the top rack, I find a black box sitting on the shelf below it.

My intuition screams that this is it. Whatever I'm supposed to find, it's in here.

There's not a fleck of dust gathered on the lid, but the edges are worn, like this box has been opened and closed hundreds of times over the years. It weighs next to nothing and there's a slight rattle inside from when I pick it up and carry it to the bed.

Taking a seat on the mattress, I open it.

When I look inside, my stomach hollows out in a way I've never experienced before. My lips part of their own accord and my breath catches in my lungs. I don't need to do much digging to know exactly what this is. What *these* are.

I tossed my own copies years ago. Partly out of anger, and partly because I no longer recognized the hopeful girl who once saw the good in everything. Who once had so many best memories she needed a way to remember them by.

The box is filled with every mixtape and CD I made for him over the years, each given to him on my birthday.

All of them, from ages eleven to nineteen, which include the two I gave him before we started meeting up on the roof, they're all in here. And it's evident they've been played endlessly over the years. They're each in their individual cases which are all cracked in one place or another. Some of the hinges are broken from overuse, from being opened and closed too many times.

It suddenly feels impossible to breathe.

I cannot believe he kept these.

Judging by the look of betrayal on his face the last time I saw him, I assumed the first thing he did was get rid of these. Burned them. Shattered them. Something dramatic to match how hurt he was.

But he kept them.

The only other thing in this box is an old piece of embroidery thread, which doesn't really make sense. I pull it out to take a closer look. It's almost unrecognizable, tattered, discolored, and worn. It takes a moment until it clicks, for me to realize what this is.

It's that old friendship bracelet I made him on my thirteenth birthday. The one he wore on his wrist and never took off until it withered away and fell off on its own sometime after he had left for college. It broke off without him realizing. I assumed it was long gone by now.

Something so small. So seemingly unimportant. But it wasn't. None of it was.

In disbelief, I move on, trading the bracelet for a cassette, thumbing over the signature I inked there years ago. I linger on the tail of the heart the way he always used to. It's such a silly little signature that I came up with when I was a kid, but I never moved on from it because I loved watching the way he'd trace it every year.

All my best memories. He kept them.

He listens to them still.

For so long, I held on to every little detail of our relationship, replaying them in my mind on a loop. I cherished the smallest moments we had together. Even at my lowest points, I was grateful that I got to be loved like that at least once in my life.

I never forgot him. I never forgot *us*.

And apparently, neither did he.

25

Rio

Throwing the comforter off, I give up on trying to sleep. It's well after two in the morning, and as per usual, I can't fucking sleep.

I've already gotten out of bed to turn the thermostat down in my hotel room. I've scrolled on my phone. I put on some TV. I tried to read.

My brain won't shut itself off. I'm too busy thinking about the game tomorrow night against Philly. Trying to remember if I took the garbage cans out to the street before I left. Wondering if the almond milk in the fridge is going to be good for the entirety of my trip, but if it's going to expire, I'm trying to figure out how I can get some delivered to the house for Hallie to use.

Hallie.

Always Hallie. That's where my mind circles back to every time I'm alone and it's quiet enough to think.

When I close my eyes, I can still picture how sinfully perfect she looked standing just outside my shower as I got myself off earlier today. How sexy she was with that lip tucked under her teeth. How raspy her voice became when she told me she wanted me to come.

Are you still thinking about me?

If she only knew.

When I think of sex, I think of Hallie. She's the only name that pops into my mind. Her face, her body, and her voice are the only things I visualize. She was my first. She taught me how to do it. We learned together by learning each other. Six years later, I think it's safe to assume there will never come a day that I *don't* think of Hallie Hart when I think of sex.

God, I miss her.

I want her back, and I'm done lying about it. To her. To myself.

Sitting up, I rest my back against the headboard before grabbing my phone off the nightstand. I text her, not caring that she probably won't respond until sometime later after she wakes up.

Me: *Can't sleep. Thinking about you.*

To my surprise, three dots immediately start dancing on the screen as she types back.

H (heart emoji): *Thinking about me, or thinking about that shower?*

A laugh warms my chest.

Me: *Both.*

Even more surprising than finding her awake is when my phone starts vibrating with a call from her. I answer immediately.

"Hey."

Her voice is tired. "Hi."

"Everything okay?"

"I can't sleep either."

It's on the tip of my tongue, wanting to ask if she went into my closet after I left. If she found all the mixtapes and CDs I haven't stopped listening to since she originally gave them to me.

I've never forgotten this girl, not even for a second, and it's about time she knows that.

With the lights off, I scoot down to lie on my back again, phone pressed to my ear. "Why can't you sleep?"

"I have a lot on my mind. Mostly you. Mostly us."

Fuck. I like that.

"Do you want to talk through it?"

"No," she whispers into the line. "I want you to talk me through something else."

Fuck. Me.

She sounds so turned on right now. Earlier today, Hallie told me she knew when I was about to come. Well, that makes two of us. I remember exactly how she sounds when she wants to get off, and I can hear it in her voice right now.

"I still feel worked up from watching you earlier," she says.

"Mmm. Well, we should take care of that. Don't you think?"

"Could you do that for me, Rio?"

There's something unguarded in the way she asks. Sure, it's just phone sex, but the bigger picture is that Hallie's not wearing her armor right now. She trusts me enough to be vulnerable in this way again.

"I can do anything for you, baby. Tell me what you're wearing."

She hums at that name. "A T-shirt."

"Yeah? What else?"

She pauses on the other line. "Nothing else."

My eyes screw shut. "Hallie, put me on a video call."

"Not this time. It's my turn, Rio, and I just want to hear your voice in my ear as you talk me through it. You owe me one, remember?"

My self-deprecating laugh is painful. "Yeah, Hal. There's no forgetting that. I've been looking forward to paying you back. Where are you right now?"

"In my bed."

"Lights off?"

"Yes."

"Door locked?"

"Mm-hmm." I hear her swallow on the other line. "But I wish you were here with me."

Something is different. She's being open and honest with me. I want to press her about it, ask her if she's feeling differently about us, but I also really want to make her feel good.

"Fingers or a toy?" I ask.

"What do *you* want me to use?"

I roll to my side, keeping the phone pressed to my ear. "Fingers. Pretend they're mine."

There's a soft rumble in her throat.

"Slide your hand down, Hallie baby. Open your legs and slip your fingers between them."

I wait to hear her tell me she's doing what I instructed, but this is torture. The best kind of torture, but still, I want to see her. I want to touch her, but I can't. So instead, I reach down and touch myself. Over my sweatpants, I run my palm down my length.

I'm hard as hell already.

She sucks in a sharp breath, and I know she's doing the same.

"How wet are you right now?"

Hallie whimpers. "Plenty."

I stroke myself over my pants. "Good. Use your fingers and rub a circle over your clit. Make yourself feel good like I would be doing if I were there right now."

She moans softly.

"Good girl, Hal. Keep doing that."

"Are you touching yourself?"

I look down, finding the obvious hard-on bulging under the fabric of my pants. "Do you want me to?"

"Yes," she breathes. "Touch yourself with me. Please."

I chuckle as I push my sweatpants over my hips and ass, letting my cock spring free. "Trust me, Hal. There's not a world in which you'd need to use your manners to ask me to get off with you."

She laughs this pretty little sound on the other end.

I stroke my cock in one long, slow slide. The head is already swollen. The veins are already bulging. "Goddamn, I wish I was there right now."

"And what would you do if you were?"

A tick of a smirk lifts on my mouth. "Are we really doing this?"

"Yes. We were long-distance for two years, and you got awfully good at making me come over the phone. Do you still remember how?"

Do I still remember how?

There's a testing note in her voice that she knows I won't back down from. I can picture the smug smile on her face as she lays there knowing I'm about to paint a picture of all the filthy things that are running through my mind right now.

I pump myself. "Are you still touching yourself?"

"Yes."

"Good. You want to know what I'd do if I were there right now?"

"Please tell me, Rio."

"If I were there, I'd kneel behind you, wrap an arm around your waist and pull your back to my chest. I'd let you feel how hard my cock is when it slides against your ass, then I'd replace your fingers with my own and make you look down between your legs to watch how well I still know your body."

She whimpers on the line.

"I'd rub tight little circles on your clit. Are you doing that right now, Hallie?"

"*Yes.*"

"I'd play with you the way I always used to play with you until I made you come, then I'd toss you on your back, bury my face between your legs, and finally get a taste of you again."

Her breathing picks up. "You always did enjoy going down on me."

Understatement of the fucking year.

"Don't be shy, Hallie. Say it how it is. I fucking loved eating your pussy, baby, and we both know it."

She moans. "More."

My muscles begin to coil, heat pricking my skin. Stroking myself, I pick up the pace.

"I'd suck on your clit until you couldn't take it anymore, until you were begging me to stop. Then I'd pin your legs to the mattress and make you come again on my tongue. And while your pussy was still fluttering with that orgasm, I'd slide my fingers inside so I could feel how insanely tight you were going to feel when I gave you my cock."

"Rio, I want you inside of me again."

"Yeah?"

She whimpers. "I wish you were fucking me again."

That makes two of us.

Running my hand over my shaft, I grip my cock as tight as her cunt always gripped me.

"Keep rubbing with your fingers, Hallie. Pretend they're mine."

"I wish they were."

My hips move in rhythm, meeting my fist in pace. "I'd open your legs even wider and slowly climb over you."

"Yes."

"Just like when we were in the hotel, Hal. Do you remember how good it felt to have me on top of you again? When your legs were wrapped around me? You felt like heaven underneath me."

Hallie's breathing is quick and short. "You felt so good. I wanted you inside of me. I haven't had you inside of me in so long."

"I know. *Fuck*." I jerk myself even quicker. "I think about it all the time. How good you felt. How well you fucked me."

"I want you to fuck me right now."

"I want to so badly. You have no idea."

"Then do it."

Screwing my eyes shut, I see it. Her on her back, legs spread wide, pussy swollen and ready for me.

"I'd suck on your neck. I'd slip my tongue in your mouth so you could see how fucking good you taste and why I'm so goddamn addicted. Maybe then you'd understand why I've been starving for you for six years now."

"Rio, I'm so close."

Shit. So am I.

"I'd slide my cock over your clit a couple of times. I'd make sure I was covered in you, and while you were squirming underneath me, eager for it, I'd drag it out. I'd torture you. I wouldn't give it to you yet. Not until you were begging for me."

"I want it," she cries. "I want you."

"And then when you were so desperate for it that you were on the brink of coming again just from me teasing you, I'd push the head of my cock down and let it slip inside your perfect fucking body."

"*Yes*. Yes. Please. I want it."

I work my hand, moving in quick, short pumps.

"And you'd be warm and wet and fucking perfect like you always have been. You've always taken me so well, baby. You remember?"

"Mm-hmm."

"Then I'd fuck you. I'd fuck you right into the mattress while also holding your hand. Because it was always more than fucking, wasn't it?"

"Yes, Rio."

"Are you going to come for me, Hal?"

She whimpers and the breath that follows is short and desperate, unable to fill her lungs with air. And that, combined with her little noises, mixed with the sound of her rhythmically moving on her mattress, means she's there.

"Hallie baby, be a good girl and come for me. Please. I need it. I need to hear how unreal you sound when you come. Fuck, I remember how pretty you are when you let go. You're doing so good. Please. If you come, it'll make me come."

"I want you to come inside of me. Please, Rio."

"*Fuck*."

My name slips off her lips like a precious, pleading cry. I can tell that Hallie is coming on the other line as her moans fill my ears. Her noises coax my own release, and I join her.

The climax is blindingly blissful, regardless that I just came earlier today. The picture I painted for her is playing like a movie in my head as I come inside of her. As she holds me to her. As she tells me she's mine and that I'm hers. I pull out and watch my cum drip down her leg before using two fingers to push it back inside of her.

Opening my eyes, I find my abdomen coated in my release.

In my ear, Hallie takes a deep inhale, attempting to find some hard-earned breaths, and I follow suit.

"Damn, Hal."

Exhaling, she giggles this sound that fills every empty crevice it can find. It burrows in my chest, making a home where she's always been.

"That was fun," she says.

"I'm covered."

She laughs again before sighing this sweet, soft sound. "I missed you, Rio."

Closing my eyes again, I let that sink in too. I allow those words to replay on a loop. "I feel like I'm still missing you, Hal."

I want her back. I want her to be open to the idea of giving us a chance.

"Maybe you won't have to feel that way for long."

I do my best not to react to that, not to ruin those words or push for more meaning. This could very well be her post-coital fog speaking for her. But I, instead, decide to assume those words mean what I want them to mean in hopes they might help me find sleep tonight.

Standing from the bed, I take my naked self over to the sink and wet a washcloth to wipe myself off, leaving the phone pressed to my ear.

"Are you feeling better now?" I ask.

I can hear the smile in her words. "Exponentially. Maybe I'll be able to sleep now."

Chuckling, I slip my sweatpants back on, dropping myself

onto the mattress again. I want to talk to her all night. I want to leave this call going and set my phone next to my bed to see if that helps, but I'm also at the place where I just want to give her anything she needs from me.

"Thank you." Her words are a whisper.

"Happy to help. Literally anytime." I swallow hard. "I'll let you get some sleep."

"Wait," she stops me quickly. "Would you... I don't know. Do you want to stay on the phone for a while? Unless you're tired."

My chest squeezes the way it started doing again after she moved in next door. It might be foolish to let myself, but there's something about her tonight that's making me feel hopeful. *We* feel hopeful.

"Yeah. I'd love to talk to you, Hal."

Tossing the comforter back over my body, I put my phone on speaker and leave it on the pillow next to mine.

And I can't help the contented smile from lifting on my lips when she says, "Tell me all about your day."

26

Rio

The rideshare drops me and Zanders off in front of my family home.

My mom's home.

The house I grew up in. Fuck, I don't even know what to call it anymore.

Regardless, as soon as the car drives away, my attention immediately drifts to the house next door. Hallie's house. Hallie's bedroom window. The roof where we spent years falling in love with each other.

Zee zips his coat for the short walk up to the front walkway. "Hallie lived there?" He nods towards the house next to mine.

"Yeah, she moved in when she was eleven and I was twelve."

"Is her family still there?"

"No, they moved out of the area sometime during my rookie year in the league."

Zee is quiet for a moment and stops before we reach the front door, clearly understanding that the Hallie talk needs to be put on hold as soon as we go inside.

"Why didn't you ever tell us about her? We've been friends for so long now, and this whole time, we all thought you had never been in a relationship before."

I groan. "It's complex, and kind of messy. And well, the entire time I've known you, I've tried my hardest to forget Hallie existed, so there's that."

A cheeky smile spreads across his lips. "I always wondered what you'd be like in a relationship. I thought you'd be a fucking idiot, not knowing which way was up. Like a too excitable puppy, but you seem...grounded."

I laugh at his analogy. "Well, my mind doesn't like to shut the fuck up most of the time, so yeah. I've got a lot of energy, but I don't know. It's always been quiet around Hal. But also, for clarification, I'm not in a relationship. She's not interested in going there right now."

He waves me off. "Give it time."

"Yeah, it's a little more complicated than that."

The front door swings open, ending our conversation. "There's my boy!" my mom bellows, arms open wide and charging to wrap them around...*Zanders.*

I'm left with a gaping mouth, watching her give all her attention to my teammate and not her only child. "Wow. Okay."

"I'm giving you shit." She lets go of him and hugs me instead. "I'm happy you're home."

"Me too, Ma." I hug her tight. "I missed you."

She's a small woman, but you wouldn't know it by her big personality or her boisterous voice. She's strong and resilient, and though she feels fragile in my hold, she's not. Which is why, the only time in my whole life that I did see her fragile and broken is ingrained in my memory like a bad dream. And I know I'd do anything to keep her from feeling that way again.

"Come on, you two." She gestures us into the house. "I made an early lunch."

My phone vibrates in my coat pocket, and I stay back on the front step to pull it out while Zee follows my mom into the house.

I discreetly check it to find my dad's name scrolling across the top of the screen. It's the second time he's called today and the fourth time he's called this week. I haven't answered a single one, and I had planned to keep ignoring them forever.

I've been upset with him for a long time, but I don't think it settled in just how angry I've been until recently. Until I realized everything I gave up after his fucked-up choices.

I don't want to talk to him, but I also don't want him to keep calling while I'm with my mom either.

"I'll be right in," I tell them. "I got to take this call quickly."

My mom checks on me over her shoulder but doesn't push. "Okay. Lunch is warm, so try to make it quick."

"It will be."

I wait until the door is closed before I answer the phone.

"Yeah?"

"Hey, son. How are you?"

I walk away from the house, trying to create distance so no one else will be able to overhear. "I'm fine. What's up?"

He chuckles. "I'm good too. Thank you for asking."

I roll my eyes.

"I've been trying to get a hold of you all week. I was hoping to see you while you're in town."

No chance of that happening.

My dad still lives in Boston, though he no longer lives in this house. But his side of the family has lived in the area for generations. He met my mom at twelve years old because they were in the same class in school, and I hate the idea that she could casually run into him around town at any given moment.

"I can't," I say with finality. "I'm only here for the day and I'm visiting with my mom."

"All right. That's no problem. I'm coming to your game tonight, so I'm hoping to see you after."

Wait...what?

"Don't piss me off right now, Dad. My mom is coming to the game tonight."

"Rio, the arena is plenty big for both of us. I haven't seen you in almost a year. You didn't visit me once while you were home this summer. I have the right to watch my son's game."

"The right?" I ask in disbelief, the anger is building quickly. "You don't have a right to anything when it comes to me."

"I'm your father. That means something, you know. When are you going to get over this? All I want is for us to get back to how we used to be."

How fucking dare he.

"When am I going to get over it?" I repeat, almost yelling into the phone.

"That's what I said."

"You cheated on my mother! I'm not going to *get over* it, Dad."

The line is silent for quite some time. My chest is heaving with anger, and I could happily hang up the phone right now and call this conversation done. But now I'm pissed, and I want to take it out on him.

"Rio—"

"You ruined our family, and now she's alone."

"I know. I know I made a mistake. But it's been *years*."

"A mistake? You made a conscious choice. And now, because of your decisions, I might have to leave all my friends, my teammates, and my home so that I can move back to Boston because she's alone. That was your responsibility, and you didn't do it. So, excuse me for not being able to get over it."

He's quiet again. I've never said any of this to him. I've simply given him the cold shoulder for years, but now that his decisions are affecting my life, I'm ready to let him know.

My eyes drift over to Hallie's old house, up to her bedroom window, and I realize that his decisions have been affecting me for a lot longer than I initially recognized.

I shake my head. "Fuck you."

"Rio DeLuca."

"No, fuck you, Dad. You have no idea how much your choices fucked me up."

"I realize that, but—"

"No, you don't!" I'm yelling again. "Because I didn't even realize until recently. I spent twenty-one years of my life chasing what you and Mom had, because I thought that's what love, or soulmates, or whatever the fuck I thought you had, looked like. But when I found out that you were full of shit, I spent the last six years trying to find the opposite. Trying to find *anyone* that could prove to me that love existed because you single-handedly convinced me that it didn't."

I feel sick. Sick of him. Sick that I let his choices dictate my own. I was twenty-one years old, and he caused most of my world to fall apart, while I finished demolishing the rest. I ran away from it all and tried to pretend none of it ever happened. I swept it under the rug and tucked it away, only revisiting my issues when I revisited this neighborhood. Chicago was my clean slate.

"How could you do that to her?"

My words are quiet and though I'm asking him the question, it feels like I'm asking myself the same thing.

How could I leave Hallie behind like that? It wasn't her fault that my dad blew up my family. It wasn't her fault that his decisions had me questioning *everything*. What the fuck is wrong with me?

"Rio, this is good. It's good to hear you say these things. You've never told me how you felt. This is good to know so we can move forward."

I scoff, tired of even talking to him. "You're the last person I want to move forward with. I'm not telling you this for your benefit. I'm getting this off my chest for me."

"Son, if I could go back in time, I would."

"Well, you can't." I swallow hard. "And neither can I. You were supposed to teach me how to be a man, Dad, and I truly hate the things I learned from you."

Before he can respond, I hang up the phone.

Fuck that. Fuck him.

Fuck *me* for being so emotionally wrung out at the time that I couldn't see straight. That I couldn't see who was truly at fault.

The front door of Hallie's old house opens, and I swear I could throw up, that's how sick I feel. I haven't met the couple who moved in next to my mom, but still, they offer me a polite wave as they take off on a walk, bundled up in their winter gear.

It's wild to think they probably have no idea about the girl who grew up in that house. They have no idea I snuck through their upstairs window more times than I can count, or that their roof might be indented from how often we laid on it together.

And I threw it all away because I couldn't see past my own hurt. Past my *mom's* hurt.

I need to talk to Hallie. I have in no way apologized enough to her, and being back here only serves as a reminder that *I'm* the one who fucked up all those years ago. Not her.

She must have been so scared and I took it out on her.

On my phone, I find her number and call. It rings long enough that eventually, I'm pushed through to voicemail. I know she's probably at the design firm, but I just need to talk to her.

I shoot her a follow-up text, asking her to call me when she can, before I gather myself and go inside.

Zee and my mom are sitting at the dining room table together, laughing about something when I close the front door behind me.

Smiling, she looks over at me. "Honey, are you okay?"

"Yeah." I shake my head, trying to shake it off. "Yeah, of course. What's for lunch?"

"Let me make you a plate." She's up and out of her seat before I can tell her not to get up.

This is her love language, though. Feeding the people she loves. Having them in her home.

I follow her to the kitchen, wrapping an arm around her shoulders and pulling her into a hug. "I love you. You know that, right?"

She chuckles, patting my back. "I love you too, *Tesoro*. Are you sure you're okay?"

"I'm good."

When I take a seat at the table, I can feel Zee watching me, but I don't look in his direction. He clearly knows something is off, but I'm not going to get into it or talk about my dad while my mom is around.

I check my phone, finding no response from Hallie when my mom sets a loaded plate down in front of me and then one in front of Zanders.

"Thank you, Ma. This looks great."

She takes a seat and the three of us eat together. She catches me up on all the neighborhood news, Zee tells her all about the new things his daughter is learning, and I sit and listen, checking my phone every few minutes.

"Big night tonight," my mom says. "Are you excited?"

I nod. "Uh-huh."

"Everyone is coming. Your uncle Mikey is dropping by the house soon. He's coming to the game too. The whole neighborhood has been talking about this for weeks. Imagine what it's going to be like when you're playing here. Hometown boy—"

"Ma." My tone is sharp, cutting her off.

Her attention flicks between Zee and me when she realizes. "Oh."

The house is silent, no one knowing how to shift the conversation with this giant elephant sitting in the room.

"I figured as much," Zee eventually admits. "You didn't sign your early extension, and there's no reason for you not to unless you're planning to leave."

He offers me a placating smile before refocusing on eating the food on his plate. But he's so clearly bummed from the confirmation that his suspicions were right. Our previous captain, Maddison, is one of Zee's best friends and he retired last season. And while yes, they're still extremely close, he doesn't have him on the ice every day the way he once did. And now, I might potentially leave too. We've played practically every shift together since I've been in the NHL. He was like a big brother when I first came into the league, and now he's one of my very best friends.

"Does, um…" I rub the back of my neck. "Does everyone know?"

"The team or the crew?"

"The crew."

He nods, shifting his food around his plate. "Everyone put the pieces together when you didn't sign last season. Indy is freaking out a little bit, if I'm being honest, but she's trying not to ask you about it. And don't get me wrong, we all understand. It's your childhood dream. Who doesn't want to play for their hometown team, you know? We're all going to be stoked for you when it happens, so don't worry about that."

"Rio, I'm sorry," my mom cuts in. "I figured you would have talked to your friends about it already."

"It's all right." I check my phone again. "Sorry. I'll be right back. I need to make a quick call."

Before I'm even out of the kitchen, I dial Hallie.

She doesn't answer, but this time when I'm sent to voicemail, I don't hang up.

"Hey," I say quietly into the phone so no one else can hear me. "Just checking in." I pause, closing my eyes. "Well, that's not entirely true. I um… I talked to my dad, and I wanted to tell you about it. I know I haven't talked about my family with you, but I want to. And honestly, my head is all over the place and you've always been the best at making it quiet down." I'm about to end the call there, but don't, continuing to say what I would've said if she answered. "I realized some things and I don't blame you, Hal. I don't blame you for not wanting to jump back into things with me now, and I don't blame you for not telling me the truth all those years ago. And I'm sorry that I did blame you for so long. It's strange being back here without you, and I'd really love to talk to you about it, so give me a call when you can. Okay?"

I end the call and go back to our text thread to find my message from earlier is still unanswered.

I find Wren's contact instead.

Me: *Hey, have you heard from Hallie lately? I've been trying to get a hold of her, and I know she's at the firm, but she usually responds by now. If you hear from her, can you tell her to call me?*

I don't wait for Wren's response before I rejoin my mom and Zee, leaving my phone on the table this time.

"Rio, I'm sorry," my mom says again.

"Don't be. I should've told everyone a while ago."

"Are you sure you're okay?"

"Yeah, of course. Big game tonight. Just got some nerves, that's all."

She rubs a soothing hand on my arm. "You'll be great. Don't worry."

I continue to eat, but glance at my phone again, finding nothing from Hallie or Wren.

My mom gestures to it with her fork. "Who are you waiting to hear from?"

Nobody is the answer that's on the tip of my tongue. I'm about to say it before I stop and decide I don't want to lie anymore.

Turning in my seat, I give my mom my full attention. "Hallie."

Her smile slowly drops. "Which Hallie?"

"You know which Hallie, Ma."

Her entire body stiffens, and I can visibly see every part of her go on high alert. "Why would you be speaking to her?"

Zanders stands from the table. "I'm going to give you some privacy," he says before leaving us alone.

"Rio," she pushes.

"Because Hallie lives in Chicago now."

Her eyes go impossibly wide.

"She moved in next door to me, and I hired her to work on my house. She's the one heading up the renovation on my place."

"Rio, please tell me you're joking."

"I'm not."

Her voice raises. "How could you do that to me?"

"I'm not doing anything to you." I keep my voice steady. "And Hallie didn't do anything to you either."

"She didn't tell me! She was practically my daughter, and she knew that your father was having an affair, and she didn't tell me. How can you even look at her now?"

"She was nineteen years old and was probably scared out of her mind. Not that I know for sure because I never gave her a chance to explain herself. She knew something that was going to break our family apart. Something that was going to break your heart and something that was going to break mine. She's not the one who ruined our family. Dad did that all on his own."

My mom is shaking her head so quickly as if she were trying to erase this entire conversation. "She played her part."

"Ma," I say softly. "It's Hallie."

I can see the fight or flight in her eyes. The panic and the trauma. Yes, Hallie played a part in the most traumatic day of my mom's life. Probably the most traumatic of mine too, but for the first time in six years, I'm thinking clearly. I'm not blinded by anger or fear for my mom. Her emotions aren't guiding my decisions this time around.

She watches me for a long time, studying, and I see the moment realization dawns on her. "You still have feelings for her, don't you?"

I exhale a long breath. "Never stopped."

"Rio, don't go there. You're going to get hurt. You two were kids. Childhood love doesn't work out the way you want it to. It's an idealistic fantasy. When you meet that young, you grow up and grow apart. Look at what happened to your dad and me."

"But we're not you!"

Her eyes widen and her lips flatten to a straight line because I have never, not once, raised my voice at my mother the way I just did.

"We're not you, Ma," I say, more even-toned. "And our relationship is not the one you had with my dad. I thought it was. I wanted it to be. I tried to shape everything off what you two showed me, and when you two fell apart, so did I. And I made a huge mistake because of it. You were hurting and that scared me, and I took it out on Hallie. But I'm not going to do that anymore. As much as you want me to, I'm not going to keep blaming her."

My phone rings on the table, and when I look down, I find Wren calling me. Which is strange because she typically would've just texted back. In fact, I don't think we've ever talked on the phone before.

"Wren?" I ask as soon as I answer.

"Hey, sorry. I just saw your text."

Every one of my senses goes on high alert. She would've just texted back if she didn't have something to tell me. "What's wrong?"

Wren hesitates. "Hallie didn't want me to tell you because of your game, but I know you'd want to know. Her dad was taken to the hospital back in Minnesota. I don't know many details other than she seemed scared. She's on her way now. She started driving about an hour ago. I just thought you should know."

27

Hallie

My knee is bouncing due to the adrenaline coursing through me. I'm sitting, watching it happen, and still, I can't stop the movement.

It's a good distraction I suppose, watching the nerves rattle in my body, knowing I can't control them.

Feels like I can't control anything right now.

Luke called me this morning to tell me that he had brought our dad into the emergency room to get checked out after he had been spiking a fever over the past two days. He was immediately admitted to the hospital for testing.

Because that's what happens when you're in your second remission from blood cancer. Something as simple as an unexplained fever or fatigue throws up major red flags for a possible relapse.

I have a vivid memory of the day we found out his cancer had come back a few years ago. He had worked so hard to fight it the first time, and just like that, we were told he'd have to do it all over again.

Hope is a dangerous thing, and I learned to stop hoping a while ago. Unfortunately, I let my defenses down, and spent the last few weeks letting hope sneak its way in again, making me believe that not only do I get to finally start living my own life, but that there's a possibility I could have Rio with me while I do.

Silly of me to get so comfortable.

Well, I'm sure as hell not letting myself hope now. I'm planning for the confirmation that my dad's cancer is back, emotionally preparing myself for it. I'll handle it, just as I did the first and second time we were told.

In a way, it gets easier to receive the same bad news. There isn't a fear of the unknown looming over me. There aren't a million questions I have rattling in my brain. I already know the steps to take. I know the emotional toll that's coming, but I also know how to control myself from breaking down or showing my fear. I'll make a plan. We'll get him back into treatment. I'll handle it.

I was only nineteen the first time we found out my dad was sick, and the one person I wanted comfort from was him because that's how it works. Parents take care of their children. Then suddenly, I was taking care of him. I wanted to cry and tell him how scared I was. I wanted to admit everything I was worried about so he could tell me not to be. But he was scared himself, so I pretended I wasn't, and I've been pretending ever since.

The waiting room is eerily quiet with only the three of us in here. Me, my brother, and his wife. My dad has been going through testing all day, so Sarah got a sitter to stay with their son so she could be here for my brother while we wait for the results.

I'm glad they have each other, and I'm thankful that my brother was able to be here and keep me updated while I was making the six-hour drive from Chicago.

While yes, Luke has had a sick parent for as long as I have, we've had very different experiences. In a way, he was able to separate himself, living out of state and not having to see the daily decline the way I witnessed it firsthand.

Luke wasn't the one who was up with him while he was sick

from chemotherapy or begging him to eat when he didn't want to, so I'm sure this is all quite shocking to him. Eventually, he'll figure it out too, how to manage his expectations. How we always have to be ready for the other shoe to drop.

He and Sarah are sitting down the row from me. He's got his hand on her thigh, holding on to her like a lifeline and she's rubbing his back soothingly. Luke is visibly stressed while Sarah is the picture of strong and steady and I'm...envious.

I'm envious that Luke has a partner to lean on. Someone he can tell how scared he is. Someone he can break down to. I'm happy for him, but envious too. Envious that during the years I spent taking care of my dad, he had the chance to start his own life and family.

My only companion today is a soap opera playing on the waiting room television in front of me. It's not doing it for me. It's too dramatic when I need it to be the opposite. Too emotional when I can't be. So, without anyone else in the room, I grab the remote and change the channel.

I don't know what I'm looking for. At least, I don't think I do until I flip to a random sports network and find commentators discussing tonight's matchup between the Chicago Raptors and the Boston Bobcats.

Rio instantly comes to the forefront of my mind, which is a nice distraction from the stress.

I haven't listened to his voicemail yet. I haven't returned any of his texts either because I was busy driving. But there's the part of me that doesn't want to respond because I don't want to lie to him.

I'm going to have to tell him everything, especially if the tests confirm what I think they will. I've spent all this time avoiding the topic, but now, I don't see how I can anymore.

This is what's been holding me back from giving us another shot. It's not that I don't want to open up to him about what the past six years have looked like for me, but I'm terrified that when Rio realizes the timeline, he won't be able to forgive himself.

I don't want to hurt him, and this is going to.

"I'm going to go grab us some coffees while we wait." Sarah stands from her seat. "Hallie, can I get you one?"

I offer her a forced smile. "That'd be great. Thank you."

She squeezes my shoulder on her way out of the waiting room.

With only me and my brother left, he moves from his chair to take the one next to me, both of our attention on the screen.

He nods towards it. "Even after all this time, you still watch his games?"

"Pathetic, huh?"

"Completely." I smack him in the shoulder with the back of my hand, but he just laughs. "Kidding."

We sit in silence, listening to the commentators discuss the matchup between Boston and Chicago until eventually, Luke speaks up.

"You didn't have to come, you know. I could've called you after the results came back."

I shake my head. "I couldn't wait around. I felt like I had to do something."

"Yeah, I get that." He sounds exhausted. "Honestly, I have no idea how you did this for so long on your own."

Well, I didn't really have a choice.

It's on the tip of my tongue, but I can't say it. Today is not the day to make him feel worse than he already does.

"And for the Raptors," one of the commentators on the television says, stealing our attention. "Forward Victor Thompson has been added to the injured reserve list and tonight, defenseman Rio DeLuca is a healthy scratch. Which is a big surprise because Boston is DeLuca's hometown, and I know he's got a whole local fan club here to watch him."

What the hell?

I grab my phone to text him, but before I can, my dad's doctor comes out of a side door, headed straight for us. My brother and I stand as she approaches, prepared to get some answers from the oncologist that's helped my dad since we first moved back here for his treatment.

Sarah walks back in the room to meet us, dropping the coffees onto a nearby side table and slipping her hand into my brother's.

"Hey, guys," Dr. Young says. "Long day, huh?"

Neither Luke nor I answer her.

"I'll cut straight to the chase here."

In that half of a second, I brace for impact, telling myself about the bad news before she can.

"His test results look good," Dr. Young says. "We ran the usual ones, and nothing is showing signs of a relapse."

"Oh, thank God." My brother exhales, hands braced behind his head. "He's okay?"

Dr. Young smiles. "He's okay. His temperature is back in the normal range, and he hasn't spiked a fever since he's been here. But he is fairly dehydrated, so I want to keep him overnight, get him some fluids, and keep an eye on him."

"Yeah. Yeah, of course." Luke immediately turns to Sarah and hugs her, holding on with everything he's got, but I don't let myself dip into the emotional relief he's experiencing.

I keep my composure, asking all the follow-up questions until I feel satisfied in knowing he really is going to be okay. Even then, the only shift in my expression is a simple smile when I say, "Thank you, Dr. Young."

"Of course, Hallie. I'm going to fill your dad in on everything, but I wanted to give you kids some peace of mind. You can go back and visit him in a bit."

"Okay. Thank you."

Luke and Sarah are hugging again, this elated relief being shared between them, and I'm just standing there, not knowing what to do with my hands. Instead, I refocus on the television because not focusing on something feels awkward and uncomfortable while my brother and his wife are sharing this emotional moment.

But then all my attention shifts to the glass windows lining the waiting room wall, watching a man in a beanie jog down the hall in this direction. He pulls the door open to scan the room, finding me in no time.

All my fear, stress, and exhaustion begin to bubble to the surface in a way I've never let it, just from seeing Rio standing in the doorway of the hospital waiting room. He's concerned, that's evident in his expression, but it's also mixed with a bit of relief and a sense of protectiveness.

What is he doing here? But also, can he get to me a little quicker?

I must be in shock because I'm telling my feet to move, to meet him partway, but I'm not going anywhere. I'm frozen in place. But my disbelief doesn't seem to slow him down, because in three quick strides he has his arms wrapped tightly around me, pulling me into his chest.

"Are you okay?" he asks quietly, lips close to my ear.

Apparently that shock has translated into an inability to speak as well.

"What do you need?" he continues, burrowing his face against the nape of my neck.

This.

I need this. My body knows it too, as it melts into him, letting go of all the tension and stress I've been carrying. Because what I've always needed is *this*.

Taking a deep breath, I inhale his scent, finally coming to when I wrap my arms around his waist and hold on. I grip his flannel shirt in my fists, bury my face against his chest, and close my eyes.

"Hallie, baby," he whispers. "I've got you."

He has literally no idea what's going on, but still he holds me, one hand slipping into my hair, palm cupping my head as he keeps me hidden against his chest, like he's some kind of shield that could protect me.

Maybe he could.

I have so many questions, and I'm sure he does too. I pull back slightly to look up at him, those green eyes boring into mine. I don't think I've ever seen him look so concerned.

"What are you doing here?" I finally ask, swallowing down the emotion in my throat.

"Wren called me."

Wren, my roommate, who also asked me to share my location with her before I started my drive.

"But your game—"

"My *job*, you mean. I took the day off. I told them I had a family emergency. My agent booked me the first flight out of Boston."

Family emergency.

"This game is too important for you to miss."

"Hallie, I couldn't care less about that game right now. It's one of eighty-two."

Which is true, but this one felt more important than the rest.

He runs the pad of his thumb over my cheekbone, fingers still threaded through my hair, and eyes searching mine. "Are you okay?"

That question alone makes me want to cry because he's not prying for answers to what's going on. He's not upset that I didn't tell him I was here or hesitate to miss his game.

"Am I allowed to say no?"

A faint smile ghosts his lips. "Yeah, Hal. You can say no."

I hear someone shift on their feet behind me, only to remember my brother and his wife are here.

Rio notices too, glancing over my shoulder. "Luke."

My brother's tone is equally dry. "Rio."

"Come with me." Slipping my hand into his, I lead us out of the waiting room and into the hallway where we could have some privacy. People pass by us, but it still feels more private than allowing my brother to listen in on this conversation.

"What can I do?" he asks.

"Nothing. Everything is okay." I throw my thumb over my shoulder. "We just found out. I'm sorry you came all this way for nothing. Everything is okay."

His eyes bounce between mine. "But you're not."

No. No, I'm not okay. I've been on an adrenaline high all day, driving here as quickly as I could, waiting for the news. And now that I've got it, I feel the come down fast approaching.

I shake my head to tell him no.

As soon as I admit that, my eyes instantly burn with tears, which feels so ridiculous because everything is fine.

"Come here." His voice is hardly a whisper as he pulls me into him again.

"I don't know why I'm crying," I blurt out as the tears start falling in steady streams.

He rocks with me, rubbing a soothing palm down my back and letting me speak.

"I don't know what's wrong with me. I never cry over this kind of stuff. I'm just tired is all."

"It's okay to be tired." His voice goes soft. "It's okay to be scared too."

The permission has more tears falling. Because yeah, that's exactly how I've spent the last six years, and I've never been able to tell someone.

I'm not sobbing or shaking or anything like that. I'm just quietly soaking his shirt with my tears, letting it out, and it feels...good.

"I've never had anyone here before," I say, hidden against his chest. "I'm just emotional over it, I guess."

Rio's hand halts along my spine. "You should've had me."

The door behind me opens, and I look back to find Luke popping his head out into the hallway. "Dad wants to see you."

"Okay. I'll be right there."

Facing Rio again, I see his calming smile before he uses his thumbs to clean up the tear streaks under my eyes. "Take your time. I'm not going anywhere."

Words aren't coming to me today, so again, I nod, feeling too overwhelmed by him, by this day. He has absolutely no idea what's going on, and he seems okay with that. He's okay with just being here for me.

Wrapping my hand around the back of his neck, I pull him down so I can kiss him properly. "Thank you for being here."

He kisses me one more time. "I wouldn't be anywhere else."

28

Rio

After giving Hallie a head start, I walk back into the waiting room. There's no one else in here other than Luke and the woman sitting next to him.

It feels strange to sit clear across the room without acknowledging my childhood friend, so I don't. I take the empty seat on the other side of him.

Leaning forward, I extend my hand to the woman. "I'm Rio."

She offers me a kind smile as she shakes my hand. "Sarah. Luke's wife."

Oh shit. I had no idea he had gotten married. But how would I? It's not like I've talked to him since I left for Chicago.

"I'll give you guys a minute," she says, standing from her seat, taking her coffee, and stepping out into the hallway.

He and I sit facing forward, not looking at each other as I start the conversation. "So, you got married, huh?"

"Yep. Had a kid too."

"No shit? Wow. Congrats, man."

Luke pulls out his phone, showing me his lock screen. "This is Hudson. He recently turned two."

I chuckle at the picture of a two-year-old boy covered in

birthday cake. "He's cute."

"Well, he looks like his mother, thank God."

We share a quick laugh, but it's a bit awkward because we're both aware of how weird this all is. We haven't spoken in six years.

"You've made quite a name for yourself in the NHL," he says, keeping up the small talk.

"Yeah, I've been lucky to stay healthy and have a solid team around me."

He nods and then I nod, because again...awkward.

"Look, Luke—"

"If you're going to apologize about something from the past, don't worry about it. It was a long time ago, and I've moved on."

"Regardless, it was a shitty thing for me to do. To never call or text you back."

"It was, but it was a whole lot shittier that you did that to my sister, and she's clearly not pissed at you anymore, so why should I be?"

That feels like a punch to the gut if I've ever felt one. It's one thing to hear it from Hallie or to acknowledge it myself, but to know the people closest to her also recognize that I made a huge fucking mistake by leaving her behind, makes me wonder if any of this is repairable.

"But I'm not going to give you a hard time for that either," he continues. "I'd be a hypocrite if I went after you for abandoning her when I did the exact same thing."

"What do you mean by that?"

Luke looks over at me apprehensively, realizing just how out of the loop I am. "What exactly has Hallie told you about our dad?"

"Nothing. I have literally no idea what's going on."

His eyes go wide. "And you're here? Missing a game for this and everything?"

"I don't need to know what's going on to know that she needs someone here for her."

Luke pauses for a moment. "Yeah, you're right about that."

My phone dings in my pocket, cutting off our conversation.

H (heart emoji): *Could you come back here? My dad wants to see you. Room 424.*

I stand from my seat. "I'll be back."

"Hey, Rio," he calls after me. "Even if I didn't want to see it at first, you guys make a lot of sense together. And she deserves to get what she wants for once, so if she wants you, I hope you stick around this time."

All I can do is hope that she wants me.

"Yeah." I nod. "I'm not going anywhere."

Down the hall, I find room 424. The door is open, but still, I knock to make my presence known.

"Come on in," Mr. Hart says.

Rounding the corner, I find him sitting up on a hospital bed with Hallie at his bedside. She's no longer crying, once again the picture of strength and resilience. Same as she seemed when I first found her in the waiting room while Luke was hugging his wife.

"Is the all-star defenseman for the Chicago Raptors here to see me?"

Hallie shakes her head. "No need to hype him up, Dad."

"Good to see you, Mr. Hart. You look good."

"Don't lie to me, kid. I look like shit and we both know it."

He's got this playful edge to his tone, so it feels okay to laugh when he says it.

Even though it's only been six years since I've last seen him, Mr. Hart has aged more than that. His hair has grayed. His skin is sunken in. He's lost a lot of weight, and you can tell that his body has been through the ringer. But still, he's looking up at his daughter and smiling at her as he always has.

I do my best not to focus on any of the information written on the whiteboard the nurses use for their rotations. I try not to play detective and figure out what's going on because no one in their family has told me what's happening, and I'm doing my best to wait until they're ready to share.

"My dad didn't believe you were here," Hallie states. "Said he wanted proof."

"I'm here."

Mr. Hart rolls his eyes playfully. "About damn time."

I chuckle. "Yeah. I deserve that."

"Dad!"

"What? I'm dying. You expect me to hold my tongue?"

"Jesus, Dad. You're not dying. Your doctor told us that you're perfectly fine. Dehydrated but fine. Though I should ask her if that fever wiped out any filter you may have had."

He pats his daughter's hand. "Hallie girl, we're all dying."

"You're so morbid sometimes, I swear."

I have absolutely no problem being the punching bag here, especially because the energy feels light and easy. The opposite of what I originally walked into in the waiting room. Hallie is smiling and teasing after having a cry, and I fucking love that.

"Dad, Rio has a long drive home, so we should let him get going." Hallie looks at me. "Oh. I drove your truck here. I probably should've mentioned that."

My smile goes soft as I look at her. "I was hoping you did."

"Or are you flying back? I can drive your car back in a few days."

I didn't really think that far ahead. I was desperate to get to her, but now that things seem settled here and she's okay, I should get back to Chicago for our game tomorrow night.

"Rio, are you okay to drive back tonight?" Mr. Hart asks.

"Yeah, I'm good."

"Good. Take Hallie home with you."

"Dad—"

"As you said, the doctor told us that I'm fine. You're going back to Chicago with him. You need to get back to your life. I'm not your responsibility anymore." He looks to me. "Rio, you make sure she goes with you, okay? And be careful with my girl."

That phrase feels too familiar. This situation feels like a

recurring dream, and my throat goes tight when I realize he said the exact same thing to me the very first time I drove Hallie home.

Nodding, I swallow. "Always, sir."

He smiles at me. "I knew I always liked you."

"All right, Dad. No need to kiss his ass. He's not that great."

I laugh. "Yeah, I kind of thought you would have hated me by now, Mr. Hart."

"Nope," Hallie cuts in. "Dad, I don't think you've missed more than a handful of Rio's games since he's been in the league, huh?"

He lifts a brow. "We both know I wasn't the only one watching."

I tilt my head as I look at her. "Oh, is that so?"

"Big hockey fan," she says. "Couldn't care less about the players themselves, though." Hallie shoots me a smile to tell me she's full of shit and does, in fact, care about one.

Mr. Hart grabs her hand again. "Hallie, go home. I love you but you need to go home. This isn't on you anymore. I'm perfectly fine."

I watch her watch him, as if she's searching for any sign that he isn't okay before she eventually gives in. "Okay. But I'm going to call you tomorrow and check in."

"I'm looking forward to it." He nods towards the door. "Go say goodbye to your brother. I want to talk to Rio for a minute."

"Dad, please don't."

"Dying man, remember?"

Her attention darts to me, an apology written all over her face.

I shake her off, silently telling her I'm fine and that I can handle this. "I'll meet you out there."

She bends down to hug her dad before giving my arm a squeeze on the way out of the door. I close it behind her, giving us privacy, grabbing a chair in the corner and bringing it to his bedside so I can take a seat.

"You're very lucky," he starts.

"I know. I know I made some mis—"

"No, I mean you're *both* very lucky. To have found each other again. Don't throw it away this time."

"I won't. I'm trying not to, at least. Hallie's not ready to forgive me, which I understand. I have no issue being patient and trying to make up for the years we missed."

"She's already forgiven you, Rio. But those years you didn't see each other were not easy for her, so I don't blame her for taking her time in letting you know that." He eyes me for a moment. "Do you know why I'm here?"

I could make an educated guess, seeing how many signs I saw plastered on the walls of this building. This hospital is one of the top cancer research facilities in the country.

"I don't know for certain."

"I'm in remission from blood cancer. Non-Hodgkin lymphoma. My second remission, actually. Today was thankfully only a scare, but that's what our past six years have been consumed by. Me and this disease."

The confirmation makes my stomach drop. It's a weird mixture of relief that he's not currently sick, and guilt knowing that he was. Not only because this man was such a kind person in my life growing up, but because Hallie loves him so fucking much, that imagining how scared she's probably been makes me physically ill.

"I need you to take care of her," he continues. "Because she's spent so many years taking care of me, but I couldn't do the same for her. I don't know that I'd still be here if it weren't for the sacrifices she made for me."

There's this ominous air lingering in the room. Like I'm about to put a lot of the missing pieces together, all while knowing I'm probably not going to like the final picture.

Regardless, I need to know.

I lean forward in my chair, knees to my elbows. "Can you explain what that means? What all happened since I last saw you guys? Because I don't know if Hallie will, and even if she did, she's going to downplay it, but I need to know the truth."

He doesn't even hesitate. "Well, for starters, as soon as I was diagnosed, she did endless research to find the best oncologists and treatment centers. We got lucky that this is one of the best cancer research hospitals out there, and I happen to be from here. I had a childhood friend who practiced here who got me into a trial. Hallie dropped out of school and moved to Minnesota to take care of me."

My eyes shoot to his.

"She eventually finished taking online courses at night or while I was busy getting treatment. She'd sit next to me the whole time and do it from her computer. That was a hard pill to swallow, knowing I was the reason she was missing out. She had worked so hard to put herself through school."

The last time I had seen Hallie was the summer after her freshman year of college. I had gotten drafted five weeks prior and was planning our move to Chicago. Hallie was looking into transferring to a university in the city so we could live together. I assumed she continued classes where she was already enrolled. I had no idea she dropped out.

"We sold the house back in Boston," he continues. "But the market was terrible at the time. We didn't make anything from the sale, and I wasn't able to work once we moved because of how sick the treatments made me. Thankfully, the trial covered housing and included a caregiver's stipend, but still, things were tight. Hallie worked any odd job she could find to get us by while also making it to every one of my appointments. She was suddenly taking care of me, when I was supposed to be taking care of her, you know?"

Nodding, my nose pricks with heat and the back of my eyes burn. There's an overwhelming sense of pride flowing through me, knowing that Hallie took this on all on her own and handled it. But that's coupled with immense guilt. Our years apart couldn't have been more different. I was busy living out my dream, while unknowingly leaving her to deal with this nightmare all on her own.

My voice is hoarse when I ask, "Where's her mom?"

Mr. Hart waves me off like she's the least important piece of the story. "She said something pretty horrible around the time of my original diagnosis that none of us have been able to forgive her for."

"And Luke?" I ask. "Where was he during all of this?"

"He was doing what any twenty-something should've been doing. Living his life. Finishing school. He wasn't ready to pause everything for me, and I can't blame him for that. Once he got married, I think Sarah opened his eyes to what his sister had been handling all on her own and that she needed her turn to live her life. They moved back to Minnesota last year, and Hallie left for Chicago shortly after that."

I'd be a hypocrite if I went after you for abandoning her when I did the exact same thing.

I'd like to go out there and give my old friend a piece of my mind for not helping his sister when she needed it, but what ground do I have to stand on? I fucking left her too.

"When um..." I clear my throat. "When did you find out you were sick for the first time?"

He eyes me for a moment, and for a man who's been so forthcoming with this conversation, he hesitates for a long while. "I think that part of the story should come from Hallie."

There's that pit in my stomach again, telling me I'm not going to like the answer.

The puzzle gets clearer, and as I suspected, I hate what it looks like.

It's no wonder Hallie hasn't wanted to give us another chance. Why would she?

I didn't just break up with her and move away. I left her when I promised her forever. And not only that, I left her to fend for herself when everyone else did too. And I'm not only referring to financially taking care of herself, but she had to emotionally take care of herself too. That was my job, and I didn't do it because I was so focused on my own life falling apart. For years, I couldn't see past my own bullshit, when all the while, she's been dealing with this.

Fuck me. I wouldn't forgive me either.

"Rio," Mr. Hart says, pulling my focus back to him. "You're adults now. Don't let your parents' lives dictate your decisions this time. You get to choose for yourselves if you want to forgive each other, and I hope you do."

I shake my head. "She shouldn't forgive me. I don't even think *I* can forgive me."

"You didn't know. I need you to give yourself a little grace, okay? I need you to take care of her and you're not going to be able to if you're too busy regretting past decisions. She needs someone to take care of her for once. Can you do that for me?"

Can I do it? Absolutely. Should she give me another opportunity to? Probably fucking not.

The things I was angry at her for so long seem impossibly inconsequential now. I was holding a grudge because she didn't tell me about my dad, while her hurt was because I left her when she needed me the most.

Regardless of what I didn't know at the time, she wins. Hallie has every right to hate me.

29

Hallie

His light is still on. It's the middle of the night, we've been back home for a couple of hours, and his bedroom light is still on.

Sure, I'm still awake too, but that's because I got to sleep most of the drive home. But not Rio. When I offered to trade off so he could have a break from driving, he refused, assuring me he was wide awake.

He still is, judging by the glaring light coming from his bedroom that I can see from mine.

His demeanor was off as soon as he left my dad's hospital room. He was quiet and in his head. The silence between us on the ride home felt suffocating, and I knew then that he knew everything.

I waited for him to ask some follow-up questions, for us to talk about the things he now knows, but he didn't say a word. But whenever I looked over at him, it felt like I could physically see him attempting to wrap his head around it all.

Standing at my window, I check on his room again, willing the light to go off next door so he can get some sleep. After traveling for work all week, catching a last-minute flight to Minnesota, and driving us all the way back to Chicago, I know he's exhausted.

I also know his mind is probably moving at a mile a minute right now.

Screw it. We can talk if he wants or I can lie down next to him so he can get some rest, but either way, I'm going over there.

I grab my keys, throw on a pair of shoes, and cross the yard to his house. It's pitch black out. Only the light from his bedroom is on. I use it to find the latch on his gate, going through his backyard and unlocking the back door with the house key he gave me.

I don't know why I didn't choose the front door. I guess I'm so accustomed to sneaking around with Rio, that slipping through the backyard in the middle of the night feels more on brand for us.

Locking up behind me, I quietly make my way through the first floor, up the stairs, and to his bedroom door. It's left open for me to see Rio sitting on the edge of his bed with his back to me. He's bent forward, elbows on his knees, and shoulders slumped.

I'm about to knock, to make my presence known, when he speaks first.

"Use the front door, Hallie."

I stay frozen in the doorway, unable to move.

"We don't need to sneak across rooftops and through windows anymore. We're adults and I'm not hiding this again. Use the front door."

Oh.

Still, he doesn't turn around to look at me, so I cross the room and round the bed. Moving to stand between his legs, I force him to sit up and look at me. It takes a second for those green eyes to make their way to mine, but when they do, the anguish in them cracks something inside of me. I think it's the rest of that armor I've been trying to wear around him.

"I take it he told you everything."

Rio's jaw tics and he pulls his eyes away from me again. He doesn't seem angry though. He looks like he's on the verge of crying and trying his best not to.

I'm exhausted. Tired from today. Tired from trying to resist this, but I can't imagine how exhausted he is. His mind has been running nonstop for at least the last six hours, but after listening to that voicemail he left me while he was visiting his mom, I'd imagine he hasn't stopped overthinking all day.

"I'll tell you everything you want to know, Rio. You can ask me anything."

He's quiet for a moment before he finally makes eye contact again. "Are you okay?" is his first question. It's gentle and sweet, with an edge of worry in his tone.

Nodding, I ask, "Are you?"

He gives me the slightest shake of his head to tell me no.

"Talk to me."

Standing between his legs, I feel him cup the back of my thigh with his palm. His thumb strokes back and forth against my skin as he mulls over something in his mind. "Why are you working so much, Hallie?"

Well, that was not the question I was expecting.

But I'm not lying to him anymore. Today felt like a shift. An important one, so I swallow my pride and tell him the truth. "Because I'm in debt."

He doesn't react at all. "And why are you in debt?"

Searching his face, I realize he already knows the answer. That's why he's not reacting. No, my dad didn't tell him because he has no idea about it, but this is Rio. The person who knows me better than anyone, even all these years later.

"I think you already know."

"Your dad's cancer trial. The insurance didn't cover as much as you let him believe."

I shake my head. "It didn't cover housing or moving expenses. There was no caregiver stipend like I told him there was. But he wouldn't have done the trial if he knew that, and I needed him to get better. So, I told him everything was covered. I took out a loan to make it happen."

Rio's brows knit together, but he doesn't say anything, so I continue.

"I was working on paying it back when he was in remission the first time. I was able to work more hours, but then he got sick again and needed me. I couldn't make the payments. Interest compounded and well...it got expensive."

Again, he doesn't say anything, and there's a part of me that wonders if I'm being judged for being careless with my money, but I didn't think it was careless back then. I still don't.

"As soon as I get hired full-time at the design firm, I'll be able to pay it down quicker. I'm just trying to stay on top of it as best I can until—"

"Hallie," he cuts me off. "You don't owe me an explanation. You were taking care of your family. I'd do the same thing if I were in your position." Shaking his head, he's having a hard time looking me in the eye again. "But you should have never been in that position in the first place and I'm so fucking sorry for putting you there."

I knew this was coming. I knew he was going to feel guilty. That he'd blame himself.

I'll admit, when I was younger, there was a part of me that wanted him to know how hard things were after he left. I wanted him to feel like shit for leaving me the way he did. But not anymore. Neither of us can change our choices, and dwelling on them is only going to fill us with regret.

I don't stop running the pads of my thumbs in soothing strokes against his cheeks as I give him a minute to gather himself.

Eventually, he tilts his head back and looks up at me. "When did you find out he was sick?"

That is something I can't tell him right now. Not when he's already so busy beating himself up from everything else he's learned today.

"Rio, it's late. Let's get some sleep."

His eyes are filled with dread as he looks up at me, like he already knows what I'm going to say. "When?"

I exhale a resigned sigh, knowing he's not going to let this go until I tell him. "The summer you got drafted. Two weeks before you left for training camp in Chicago."

I watch as he tries to process it, as he tries to understand the timeline. I see the moment it clicks because he looks like he got the wind knocked out of him.

"Please tell me that's not true."

All I can do is offer him a sad smile and watch his entire demeanor deflate more than it already was.

I hadn't gotten a chance to tell him about my dad's diagnosis all those years ago because twenty-four hours after I learned about it, I found out that *his* dad was having an affair.

I was so scared for so many reasons, and suddenly, I didn't know how to tell him anything.

Leaning forward, he drops his forehead to my stomach to hide his face from me. "You weren't yourself at all those last two weeks. I remember that. After everything came out, I figured it was because you had known about my dad and were trying to keep it from me."

I run my fingers through his hair, attempting to soothe him. "It was partly that. But I was also scared about my dad being sick and not knowing what that was going to look like for us. I was supposed to move to Chicago with you, and I didn't know how to tell you that I might not be able to go anymore."

He shakes his head. "What the fuck is wrong with me?"

"Rio—"

He lifts his head to look at me, and I don't think I've ever seen him so heartbroken. He's trying his best not to cry. To keep it together.

"I left you to deal with all of that on your own, Hallie. Do not try to make me feel better about this."

"You didn't know."

He breathes a self-deprecating laugh. "Because I never gave

you a chance to tell me. All this time, I thought if you could forgive me for leaving, then maybe we could have another shot at us. But this?" He shakes his head. "I wouldn't give me another chance either."

"Rio, that's not... Maybe initially, yes. I didn't want to give you the time of day because you hurt me. But when things started to shift, when it started to feel how it used to feel between us, I knew I was going to have to tell you everything and I was terrified to. I didn't want you to blame yourself."

His eyes go wide. "You were afraid that my own actions would hurt my feelings? Jesus, Hallie. You should hate me, not protect me."

"But I've always protected you. At least I tried to, and that hasn't changed."

He watches me for a moment, eyes searching my face. "For a while, I convinced myself that I had every right to feel the way I did, but before I even found out about your dad, I knew I was lying to myself. I even called you about it earlier today. I wanted to try to explain how fucked up my head was at the time, but to find out I left you with all of this? I should've been there."

I shake my head to tell him no. "You don't need to explain anything. When I'm logical about it, I know why you left. Rio, you were heartbroken over your parents."

"Don't make excuses for me. Your parents split up too. I'm assuming that's what your dad meant, and I've spent all this time focused on *my* family falling apart, while you were going through the same fucking thing."

"I wasn't though. My parents' divorce did not affect me the same way yours did."

His brows furrow. "What are you talking about?"

"You held your parents' relationship on a pedestal as this ideal picture of what love should look like, but I didn't view my parents' relationship that way." I take his face in my hands, making sure his attention is on me. "That's how I viewed *ours*."

He stares at me, and this time he doesn't fight the tears from welling in his eyes. He doesn't wipe them away when they fall either. So, with my thumbs I gently clean them off.

"You have every right to hate me, Hal. You have every right to believe that I forgot about you, but I didn't. Not one day went by that I didn't think of you. You were everywhere. In the music I listened to. In the house I live in. I tried to compare every single person I met to you, but there was no comparison. And I will spend the rest of my life regretting leaving you behind all those years ago."

There's no point in telling him I forgive him or asking him to forgive himself right now. Anything I say will fall on deaf ears. He won't be able to hear me take responsibility for my part in our breakup, or when I tell him I don't blame him for something he didn't know about. He's just going to be hard on himself for a while.

Instead, I go into his closet, retrieve the black cardboard box I found last week, and set it on the nightstand.

His eyes flick to it as I open the lid.

"Rio, I know you didn't forget about me."

He studies the box for a minute, and I'm hoping he's not going to be so hard on himself right now that he brushes this off. To anyone else, him keeping these might seem like no big deal, but to me, this is our everything. Not just the songs, but the moments they represent too.

"Come here," he says, tugging at my hand to pull me onto his lap.

I go willingly, thankful that he's open to this conversation.

"When we were in New York, you asked me why I never upgraded that old boombox. Do you remember that?"

I nod.

"This is why," he says. "I didn't have any other way to play the tapes and CDs, and not playing them wasn't an option for me. For years, I've taken this fucking boombox everywhere with me.

Held on to it, like if I could keep rewinding and replaying these moments we had, then maybe it wasn't over." He pulls a random cassette tape out of the box, running his thumb over the inked heart. "I don't want it to be over, Hallie."

Using the tip of his finger, he covers the tail of that overdrawn heart, and it makes me want to cry. Not from sadness or painful nostalgia. But from hope.

Hope that now that everything is on the table, maybe we can move forward.

I lean my head on his shoulder. "I can't believe you kept them all this time."

"Well, I know that technically, these are *your* best memories, but they're mine too. Meeting on that roof, listening to music. Getting the opportunity to fall in love with you is *my* best memory, and all I can do is hope that one day you'll let me do it again."

Hallie

(AGE 18)

"Hey, Dad," I whisper, closing the front door behind me. He's sitting on the couch, reading a book, and waiting for me to get home as I knew he would be.

"Hey, Hallie girl. Did you have a good time?"

I try to put on my best smile. "It was all right. I think maybe the idea of senior prom was a little more exciting than the execution."

Mostly because I didn't get to go with the person I wanted to. Rio had the last final of his freshman year of college today and couldn't make it back to Boston in time, so I went with my platonic guy friend instead. It just wasn't what I had always pictured prom would look like.

"Well, you look beautiful," my dad continues. "I can't believe you're almost done with high school."

"Dad, don't get all sappy on me now. At least let me get to graduation before that."

He smiles at me, but it's kind of sad and I know that all he's thinking about right now is that in a few short months, I'll be off to college, just like Luke. He and my mom will officially be empty nesters, but the DeLucas next door already are, so at least they'll have each other.

"Where's Luke?" I ask.

My brother's lacrosse season is still in full swing, but they play Boston College tomorrow, so he's home for the night.

"He went out to catch up with some old friends he hadn't seen in a while, but he was in a foul mood when he left. I have no idea what's up with him."

"Weird. I'll check in with him tomorrow and make sure he's okay."

"Please do."

"Well, I'm going to get some sleep."

"All right, Hallie girl. Love you."

"Love you too." Halfway up the stairs, I turn back and ask, "Hey, Dad, do you want to go get breakfast tomorrow? Just the two of us before Luke's game?"

His previously sad smile turns up at the corners. "I'd love that. I'll see you in the morning."

Slipping my heels off, I carry them the rest of the way to my room. The house is quiet tonight, like it's been all year. Without my brother around, without Rio here, it's just...quiet.

Senior year was fine, I suppose. I hung out with my friends and did all the high school activities you're supposed to do in your final year, but I spent most of the time counting down the days to when Rio would be home for his breaks. Unfortunately, it wasn't very often with his college hockey season running straight through from October to April.

His visit for Christmas only lasted forty-eight hours because of their game schedule. He was traveling for hockey during his spring break, and of course, I already knew he wouldn't make it home for my birthday.

Playing a division one sport may as well be a full-time job on top of being a full-time student, so Rio's free time was limited all year. I knew how this transition year was going to go, but knowing something doesn't make it any easier to accept.

It was hard. I was lonely, and it's not like I could hop on a plane and go see him. I had my own school schedule to stay on top of, not to mention the little detail hanging over us that neither one of our families knows we're together.

He's been especially off these last few days, blaming it on his finals schedule, but I don't know. I'm trying to not overthink the distance or that he still hasn't told my brother about us, but I'm human and it's difficult not to.

He'll be home later this week, so I suppose I'll find out soon.

Closing my bedroom door behind me, I'm instantly hit with a draft of cold air. And when I flip my light on, I find my window pushed open all the way, my curtains dramatically blowing in the breeze.

That window hasn't been open in months, and I could count on one hand how many times it's been open this year since Rio hasn't been home to sneak through it.

Unless he is...

I rush across the room, hands braced on the windowsill to find him sitting smack dab in the middle of our houses on the roof. *Our* roof. He's got his knees bent and his arms leaning on them, hood covering his face, but I know it's him.

What is he doing home already? And why didn't he tell me he was here?

I don't waste time by grabbing a sweatshirt to wear over my prom dress. I don't bother with putting shoes on my bare feet. I just need to see him. So, while wearing my floor-length satin dress, I climb out my window.

"Rio?" I tentatively ask, staying close to my house. "What are you doing home already?"

He shakes his head, exhaling a defeated laugh. "I was trying to surprise you by making it home in time to take you to prom, but my flight got delayed."

What?

"You were?"

"I bought an earlier plane ticket home."

"That's why you've been so distant the past few days?"

"I'm not a good liar, Hal. I didn't want to risk ruining the surprise." He doesn't fully turn to face me, only giving me his right profile, but still his eyes slowly work their way up my body. "You look beautiful, baby."

I take a step closer. "Thank you. But I wish I knew you were coming. I would've waited for you."

"I only got here thirty minutes ago and telling you I was trying to make it would only disappoint you on your big night."

I huff a laugh. "It wasn't all that big. It was pretty uneventful, actually."

I watch the outline of his jaw tic. "And your date?"

"My *friend*," I correct. "I spent the whole time hyping him up to go ask the girl he's been crushing on if she wanted to dance."

His body moves in a silent laugh.

I step closer. "But the whole night, I was wishing I was with you."

Finally, he turns my way, fully facing me and allowing the light from the moon to illuminate his entire face.

His very *swollen* face. Particularly his left eye that's already forming a bruise.

"What is... Is that from hockey?" I rush to him, kneeling to make myself eye level. Gripping his chin, I push his hood off so I can get a better look. "Did you take a hit in practice?"

His eyes drop to my lips. "No."

I run a gentle thumb over a split area, and he flinches slightly.

"What the hell happened?"

"Luke."

"What do you mean *Luke*? He hit you?"

Rio shrugs like this is the most casual conversation. "Well, I let him, but yeah."

"Why would you let him? And why would he do that?"

"I let him because I deserved it for lying to him for so long, and he hit me because he was furious after I told him I was in love with his sister."

My eyes go impossibly wide. For multiple reasons.

I fall back to a sitting position, my yellow satin gown falling around me. "What?"

"I told him. I couldn't hide it anymore, Hal. This year was fucking miserable without you, and I can't do another that way. You were on my mind practically every minute of every day. I wanted to fly you out to Michigan so many times. I needed to see you, but I couldn't because your family didn't know. I wanted to—"

"You love me?"

"Well, yeah." He softens with a smile. "Isn't that obvious?"

"You don't think you should've told me before you told my brother?"

"Shit." Realization dawns on his handsome but bruised face. "I didn't think of it like that. I mean, I've loved you since I was twelve. I thought that was another one of those unspoken things."

I can't help but laugh because, wow, that feels good to hear after a year apart. "This is something that should maybe be spoken out loud."

"Well, then." He takes my hand, pulling me towards him. With my long dress gathering above my knees, I straddle his lap, putting us face to face. "I love you, Hallie Hart. I am *in* love with you, though I hope that doesn't come as a surprise. Because if so, I've been doing something wrong all these years."

I shake my head, smiling. "No, you've been doing it all right. I've just been missing you, and it's nice to hear it said."

"God, you have no idea how lonely I've been without you."

"So have I."

"We're not hiding this anymore. I'm done pretending like we haven't planned out our entire future. I'm done acting like you're not mine."

I wrap my arms around his shoulder, smiling against his lips. "But I am yours."

"Damn right, you are."

"Mmm." I teasingly kiss along his jaw. "And you're mine."

"Always, Hal."

"Rio?"

"Hmm?" he asks, lips dotting a path of kisses along my collarbone.

"I love you too."

I feel him smile against my skin before he pulls back so I can see it. "Stay with me tonight?"

I quickly agree. "Your room or mine?"

"Mine." He pauses for a moment, giving the words a chance to sink in. "My parents aren't home."

Oh. *Oh.*

I search his face, and I don't think I'll ever get over the way this boy looks at me. He looks like he loves me and has since the first day he saw me. I understand that sentiment all too well.

"Only if you want to," he continues. "We can wait—"

"No," I quickly disagree. "I don't want to wait any longer."

His smile turns up before he leans in and presses his lips to mine softly. We take our time, kissing for a long while, moving together.

"Come with me," he whispers against my mouth.

He helps me stand from his lap before he takes my hand and walks me back to his bedroom window, letting me go through first.

I've been in his room countless times over the years but tonight, everything feels different. Bigger. More charged.

He puts on some music and the sound helps drown out the pounding beat of my heart.

Rio crosses the room and locks his door before leaning back on it as he watches me move around his room, nervously checking out things I've already seen a thousand times.

Eventually, my eyes track back to him, and I don't think I've ever seen his eyes so heated.

"I love that dress on you, baby."

"Thank you. It's—"

"Take it off."

My lips part of their own accord because, wow, I *like* this version of him.

Reaching behind me, I unclasp the hook at the center of my back with trembling fingers as Rio slowly makes his way back over. Standing in front of me, he slips his hands around my waist and places his hands over my shaking ones to stop me.

"Are you nervous?" he asks softly.

I nod. "Are you?"

He nods too.

That makes me smile and it makes me settle. The way he always does.

"You tell me to stop if you want me to stop." He takes over, slowly unzipping my dress, his eyes trained on my face the whole time. "We'll take it slow and figure it out together, okay?"

My hands aren't shaking anymore. My heart is no longer racing.

I watch him slowly slip a strap off my shoulder.

"I'm glad it's you."

He breathes a small laugh before pressing his smiling lips to mine. "It's always been you, Hallie."

31

Rio

"Miller, can I get you another?" Stevie asks, standing from the floor where she's sitting next to me.

Miller holds up the same Corona she's been nursing all night. "I'm one and done these days."

"Says the woman who met her husband while literally double-fisting on a weekday morning." Kennedy's head falls back in laughter.

"Yeah, well, your girl has two kids and two businesses now. I can't afford to wake up hungover."

Stevie silently takes inventory of Kennedy's and Indy's empty drinks before turning to me. "Rio, another glass of wine?"

I check my glass to see how much is left, only to realize I've barely had any, regardless that I poured it over an hour ago.

"I think I'm going to be one and done tonight too."

"Girls' nights have certainly changed, haven't they?" Stevie says, heading into Indy's kitchen to grab another round for everyone but me and Miller.

I can feel Indy watching me from the couch. "Rio, are you all right?"

Nodding quickly, I tell her, "Of course, I am."

Her eyes narrow suspiciously, but thankfully her attention is pulled away when Stevie returns with a new drink for her.

I probably should've bailed on hanging out tonight, seeing as I've been feeling off for days. But it only happens once in a while that these girls can get together without their kids or the guys, and though I fall into the "guys" category and technically shouldn't be included in girls' night, it's never stopped me from attending before.

After spending all day, every day with a bunch of dudes, I value my time and friendship with these four. Plus, I was hoping that seeing my friends would pull me out of my head.

It hasn't.

I've played like absolute garbage in the two games since we got back from seeing Hallie's dad. I can't focus. I can't stop beating myself up. I barely sleep, and though that's nothing new, I wake up from the few hours I do get feeling like I got kicked in the stomach when reality sinks in again.

I've still seen Hallie almost every day, either at my house when she's meeting with contractors, or when I drive her home at night from the bar. But it feels different.

I'm making it feel different because I can't look at her and not hate myself for letting her go. Honestly, I don't know how she can even look at *me*. I can't change the past now, but I don't know how she'd ever be able to move on from what I've done and see a future together. And that is a terrifying realization that's been constantly floating around in my head this week.

"Rio?"

Kennedy's voice pulls me out of my head, and I snap out of it to find all four of them looking at me. "Huh?"

"I was saying that we're all coming to your game against San Jose at the end of the month. It might be the last one that Isaiah and I can make it to for a while since we leave for spring training soon."

"Oh." I nod. "Cool."

"Do you think Hallie would want to join us?" Miller asks.

"Yeah...um. I don't know. Maybe."

Indy nudges Miller's shoulder. "Should we bring the kids, or do you think your hot dad would be up for babysitting?"

"Gross." She grimaces. "You guys have got to stop calling him that."

"We can't," Stevie chimes in. "Even my husband refers to Monty as Miller's hot dad."

Kennedy is trying to hold back her laughter. "Who started that?"

"Ryan," Indy and Stevie say at the same time.

"I think the boys might be in love with him," Indy continues. "Both of them always talk about hoping to look as good as him at that age. And 'did you see how fucking jacked Miller's hot dad is?'"

"And Zee is constantly drooling over Monty's tattoos," Stevie adds.

"Why?" Miller could not look more disgusted. "Zee is fully tatted up himself."

"Yes, but they're not Miller's hot dad's tattoos."

Miller closes her eyes. "I hate this so much."

Kennedy can't stop laughing, but she doesn't chime in on the conversation. Probably because Miller's dad is not only her colleague, but also Isaiah's coach, and that would just make things weird.

Stevie swats my leg. "How does that make you feel to know that Ryan Shay has himself a man-crush, but it isn't you?"

I shrug.

Everyone's eyes narrow.

"I mean, yeah," I amend. "Have you seen Monty?"

That doesn't do anything to sway their suspicion. Probably because I'm mentally checked out and there's no playfulness in my tone the way there is ninety-nine percent of the time.

"Rio," Indy says softly. "Something is up. Is Hallie's dad okay?"

They're all aware I missed the Boston game and of course, I told Zee what was going on before I left for the airport, so I couldn't exactly keep certain facts from my friends.

But they don't know the details. Only that Hallie's dad had a scare, and I wanted to be there.

I shake my head. "Yeah. It's not that."

Well, not entirely.

Indy watches me. "You know you can tell us anything, right? If you need to talk about something."

My attention bounces around the room to each of them. I've seen every single one of their relationships form from the beginning to now. I was on the plane the day Stevie met Zee. Indy stayed at my house in the few days she wasn't sure Ryan saw a future with her or not. I still remember the night when we all figured out that Miller was in love with Kai, even if she hadn't realized it herself. And Kennedy... Well, I watched Isaiah obsess over her for years before she married him.

But I've never needed advice in the relationship department because for the last six years, I didn't take anything past an introductory date.

Because no one else was the girl I had been in love with since I was twelve.

"Rio," Kennedy says cautiously. "Do you want to talk about something?"

"I think I need some advice."

Four way too excited smiles reflect back at me, like they've been waiting the entire duration of our friendship for this opportunity.

"But this stays here," I continue. "There are two reasons why I never talked about Hallie before. One, is that when I left Boston, I tried my best to pretend that part of my life didn't exist. And two, because I blamed Hallie for the reason I wanted to forget it all, and I didn't want any of you to think less of her. But I've recently come to the realization that I was the one who fucked everything up, and I'm perfectly okay with you guys thinking less of *me*. I need to get this off my chest because I don't know where to go from here."

Miller leans forward, chin in her hands as she listens intently. "Tell us everything."

And so, I do.

"It all started when I was twelve. I was outside playing hockey when our new neighbors pulled into their driveway for the first time."

I continue to tell them everything. How we met. How we became friends. How we spent her thirteenth birthday and every one after that. I tell them how we fell in love. How I viewed my parents' relationship and how I thought I had found the same thing. How Hallie was and still is the only woman I've *ever* loved.

I tell them why we kept it a secret from our families and how when we finally told them about our relationship, everyone but her brother had already figured it out.

I tell them about the summer I got drafted and about all the plans we made for our life here in Chicago. I tell them about my dad and what Hallie accidentally found out. I tell them about how angry I was that she didn't tell me, and how broken my mom was afterward.

I tell them how fucked up their divorce made me. I tell them about the grudge I held for years over Hallie not telling me the truth. I tell them about how I essentially ran away, thinking I left everything behind, only to spend the next six years comparing every person I met to her.

Without giving details that aren't mine to share, I tell them that her dad had been sick, and I only recently found out. I tell them the timeline of when she got the news and how it only added to the reason why she didn't tell me about my own dad, though I had already forgiven that detail before I knew anything else.

I tell them what she was left to deal with and how mad I am at myself for putting her in that position. And I tell them how I haven't been able to stop thinking about how badly I fucked up and ruined the best thing I've ever had in my life.

But I don't tell them the small things. The pieces that really make our story *ours*. The things that are special because only Hallie and I understand their significance.

"So yeah," I finish. "That's the whole story."

The room is completely silent. Looking around, I find four gaping mouths unable to find any words to say.

And then there's Indy...

"Indy." I furrow my brows. "Are you crying?"

"Of course, I am!" She wipes at her face. "I'm always crying, so I don't know why you're surprised. But that is the most beautiful story I've ever heard, and I just love love, okay?"

"Did you not hear the ending? I fucked it all up."

The other three who aren't crying, start laughing instead.

Stevie shakes her head, trying to contain her smile. "No, you lovable idiot. You didn't."

"Damn," Miller exhales. "If Kai hadn't already convinced me, that right there would've made me believe in love."

"That story makes me want to go home and see Isaiah." Kennedy leans her head on her sister-in-law's shoulder. "Then ask him why he only pursued me for three years before we got married when he should've started thinking about me at the age of twelve."

That finally makes me smile, which feels nice.

Indy keeps wiping at her face, cleaning herself up. "I always thought that the first time you brought someone around, we'd have to interrogate them or something. Figure out their intentions and decide if they were good enough for you. Like four overbearing and overprotective sisters, but..." She shakes her head. "I like this outcome so much more."

I set my still full glass of wine on the coffee table in front of me. "I know you all thought I had literally no game, and that's why I had never been with anyone the whole time I've lived here. But the reality is, I just wasn't interested. I wanted to be. I really wanted to prove myself right that Hallie wasn't the one, but every person I met further confirmed that she was."

"Stop." Stevie falls back onto the floor next to me. "I love hearing you talk like this."

Miller is laughing. "No one actually thought that, Rio."

"You really think we believed you went on these first dates and not a single person was interested in a second?" Indy laughs. "First of all, have you looked in a mirror? And secondly, you're you. Who wouldn't be interested?"

"What the hell?" My voice raises. "I hit on every single one of you over the years. And none of you were interested."

Kennedy rolls her eyes. "We don't count."

"I'm just saying," Indy continues, "we knew you weren't as hopeless as you led us to believe you were, but I wasn't going to push you to tell me why you wanted us to think that."

I huff a laugh. "I guess I thought it was easier to sell that story than have to explain why *I* wasn't interested in anyone. I didn't want you to know about Hallie because I know what you all would've said."

Indy lifts a brow. "That you should go get her?"

"Exactly."

Stevie sits up. "Well then, we'll say it now. Rio, you should go get her."

Miller holds up her nearly empty beer. "Take it from me. There's no point in running away."

"Again," Kennedy tacks on.

I shake my head. "She's not going to forgive me."

"Honey," Indy coos. "I saw the way she looked at you the night she helped watch the kids. She already has. It sounds like the only person who hasn't forgiven you is you."

"Yeah," Miller agrees. "Stop feeling sorry for yourself."

I can't help but laugh at the directness. "Well, damn."

"I'm sorry, I'm not great at soft and sweet, but Rio, come on. You running away again is not only punishing you, but it's also punishing her. You said it yourself, you've already fucked up once, so don't go fucking it up again. Simple as that."

"I'm not running away."

"Does she know that?"

My attention flicks to Kennedy, Stevie, and Indy to confirm at least one of them is going to cut in and say something to the effect of "of course she knows." But they're all looking at me too, silently asking the same question.

"Yes," I finally say. "Of course, she knows I'm not. I put the ball in her court weeks ago. I told her that when she was ready to give us another chance, so was I."

"Oh my God." Kennedy falls back onto the couch. "Have we taught you nothing?"

"Rio," Stevie scolds. "Come on."

Miller is shaking her head. "Ind, do you want to take this one? You're going to be nicer than me."

Indy smiles at me weakly. "Rio, honey. My sweet angel of a best friend, you're killing me here. I get that Hallie had time to forgive you because she had years to process this all, and that you needed time to forgive yourself, but the ball is in *your* court right now. If she understands you as well as it seems she does, I'd suspect she knows that you're busy beating yourself up over all of this and she's waiting for you to tell her when *you're* ready to let that go."

"No," I argue. "No, I'm waiting for her."

They all wait for me expectantly.

Hallie hasn't seemed off since we got home from Minnesota or acted differently at all. She hasn't given me the cold shoulder or actively avoided me. She still shoots me that same excited smile anytime I show up at her work to drive her home. She still texts me a thank-you message with about a thousand exclamation points each morning after she finds the latte I left for her on her doorstep.

Holy shit. I'm an idiot.

I shoot up from my seat. "Why didn't you guys tell me?"

Kennedy cocks her head. "We just did."

"*Fuck me.* You would've thought I learned something in all the years I've been coming to these girls' nights, but apparently not." I race around the house, gathering my keys and jacket. "I've got to go. I have to tell her."

"Hell yeah, you do!" Miller cheers.

"Good luck!" Kennedy chimes in.

Stevie holds a hand over her heart. "They grow up so fast."

Lastly, I look to Indy who is fucking crying...*again.*

"Ind, really?"

"I'm not crying! I'm fine. I'm just really happy that you're happy." She cleans up under her eyes. "You deserve to be happy, Rio. You both do."

I offer her a coy smile before I'm out the door and racing to my truck.

Because she's right. *We both* deserve to be happy.

Parking in my driveway, I jog across the lawn and up the steps to Hallie's front door, knocking frantically and praying that she's home.

I pace the front porch, impatiently waiting for someone to open the door while reviewing everything I rehearsed on my drive home. There's no answer, so I knock one more time, just to be sure, before I get back in my car and try to figure out where else she might be.

Finally, the porch light flips on and the door cracks open.

"Rio?" Hallie peeks outside. "Is everything okay?"

And suddenly, everything I had prepared to say flies out the window.

God, she's beautiful. Has she always been this beautiful?

The easy answer is yes. I've known almost every iteration of this woman and have loved each version. She has been my favorite person since I was twelve, and fifteen years later, that hasn't changed.

"I didn't tell you something the other night," I finally blurt out. She lifts a brow in interest.

"Well, I didn't tell you a lot of things, but the biggest one is that even though I am mad at myself, I am so proud of you."

She opens the door fully, leaning on the doorframe to listen.

"I am so proud of you for taking care of everything you did these last handful of years. I fucked up. We both know that now, and I am so sorry. I'll never be able to say that enough. I'd offer to start over with you, but I'm afraid if we do that, you'd end up introducing yourself again and I feel like twice in a lifetime is plenty."

Her head falls back with a laugh, and the sound is so fucking lovely. It's all the encouragement I need to keep going.

"And honestly, Hallie, I don't want to start over with you. I want to accept that we went through some shit, you more than me. We hurt each other, and I made mistakes."

"I did too," she cuts in.

"And those mistakes changed us in certain ways, but in others, we've remained the exact same. It wouldn't be our story if we ignored all the bad parts, so I'm not going to. I'm not going to run away because where could I go? Hallie, you're in here." I tap my chest. "Regardless of the years we spent apart, you're still in here."

She's trying to hold back her smile, which seems like a good sign. "Are you sure that's not just a first-love thing?"

"No, baby. It's a last-love thing."

I take a step closer, into the doorway, bracing my hands on either side of it and subsequently her. But I don't go any farther because I have one more thing to say and I won't be able to if I get my hands on her.

"The other night when I said I hoped that one day you'd let me fall in love with you again, what I meant to say was that I hope to *earn* the chance to fall in love with you again. And that's not going to happen if I'm too busy regretting the past. So, yes. I made the biggest mistake of my life, and it's probably going to take some time to fully forgive myself for it, but I don't want to waste that time without you." With both hands, I cup her jaw, sliding my fingers into her hair. "It's always been you, Hallie, and I think we both know it."

She's just standing there, smirking up at me.

"So, yeah…" I stumble. "That's my big speech."

"Are you done?"

"I'm done."

"Then you should probably kiss me now. We already lost six years. I don't feel like wasting any more time."

I quickly agree. "I probably should."

Smiling, I lean down and press my mouth to hers and it feels like the biggest sigh of relief, the way our bodies melt into one another. She wraps her arms around my neck, parting her lips and letting me kiss her deeper, harder, more urgently.

"That was adorable, you two!" Wren shouts from somewhere inside. "But if you're going to finally fuck, can you do it at Rio's house? I need to study."

Hallie pulls her lips away from mine when we both start laughing, dropping her head to my chest.

But I think it's the feeling of lightness between us that has us acting all giddy. It finally feels like it should. There's no heaviness hanging over us. There's no animosity.

She tilts her head back, chin on my chest, as she looks up at me, and I take my time searching her face for the answer. Because we both know what it means if we go there. We're doing this again. We're fully in it. Me and her.

I tuck her hair behind her ear. "What do you say, Hal?"

She nods. "I think you should take me to your house."

I can't hold back my smile. "Did I ever tell you how much I love the convenience of us being neighbors?"

Reaching down, I cup her ass with both hands, lifting her to wrap those pretty legs around my waist. She crosses her arms around my shoulders and lets out a little squeal when I quickly take off to my place across the yard.

I've got my house key in the lock when she runs her fingers through my hair and says something that stops me in my tracks.

"Rio." Her eyes bounce between mine. "You should know. It's always been you too."

32

Hallie

Rio carries me through all the construction that's happening in his house and still doesn't put me down even after we've made it to the bedroom.

He kicks the door closed behind us before turning and pinning me against it, his mouth immediately finding mine. There's nothing soft about this kiss. It's urgent. It's needy, and it only becomes more frantic when I tighten my legs around his hips and pull him into me.

I immediately find a bit of needed friction, and so does he it seems with the way one of his hands grips my ass, the other slamming flat against the door by my head to keep himself steady.

He rolls into me again, and the movement has my lips falling open and my head dropping back to the door behind me.

"*Fuck*," he exhales, resting his forehead on my shoulder and looking down to watch us move together. "I could come like this and not even be embarrassed about it."

Chuckling, I slide my fingers into his hair, working my lips up his neck. "You're hard already."

"Mmm," he moans, fingertips digging into my ass. "That's a constant when around you, Hal. It's quite inconvenient."

I drag my tongue over his lower lip and watch his eyes flutter before I kiss him again. "We should probably take care of that."

Unwinding my legs, I find the ground, ducking under his arm to move closer to his bed.

Rio leans back against the door, arms crossed over his chest as he watches me toy with the bottom button of the cropped sweater I'm wearing.

He nods towards it. "Take it off."

And so I do, undoing one button and then the next. *Quickly*, because I'm eager and ready and I've missed this part of us.

He shakes his head. "Slowly, Hallie. It's been a long time. Let me savor this."

And dear God the way his eyes are hooded over, the way his bottom lip slips between his teeth as he rakes his gaze up my body. I hope he plans to savor me all night. Over and over again.

I make a whole show of it, slowly undoing each button and letting my sweater open a bit at a time, teasing what's underneath. My bra isn't anything special, plain white with a touch of lace over the cups, but Rio is watching me like I'm unwrapping a gift he's been asking for his entire life and is finally about to get his hands on.

He takes slow steps towards me, green eyes tracking every inch as I give him his own personal striptease. When my sweater opens fully, he wets his lips. When I slip an arm out, his throat bobs with a harsh swallow. When I let the entire thing pool on the floor by my feet, leaving me in only my bra and midi skirt, he stops dead in his tracks.

Rio shakes his head in disbelief and that alone has me standing straighter, shoulders pushed back.

His eyes roam, cataloging every inch of me. He's seen me naked countless times before, so I'm not sure if he's looking to see if anything has changed since the last time, or maybe it's been so long that he doesn't remember.

"Fucking beautiful," he murmurs under his breath. "It's been a long time."

So, it's the latter of those two options. But who remembers every little part of a person they had sex with six years ago?

Well, *I* do, but that's because I haven't been with anyone else since him.

"But I still remember everything," he says.

"It's been an awfully long time, Rio. Are you sure you're remembering correctly?"

His brow furrows. "Did you not believe me when I told you I picture you whenever I'm getting myself off? Do you think I made up an image of what I thought you looked like? No. Your body has been ingrained in my mind since I got to see it for the first time when I was nineteen. I remember everything."

Reaching out, he cups my elbow, his index finger running over a bit of raised skin. "I know you have a scar right here from falling off your bike when you were eleven."

"Well, I'd hope you remember that. It was your fault. You were going too fast, and I was trying to keep up."

Chuckling, he wraps his other hand around my hip, running the pad of his thumb over the inner part of my upper thigh. Even though I'm still wearing this satin skirt I can practically feel the warmth of his skin on mine, and it sends a rush of heat about two inches north, right where I wish he were touching me instead.

"I know you have a freckle right here." He softly strokes that same spot. "That I loved to lick before I tasted the rest of you."

Jesus.

He steps into me, trailing his lips along my jaw and down my neck until they meet the dip that connects with my shoulder.

"And I know that when I bite right here…" He does exactly that, pulling an instant whimper from my lips. "You'll make that fucking noise."

I'm writhing into him with my head thrown back as he kisses a path across my throat and up my jaw until he finds my mouth again.

"So yes, baby, I remember everything. Including all my favorite ways to make you come." He runs his thumb over the lace of my bra. "I was staring because I can't get over how innocent you look in white when we both know that you're not."

I hum. "That's your fault too."

He smiles against my skin, dragging his warm, wet lips over every inch of my neck and collarbone, his thumb still drawing languid strokes against the fabric of my bra, but I want his skin on mine, so I reach back to unclasp it.

But before I can, Rio has his arms around my waist, his hands covering mine to stop me.

There's an overwhelming sense of déjà vu from the very first time we did this together.

"Are you nervous?" he whispers.

I shake my head no. "Are you?"

"Not even a little bit."

I softly smile up at him as he draws small circles on my spine, but still, he doesn't undo the clasp.

He watches me for a long moment, toying with the fabric back there, until eventually he pulls his hand away, leaving my bra in place.

"What's wrong?" I ask.

He shakes his head to tell me nothing before reaching over his head to take his shirt off in one fluid motion, tossing it to the floor.

He's stunning. Tan skin, defined but lean muscles, and ink. Black and sprawling over his left side. And when he doesn't make a move to touch or kiss me again, I realize he's waiting for me to look at it in more detail.

There are a few tattoos, and I'd call all of them new because they're new to me, but I couldn't tell you what the others are. My attention is fixated on only one.

"Hallie," Rio says tentatively. "Say something."

I can't. I'm speechless. Because how am I supposed to speak when my eyes are glued to what is essentially my last name, tattooed as a heart, inked over his *actual* heart?

Hesitantly, I reach out, gently running my fingers over the black ink, following the curves and the dip until I stop to cover the overdrawn portion where it was supposed to stop, but never did.

My heart.

His heart, really, when I think about how many times he fixated on my signatures from the mixtapes and CDs I gave him.

It's my favorite part.

"In case you're still wondering if I ever forgot about you," he says softly. "I got this three years ago. Three years *after* I saw you last."

"Why?"

"I'm pretty sure you know the answer to that, Hal."

"Tell me anyway."

I can't stop running my fingers over it, pausing at the same point where he used to stop. It's an exact replica of my handwriting and everything, clearly taken from one of those tapes or CDs.

"Because it's always been us." With his knuckle, he tilts my chin up, so I look at him. "Even when I thought I didn't want it to be, I knew it was us. I sat there getting this permanently inked onto my skin, trying to convince myself I was only getting it as a reminder that love existed when the whole fucking time, I knew it only existed with you."

Well...*shit.*

His complete and utter honesty has my lips falling open. It has my heart racing and my skin heating.

I didn't know being someone's everything could be such a turn-on.

I run my fingers down, brushing over his ribs and abs, tracing the lines of that V that may as well be a road map to his dick. I unclasp his pants, unzip the fly, and push them over his stupidly perfect ass, past his thick thighs, until they're pooling on the floor.

He kicks himself out of them, fingers pushing my hair out of my face. "You like hearing that?"

Nodding, I lean in and kiss him, dragging my lips over his jaw and down his neck, working a path over his chest as I begin to kneel.

"Wait, Hal. I want to take care of you first."

Shaking my head, I continue to drop, brushing my lips over my tattoo before I'm too low.

"*Fuck*," he exhales, tossing his head back.

I use his thighs to hold on to, looking up at him, and really playing up that whole doe-eyed thing.

"Look at you," he murmurs. "You look so pretty on your knees."

"Is this what you picture when you're getting yourself off?"

He nods, eyes trailing all over my face and body, hand running languidly through my hair. "You look like an angel in white, but the way your tits are propped up right now is downright sinful."

Squirming, I push my knees together, searching for a bit of friction.

He was always fantastic at giving affirmations, so it's not surprising to hear them. The guy could hardly go through his normal everyday life without praising me for something. But it's been so long since I've heard it, I almost forgot what it felt like to glow under his encouragement.

As a reward, I push my skirt down over my hips to let him see a peek of my matching white panties.

"Fuck me, Hal. Take that skirt all the way off. I want to watch how wet you get when you put my cock down your throat."

And so I do as I'm told, slipping my skirt down over my thighs and past my knees, before tossing it to join the rest of our discarded clothes.

Running my hands over his stomach, I toy with the waistband of his boxer briefs, watching his muscles bunch in anticipation. Rio keeps running his hand over my hair, moving it out of the way as he waits.

Bracing my hands on his thick thighs, I lean in and press my lips to the bulge in front of me, right over his boxer briefs.

He hums in approval. "Tease."

I can't help but smile at that because I have about six years of teasing to do. He wants to savor tonight? Oh, we can savor it all right.

Fingers slipping into his waistband, I pull them down only an inch, letting the tip of his cock slip out.

I lightly kiss that too.

"Fuck, Hallie."

The torture in his tone sounds like music to my ears so I decide to twirl my tongue over the head and see what kinds of noises I can earn from that.

It's the most desperate whimper I've ever heard.

"Are you punishing me, baby?"

I look up, put on my most innocent expression, and nod.

"Fair." His chest is moving rapidly with ragged breaths. "I'll happily take this punishment."

Pulling his briefs down another inch, I flick the underside of his crown with my tongue.

His legs are already trembling. His abdomen muscles are already spasming. The hold he has on my hair gives my scalp a delicious burn.

"I should warn you, Hallie, there's a good chance that I'm going to come in your mouth as soon as you wrap your lips around me. It's been too long."

I smile against him, swirling my tongue around the head again.

"You want me to come too quickly, don't you? You want to see how fucking weak I am when it comes to you?"

Nodding, I kiss a path down his cock.

I'd just like to remind him, is all. That regardless of what he's done with anyone else over the last six years, I was his first and I fully plan on being his last. That even though I had no idea what I was doing the first time, I learned how to give a proper blow job by giving them to him. I, better than anyone, know what he likes. I learned his tells. I learned his sounds.

And I haven't forgotten any of it.

I pull his briefs down the rest of the way, letting his cock spring free in front of me. He's as blessed as I remember him being and though I was recently reminded of his size when I saw him fucking his fist in the shower, it's a whole different reminder when you're on your knees, trying to remember how you're going to breathe when he fills your mouth.

I tease him by licking a slow path up his shaft, circling the tip with my tongue before wrapping my lips around him and gliding them down until his crown hits the back of my throat.

"Goddamn," he breathes like a sigh of relief, fingers tightening in my hair. "That's it."

Pulling back, I use my lips to stroke him, twisting my hand on the remainder of his shaft. I continue to work him in my mouth, quickly finding a familiar rhythm.

His breathing is labored, coming out in short spurts.

"So much." He loses his words for a second. "So much better than I've been imagining."

I continue sucking and swirling, humming around his length and I can almost see the vibration tremble through his entire body.

"Careful, Hal. I need to make this last. I need to get inside of you at least once before this is over."

I don't slow down at all.

He looks insane from this view. Big and strong, but weak when it comes to me. He throws his head back, his Adam's apple bobbing in his throat and there's something about knowing that I still have this power over him that has me shifting and moving, trying to find friction between my legs.

"You need to touch yourself?"

I quickly nod as saliva pools around the corners of my lips.

"Put your fingers on your clit."

Eyes fluttering, I meet his gaze.

"Touch yourself. Make yourself feel good until I can."

Shifting, I make sure he can fully see me from his view before

I use one hand to run over the waistband of my panties, the other continuing to twist and stroke him with my mouth.

I trail my fingers over the fabric, right over my sensitive clit before tugging them up, using the friction to my advantage, while also showing him.

"Jesus," he murmurs. "You're soaked, Hallie baby. Is that all from having me in your mouth?"

I agree, creating tight little circles right over my clit for him to see. I run my middle finger over my seam, watching the way he's completely mesmerized by it.

"Let me see that."

As I hold my finger up, he takes it, slipping it into his mouth and sucking it clean with this growl of satisfaction. My eyes go wide at the sight, because *holy shit*. And more heat pools low in my core when he licks his lips to make sure he gets all of it.

His cock is still in my mouth, so I try to refocus on that, but all I can do is stare at him, noting the feral hunger on his face.

"I need to touch you," he says, standing over me.

But because he can't, I decide to touch him, reaching down and cupping his balls.

He falls forward, jerking in my mouth, his legs starting to shake before he tugs my hair to pull my mouth off him.

Looking up, I smile. Big and wide and not at all innocent.

"What happened to making this last?" he asks between labored breaths.

"We have all night to make this last."

He tilts my head back so he can kiss me, tongue drawing a path over my lower lip. "Do you want me to come in your mouth? Is that what you're saying?"

I nod eagerly.

He smiles against my lips, kissing me one more time.

Standing straight, he cups the back of my head with one hand, gathering my short hair there, before he uses the other to guide his cock back into my mouth.

"Then do it," he says. "Make me come, baby."

Holding my head in place, he rocks his hips into me.

With my hands free, I take the opportunity to touch him. Running over his cut thighs, over his ass, nails raking against his skin. He sets a punishing pace, and it doesn't take long before his thrusts turn sloppy, his hips jerking without restraint.

He's close. I can tell by the way he's breathing. By the sounds he's making. By the lack of control he has over his own body.

"Gonna come," is all he says as his grip on the back of my head loosens, giving me the opportunity to pull away.

But I don't. I pull his hips into me, feeling his tip pierce the back of my throat before I swallow around it.

"*Fuck*, Hallie," he cries out, throwing his head back.

His eyes screw shut, his fingers grip my hair, his hips jerk and twitch as he starts to come down my throat. He keeps coming, holding me steady and I just watch, fascinated by him. Fascinated by what I can still do to him.

Once his muscles relax and his body uncoils itself, his grip on me loosens. Slowly, he pulls himself out of my mouth.

I wait until those hooded eyes are on me before I make a show of it and swallow.

He shakes his head in disbelief.

"So good." Rio crouches his naked body, making himself eye level with me. "But I haven't had sex in a long time. We probably should've started slower than that because I don't know how I'm ever going to recover from this."

I chuckle, wrapping my arms around his neck. "You're telling me."

He grabs my ass, picking me up and carrying me to the bed. Protecting my head, he lays me back before draping his fully naked body on top of mine, pressing me into the mattress. We're chest to chest. My legs are open around him. And I'm so sensitive, so needy right now, that I can't help but lift my hips and grind myself into his still partially hard cock.

He plants a hand on my hip, keeping me from moving as he looks down at me, his eyes bouncing between mine. "I don't think you get what I'm trying to say. I haven't had sex in a long time."

It's the exact same sentence he already said, but the speed with which he repeats it tells me there's an open door to ask.

I'm cautious though, because most of me doesn't want to know the answer. "How long is a long time?"

He cradles my jaw, his thumb stroking over my cheekbone and while his eyes are boring into mine, I look away, hoping I can keep my reaction neutral if I don't have to see his face when he says it.

"Six years."

My eyes shoot to his.

"I've only ever been with you."

33

Rio

I can't tell what's going through her head. Her eyes are wider than I've ever seen them. Her lips are parted slightly.

I push her hair away from her face. "What are you thinking, Hallie?"

She's quiet for a moment and I try not to focus on how fucking stunning she is, lying underneath me, tits perched up against my chest, pussy lined up perfectly with my cock. I'm attempting to be a gentleman and give her a moment if she needs to freak out after realizing how utterly gone I've been for her for the last fifteen years of my life.

She shakes her head. "That can't be true."

"Oh, I can promise you, it is. I'm practically a born-again virgin at this point, so if you can do me a favor and deflower me again, that'd be great."

Okay, well, that didn't work. I'm trying to make light of the situation, but I just used the word *deflower* in a sentence, and she's still lying there in utter disbelief.

"But you said you've been dating all this time."

"I've been *on* dates. First dates that don't lead to a second." I laugh at myself again. "I haven't even kissed someone else."

She shakes her head again. "Why?"

"Do you realize how unfair it'd be if I actually got in a relationship with someone else? When all I think about is you? When I compared every person to you? There *was* no comparison to you."

"Rio."

I wait for her to say something else, but she doesn't. I wait for the shock to pass, but it won't.

Then suddenly, those wide hazel eyes looking up at me in disbelief begin to gloss over.

"Hey," I say softly but urgently. "Hallie, baby, don't cry."

This is not at all the reaction I was expecting. I kind of thought she'd tease me a little bit before putting me out of my misery. But then I realize that me telling her this might not be reassuring. It might make her feel bad that I waited for her, but she didn't do the same. But I would never expect her to wait, especially after I ended things the way I did.

"Hallie." I wipe away a rogue tear that falls out of the corner of her eye. "There's no need to cry about this. I would never expect you to wait for me."

"But I did."

I rear back slightly, my thumb halting mid-stroke of her cheek. "No, you didn't."

She huffs a laugh, but it sounds as shocked and startled as I feel. "I've only ever been with you."

"Why?"

"Why did *you* wait?" she counters.

Because I've only ever wanted to be with you.

My own answer hits me square in the chest, knowing her sentiment is the same.

She's not crying anymore. Now she's laughing, her head falling back to the pillow behind her while I'm lying on top of her completely naked and in shock.

I'm such a goddamn idiot for staying away as long as I did.

"What the hell is wrong with us?" I ask, somewhat rhetorically.

"I have no fucking clue." She can't stop laughing and apparently, it's contagious because now I'm laughing too.

I hide my face in the crook of her neck, and she wraps her hand around my back and it feels good. It feels good to be able to laugh with each other instead of regretting the time lost. What else are we going to do about it now other than laugh at our own stubbornness?

She bends her knee at my side, and I palm it, running my hand down the length of her thigh.

"What are you thinking?"

She's got this brilliant smile on her lips, those hazel eyes now clear and sparkling.

"I'm thinking..." She runs her fingers over my ribs, and I can't get over how fucking unreal it feels to have her touching me again. "I'm thinking that you should probably fuck me now. I've been awfully patient."

She has been. And realistically, I could go again already. I'm not going to lie, I got pretty fucking turned on hearing that she waited for me, but between that incredible blow job and the whole shower thing, she's gotten me off twice before I've even given her one, if we're not counting that phone call.

"I've got some work to put in first," I say against her lips, leaning in to kiss her.

There's nothing fumbling or frantic about this kiss. It's soft and languid, taking our time as our bodies move together. Reaching between her and the mattress, I unclasp her bra, pulling it off her and tossing it to the floor.

Perfect fucking tits on full display as they should be.

I take a handful and squeeze, circling my thumb over her nipple before I pinch it between my fingers, memorizing every little sound that comes out of her mouth.

"I want you inside of me," she breathes.

Fuck me, those words alone could make me come again, which only acts as a reminder I need to take care of her at least once before I do. I create a path, licking and kissing down her neck and chest before taking one nipple in my mouth and flicking it with my tongue.

"*Yes*," she hisses, arching into me. "More of that."

I do as I'm told, moving to the other to give equal attention. I swirl and flick, offering her a preview of exactly what I'm about to do to another part of her, before I work my way down her stomach. Kissing her soft skin. Gently biting when I can't resist. And when I'm lying all the way between her legs, I don't stop, continuing to lick a line straight down her already-soaked panties.

"Fuck," she cries. "More, please."

"Such good manners, baby. But you don't have to say please. You tell me what you want and it's yours."

"I want you to fuck me."

I smile against her, rolling my tongue in a stiff circle over her clit. Her head is thrown back, her fingers gripping the sheets at her sides.

"I will but tell me what you want before I do that."

She's so fucking sensitive, so responsive, that when I take the waistband of her underwear between my teeth and let it snap back against her skin, she's trembling.

"I want you to take those off of me and lick me until I come."

"There we go."

I stand from the bed, between her legs. My cock is already hard again, proudly pointing right at her. She's got her eyes fixated on it, licking her lips, so I give it a couple of tugs, working my fist over myself.

"Don't tease me, DeLuca. It's my turn. Get on your knees and get to work."

"Yes, ma'am." Chuckling, I shake my head at her, pulling her underwear down her legs and tossing it to the side.

There's not a shy bone in her body when she bends her knees and widens her legs, letting me get a proper view of her.

I groan at the sight, all swollen and wet. "Goddamn, baby, I love your body."

She hums under the praise. "I was just thinking how much I love yours."

"It's a little different from the last time you saw me naked, huh?"

I would almost call my old body scrawny compared to the build I've earned over the last six years. I run a hand over my chest and stomach, bringing her attention to some of the things that have changed.

She shakes her head. "I loved that one too."

Dear God, I'm obsessed with her.

How rare to find someone who understands and appreciates you for exactly who you are at each phase of your life. She liked me before anyone else ever did. She saw my potential when I couldn't. She doesn't give a shit about my job and that alone is refreshing. Fuck, she's the reason I'm even playing hockey. If it wasn't for her encouragement all those years ago, I would've quit a long time ago.

Sinking to my knees, I hook my hands around her hips, pulling her to the edge of the bed to show her just how appreciative *I* can be. But I have to give myself a moment to get my shit together because being this close to her, smelling her, knowing I'm finally about to taste her again, I could easily lose any restraint I'm pretending to have.

"You're soaking, Hallie."

She nods to herself, squirming against the bed.

"Do you need me to take care of this for you?"

"Pl—" she stops herself from being polite. "Yes."

I hold her legs down, spreading her wide, and my eyes fall to that little freckle on the inside of her thigh.

I lick it and Hallie bucks off the bed.

"So sensitive."

She whimpers.

I can't help myself from groaning like a starved man when I lick a long path over her center, swirling around her clit. A desperate sound escapes her before one hand slaps over her mouth, the other fisted in the sheets.

"Take your hand away."

"I'm too loud."

"I don't give a fuck. This is my house. We aren't hiding shit here. Scream all you want. I want to hear what I'm doing to you."

She takes her hand away, so I give her clit another flick with my tongue to see if she puts it back.

"Good girl," I praise when she doesn't. Instead, she cries this sweet little sound that goes straight to my cock.

Hallie lifts her hips, bucking and rolling, seeking my mouth.

So I give it to her, latching onto her perfect fucking pussy, sucking her clit before rolling over it with my tongue in a way I know she loves. It doesn't matter that it's been six years since I've done this. It quickly comes back to me. My body knows her body almost better than my own.

The noises coming out of this woman's mouth are going to haunt me in my dreams in the best way possible. I'll be adding this soundtrack when I'm on the road again and back to fucking my own fist.

I do this thing with my tongue that I remember always drove her mad. It has her tightening her thighs around me as a tremor runs through her body.

"You know exactly what I like. That's so good, Rio."

Hearing her say my name while like this has my balls unexpectedly tightening. I quickly grasp the base of my dick, needing to slow myself down, focusing all my attention on making sure I don't come again.

Her tits are heaving when she perches up on her elbows to look down at me. "What's wrong?"

"Almost came from you saying my name."

She gets this satisfied smirk on her lips.

"Don't get so cocky, love. If you make me come again, you're going to have to wait that much longer until I can fuck you."

She shrugs casually, lying back down. "I know of some ways you can pass the time."

Damn. I missed her. I missed everything about her.

I bury my face between her legs again, letting her know just how badly I've been missing her. I concentrate on her clit, because I know that's what she likes the most, while circling her entrance with my fingers, coating myself in her before I sink them inside.

"*Yes.* Yes. Oh God," she cries, fingers pinching her nipples. "So close."

I brush my fingertips forward, teasing her front wall, and just like that, she's tightening around them, her entire body contracting as she comes on my fingers and tongue.

I don't stop, letting her ride it out, and goddamn is she stunning while she does. She's practically levitating off the bed, her nipples tight as she teases them, her hips erratically bucking against my face.

When she settles back onto the mattress, she's still spasming around my fingers and it takes a moment for me to slowly ease them out.

Flushed cheeks and chest. Glistening pussy. Perfectly fucking wrecked.

I climb my naked body right on top of hers, kissing a path up her heated skin. "Tell me what else you want, Hal."

She's completely dazed, living in that post-orgasm fog when she says, "Everything."

And that's exactly what I plan on giving her. For a lot longer than tonight.

Slipping an arm under her body, I take her with me when I pull myself to sit up against the headboard. With my legs sprawled out in front of me, taking up most of the bed, Hallie straddles my lap.

"Shit," I hiss from the blinding bliss when she scoots closer, sliding her pussy over my very ready and equally willing cock. "You're so fucking warm, Hal. So goddamn wet."

I run my hands over her thighs, still not fully convinced she's here, that this is happening, and that I somehow got so lucky to find her again.

Hallie brackets my face, bringing my attention to her and just like that, the tone in the room shifts completely. It's still charged, but sweet and heavy, like we both know what we're about to do isn't as simple as calling it sex.

She runs her thumbs over my cheeks, her hazel eyes boring into mine. "I missed you so much."

Those words have my heart lurching in a way I forgot it could.

"You're everything to me, Hallie. I've been addicted to you since I was a kid, and clearly nothing has changed. I don't want to be without you again."

She shakes her head to tell me we won't be, leaning in and placing a gentle kiss on my lips before resting her forehead on mine.

"Condom. Nightstand."

She chuckles but doesn't make a move for one. "And how old are those?"

"I bought them a couple of months ago. Just in case."

"How forward-thinking of you," she teases. "But we don't need them. I got back on birth control."

I smooth my hands down her spine. "And when did you do that?"

"A couple of months ago. Just in case."

"Hmm," I hum. "I think that was around the time you threw me a middle finger and told me to go fuck myself."

"Yeah, and you deserved it."

I huff a laugh because yeah... I did deserve it. I probably still deserve it, but I'm trying to not think about that while I have her naked and sitting on my lap.

Her hips start moving again, running over my length.

"Put me inside you and let me watch you do it."

She moans at my words, her hips circling over me and I'm

sitting here fucking dying in anticipation. She lifts on her knees, taking my cock and running it over her core, coating me in her.

"You're killing me." I throw my head back to the headboard behind me. "Keep doing it."

So she does, running herself over me, using her hand to stroke me in tandem. She taps the head of my cock against her clit, and it's a maddening tease, but that's nothing in comparison to when she lines me up with her entrance and sinks down only a centimeter or two.

It's as if time stands still in that moment, like it's a last-second reminder that we're putting the past behind us and moving forward.

Hallie checks on me. I check on her.

Her legs are trembling from holding herself in place without sinking down, so I wrap an arm around her waist to hold her up, so she doesn't have to. Then I lean in and kiss her collarbone before slowly lifting my hips.

I only go in an inch or so, letting her adjust slowly.

I try to focus on the way her pupils are blown out, on the way she can hardly catch her breath. But so much of my attention is locked in on how fucking unreal she feels.

"So good, baby," I praise. "You're doing so good."

She reaches behind me, bracing her hands on the headboard to give herself leverage. "I have to go slow."

"Take your time. You already feel incredible."

I run a hand over her hips until my thumb grazes over her clit.

She moans, sinking down another inch.

"Good girl, Hal. Just like that."

Cupping the back of her head, I pull her down to kiss me.

It's hot, the way her tongue slips into the mouth when she drops another inch. The way she scratches the skin of my chest when she takes another.

But when she fully sits, letting me sink inside her...*holy hell*. There are no words to describe that.

Neither of us moves as we try to catch our breath. I hold her tightly to me, allowing her to get her bearings.

"Are you okay?" I ask quietly.

She nods, lifting her face away from me to smile. "Perfect."

She rocks her hips forward, rubbing her clit against my pelvis. "That's it," I encourage. "Use me, Hallie. Make yourself feel good."

She rocks back and forth in little motions, and it doesn't take long before I can tell she's close again. Which is for the best, because I know I'm not going to last long. As if we were thinking the same thing, she lifts up and drops back down, giving me the green light to go.

Two hands on her ass, I hold her in place as I push up into her, fucking her from underneath. I work us together, our sweat-slicked bodies clinging to one another. She latches her lips on my neck as the room fills with the sounds of slapping, wet skin, and I suck on her nipples as she adds her pretty little moans into the mix.

I give her a chance to take over. Her tits bounce as she rides me and for a moment, I lean my head back and watch. My perfect fucking girl. She's *always* been my perfect girl.

"You know exactly what I like, baby. You've always known what I like."

She whimpers.

"Do you know what else I like?"

She nods frantically. "When I come while you're inside of me."

Jesus. Hearing her say it out loud puts me that much closer to the edge.

"Can you do that for me?"

She's a panting mess, her lips finding mine again. "I think I'm…"

I know she is. She's tightening around me, so I don't change anything. I do exactly what I'm already doing until her hips stutter and stomach pulls taut, falling completely apart on me.

It might be the most beautiful I've ever seen her. Untethered. Undone.

Mine.

And the realization that I may have gotten so lucky that for the second time in my life, she may actually be mine, has me coming with her. I spill into her while chanting her name like a fucking prayer against her lips.

Which is fitting because she feels like my answered prayer.

And as we come down together, I make sure to tell her that.

Hallie 34

I wake with a head of dark messy hair on my chest, arms wrapped around my waist, and a giant man between my legs, sleeping peacefully. Sleeping like I've never seen him sleep before.

Which is probably for the best because we were up most of the night.

After the first round, Rio took me downstairs and fed me. I'm not sure if any of his friends know, but the guy is one hell of a cook. All those cooking lessons his mom gave him while growing up have clearly stuck. He whipped up a homemade pasta sauce that he promised would be better if it got to meld together longer, but I didn't know how that was possible because it was already delicious.

He watched me eat my bowl of pasta, unable to keep his hands off me the whole time, but I didn't mind. After so long without being touched in that way, it felt good to be needed. It felt good to be taken care of too.

And as soon as I finished eating, he sat me on the kitchen counter and took care of me in another way.

Unlike the first time, the second time was hard and fast. He had a hand cradling the back of my head so it wouldn't slam against the kitchen cabinets, and once we both came again, he carried me to his shower to clean me off, where he dropped to his knees and threw one of my thighs over his shoulder. He made me come again with his mouth, as if he were on a mission to give me all the orgasms I missed over the last six years.

We both passed out asleep after that.

And as much as I'd love to lie around with him all day and try to find the energy to return the favor, I have a job I need to get to.

I peel myself out from under him, making sure not to wake him up, before finding one of his flannel shirts tossed on a chair. I slip my arm through that, buttoning it all the way down the front before heading downstairs.

Thankfully, it's not a construction day at Rio's house, so I'm not worried about anyone walking in on me wearing my client's shirt as a dress with nothing on underneath.

When I get to the kitchen, I put on some music, letting it connect to the speakers only on the first floor. I choose something soft and melodic to start my morning before turning on Rio's espresso machine.

At the fridge, I contemplate grabbing the dairy milk instead of the almond since he's not awake and can't have a taste of my coffee anyway, but something about it feels wrong. So, I grab the almond milk instead.

I'm pulling a shot when I hear a sleepy, raspy voice ask, "What do you think you're doing?" from behind me.

I look over my shoulder to find Rio, leaning his hip on the kitchen counter, right where he fucked me a few hours ago, sweatpants hung low. Smirk on his face and not wearing a shirt, showing off *my* tattoo.

Mine.

Only mine.

I'm still processing his confession last night, that he hasn't been with anyone but me.

I've forgiven him for our past. I understand where his head was at when he made the choices he did. And though I know there's a part of him that thinks it's going to take more or that he should continue to punish himself over it, I think the fact that he tried so hard for six years to get over me and couldn't was torture enough.

And I kind of love that he couldn't do it.

"What are you smirking at?" he asks.

"Just thinking about what a terrible time you had trying to get over me."

He laughs to himself, crossing the kitchen to me. "Ain't that the fucking truth." His palm slides against my lower back. "And my other question. What do you think you're doing?"

"Making myself a latte."

"That's my job." He takes the almond milk from me at the same time he leans down and plants a soft kiss on my lips.

"You were sleeping."

"Then you got out of bed. I think you know by now I only sleep when you're next to me."

"So honest today."

"Yeah, well I just got laid for the first time in six years, Hal. I'll tell you anything you want to know as a thank you for fucking me."

Laughing to myself, I curl into him, hiding my face against his chest. He wraps his free arm around me, holding me close as he continues to work on my latte.

"Hi," he says quietly, lips brushing my hair. "Are you tired?"

"Exhausted." I pull back to look at him. "But happy."

The most stunning smile spreads across his lips. "I'd hope so. I put in a lot of work last night to make sure you're happy."

Chuckling, I rest against him again, wrapping my arms around his waist.

"I'm happy too." He leans down and kisses me. "Your latte is ready."

I find it on the counter. "What's the art today?"

"Well, clearly, that's a dragon. I'm not sure how you're not seeing it."

It's literally a blob of foam in the center of the cup.

"But I only had one hand," he continues. "So just imagine what I could've done with two."

"I've spent a lot of time imagining and *remembering* what you can do with two hands."

"Don't flirt with me, Hart. Not when you're about to leave me all day."

"Do you want to try it first?" I ask, holding the mug out in his direction.

His smile is sweet when he brings the mug to his mouth and takes a sip, but our little moment is interrupted by his phone ringing in his pocket, and when he pulls it out, his mom's name is obvious enough that we both see it.

"Sorry," he says, switching the sound off. "I'll call her back later."

"You should answer it, Rio. I don't need another reason for her to hate me."

He gives me this look, as if he wants to argue, but then it softens to something laced with sympathy. Because we both know he can't tell me that I'm wrong.

"Please answer it," I plead.

He hesitates for a moment before he leans down and brushes a kiss on my hair, answering his phone at the same time.

"Hey, Ma," he says, leaving the kitchen to take the call in another part of the house.

The reality of the broader situation comes into focus again.

Rio and I may have forgiven each other, but his mom hasn't. And not only does that worry me because I know how close the two of them are, but there's a part of me that misses her too.

Not only was Mrs. DeLuca my mom's best friend, our neighbor, and my boyfriend's mom, but she was practically my second mother as well. As soon as we moved in next door, she treated me like the daughter she never had.

The day she found out about her husband's affair, I'll never forget the way she looked at me when she realized I knew and didn't tell her. It was this agonizing mix of betrayal and disappointment on her face, and it's been ingrained in my mind ever since.

She looked at me like she hated me with every fiber of her being and I can't exactly blame her for it. Every day for the last six years, I've regretted not telling Rio sooner, but I equally regret not telling her.

I have missed her for as long as I have been missing him.

Trying my best not to focus on those facts or what is most likely a less-than-cordial phone call happening in the other room, I grab my own phone as a distraction. I have new progress photos of Rio's house that I should share on my Instagram.

I didn't have any social media until I moved here last spring and realized what a huge part it played in growing a clientele. I started an Instagram page after I learned that every designer at the firm had one, and I began posting consistently while I was working on Wren's house. I don't have a large following, and most of the comments are from my dad, but I figured it would only aid in helping me land a full-time position at Tyler Braden Interiors if I could start curating an online presence and personal aesthetic.

Except this time, when I open the app, I find a lot more than the few hundred followers I had before. Now, I'm just shy of thirty thousand.

There are new comments on every single post. Some are asking how they can request to work with me, others thanking me for listing the paint colors I used in the captions, and even more simply gushing over my style.

"What's wrong?" Rio asks, coming back into the room.

I hold my phone up to show him. "I have almost thirty thousand new followers on my design account this week."

"Hell yeah, Hal!" His smile lights up his whole face. "I've been sharing all your posts about my house, and my friends have been too. Zee has an obscene number of followers, and Miller's account for the patisserie has a big local following. And of course there's Ryan, who is almost never online, but when he is, his engagement is wild. I think he shared your account in his stories yesterday."

My throat does this odd tightening thing. "That's so nice of them, but they barely know me."

"Well, they know *me* and how I feel about you, so whether you like it or not, you're already part of the group. I'm pretty sure the girls are ready to ban me from girls' nights in hopes that you'll start joining instead."

That sounds overwhelmingly lovely. I have craved friendship and community for so many years now. I was a social butterfly before my dad got sick and I'd like to get back to that part of who I am.

"You go to their girls' nights?" I ask playfully. "Why does that not surprise me in the least?"

"They have way better snacks than what the guys have when they get together." He takes my mug, setting it on the counter. "Come here for a second."

Taking my arms, he guides them to wrap around his neck, his own going low around my waist as he holds us together.

"I like this song," he says.

He begins to sway, dancing with me in his under-construction kitchen while we're both barefoot and I'm only wearing his shirt.

"What are you doing?" I ask.

"Dancing with you."

"Why?"

"Because *I* want to."

A flash of an old memory comes back. He told me he'd catch his parents doing this all the time in their kitchen. I know he spent the last six years trying to distance himself from anything that resembled their relationship, so him saying this is something *he* wants to do feels a bit bigger and more important than simply swaying in his kitchen together.

"Was the call that bad?"

His jaw flexes before he nods to tell me yes.

"She's upset with you because of me."

"I don't care, Hallie."

"But you should. I know how important she is to you."

"Of course she is. But I also let her feelings sway mine for six years longer than they should've. I'm finally doing what I want."

"Rio." I toy with his hair at the nape of his neck. "She hates me."

"I think we both know it's not actually you that she's angry with." He lets that truth hang in the air for a while before he adds, "I'm not letting anyone ruin this again. Not her and not me. Please don't worry about it. I think she'll come around one day and if she doesn't, well, that's her own problem. But I'm not fucking this up again."

I want to argue back and remind him that there's no way in hell that he's going to be okay for long if his mother is opposed to us being together. He respects her too much to allow this riff between her and the woman he's seeing. I just hope that one day, I'll get the chance to change her opinion of me.

"Hallie," Rio whispers, still dancing slowly with me in his kitchen. "Are we doing this? You and me. Because I'm all in."

I laugh lightly. "I thought last night kind of answered that."

"I'd really like to hear you say it, to make sure I'm not assuming anything here."

He has this sweet, pleading look in his eyes as he waits for my confirmation.

"You're not assuming anything." I pull him down to kiss me. "I'm all in too. It's you and me."

Again is what I'm tempted to say, but *for good* feels more accurate.

Rio

(AGE 20)

"I decided I'm going to enter the NHL draft this year."

I've been waiting to tell her until I got to see her in person, and apparently, the moment we collapsed onto my bed together, tangled limbs and hard-earned breaths, was the opportunity I saw fit.

Hallie rolls onto her stomach, propping her naked body on my bare chest to look at me. Wide eyes and a big smile on her lips. "You are?"

I push her long, messy hair behind her ear. "I know it's earlier than I originally planned, but my agent feels like it's the right time. Worst-case scenario if I don't get picked up, at least I still have two more years I can play here."

"You're going to get picked. *Early*, I bet. The amount of attention you've had from scouts this season is wild."

I run my fingers down her bare back, listening to this year's playlist she put together. Now that Hallie is in college for interior design and has a more flexible schedule, she's been able to come out to Michigan to see me more often, and since I couldn't get to her for her birthday, she hopped on a plane to come to me.

Thank God.

Unlike last year when she was finishing high school, now we don't go more than a month without seeing each other. Our families both know about our relationship, though they apparently knew before we ever confirmed it. They're fully on board. My mom might be the most ecstatic of all, but that's not all that surprising. She has adored Hallie since the moment the Harts moved in next door.

And while yes, Luke spent the entire summer after finding out, furious with both of us, it's now been almost ten months since he learned about his sister and me, and he's slowly starting to come around to the idea.

"What's this song from?" I ask as the next one begins to play through the boombox speakers.

"You don't remember? This is the song you played right before our first time."

"I remember. I just like to hear you tell me about each one. And I'm glad this song made the cut. I'll happily rewind it back and replay that night over and over again."

Chuckling, she settles onto me, resting her head on my chest, and wrapping her arm around my middle.

We lie there for a long while, holding one another and listening to music before I finally gain the courage to ask what I've been wanting to ask.

"Hal?"

"Hmm?"

"If I do get picked up by a team, will you go with me?"

She lifts her head, whipping her attention in my direction to check if I'm being serious.

"I know it'd mean you'd have to transfer schools next year, but I honestly can't see myself playing in the league without you by my side. You've been there for every part of this. It's only right that you're with me for the next."

Her face softens with a sweet smile.

"I want to start our lives now," I continue. "I want to buy us a house. One that's all ours. I want you to be at every one of my home games. And though I'm glad I get to see you once a month now, I spend all the days in between waiting for these ones. I don't want to be away from you anymore."

"And if I'm not ready to go with you now?"

"Then I'll still buy you a house and it'll be waiting for you." I run my fingers through her hair. "And so will I."

"I'm kidding." She leans up, pressing her lips to mine. "Of course I'll go with you. I'd go anywhere with you."

"Yeah?"

"We both know it's going to be us in the end. What's the point in wasting time?"

"That's exactly how I feel."

I watch the excitement grow in her expression. "What if you get picked up by Boston? How amazing would that be to play for your dream team right away?"

"I can't even let myself think about that. Obviously playing in the league is the goal, but playing for my hometown?"

"It'll happen one day," she states. "I know it will."

I bask in her confidence in me. The same confidence she gave me that night on the roof when I was about to quit playing hockey for good. The same she gave me when I was too nervous to kiss her for the first time. The same she's had in us and our relationship since the day it began.

"So," she begins excitedly. "What kind of house are you going to buy us?"

I chuckle at the change of subject. "What kind of house do you want?"

"A big one. With four or five bedrooms that we can fill with kids one day."

I can't wait for that. I can't wait to marry her either.

"I'm assuming you want something colorful and pretty that fits your vibe."

She shakes her head no. "White walls. Boring. Like a big plain box, so when we get there, I can start renovating it to be ours. I'll paint every wall exactly how we want them, and I can add all the finishes we decide on together. It'll be my very first design project, and I'll make it into our dream home."

I'm having a hard time holding back my smile as I listen. "Is this house in the city or in the suburbs?"

"It depends on where we end up, I suppose. But ideally, we'd live a short drive from downtown so you can get to work, but in a family area that's a bit quieter. Like the neighborhood we grew up in back home."

I make a mental note of those items because if there's one thing I'm going to do, it's make sure this girl gets everything she wants in life.

"But what do you want?" she asks.

"You," I answer quickly. "I just want you."

"But you already have me."

"Then I'm happy."

"I'm happy too."

"Happy birthday, baby." I sigh. "My favorite day of the year."

Chuckling, she leans her cheek back on my chest as we continue to lie together, listening to her playlist.

"Tell me more about our dream house, Hallie."

And she does, while I lie there with a ridiculous smile on my face, listening as she goes into detail and paints a picture of the life we're about to have.

♥ Hallie 36

I clock in on one of the computers before saying hello to my coworkers at the bar. It's happy hour and there's a Raptors game later tonight. With their arena only a few blocks away and still a couple of hours before the puck drop, this place is packed.

And regardless that I will probably make good money tonight, I have no desire to be here.

This is my last shift of the week, and I made such good tips from the previous nights that I was tempted to try to get this shift covered. I'm not entirely sure why I didn't, other than I've never given up a shift before.

You could say I officially have senioritis from this job. My internship at the design firm will be over in a couple of months and with how smoothly Rio's home project is going and the way my social media content has been blowing up the last few weeks, thanks to some of Chicago's biggest names continually sharing it, a full-time position at Tyler Braden Interiors feels inevitable.

Tyler has said as much.

I can finally see the light at the end of the tunnel with a higher salary and more free time, but I wish that time was already here.

I'm enjoying my personal life far too much these days to bury myself in work.

Carson, or Ken as Rio still refers to him as, pushes through the swinging side door that connects the back of the bar to the storage room. He stops short when he sees me standing at the computer. "I thought you were off tonight?"

I furrow my brow. "I thought *you* were off tonight."

"Shit," I hear from behind me. "I was trying to get here before he did."

Turning, I find Rio pushing himself through the crowd to get to the bar. Which isn't all that difficult for him because people are staring at him in disbelief, shocked that one of their favorite players is here. It's the same way they look at him almost every night he shows up to wait for my shift to be over.

He's in his game-day suit and looks sinfully hot.

"Hey." There's plenty of surprise in my tone because he should be on his way to the arena right now. "What are you doing here? I thought I wasn't going to see you again before you left."

He leaves straight for the airport tonight from his game, which is why we said our goodbyes this morning when he dropped me off at work.

"What do you think about coming to my game tonight?" he asks. "We're playing against Boston, and I could use my good luck charm."

A spark of excitement blooms before I quickly put it out. I've been wanting to go to one of his games for weeks. But there hasn't been a home game on a night I'm off work.

"I wish I could, but I have a shift."

"Actually," Carson cuts in. "I'm covering for you. Your boy begged me, so here I am."

I whip my head in Rio's direction. "You did?"

He rubs his palm over the back of his neck—his adorable, but nervous tell.

Rio and Carson have gotten to know each other a bit from all the time Rio has spent here sitting at the bar. Carson even enjoys his little nickname, but I didn't know they were on the level of calling in favors.

"He also bribed me with two tickets to the game on my boyfriend's birthday," Carson adds. "So here I am."

"I did do that." Rio's smile turns cheeky. "What do you say, Hal? Think you could take the night off?"

I check back in with Carson, who gives me the go-ahead.

"Yeah." My smile gets way too big, way too fast. "I'm in."

"Let's go!" he cheers, knocking his fist on the bar top. "I'll meet you around back. Thanks, Ken! I appreciate you!"

Rio jogs out the front before either of us can say anything else.

I look at my coworker. "I can tell him to stop calling you that, you know."

Carson lifts a brow. "Um no...have you seen him? Don't tell my boyfriend, but yours can call me anything he wants."

"Back off," I tease, clocking out on the computer before I say a few quick goodbyes.

When I walk out the back door, Rio is waiting by the passenger door of his truck, holding it open.

"I should've asked, but are you sure you're okay taking the night off work? I'm probably being selfish here, but I've been kind of desperate to get you to a game and it hasn't worked out yet."

"I'm sure." I lean up and kiss him. "I've been wanting to go see you play live instead of watching you from that TV in the corner of the bar."

I round the door to my seat to find a folded jersey waiting for me on it.

"What's this?" I ask, already knowing.

"Well, I couldn't exactly give you my extra jersey like I used to in high school since the equipment guys keep them, so I got you your own."

Opening it, I hold it up to my body to check the size and that's when I see his last name stitched on the back above his number thirty-eight. An overwhelming sense of pride takes over because how the heck did he go from the kid who couldn't even stand on a pair of rollerblades to this?

"And," Rio continues, "I wasn't sure what you'd want to wear with it, so I kind of raided your closet and brought you a bunch of options."

He opens the back door and right there on the bench seat is what looks like half my closet.

"I thought I'd know what you'd want to wear, but then I got in your closet and realized you have way cooler style than me, so I brought a bit of everything. Apologies for how annoying this is going to be for you to put back later, but I got nervous."

The way this man knows me.

I snag the pair of wide-legged checkered denim that I love but then find one of his hoodies tossed in the back seat, so I grab that too. He even brought some of my favorite jewelry pieces, so I add that to my pile, making sure to select a mix of silver and gold.

"Thank you for doing that."

His eyes bounce between mine, and I don't think I'll ever get over the way he looks at me. It's the same way that it was when we were younger. "Anything for you, Hal."

He waits until I'm in my seat to close the door. Rounding the truck, he gets behind the wheel while I take a quick inventory of my surroundings to find no one else in the lot.

I lift my shirt up over my head, leaving me in only my bra for a moment.

"*Fuck me,*" Rio groans from next to me.

I can't help but laugh. "Let me change real quick before we get to the arena."

Slipping my arms and head through his hoodie, I situate my new jersey over it, pulling the hood out of the neck hole. Then I unzip my work jeans and push them down my hips.

"Maybe I could be late."

Looking over, I find him fixated on my partially naked body, hooded eyes, parted lips.

"You need to focus on your game," I tell him as I pull the checkered denim on.

"I don't care about my game right now."

I zip and button them, fully covering myself. "Well, you should. This is a big one. You missed your last Boston game because of me. You need to do well tonight, right?"

He offers me a sweet smile and a nod. "Yeah, but I'm glad you'll be there."

I smile right back at him. "Me too."

He laces his hand with mine for the short drive.

I can tell he's mulling something over in his mind, and he hesitates before finally asking, "Could you ever see yourself living in Boston again?"

I knew this conversation was going to happen at some point, so I've already been thinking over my answer to his question.

"One day, yes."

He quickly looks in my direction, utterly surprised, before refocusing on the road.

"If that's where you're going to be, then one day, I'll be there too," I continue. "I'm not going to lie to you and say I'll be ready to move before your next season starts. I'm just beginning my career here and I have a huge opportunity at this design firm. Plus, this is my first time living away from my dad since he got sick, so knowing I'm within driving distance is comforting. But I think eventually, yeah, I'd feel okay being farther away."

I can see his wheels spinning as he nods.

"But we're going to be fine either way," I tack on. "After everything we've been through to make it back to this point, a bit of distance while you're in season isn't going to break us. You need to chase your dreams, like I'm chasing mine."

His lips tilt into an understanding smile. "I just don't want the idea of chasing my dreams to mean that I'm losing you again."

"It doesn't. I promise."

He lifts my hand to his lips to leave a kiss there.

"Since you're coming early with me," he says. "There's a room where all the players' families hang out pre-game and again post-game. It's right outside of our locker room. I'm going to take you there. All the other wives and girlfriends will be there, and Stevie will make sure to show you how it all works."

That is *not* what I was expecting. I kind of thought I'd have a ticket with a seat number that I could sneak into while I waited for the game to start.

As if he can read my mind, he asks, "Does that make you feel nervous?"

"A little bit."

His voice is soft. "Why does that make you feel nervous, Hal?"

"I don't know."

"Yes, you do."

I huff a small laugh because what's the use in lying to this guy? He knows me too well.

"I think because for six years, I watched your life move into this new, impressive phase. You have all these new people around. I mean, you're literally famous now."

"Gross."

"But you are, and sometimes I get nervous that because I'm part of your old life, I won't fit into the new."

He's quiet for a long moment before he says, "But you're not just a part of my life. You're the center of it. So, if something isn't fitting around us, that piece needs to change, not you." He runs his thumb over my knuckle. "And yes, I'm in a different phase of my career than the last time we were together, but you've been with me since the beginning of all of this. So, if anyone should feel out of place, it certainly isn't you."

I squeeze his hand in mine.

"You have no idea how many times I've wished you were there, waiting for me after these games the way you used to. But I also don't want you to feel uncomfortable about it."

That hits me right in the heart, thinking of how many times he came out of the locker room post-game to find no one there for him.

I shake my head. "I'll be there."

Rio parks in the private lot behind the arena. He opens my door for me and immediately slips his fingers through mine as he leads me to the private entrance.

An older man in a black blazer opens the door for us as we approach. "Rio!" His face lights up. "Good to see you, man. How are we feeling?"

"Great. Excited to play tonight." Rio puts his free hand in his. "Bruce, this is my girlfriend, Hallie. Hallie, this is Bruce. He's worked here since the United Center was built and hasn't missed a single game as long as I've been playing here."

"That's right," Bruce says proudly.

"It's nice to meet you." I offer him a smile.

"You too. Rio has never brought someone with him to a game other than his mom when she's in town, so I take it we'll be seeing you again?"

"You'll be seeing her a lot," Rio adds for me.

"I like that." Bruce smacks him on the shoulder. "Good luck tonight."

We say our goodbyes before taking off down a hallway that's lined with photos of previous Chicago teams. It only adds to the surreal nature of it all. To see him in his fitted suit, headed to the locker room, and finding him in six of these previous team photos along the wall.

He's really doing what he always dreamed of.

"So," I begin. *"Girlfriend,* huh?"

"Oh, I'm sorry. Do you think we should take a couple more decades to get to know each other before I start calling you that?"

"I just didn't know I was, is all."

"I assumed this was another one of our unspoken things." He drapes an arm over my shoulders as we continue walking. "But in case it needs to be said out loud... Yes, Hallie Hart, you are my girlfriend. Though, you should know, there's a good chance I'll be changing both that title and that last name one day."

He pops a quick kiss on my hair as we continue walking.

It feels nice to hear him say it, but we both know what we're doing here. There's so much history between us that getting into a relationship only a few weeks ago does not make our relationship new. It feels like we're restarting right where we left off six years ago when we had our entire future planned with one another in mind.

"Rio," a man calls out, walking towards us. He looks vaguely familiar, but I can't place him.

"Hey, Will. I didn't know you were coming tonight. I would've gotten you a ticket."

Will and Rio put their hands in each other's.

"I'm not sure if you remember each other, but Will, this is my girlfriend, Hallie. Hallie, this is my agent, Will. He started representing me towards the end of my second year at Michigan."

That's how I know him. He was there the night Rio got drafted.

I watch as Will puts all the pieces together before a genuine smile lifts on his lips. "Of course, I remember you." He nods as if he were approving of the whole situation. "It's really good to see you again."

"You as well."

He returns his attention to Rio. "Do you think I could talk to you for a moment in private?"

Rio looks down both ends of the hallway. "We can talk now. Anything you need to say, you can say in front of Hallie."

Will keeps his voice quiet. "The reason I'm at the game tonight is because Boston's general manager invited me to join them in their box."

Rio's brows lift in surprise. "Really?"

"Apparently they're not planning on re-signing Eriksson after this season."

"No shit?"

"Who is Eriksson?" I ask naively.

"He's one of Boston's defensemen," Rio explains. "And his salary is about the same as mine, which means…"

"They're making room in their budget for you," Will states.

I watch as the realization sinks in for Rio and this childlike smile graces his mouth.

"Of course, nothing is official," Will continues. "And any discussion I have with their GM tonight is all hypothetical, but they're making it clear that they want you."

"I've always dreamed of playing for the Boston Bobcats."

I squeeze Rio's hand in mine. He was always a huge fan of our local team. His childhood room was covered in their memorabilia.

"I know. And we're going to make it happen." Will gives Rio's shoulder a smack. "Good luck out there tonight. I'll call you after and let you know what I find out. Hallie, I'm sure we'll be seeing plenty of each other in the future. Have fun."

He takes off with that, leaving the two of us alone.

"That's exciting!"

There's an edge of disbelief on Rio's face. "I knew it was a possibility of happening, but their lack of cap space in the budget was always going to be an issue."

"And now it's not."

"And now it's not," he repeats.

I swear I watch him go through every emotion. Excitement. Disbelief. Concern. Sadness when he looks at me and remembers I won't be going with him right away. But then that all settles and he seems centered and content, and I'm hoping that the reminder I gave him in the car is repeating in his mind. That whether we're living next door to each other or there's a few hundred miles between us, we're good.

We continue down the hall, approaching a door.

"All right," he says, "this is where I leave you. Are you sure you're okay?"

With a bit more confidence thanks to Rio's little speech from earlier, I nod.

But before he opens the door, he turns to face me. "I know this is just another in-season game and there's not much significance to it for anyone else, but it feels significantly more important now that you're here. You should've been at my very first pro game, Hal. But seeing you in my jersey again?" He shakes his head in disbelief. "It feels nostalgic. Finding you in the crowd was always my favorite part of my high school games."

I lightly laugh. "You never told me that."

"Every week I looked forward to game day like it was Christmas morning because I viewed it as my chance to impress you. Today feels like that, but amped up to a million."

Reaching up, I wrap my arms around his neck. "I don't think I could be more impressed by you if I tried. And I just feel lucky that I got a chance to see it all happen."

"That's exactly how I feel about you renovating my house. Do you know how many times I watched you repaint your bedroom walls growing up?"

"Just be glad I'm not still in that lemon-yellow phase now that I'm working on your house."

"Baby, I'd happily live with yellow walls, knowing you're the one who chose them." He gives me a quick kiss. "Ready?"

When he opens the door, every pair of eyes turns our way. I find Stevie first, which settles me more than I was expecting, and I give her an excited wave. It's nice to know that even though I'm the new girl around here, she's been doing this for years and can show me the ropes.

"Everyone," Rio announces, "this is my girlfriend, Hallie. Be nice to her or I'll literally never talk to you again." There's a collective laugh throughout the room before Rio tilts my chin up to him. "See you after."

"Good luck."

He drops a quick kiss on my lips before taking off to the locker room.

Stevie instantly greets me with a hug. "Don't be nervous. I was working for Zee's team before I ever showed up to one of his games as his girlfriend, and I was terrified. But we're all here for the same reason. Everyone is so excited to meet you."

We spend about an hour in the family waiting room and any nerves I did feel about being the new girl quickly dissipate. Everyone is kind and excited for me to be there, and apparently, they've been curious about me for weeks, ever since Rio told his teammates that we were together.

They seemed invested in getting to know me, which I think could be attributed to Rio telling his buddies that I was his high school sweetheart. It helped affirm the fact that my being here tonight isn't temporary.

About fifteen minutes before warmups begin, Stevie leads me up to their family's box. Apparently, this box belongs to the Zanders and Shay families all season long, with Zee playing here some nights and Ryan on others.

When Stevie opens the door, I find it full of people. *Familiar* people this time.

They all turn to face me as I stand in the doorway, but I'm not as nervous as I was downstairs. Because these people I've all met at one point or another. Ryan and Indy are here, as are Miller, Kai, Kennedy, and Isaiah.

I lift my hand in a wave. "Hi."

"Hell yes!" Miller cheers.

"Finally," Kennedy says with a smile.

"I am so glad you're here!" Indy tacks on, rushing me with a hug.

I say my hellos to them and to their husbands too. They give me a little tour of the suite, showing me where the food and drinks are, and we hang out while we wait for the game to start.

It's nice. It's *really* nice.

They don't just make me feel like I belong, but they make it seem as if I'm right where I'm supposed to be. Any fears I had about fitting into Rio's new life are quieted. His "new" friends are exactly the kind of people I'd hope for him to have in his life.

Outside of Zee, I learn that Stevie and Indy have known Rio the longest, since they started working on their team plane at the beginning of Rio's second year in the league. It's clear how much they care about him. They seem like a pair of older sisters without the intimidating aspect.

I don't even have to ask to know that Indy is his closest friend here, and that Ryan, her husband, loves Rio but won't admit it out loud.

The Rhodes families met him a couple years later, rounding out these five athletes and their wives who formed this unique little friendship group. But it's wild to me that Rio met Kai and Isaiah last because every time Isaiah opens his mouth, I can't get over how similar it sounds to some of the goofy things I've heard Rio say over the years.

The way they all speak about him—highly, while still giving him a bit of shit—makes it so clear how loved he is by these people. They seem like the definition of *his people*. Like they'd do anything for him.

I understand that sentiment all too well.

We take our seats as the team skates out for warmups, and I'm smack dab in the middle of the girls, with two on my left and two on my right.

The jumbotron plays the team's intro video, but I can't peel my eyes away from the rink, following Rio as he skates onto the ice and takes a few laps on their team's side. Even with the arena dark and the light show bouncing over the ice, I watch him.

Which is nothing new, I suppose. Thirty-eight has had my attention for fifteen years now, even when he was wearing a different number.

"Does this all feel surreal to you?" Stevie asks.

I nod. "That's exactly how I would describe it. I started watching his games when he was in middle school, but I haven't seen him play live since his second season in college."

"All of us met our husbands after they were already playing in the pros," Miller says. "How do you feel, getting to see his career form from the beginning to this point?"

Still focused on him on the ice, I simply say, "Proud."

Once the lighting lifts again, I watch as Rio drops his helmet and gloves off at the bench before slowly skating along the length of the rink closest to us, eyes up in our general direction. I note the moment he spots Zanders' box, and more specifically, me, because his face lights up with a beaming smile in a way I feel possessive over. In a way I've only seen directed at me.

Rio lifts his stick in the air, pointing it in my direction then tucks it under his arm to form his hand into a heart. And I don't miss the way he lets one thumb overlap past the other to create a little extra piece, not letting it connect where it should.

Too many people sitting in the section below us turn over their shoulders to see who he's pointing at. My cheeks are most likely flaming right now as I shake my head at him, but I also can't fight the stupidly giddy smile on my lips.

This man has no shame, acting like a love-sick idiot on the ice with twenty thousand fans watching him.

But I'm a love-sick idiot too, so I somewhat discreetly make the same heart, *our* heart, with my hands for him to see.

That smile on his lips only grows before he skates back to the bench, grabs his gloves and helmet, and refocuses on warming up.

"That boy is so in love with you," Indy states.

Spoken or unspoken, I feel the exact same way.

37

Rio

Whiskey in hand, I sink into the hot tub, making sure to align my body with the jets. We just got home from a two-game road trip where both of them went into overtime, and thanks to the added minutes on the ice, my body is aching.

It always does around this time of the year, though. We're at the mid-point of the season with games, practice, or travel happening almost daily.

So even though I should probably be getting some sleep, seeing as it's close to two in the morning, I know it'll be a futile attempt until Hallie gets home from her shift at the bar. She was cleaning up to get out of there around the time our plane landed, so Zee dropped me off at home to wait for her here.

With one arm spread wide on the ledge of the hot tub, I grab my whiskey and take a long pull, letting the liquid burn as it goes down.

I fucking need it.

I called my mom today and tried for what felt like the hundredth time to explain Hallie's side of things. She wouldn't even let me get past her name. I understand she has so much resentment built up towards my dad and the whole situation in general, but she's taking her anger out on the wrong person.

Same as I did.

If she heard Hallie's side of things and saw the big picture, she'd be a lot more gracious and understanding. I know she would be. But I don't think she wants to understand anything when it comes to my dad's affair.

They're the two most important women in my life, and it's stressing me the fuck out.

It's not like Hallie is asking me to choose between them. Shit, she doesn't even know how bad it's been between me and my mom lately. But if there ever comes a time that I need to choose which relationship to keep safe, I won't make the same mistake twice.

I'll choose Hallie every time. I just hope my own mother doesn't put me in that situation.

And there's Boston.

Because yeah, I think that's happening.

My agent got quite the insight during our last home game. Boston's front office is making way for me to join their lineup. Which is my dream. It's everything I've ever wanted.

But there's another part of me that doesn't quite believe that anymore. Because I recently got everything I've ever wanted, and those dreams are wrapped up in one single person, not in a career achievement.

Fuck me. I'm exhausted.

I've been on this endless loop of what-ifs whenever it's quiet and I'm forced to think. My brain hasn't stopped spinning since I was home last, so I take a long swallow of my whiskey and hope that'll be enough to quiet things until Hallie gets here.

The steam billows around me as the jets go to work on my sore and aching muscles. I sink into the water, trying to tune it all out for a moment when a flash of headlights bounces off my back fence, the way it does whenever someone turns down our street, and I instantly know it's her.

By the sounds of it, Hallie pulls into my driveway and parks my truck there.

I hate that she gets home this late. I hate that she's working a second job, but even more, I fucking hate the reason why.

I'm about to get out of the hot tub to go find her inside, when, through the back-door slider, I find her marching through my house, straight towards me. She opens the back door, and the force in which she does, tells me something is wrong.

"Rio DeLuca."

Oh, she's pissed. At me, it seems.

She stops at the base of the stairs that lead up to the hot tub, arms crossed and hip cocked out with attitude.

"Hi, baby." My tone is cautious. "I missed you."

She simply raises a brow, as if she's expecting me to explain myself.

"So much?"

"What the hell, Rio?"

I stretch my arms out wide on the ledge of the hot tub. "I'm going to need you to be a little more specific."

"Do you want to explain to me why I went online to make a loan payment, only to find that it's fully paid off? In fact, both of my loans are."

I should probably be concerned that she's clearly upset, but I really enjoy it when she's feisty like this. She also looks so fucking cute, fully bundled up in her wool trench coat and beanie pulled down over her ears, only allowing about an inch of the ends of her hair to peek out.

"Hallie, let's go inside and we can talk about this. It's freezing out."

"No."

Her quick defiance is fucking hot, so I stay seated, tracing the rim of my glass with my fingertip. "Then get your ass in here."

She seems thoroughly unimpressed with the idea of joining me and judging by the way she doesn't move to do that either, I know she's not going to give up until I give her an answer.

"Fine." I take a long swig of my drink. "I get that you feel prideful when it comes to money, especially towards me. But we aren't on opposite teams anymore, baby, so put down the armor."

I watch as her shoulders loosen an inch.

"I had every intention to pay them off the morning after we got back from seeing your dad, but I didn't want you to think I was trying to buy your forgiveness. Because I wasn't. I'm still not. But, Hal, if I were around when your dad got sick in the first place, the way I should've been, I would've taken care of the financial aspect anyway. You know that. And I think that's why you were so against my help before."

Her features begin to soften, and it's the confirmation to know I'm right.

"I would've told me to fuck off too," I continue, and I watch as a spark of a smile lifts on her lips. "But this isn't me swooping in like some kind of knight in shining armor, trying to save you. To be frank, I fucked up that opportunity years ago and I'm so fucking sorry."

"Rio," she interrupts, shaking her head. "I need you to stop apologizing."

I allow that request to sink in. I know she doesn't want to hear it because she's long forgiven me, but it's different from my perspective.

"You should know I'm partly doing this for me," I continue. "I'm trying to forgive myself for past mistakes I made, and watching you work as hard as you're having to work isn't helping that. I feel guilty when I sit at the bar and watch you serve drinks all night. I feel guilty when you get home after two in the morning, knowing that in a few hours you're going to have to wake up to do it all over again. So, while yes, I paid them off so you won't have to worry about them anymore, I also paid them off for me."

Her stance shifts, softening from the defensive mode she was in.

"Because I *should've* been there, Hallie. I should've been there to take care of it then, so I'm taking care of it now. And I need you to let me."

Once again, I stretch my arms up over the ledge, taking up the entire corner of the hot tub. Absent-mindedly, I swipe some of the condensation off my whiskey glass as I wait for her answer, but we both know I'm not backing down when it comes to this. There's no compromise in this situation.

She hesitates for a long while before she finally says, "Okay."

I give her a single nod in agreement. "Now get in here."

She exhales a disbelieving laugh. "You're out of your mind. It's too cold out."

"I'll keep you warm." I bring the whiskey to my lips. "Take your goddamn clothes off."

Hesitating for only a moment, she complies.

She slips the buttons of her jacket through their looped counterparts before peeling it off her arms and tossing it onto a nearby snow-covered table. She does the same with her beanie and the rest of her clothes, kicking her shoes and socks off last.

She's left wearing only this little dark red matching set and a million goose bumps painted on her skin.

She's a fucking stunner in red. Stunner in every color under the sun, if we're being honest.

"Holy fuck, love."

Her bottom lip quivers but it tilts with a shy smile.

"It's no wonder I've been obsessing over you for fifteen years."

Her laugh is small as she quickly bounds up the stairs to join me in the warm water, and her shivering stops almost immediately when she sinks her shoulders below the water's surface.

She wades over to me, straddling my lap when she gets to my far corner, slipping her hands behind my neck.

"Hi," she says softly.

"Hi, baby." I run a hand over her back, pushing her ass down onto my lap because she's so fucking buoyant right now I can hardly feel her.

She rolls her hips against mine as soon as they make contact. "I missed you."

"I missed you."

"Thank you." She holds eye contact. "I never would've let you pay those off if you asked."

"I know. And that's why I didn't."

"I'm not sure you understand how much that means to me." She inhales deeply through her nose, as if she were taking her first breath without a heavy weight sitting on her chest. "I don't know how I'm ever going to be able to say thank you enough."

Which is exactly what I don't want. I didn't do it to hold it over her head.

"Let's make a deal."

Her brows cinch. "What do you have in mind?"

"You're not allowed to thank me for it anymore, and I'll stop with all the apologies."

A slow smile lifts on her lips. "I like that deal."

"Good." Slipping my fingers through her hair, I pull her in for a kiss. "Can you quit your job now?"

She chuckles against my mouth. "I haven't thought that far. I make good money there."

"You're working too much, and I want you at more of my games. To hang out with my friends. To come to family dinners."

"Let me think about it."

"Fine." I kiss her again. "So would now be a good time to also tell you that I bought you a car?"

She freezes, her lips still on mine before she pulls back to look at me. "Rio!"

"Hallie!"

Her eyes narrow. "Stop trying to be cute right now."

"I'm not trying. It just comes naturally to me."

"Well, then..." That smile she was trying to fight breaks free. "Stop being naturally cute."

"Will it make you accept it quicker if I tell you I didn't do it for you?"

"You did it so I'd stop stealing your truck?"

"Fuck no. I literally get hard just thinking of you driving my truck, but if I do end up back in Boston, you need something to drive here, and I need the peace of mind that you're safe."

She waits for a moment, her eyes bouncing between mine before she simply says, "Thank you."

I shake my head. "No more saying thank you."

"Fine. Then instead of saying it, I'll show you."

The tempting little smirk toying on her lips in combination with the way she rolls her hips against me, has me instantly fucking hard. Her arms tighten behind my neck, pulling her into me and pressing her tits right up against my chest.

The warm water. Her warm body. Fuck me, this is heaven.

Reaching behind her, I unclasp her soaked bralette and toss it aside, letting it float away in the water. Eyes raking over her, I bring my whiskey to my lips and take a drink.

She tracks the drip that lands on my lip, but before I can clean it off myself, she leans in and drags her own tongue to do so.

"*Fuck*," I groan, head falling back to the ledge behind me.

"Mmm," she hums. "Tastes good."

"Yeah? Do you want some more?"

Biting her lip, she nods.

I put the whiskey in her hand, but before she can even bring it to her lips, I stand from my seat, taking her with me and turning to sit her on the corner ledge. Wet skin, heated hazel eyes, peaked nipples, and spilled whiskey running down between her tits.

Bracing my arms on either side of her body, I lean down and lick it off her with a long, rough slide of my tongue.

"Holy shit," she murmurs under her breath as she watches me.

"You're right. That is good, but there's something else I want to taste. Spread your legs for me, baby."

She does as she's told, placing one foot on the ledge on either side of me.

"Good girl, Hallie. Now drink that whiskey to keep you warm while you're out of the water."

She's almost compliant when she brings the drink back to her lips, but then I see the mischievous tilt in her smile behind the glass. Before the rim makes it to her mouth, she pours a bit down the center of her body instead.

"Oops."

It's the least innocent sound I've ever heard and I'm fucking feral for it. My eyes are glued to the liquid trail as it takes a direct path down her chest, between her tits, and over her stomach. Before it can reach her belly button, I lick her clean, dragging my tongue all the way up her body, until take her mouth with mine to let her taste how deliciously it burns.

She's writhing beneath me as I kiss her, my tongue sliding against her own.

Between us, I drag my thumb slowly over the center of her panties and the moan she hums into my mouth feels like a direct line to my dick, the way all my blood rushes in that direction.

She's desperately seeking more friction, pushing her hips to meet my hand in pace when she pulls away from my mouth to look at me with heavy eyes and swollen lips. My attention is glued on her heaving chest when she spills more whiskey right over her body for me to taste.

I do as I'm told, sucking it off her tit and circling over her nipple, but I meet her gaze when I use my tongue to flick it, exactly how I'm about to do to the spot between her legs.

"That's so good," she cries, rhythmically rolling her hips into my hand where I haven't stopped creating stiff little circles on her clit.

She pours more whiskey over her other nipple, and I do the same to that one, circling with my tongue and lightly biting between my teeth.

"*Oh my God.*" She throws her head back. "I want to come. Will you make me come?"

"Of course, baby."

"Yeah?"

"Mm-hmm. I'll make you come if you quit your job."

She laughs but it's interrupted by a little moan. "Fuck you."

I smile against her skin, biting and sucking on her tits. "Give me what I want, Hallie, and I'll return the favor."

When she doesn't answer, I lighten my pressure on her clit to barely a brush.

"No," she whines. "More."

"Tell me what I want to hear."

She swallows, trying to catch her breath, and I can't help but run my lips over the curve of her throat.

"Fine," she finally agrees. "But I'm only quitting because I was planning to once I paid off those loans, and not because you told me to."

"Works for me."

"And I'm putting in a two-weeks' notice."

I chuckle against her, kissing a path over her stomach as I drop to my knees. "So responsible of you."

She's trembling as she looks down at me between her legs.

"Drink that whiskey, Hallie, and I'll make you come so you stay warm."

This time she does as she's told, bringing the rim of the glass to her lips to take a sip and it's so fucking sexy, I'm gritting my jaw to keep from coming myself.

I rip the center of her panties in two, opening up the lace to give me access to her perfect fucking pussy.

I place a quick kiss on my favorite freckle on her inner thigh before I bury my face between her legs. She's fucking soaked and not from the water. Her clit is swollen and only becomes more so when I suck it between my lips.

She makes this pretty little sound of approval, so I do it again and watch her reaction. I watch the way her chest heaves and the way her stomach quivers. I watch the way her legs try to tighten around my face.

"Oh God," she whines, fingers threading into my hair and gripping hard.

I circle her entrance with my fingers before I push two inside. She's already convulsing, her pussy squeezing me tight.

"Damn, Hallie, you're going to come already."

She nods frantically, chasing her orgasm as she rides my hand and face.

"That's it, baby," I encourage from between her legs. "Take what you need."

Pumping in and out of her, I feel her walls tighten around my fingers while I lick the rest of her.

"I'm close. I'm close. I'm close," she chants. "I didn't touch myself once while you were gone."

I hum against her core and watch her whole body shiver. "You waited for me, Hal?"

She nods frantically. "It's not as good without you. Only you."

Fuck, I love that.

"Always only you, Rio."

I'm going to fucking come apart in my swim trunks with my tongue on her pussy and my name on her lips.

I stroke her two more times before I feel her come apart around me. And fuck, is she pretty when she does. Flushed chest, trembling muscles, lip tucked between her teeth.

I stand as I let her ride it out, keeping two fingers inside her and replacing my tongue with my other thumb. And I swear, I'll never get over watching this woman fall apart.

But then she does something to remind me I'll never get over this woman, period.

She reaches out and slowly traces the lines of her tattoo.

I slowly pull my fingers from her cunt, but she's pulsing so hard, I can hardly remove them. All it does is make me eager to feel her tighten around my cock.

Pushing my swim trunks down enough to free myself, I wrap a fist around my dick while Hallie continues to follow the lines of her tattoo.

"Fuck, baby." I stroke myself. "I love when you do that."

We stay there for a moment, her recovering from her orgasm as I pump myself while standing between her spread legs.

Eventually, those legs wrap around me, pulling me into her. Opening the torn lace of her underwear, I run my cock over her center, coating me her in release, and letting the torture build. Letting the anticipation turn unbearable.

She's still gripping that almost empty glass in her other hand, the one that's not running over the inked lines, so I take it from her and down it in one go. Then I grip the back of her head and pull her mouth to mine to give her the last taste on my tongue.

"You ready?" I ask against her mouth.

"Please," she whispers. "Put it in."

I tap my cock over her clit a couple of times before I push down on the head and drive inside of her.

Her mouth pops open and I watch as she loses her breath. Her nails are practically drawing blood in the way they're digging into my flesh, and I'd typically check on her and ask if she's okay, but I know she is.

Sometimes we're sweet together in bed, but sometimes the vibe calls for something different. Right now, it feels like the latter. Like she doesn't necessarily want me to be soft and sweet.

I drop my face to hide in the crook of her neck, concentrating on not finishing too soon. But she's still fucking pulsing from her previous orgasm and it's enough to make me come if I allow it. But if she wants me to fuck her the way I can tell she does, then I need to hold it together.

"Jesus, Hal. The way you're pulsing over my cock right now."

As soon as the words are out of my mouth, I feel her tighten even more, gripping my cock with her pussy.

"Fuck, baby. This is going to be over way too fast if you do that again."

And she does it again, like a brat who wants to test the theory, and I fucking love it. I love when she does what I tell her to, and I equally love when she doesn't.

Honestly, I just love her. But that's nothing new.

When I pull back to look at her, she's smiling wickedly.

"You're not being a very good girl tonight."

She shakes her head no.

"Do you want me to fuck you hard? Is that it?"

That smile turns up. "I want you to take what you want."

And so, I do, pulling my hips back before snapping them forward.

Hallie's lips are formed in the perfect O, and the little lines between her brows are creased.

Gripping the side of the hot tub with one hand and the back of her head with the other, I set a steady pace, watching myself rock in and out of her. It's fucking mesmerizing, the way she takes me, the way she meets me, the way she fucking cries my name.

She grips onto my forearm with everything she's got and it's not long before she's tightening around me again.

"You going to come on me, Hallie?"

She squeaks out this desperate noise, so I don't change my pace or position.

Hallie reaches between us and circles her clit with her fingertips, which I'd do for her if I didn't already have my hands full with keeping us upright on the ledge of a hot tub.

"That's it," I encourage. "Fuck, Hallie, you feel incredible. Do you know that? Do you know how lucky I am to be with you?"

She grips the back of my head with her other hand, pulling my lips down to meet hers and as soon as my tongue plays with hers, she comes, every muscle in her body tightening at once.

Because, yes, it's fun to fuck, but we always end up here, kissing slowly, giving praise, letting hands roam and wander before they end up intertwined with one another.

I keep a consistent pace until I feel her starting to come down and once she does, the moment changes to something more tender. She wraps her arm around me as we kiss, and her fingers find her tattoo again while I keep a languid tempo with my hips. It doesn't take long before I join her, falling right over the edge and coming inside of her.

She continues to run her fingers over the ink.

"You like that, don't you?" I ask through hard-earned breaths.

She nods against me.

"You like that you're permanently under my skin."

"I love it. It feels like you're branded and mine."

"That's because I am."

Her smile turns possessive, which is well-deserved. I'm completely and undeniably hers.

Pulling back to rest my forehead on hers, I know we're a tangled mess of damp bodies and shared breaths, but her hazel eyes are locked on mine trying to tell me something she hasn't said in six years.

It's okay that it's one of those unspoken things. I know that Hallie loves me the same way I love her.

Slowly, tortuously slowly, I pull out of her and watch as my cum drips down between her thighs.

It's fucking hot, seeing her full of me. It makes that possessive side roar to life when I clean it up with two fingers and push it back inside of her.

Lips on hers, I whisper, "Still mine."

She kisses me as our breathing evens out until she giggles this cute laugh.

"What's so funny?" With a smile on my face, I pull back to look at her.

"I'm absolutely freezing right now."

Chuckling, I tug her down into the water with me as I fix my swim trunks, making a mental note to drain the hot tub tomorrow.

But fuck it, it was fun and completely worth it.

I bring her with me to the steps but have her wait while I get out and grab a towel. Wrapping it around her naked body, I quickly carry her inside the house with me. I don't care that we're leaving a trail of water behind us, I start to take her right upstairs and into the warm shower.

She's dotting languid kisses along my neck when she quickly sits up and looks around.

I pause halfway up the stairs. "What's wrong?"

She takes in her surroundings before her attention is back on me. "What do you think of the house?"

Even more of the renovations have gotten done since I was home last. Walls have begun to get painted. Flooring will be installed next week.

I keep my focus on her and not on the space around us. "I love it."

And you.

Her grin proves she's so proud of herself and I fucking love that too.

She should be proud. Her designer eye, her time management, her organization. She is so good at what she does, and I don't think she fully understands that yet.

Hallie renovating this place and putting her touch on every square inch of it is reason alone that I wouldn't sell, but there's plenty more reasons too.

She's going to need a place to live once Wren's house next door sells.

I need somewhere to stay when I come to visit her and my friends, but my stomach sinks when I picture Hallie living here without me. Living here alone. That was never the plan for this house. We were supposed to live here together. Rooms were supposed to be filled.

"Thank you for giving me the chance to do this," she says quietly. "You basically let me design my dream home."

This *is* her dream home, and that's the whole fucking point. I don't know how she hasn't put the pieces together yet, but that's the final and most important reason why I won't sell. Six years ago, even after things fell apart between us, I bought this house for her.

It's everything she told me she wanted, and there was a part of me that hoped if both it and I were here waiting for her, she'd somehow find her way home.

38

"**A**re you sure you're okay?" I ask Rio as we wait around the kitchen island for dinner to be plated so we can carry it into the dining room.

"Of course, I am." He forces a smile on his face, running a hand down my back. "Don't worry about me, Hal. I'm good."

But he's not. Rio has been quiet and unlike himself ever since he came out of Indy's home office a couple of hours ago. It's Sunday and he doesn't go a Sunday without talking to his mom. Only today, she didn't answer his call, and I can tell it's bothering him. The strain in their relationship has been weighing on him for weeks, regardless that he thinks he's doing a good job of hiding it from me.

Mia DeLuca, Rio's mom, is such an integral piece of his life, and they're barely communicating because of me. When they do get on the phone, it quickly turns sour when my name is brought up.

Watching it happen firsthand is making me even more understanding as to why he made the choices he did all those years ago. Twenty-seven-year-old Rio is struggling with them not getting along. It's no wonder twenty-one-year-old Rio did what he thought was right by her when her life was falling apart.

I hate to see him hurting this way, but I don't know how to fix it if Mrs. DeLuca doesn't want to listen.

Rio places a quick kiss on my hair before taking one of the entrée plates into the dining room. I grab the salad bowl and follow behind, placing it with the rest of the dishes in the center before taking a seat next to him at the Shays' massive dining room table.

It's evident that their house was chosen with the want to host in mind. It's warm and inviting, as are the people in it.

This is the first family dinner I've been able to attend now that I've quit my second job, but Rio has been trying to get me to join for weeks. I finally have weekends and evenings free and have spent the month of February going to all his home games, working on finishing his house renovations, and getting to know these other eight people around the table.

But even if I could've joined a family dinner over the past couple of weeks, this is the first one that everyone has been able to attend anyway.

Kennedy and Isaiah have been gone for spring training, but were sent home early so Kennedy could get her department in order before Opening Day and Isaiah could train here while giving some of the new guys a chance to get some playing time.

"Indy," Rio says, trying not to laugh. "What's wrong?"

I look over to find her brown eyes glossing over from her seat at the dinner table.

"Nothing." She shakes her head. "This is just really nice. Everyone is here. It finally feels...complete."

She looks over to me and smiles.

"Blue," her husband chuckles, running a soothing hand over her back. "There's no need to cry over that, baby."

"I can't help it! It's who I am."

The table as a whole laughs, which I'm quickly learning is acceptable when she cries about something that isn't sad.

Ryan wraps an arm over her shoulders to pull her into his side, kissing her on the top of her head. "It's one of the many reasons I love you."

"Thank you for having me," I cut in. "Your home is beautiful."

She wipes under her eyes, smiling. "It is so good to have you here, Hallie. You're the final piece, even though I guess you were technically the first piece, knowing him as long as you have."

Under the table, Rio runs his hand over my thigh, squeezing it.

I've loved getting to know these people, especially the other four girls. But knowing how close Indy and Rio are, it's been especially nice to get to know her. I can see why they've become as good of friends as they are.

"Speaking of beautiful homes," Kennedy begins. "Rio's place looks amazing already. It's been fun to follow the progress on your social media."

I find him watching me with a proud smile as food is passed around the table. With each dish, he puts some on my plate before adding a serving to his.

"I can hardly recognize it," Kai adds. "Mills was showing me the pictures online."

"It's coming along," I say. "Also, if I haven't already said it enough, thank you all so much for sharing my stuff on your accounts. The firm has been buried with inquiries and it's a huge reason why I was offered a full-time position after my internship ends."

"Hell yeah, you were!" Miller raises her Corona in the air.

"That was all you," Rio says from next to me as we begin eating. "We just made sure more people got to see how talented you are."

"I filled out an inquiry form last week," Zanders says plainly.

Every pair of eyes turns to him in confusion.

"Tyler was asking me about it," I tell him with excitement. "He's hoping to use your project for an upcoming episode of his show."

"That'd be great." Zanders nods to himself. "More exposure

for the center, but I want you to be the designer on the project."

"I definitely will be."

Stevie looks at him, more confused than anyone else. "What project are we referring to?"

He tries to act completely nonchalant about it, moving food around on his plate. "Well, you and Cheryl have been talking about moving Senior Dogs of Chicago into a bigger building. I found one. I bought it. I want Hallie to design it so there's more room for people to come visit the dogs, hang out with them, and take them on walks."

She stares at him, dumbfounded.

"What?" he asks, trying to bite back his smile. It's drastically different from the arrogant version I've gotten to know.

"How people ever thought you were an asshole, I'll never understand."

Zanders chuckles. "Stevie girl, I hate to break it to you, but you were one of those people."

"We're five years past that." She waves him off. "Zee, we can board so many more animals in a bigger space."

"Plus, Tyler's show is huge," Rio cuts in. "If you guys do an episode with him and get some of the guys from the team involved too, you could get so much exposure for the center. You'd have people wanting to adopt from everywhere. Not only Chicago."

"Thank you," she says quietly to her husband with a beaming grin.

He's acting as if buying her business an entirely new building is no big thing, smiling at her knowingly without saying anything more about it.

"Was the other house on your Instagram account your first project?" Indy asks me.

"My first *official* project, yes. Outside of redoing my childhood bedroom a million times growing up."

I watch Rio smile to himself as he chews his dinner.

"That house on my account is my roommate's home. Actually,

Ryan, you might know her brother. Cruz Wilder."

He pauses with his fork midway to his mouth. "Cruz Wilder?"

"Yeah, he plays basketball too."

"I'm sorry, what?" He places his fork back on his plate, turning to Rio. "Your neighbor is Cruz Wilder's sister?"

"Yeah." He shrugs casually. "He owns the house. She's living in it while finishing school."

Ryan's eyes go impossibly wide. "You're telling me you've been living next to Cruz Wilder's sister for..."

"Four years."

Ryan laughs but it's laced with disbelief. "You've lived next to Cruz Wilder's sister for four years and you've never once mentioned it? Those brothers are huge names in their own respective sports. The oldest Wilder is going to be inducted into the NFL Hall of Fame one day, and the youngest brother was the MLB Rookie of the Year a few years back."

"Wait," Isaiah cuts in. "Easton Wilder? He's a beast, and he's only in his third season in the league. You're living next to his sister?"

Kennedy's eyes go wide. "He's amazing. Every time we play against him, I'm shocked by how good he is already."

"Okay." Isaiah holds his hands out to stop her. "He's not *that* great, Ken."

"I don't know," she teases. "He's pretty great."

Isaiah takes her left hand and places it flat on the table. "Okay, just making sure it's still there."

She laughs. "I haven't taken off my wedding ring in three years, you caveman. Still your wife. Still fully obsessed with you."

Isaiah wraps his arm over her shoulders. "Hell yeah, you are."

"The Wilder family is West Coast sports royalty," Zanders says. "They're all playing in the same city now, close to where they grew up, I think. It's a huge fucking deal."

"You've been living next to their sister this whole time and never mentioned it?" Kai shakes his head with a laugh. "And you've spent all these years fanboying over Ryan?"

"Well yeah, he's Ryan fucking Shay." Rio turns to him. "Don't worry, honey. Cruz Wilder will never be you."

"But he basically is. He's the West Coast version of me." It sounds like Ryan is fanboying now. "I'm a huge fan of his, even when I have to pretend I'm not a few times a year when we play each other."

"Wren is great too," I chime in.

Rio chuckles. "Wren *is* great. She's been an awesome neighbor and I'm going to miss her when she moves."

"She's moving?" Ryan asks, outraged. "You had four years to tell us about her and her family and now she's moving?"

"Damn, Ry," Indy teases. "Do you need him to get you an autograph or something?"

"Yeah. Kinda."

"Where's she moving?" Kennedy asks.

"Back home to Northern California," I tell her. "Now that all her brothers are playing for their hometown, she wants to get back home too. I hope to visit her at some point, though."

Rio smiles at me. "We'll definitely do that."

"Yeah," Ryan agrees. "Maybe we should make that a group trip."

Miller cackles. "Fanboy Ryan Shay might be my new favorite."

"Back to the house," Isaiah cuts in. "Are we having a housewarming party or what? With you most likely moving this summer, we should enjoy the new house while you've still got it."

The entire room goes silent, and Kennedy smacks him in the shoulder.

"What?" Isaiah asks with an edge of innocence. "We all know what's going on. I don't know why we're pretending like we don't."

"Fuck it. We can talk about it." Rio sits back in his seat. "Boston is going to make an offer after the season ends as long as I don't re-sign with Chicago, and it's my childhood dream to play for them."

When he looks in my direction, I give him a wink, telling him I'm on board.

"And I'm sorry I didn't say something before," he continues. "But leaving you guys isn't exactly something I've been stoked to talk about."

"Rio, you've got to do what's best for you," Zanders says. "I think we all understand the appeal of playing for our hometown team."

Rio nods.

Kai sits forward, forearms on the table. "And it's not like you're going to leave and that's it. You're going to be back here to see Hallie, right?"

"Of course."

"Don't worry about all of us," Stevie adds. "We're all going to still love you."

Rio's attention shifts to Ryan. "Is that true, Ryan?"

The tension dissipates with a laugh from everyone, thanks to Rio's futile attempts to get the basketball superstar to admit he loves him.

Ryan shakes his head. "I have no idea what you're talking about."

Indy tries to discreetly wipe her cheeks again.

Rio sighs when he spots her. "Ind."

She offers him a placating smile. "Just going to miss you is all."

"We'll chat later, okay?"

She nods to agree.

There's still a heaviness lingering over the room.

"So, uh..." Isaiah begins again. "Are we having a party at your house or what?"

Kennedy shakes her head at him. "One-track mind, I swear."

"Hell yeah, we're having a party. I was hoping the house would be ready for Hallie's birthday, so we could celebrate both, but a couple of the projects got delayed. We'll get something planned in April or May for the house."

Indy's sadness begins to shift when she sits up excitedly. "Wait. Hallie, when is your birthday?"

"Next Saturday."

"What? We have to do something! Next Sunday's dinner has to be a birthday dinner."

"I'll make a cake!" Miller chimes in.

Rio squeezes my thigh again and I don't do a great job of hiding my smile. It feels really nice to make new friends again.

"Wait, when do we get home?" Zee asks him.

"We'll get back late Saturday night. Coach wants to stay an extra night to see his family in Montréal. I already tried to convince him to let us fly home Friday after the game instead, but he's not into it."

"Sunday dinner will be fun," I interrupt. I don't need him to feel bad about something he can't change. And honestly, whenever we do celebrate, I know it'll be the best birthday I've had in a long time. "I'm looking forward to it."

"Speaking of March birthdays." Miller sits up in her seat. "Did you all get the invite to Max's party?"

"How the hell is he going to be five already?" Kennedy asks rhetorically.

Kai shakes his head. "I can't talk about it."

"The baseball theme is so cute," Stevie says with a sweet smile.

Ryan chuckles. "Was that his idea?"

"Oh yeah. He's obsessed with baseball right now." Miller pulls out her phone and holds up a picture for all of us to see. "He's starting T-ball, and we just picked up his very first uniform."

Right there on her phone screen is little Max, a big smile on his face, wearing his brand-new uniform with number twenty-one on it.

"He's wearing his dad's number." Zee grins. "Did he choose that himself?"

"I seriously cannot talk about this." Kai takes off his glasses, pressing his thumb and forefinger against his closed eyes.

Miller laughs but runs her hand over her husband's back.

Isaiah smiles. "We asked him what number he wanted to wear, and he said he wanted his dad's number. It was fucking adorable."

"I fucking love that kid." Kai sighs. "But I have no idea how he's old enough to play already. Where did the time go? It feels like yesterday Miller was bringing him to the field to take his very first steps."

Miller smiles softly at him, giving his shoulder a squeeze.

"How'd you pick your jersey number in the first place?" Indy asks. "Does twenty-one mean something?"

"Oh, *fuck me*," Rio mutters under his breath for only me to hear.

"Great question, Indy!" I drape my arm over Rio's shoulder, excited for this conversation.

"Not exactly," Kai says. "I was twelve years old and didn't know what number to pick, so I flipped the numbers of my age because that's how my twelve-year-old brain worked."

Isaiah chuckles. "And I'm two years younger, so I picked the number that was two less than his. Nineteen."

Rio is completely silent next to me, and I know he's hoping for this conversation to die, but I refuse to let it. "Ryan, how about you?"

"I don't have a good reason. I was, what? Five or six years old when I first joined a team." He looks to his sister for confirmation. "And I was sick the day they picked numbers, so they handed me a jersey with number five on it when I came back. I haven't changed it since."

"How consistent of you, baby." Indy laughs, dropping her head to his shoulder. "Zee?"

"Mine is simple. Number one was taken at the time and I figured that number eleven was even better because it's number one twice."

There's a small laugh among the group because from what I've gotten to know of Zanders, that thought process tracks.

Everyone turns their attention to Rio, but he doesn't answer.

"Rio?" Stevie pushes. "What about you?"

He hesitates for a long moment, not looking in my direction.

I'm just sitting here with a smug smile on my face and my arm draped over his shoulder, ecstatic that I'm finally going to get the answer to the question I've been curious about for months.

"Well," he begins slowly. "I was always number eighty-three growing up."

"So, you flipped the numbers?" Miller guesses.

"Not exactly. I didn't know what number to choose when I was a kid, so I picked the number of my favorite day, which was, of course, my birthday. August third. Eighty-three."

Realization finally dawns on me. I forgot that his old number was his birthdate. Which means his new number is…

"When I got to training camp in Chicago, they asked me if I wanted to keep eighty-three, but I decided it was time to change it to my *actual* favorite day."

My birthday. March eighth. Thirty-eight.

He's been wearing my birthdate on his jersey for six years and I had no idea.

He slowly turns over his shoulder to look at me.

I lean my chin on my arm that's resting on him, a painfully big smile on my mouth. "So, you like *really* like me, huh?" I tease quietly for only him to hear.

"I think we both know it's a little deeper than that, even if we're still pretending it's one of those unspoken things." He turns to press a quick kiss to my lips. "And I have for fifteen years, Hal. You've had me hooked since the day you became the girl next door."

I drop the last dirty dish by the sink while Ryan finishes washing them.

Isaiah is cleaning up the table, Kennedy is putting the leftovers in Tupperware, and Kai, Miller, Stevie, and Zanders are grabbing their sleeping kids from upstairs to take them home.

It's getting late and we're all ready to go, so I sneak away to

Indy's home office where I hung my coat in the closet when I first got here, but when I get to the office door, I find it locked.

I'm about to go ask Ryan if I could get in there when I hear Rio's voice coming from inside the room.

"I'm going to sign."

"You are?" I hear Indy ask, but I don't know how to read the tone. Is she surprised, or is she simply agreeing with him?

"But I don't know how I'm going to tell her." There's an edge of panic in Rio's tone. "How is she supposed to come visit? My mom refuses to even let me *talk* about Hallie, and I'm supposed to assume they'll be able to be in the same room?"

My stomach drops.

It's not hearing that he's going to sign with his hometown team that makes me feel sick. I've known that for a while. But instead, it's the confirmation that his mother's disdain for me has been eating away at him as I suspected it was.

"It'll work itself out," Indy tries to soothe.

"It's not that simple, Ind. It's actually very fucking complicated. I can't give you all the details of why that is but trust me. The history between them is not some kind of small misunderstanding that will go away on its own."

He's right about that. Our situation is nuanced. Only he and I will ever fully understand.

"Rio, you have to do what's best for you."

"I know." There's a long pause. "But it makes me sick to think that for the rest of my life my mom isn't going to approve of the woman I love. How the fuck am I supposed to be okay with that, Indy?"

I walk away before she responds because I shouldn't be a part of this conversation.

I create as much distance as possible between me and the door as I hear my pounding heart in my ears. And not because Rio just admitted that he loves me. I already knew that too. My heart is racing because he's right.

He *shouldn't* be okay with his mother not liking the woman he's with. And I know with every fiber of my being that I can no longer be that woman.

That realization is so painful that I think I'm going to be sick.

I just...I don't know how I could even get the words out. The thought of that conversation, which is one I believed I'd never have to have, makes me physically ill. Not to mention, how will I ever find even courage to do what I know has to be done?

Rio's mom is his only family. He loves her the same way I love my dad, and I won't be the reason that relationship falls apart.

I refuse to be.

39

*Rio*

"Thanks, man," I say to the rideshare driver as he drops me off at the airport. "Appreciate it."

Grabbing my bag, I head inside the Montréal airport.

We just won our game, and I'm eager to get home. Hallie's birthday is tomorrow, and I refuse to miss another one, so I got approval from team management to catch a commercial flight home tonight instead of waiting for the team plane to leave tomorrow afternoon.

I haven't told her yet. I've been keeping this surprise to myself, and I can't wait to see her face when I walk in the door tonight. I should be able to get there before midnight and spend every second of my favorite day with my favorite girl.

Heading straight for the security line, I pull out my phone to check in with Wren, wanting to give her a heads-up that I'll be sneaking into her house later.

Me: *Hey, Wren. Keep this between us, but I'm catching an earlier flight home. Hal doesn't know, but I should be there before midnight. Wanted to give you a heads-up that I'm going to come over when I get there.*

Wren: *So cute, Rio! But I don't think Hallie is in town right* *now. She left early this morning with a suitcase.*

Me: *What are you talking about?*

Wren: *She left while I was still sleeping, but I checked my doorbell camera and saw her leaving with a bag.*

Me: *And you have no idea where she went?*

Wren: *No. I texted her but haven't heard back. I kind of assumed she was headed to meet you on the road.*

Could she be headed here? No. No, there's no way. She doesn't know where the team is staying, and if she got that information from Stevie, Zee would've stopped me from leaving if he had any inclination that she was on her way.

Me: *Can you let me know if she comes home?*

Wren: *Of course.*

Something feels off. Something in my gut is telling me to not get in the airport security line, so I don't. I stand off to the side and text the girls to see if any of them have heard from her.

They haven't.

I didn't call Hallie after my game because I was trying to surprise her, and I'm shit at lying but fuck it. I dial her number, but after it rings too many times, it goes to voicemail.

Panic starts to take over because the last time she left the house with a bag and wouldn't answer her phone was when her dad was in the hospital. Did she go back to Minnesota again?

If Hallie isn't going to answer her phone, there's only one other person to ask.

I call Luke.

Things were fine between us at the hospital, but Hallie is going to be in my life forever. Things between her brother and me need to be better than fine, so I got his phone number from her a few weeks ago with the idea of inviting him and his family down when the house renovation is finished.

"Hello?"

"Luke? Hey, it's Rio."

He hesitates for a moment. "Hey, man. Is everything okay?"

I glance around me, watching the security line build up with passengers. "I'm not sure, actually. Is Hallie there?"

"Is she here in Minnesota? No..."

Fuck.

"Is your dad doing all right?"

"Yeah, he's doing pretty great actually. I don't think she's headed this way unless she didn't tell us."

"She would've been there by now. She left early this morning."

There's a long beat of silence on the line.

"Let me call her," he suggests. "I'll text you back when I know more."

"Yeah. Thanks. I'd appreciate that."

"I'll let you know."

He hangs up the phone and I pace the airport as I dial her again.

No answer.

Something feels off. Something isn't right.

When I analyze everything a little more, she has been a bit distant this week. Calls were shorter than usual. Texts were more infrequent. I summed it up to her being busy with the renovations because that's what she told me, but now I'm thinking there was something going on that I wasn't aware of.

I lift my phone to call her again when it dings with a text.

And the message on the screen is one I never thought I'd read.

My attention snags on the house next door, following the roofline that connects it to this one. I take inventory of the red brick exterior and the new ivy that's grown along the front wall since I lived there.

The car parked in their driveway is not my family's car. The pots and planters on the top step are different from the ones I walked by every day growing up.

It's been a long time since I was last here, and my nerves are rattling.

I've spent the entire week thinking about this conversation. Going over all the things I need to say and writing it down in the form of a letter in case she doesn't want to listen to me.

Rio's team plane lands back in Chicago tomorrow afternoon, so I took the day off today, knowing I need to get back home before he does. He doesn't know I'm here, nor does he have any clue that I've been planning this. I didn't want him to try to talk me out of it.

Yes, it's his mom, but this conversation also doesn't really have anything to do with him.

I truly have no idea how this is going to go. The last time I saw

Mrs. DeLuca, she told me she never wanted to see me again. Yet, here I am, six years later, standing on her doorstep.

Inhaling a deep breath, I steel my spine and knock on the door.

Standing outside, I slip off my coat as I wait. It's early March in Boston, but it's a warmer day than I expected.

The door finally opens with a smiling Mia DeLuca revealed behind it, but as soon as her eyes land on me, that grin drops.

I swallow hard. "Hi."

If there's one thing I know for certain, she hasn't lost that intimidating factor one bit. Standing in the doorway, she looks me over from head to toe, but when she makes it to my face, she can't meet my eye.

I know exactly what she's thinking. I can see the pain in her eyes.

Exhaling, she drops her shoulder an inch as she opens the door wider. "Well, I can't exactly leave you out in the cold, now, can I?"

The smallest tick of a smile lifts on my lips before I slip past her into the house where I spent so much of my childhood.

As soon as I'm inside, an overwhelming wave of nostalgia passes over me. It's the exact same as it's always been. It's the same kitchen we used to bake cookies together in. The same dining room our families shared so many dinners together. The same living room where I watched TV after school with Luke and Rio.

The front door closes behind me, pulling me out of the past and reminding me why I'm here.

"Can we talk?" I ask, an edge of desperation in my tone.

Because I am desperate. I'm desperate to fix this for him.

His mom doesn't answer right away, walking past me to her coffeemaker. She takes her time grabbing a mug and pouring a cup, until finally, she asks, "Why?" with her back to me.

"Because I love your son, and I won't be the reason you two aren't talking. And when he moves back to Boston, I'm going to be visiting often until I eventually move back here too. It'd be nice if we could be in the same room. For him."

Her shoulders deflate, then she grabs a second mug to pour another coffee.

She's not looking at me still. "You cut your hair."

"I did."

"Rio's not with you?"

"He doesn't know I'm here."

Finally, she peeks over her shoulder at me.

"If you're up for it, I'd like to explain myself. And if you don't want to hear me out, I wrote it all down." I slip the letter out of my back pocket and hold it out to show her. "If you still hate me afterward, I'll have to live with that, but it's killing him that you two aren't getting along, and I love him too much to not try to fix this."

She turns to face me, leaning back on the counter, assessing me. "I don't hate you, Hallie. But you were practically my daughter, and you didn't tell me."

My throat goes thick. "I didn't, and I have regretted that choice since. It not only lost me him, but it lost me you. I can't change it, but I'm hoping if I can explain why I didn't say something at the time, you might understand."

Her jaw tics as she processes.

"I'm not here to give you an excuse," I continue. "But I'd really like to see if there's any way we could move forward."

"For Rio?"

I nod. "Maybe for us too."

Finally, she grabs the two mugs of coffee and brings them to her kitchen table, placing each on a coaster.

"Come on." She takes a seat, gesturing to another empty chair. "Let's talk."

I join her, both of us bringing the coffee up to our lips and taking a drink.

"Thank you," I tell her quietly.

"It's your birthday tomorrow."

My eyes flit to hers, shocked at her memory. "It is."

"Doesn't Rio want to spend it with you?"

I nod with a soft smile. "I have a flight home in the morning. I'll get back there before his team lands in Chicago."

"That's good." She takes another drink of her coffee. "I feel like I should've added alcohol to this."

"You're telling me."

She chuckles and it's nice to hear. This isn't comfortable by any means, but she could've closed the front door in my face instead of sitting down and drinking coffee with me.

Mrs. DeLuca stands, going to the fridge before coming back with a bottle of Bailey's, pouring a healthy amount in mine, then taking her seat and adding some to her own coffee.

"So, what is it you want to tell me?"

I take a long sip of my drink. "I need to tell you what happened two weeks before you found out about everything."

She nods, and I can practically see her mentally preparing herself. "I'm listening. Tell me what you came here to say."

Taking a deep breath, I do exactly that.

Hallie

(AGE 19)

I'm supposed to be looking for a place for us to live, but every time I open my laptop to do so, I end up typing in the words *non-Hodgkin lymphoma* in the internet search bar.

Because right now, that's all I care about.

I need to know everything. I need to find the best treatment options. I need to know how sick he's going to get so I can prepare myself. But most importantly, I need to know how to fix him.

I'm frantic and desperate to fix him.

I'm also terrified, but I don't know how to handle this fear other than doing everything in my power to change this outcome.

The past three weeks have felt like a dream. Rio got picked up in the first round of the NHL draft, which for anyone is a huge deal, let alone a defenseman. We celebrated with both our families, some of our old high school friends, and the entire neighborhood. I immediately started packing for our move and working on my transfer paperwork to a Chicago-based university, and each day since, I've spent looking for the right apartment for us to rent until we can find our dream home.

But everything changed last night when my parents sat me and my brother down to tell us that my dad has cancer.

Two weeks ago, the idea of living a thousand miles away from my parents seemed like no big deal. But today, that distance feels unfathomable. After crying myself to sleep last night, I woke up with the determination to fix this...right now, ideally.

There's so much of me that still wants to go with Rio, but the terrified side of me doesn't want to be more than ten feet away from my dad. Yes, I'm panicked and frantic, and probably not thinking clearly because this is all so fresh, but I don't care about logic at the moment.

I need him to be okay. I'd give up everything to make sure he's okay, and last night, as we found out everything was about to change, it seemed like I was the only one of us who felt that way.

Luke was completely checked out after we got the news. I had hoped to talk to him because he's the only person who can understand how I'm feeling right now, but his bedroom door was closed all night. However, I heard him on the phone for hours, talking about it to his new girlfriend, Sarah, who I haven't met yet.

Then there's my mom, who hasn't seemed like herself since I came home for the summer. I thought it was strange until last night when I realized that my dad had probably been showing signs of being sick for weeks leading up to his diagnosis. She must have been so worried about him.

All I wanted to do was go to my parents for comfort, but how could I? My mom just found out that the love of her life is sick. And from the research I found, his treatment journey is going to take its toll on her too. She didn't need me crying to her about it.

Then there's my dad, who is probably the most scared of all. This is happening to him after all.

The only other person I wanted to go to was Rio, but I couldn't tell him. As soon as I say the words out loud, it'll mean they're real, but I'm not ready for them to be real yet.

So instead, I cried myself to sleep and have never felt more wrung out as I do this morning.

Which is why I thought coming to a coffee shop would be a

good place for me to bring my laptop to apartment hunt. I was hopeful that the caffeine would help me focus, but I've been here for over an hour, my coffee is untouched and cold, and my internet search has nothing to do with Chicago and everything to do with a cancer research hospital I found in Minnesota.

I don't understand how everyone around me in this coffee shop is having a normal fucking day while I'm sitting here more terrified than I've ever been in my life.

I need to tell Rio.

If I decide I'm not ready to go with him yet, he'll understand. I know he will. I just don't want to blindside him two weeks from now when we're supposed to be loading up our cars and driving to Chicago together.

The mere thought of this conversation has my eyes burning with tears, but I guess that's what happens when you've been crying a lot. It starts up again at the drop of a hat. So, before I end up breaking down in the middle of this coffee shop, I close my laptop and start the short walk home where I can do so in the privacy of my own room.

Or rather, his room.

Rio is at a training session but should be done soon. When I get back to our street, instead of going to my house, I go to his. I'll wait for him in his room and tell him about my dad before I lose the nerve to do so.

His parents are both at work, so I find their hidden spare key under one of the planters and let myself inside.

Technically, I live in the house next door, but Rio's feels equally like home. I've spent so much time here with him. I've enjoyed countless hours here in the kitchen with his mom. Our families have endlessly bounced between this house and mine for years now, so letting myself into their home isn't strange in the slightest. Rio does the same with our place.

Leaving my laptop by the entryway, I head straight upstairs. His parents' room is at the top of the landing, so when I pass their closed door, I take a right, down the hall to Rio's bedroom.

His door is closed too, but when I reach to open it, another door opens instead.

Over my shoulder, I watch his parents' bedroom slowly creak open, but the woman who exits isn't Mrs. DeLuca.

"Mom?"

Adjusting her blouse, her eyes snap up to mine.

I've always been told I am the spitting image of her, and right now it feels like I'm looking in a mirror due to the complete and utter shock on her face that I know is reflected on my own.

She's in her work clothes, though her heels are dangling in her hand. Her cheeks are flushed, her hair is a touch tangled, and she's frozen in place outside of her best friend's bedroom.

"Hallie." My name is hardly a ghost of a whisper past her lips. "What are you doing here?"

My eyes go wide. "What are *you* doing here?"

Because what the hell is going on?

My attention flicks to the open bedroom door, but she steps in front of it to block my view.

"It's not what it looks like."

"What does it look like?" My heart is pounding. I can hear my pulse ringing in my ears. "What are you doing here?"

"Mia...needed..." She throws her thumb over her shoulder towards the room. "Mia needed me to grab her something."

My gaze drops to her arms. She's carrying nothing but her shoes.

"Mom?" my voice cracks, laced with a panic plea. "Please tell me what you're doing here."

"Steph," Mr. DeLuca's voice calls out from inside the room. "Did you want—"

His sentence cuts short when he steps behind my mom and spots me down the hall, standing in front of his son's bedroom.

And just like that, everything I was hoping I'd falsely assumed is confirmed.

His shirt is untucked and partway unbuttoned. His belt is still unfastened.

"Hallie," he breathes out, eyes impossibly wide.

I can't speak. I can't move. This can't be fucking happening.

"Go back inside." My mom puts a hand on his chest, urging him back. "I'll handle this."

"Steph." His tone is desperate. His eye contact is pointed.

"She won't say anything."

My mom sounds so sure of herself as she closes the door, leaving only her and me in the hallway together. If I could get out of this house without having to pass by her, then I would. I'd run.

My mom turns her attention back on me. "Hal—"

"How could you?!" I practically scream.

She closes her eyes. "Hallie, let me explain."

"Let you explain?" I laugh sardonically. "Let you explain what? What kind of explanation could you possibly have for sleeping with my boyfriend's dad? What the hell are you thinking?"

"I know," she says calmly. "I know."

"How long?"

"Hallie."

"How long have you been fucking your best friend's husband, *Mom*?"

Her jaw tenses as she rolls the answer over in her mind. "It started last fall, after you left for college."

I shake my head. "Unbelievable."

"Things changed between me and your dad once you and your brother left the house. It was different without—"

"Do not blame us!" I point a finger at her. "Don't you dare blame us for what you're doing to our dad."

Oh my God. My dad.

Those tears I was trying to delay begin stinging the back of my eyes again. "Why would you do this to him?" I can't even recognize the woman standing in front of me. "Dad has cancer and you're off having an affair with his closest friend?"

She takes a frantic step in my direction, but I hold my hands out to stop her.

"I was ending it," she attempts to claim. "That's all this was. I was ending it for your father."

"For my father?" The laugh that rips out of me sounds manic. "How about not cheating on him in the first place? This is going to destroy him. And Mia."

And Rio.

Oh my God.

This is going to devastate him. His parents' marriage is *everything* to him. It's the foundation on which he's built his own ideas of what love looks like.

It'll be entirely dismantled because of this.

I choke back a sob. "Rio's heart is going to be broken, Mom."

"No," she says firmly. "Hallie, you cannot tell him."

My eyes shoot to hers because what the hell does she mean I can't tell him? Of course I'm going to tell him. I have to. And screw her for making me be the person to break his heart.

"You can't tell Mia either."

"I have to! I'm not going to lie to Rio about this. We're about to start our lives together and you expect me to keep this from him? No way. I'm not protecting you."

"I'm not talking about protecting me."

My eyes narrow in confusion.

"I'm talking about protecting your dad. You cannot tell anyone, Hallie. If your father finds out, this *will* kill him."

All the air leaves me.

Did she really just say that?

And is she right?

Fear takes over again, pushing my rage to the side. I'm not sure what a broken heart would do to my dad when he's fragile already, but no part of me wants to test her theory.

"Think about what this information could do to your dad's health, Hallie. Do you really want to be the one to tell him?"

42 Hallie

"Then two weeks later, you found out anyway," I say to finish.

For the two weeks following that day, I kept my mouth shut. I kept my mouth shut about *everything*. I was terrified that my mom would be right, and that if I said something, it would be detrimental to my dad's health.

Of course, now looking back, I know that's not true, but for those two weeks, I was living in paralyzed fear that it could be.

If I would've known better, I would've told Rio and his mom as soon as possible. Maybe then I wouldn't have lost him for so many years. Or her.

Mrs. DeLuca is sitting across from me, tears silently streaming down her face. It's an entirely different reaction from the day she found out that her husband and best friend were having an affair.

In her house. In her own bedroom.

Rio and I were headed to pack up his room when we walked in to find his typically strong mother broken in a way I've never seen her. Broken in a way I'd never seen *anyone*. I watched the panic consume him as soon as we heard her blood-curdling cry. I noticed when the protectiveness took over as he picked his inconsolable mother off the ground.

I witnessed his heart crack when she told him about his dad, and I watched it shatter completely when she told him that I knew.

I'm not sure what hurt worse that day. The way she looked at me with complete and utter disgust, or how it felt to have the only man I've ever loved, tell me to get out of their house.

Across the table, Mrs. DeLuca brings her coffee to her lips as she watches me from over her rim, tears still falling of their own volition. "You look just like her."

My heart sinks at the reminder. It's a suspicion I've had for a long time, that maybe she looked at me the way she did that day because physically, I'm practically a carbon copy of her former best friend. And now, how could I expect her to look at me when I'm the spitting image of the woman who tore her family apart?

We both know it's not actually you that she's angry with.

"I know." I offer her an apologetic smile. "I'm sorry about that."

Shaking her head, she tells me not to be.

"That's why I cut my hair. I didn't want to look anything like her."

"*Hallie.*" More tears well in her eyes and she reaches across the table to put her hand over mine. "You're not her, honey."

"I am so sorry for what she did, and I'm even more sorry that I didn't tell you when I had the chance."

She inhales a shaky breath. "I had no idea that she said that to you. I had no idea your dad was sick. Is he…"

"He's good." I allow the genuine smile to lift. "He lives in Minnesota with my brother's family now."

"Luke has his own family?"

"He does. A wife and a son."

"Wow." She nods to herself as a long beat of time passes between us. "Hallie, I am so sorry that you were put in that position with an impossible choice to make."

"And still, I made the wrong one."

"You're only feeling that way because hindsight is 20/20. I know how much your dad means to you. You must have been so scared."

"I was terrified."

"And then I was horrible to you."

I shake my head. "If I were in your shoes, I probably would've been horrible to me too."

"If I can explain my side, at the time, it felt like everyone was lying to me. Your mom was my best friend. He was my partner for over thirty years. And I thought of you as my daughter. Then, just like that"—she snaps her fingers—"it was all taken away, and all I had left was my son."

I nod in understanding.

"Hallie." She exhales a long breath. "You should know that the reason Rio ended things with you the way he did is because of me."

"He was a grown man. That was his choice."

"Yes, but much in the way your mom made the choice for you by scaring you when she told you not to tell anyone about what you knew, I made the choice for my son."

She allows that statement to linger for a long while.

"I was alone for the first time in my life. I had just lost my husband and my closest friend, and I needed someone, anyone to be on my team. I was so angry and so hurt that I made sure my son felt that same hurt too."

"I can understand that. You wanted him to have your back, but he always has."

"He has, but I wasn't thinking clearly at the time. To be honest, whenever I reflect on that time in my life, logic flies right out the window. There was no part of me that was okay with the only person on my team having a relationship with *her* daughter." She closes her eyes for a moment. "And I made sure he understood that. Without saying the words, I made him choose."

She looks up at me cautiously, like she's expecting some kind of explosive reaction from me. But nothing about that admission is surprising. I saw her that day. She was in fight or flight mode, and from what Rio has told me, those survival instincts have lasted for years.

How exhausting for her.

"He was all I had left, Hallie."

"I know."

"I just wanted my family back, but he was all I had left." She shakes her head. "If he was with you, it meant he was on her side and that your mom had won. I know it sounds ridiculous now, but it made complete sense to me at the time. She would've taken every part of my family."

Realization dawns on me. "All this time, you thought I was protecting my mom by not telling you about the affair."

She smiles regretfully. "I did."

"No," I quickly say. "I was always on your side. I was always on Rio's side. I'm on Luke's side, and my dad's side. We haven't had contact with her in years. Not since we moved away from here."

Mrs. DeLuca's brows furrow and I watch as she lets all those pieces fall into place.

"We were all on the same side," I tell her. "And I'm sorry I didn't make that clearer at the time by telling you when I had the chance."

She uses the back of her hands to pat at her face. "I've spent about six years trying to avoid the regret I have from putting my son in the position to choose. There's this stubborn part of me that hoped if I never acknowledged what I did was wrong, or if Rio never talked about you or your family again, that regret would be irrelevant. I could bury those feelings.

"Then, a couple months ago, when he visited last, he talked about you, and as soon as he did, my walls went up. I was terrified that my only child was going to hate me for making him choose all those years ago, but at the same time, I couldn't stop myself from doing it again. I wasn't ready to dissociate you from your mom.

Regret is not easy to live with, and I tried to convince myself that I didn't regret my choices, but Hallie, I do."

"I know." I quickly nod. "I've regretted my choices for just as long."

She offers me an understanding smile. "It can feel suffocating once you let it in. Consuming and debilitating. But I was wrong. What I asked of him was wrong. When he told me about you living next door to him again, I was triggered, but it wasn't necessarily *you*, Hallie. It was the memory of how painful that time was. I didn't want to relive it."

"Then I show up at your door and here we are, reliving it."

She laughs and it sounds like there's an edge of relief in it. "Here we are."

"I'm so sorry."

"Oh God." She shakes her head. "No, *I'm* sorry. I mean I knew Rio loved you then, but I clearly didn't understand the extent of it. He's loved you for most of his life, and I will forever be sorry that I'm the reason he lost you for so long."

She squeezes my hand, and I realize then she's still holding it, so I squeeze hers back.

"I don't know that this will help that regret at all," I say. "But I think about what the last six years would've looked like if things happened differently. And I don't know. In a way, it was a good thing that going to Chicago with him back then was no longer an option. I would've been torn between two places at once. The strange silver lining of it all is while my dad needed me, there was nowhere else I wanted to be. Of course, I wish I didn't lose that time with Rio, but life had a funny way of working itself out in the end."

"Now, don't try to make me feel better about it."

I huff a laugh. "I'm not. I'm just saying, it's hard to regret the past when he and I are right back to where we were always meant to be. We just had to take a little detour to get there."

She studies me from across the table. "You've always loved him, haven't you?"

"Always. He's good and kind. And he's good *to* me, which I know is because he grew up learning to be good to you."

She's quiet for a long moment before she finally says, "I missed you, Hallie girl."

"I missed you too."

"Can I give you a hug?"

My smile blooms in an instant. "I'd love that."

She stands the same time I do, rounding the table to hug me.

"I'm so sorry," she repeats, holding on to me.

"I know. And I know you're not my actual mom, but you always treated me as if you were. And I'm sorry that I hurt you."

She exhales a long breath, and I do the same.

It feels like the final weight is lifted.

We unwrap ourselves after a long while, but she holds me at arm's length. "Do you have anywhere you need to be tonight?"

"No. I only came here for you. My flight doesn't leave until the morning."

"Would you stay for dinner? If you're up for it, I mean. I'd really love to hear about your life."

"Yeah." I can't hold back my smile. "I'd love that."

Rio

U sing my key, I unlock the front door of the house I grew up in.

But before I open it, I do my best to tamp down the anger that's simmering in my veins.

Once I landed in Boston, I got a second text from my mom, asking if I knew what Hallie's mother had said to her all those years ago when she accidentally caught our parents together. Of course I had no fucking clue, but now that I do, I can say with certainty, I've never actually felt hatred for a person up until now.

How fucking dare she put the burden of her choices on Hallie's shoulders. How dare she use the person her daughter cared for most as a ploy to scare her into keeping that secret.

Shit. I'm getting amped up again, just as I was the whole drive over here, but I do my best to swallow it down as I step inside. When I catch Hallie's eye as she's turning around from the couch to find me dropping my bag in the entryway, that anger all but disappears.

Her jaw goes slack, and her hazel eyes widen in surprise. "What are you doing here?"

She stands, rounding the coffee table to meet me, practically slamming into my chest. It's the best hit I've ever taken, and I instantly wrap her in a hug. Hallie has always been this grounding force in my life, and that's no different now.

I exhale, holding her tighter. "I was at the airport, about to catch an early flight back to Chicago to surprise you for your birthday when I found out you weren't there. Thankfully, there was a flight to Boston that still had room for me." I glance back into the living room. "Thanks for texting me, Ma."

She looks over the couch with a knowing smile on her lips.

I'm still in a bit of disbelief from the first message that landed on my phone while I was about to go through security at the airport, telling me that Hallie was in Boston and that she and my mom had talked through some things.

I went to a desk agent and booked a new flight right then.

Hallie rests her chin on my chest as she looks up at me and a bit more of that sickening feeling dissipates. More centered. More grounded.

"You were coming home early for my birthday?" she asks.

"Hell yeah, I was. It's my favorite day of the year."

She huffs a laugh as I push her hair out of her face.

"You okay?"

Her smile is sweet and genuine as she nods to tell me yes.

"Ma," I call out. "You good?"

She throws a thumb up in the air, which I can see over the back of the couch. "I'm good."

I do a double-take between them again. Part of me wasn't sure what I was going to walk into. From the text my mom sent me while I was at the airport, I knew the two of them had talked, but I wasn't sure what that talk looked like. Was there screaming involved? Crying? Did my mother break anything? Don't get me wrong, I love the woman, but her Italian blood runs hot. I didn't exactly expect to walk in and find the two of them sitting on the couch watching *The Great British Bake Off* together.

My mom stands from the couch, and Hallie slips out of my

arms to let me greet her with a hug. It's a bit tighter than usual because we haven't been okay for a while now, and I fucking hated that.

"Are we good?" I ask quietly.

"No." Pulling back she puts a hand on either side of my face. "I have a lot to apologize for before we're good."

I shake my head. "Ma, we're good."

"I'll get out of here and let you two chat, but I hope we can talk later."

"We will," I promise her. "But you don't need to go anywhere. Hallie and I can talk upstairs."

She smiles at me, but I can tell she's both tired from today and regretful from some of her actions lately. "I love you, Rio. I'm sorry we haven't been okay."

I bring her in for another side hug. "We're okay now, and I love you too."

Hallie is already a few steps ahead of me as I start up the stairs, and when she gets to the top of the landing, I slip my hand into hers to stop her.

"Wait, Hal."

She turns around, confused, as I stay two steps below her.

"Why didn't you tell me what your mom said to you?" The anger towards that woman starts simmering under my skin again. "I feel sick. You should've told me after I learned about your dad."

She shakes her head. "I didn't need to add onto your plate with how you were feeling at the time. You had already forgiven me for not telling you about the affair. It didn't matter then. You already understood without that piece of information added on."

"I think I hate her."

She huffs a laugh. "Get in line."

"This is what your dad meant when he told me she said something unforgivable around the time of his diagnosis."

Hallie nods.

"And none of you talk to her anymore?"

"No." There's not an ounce of sadness on my girl's face. "My dad offered to forgive her because he knew if he didn't, it meant I'd be the one taking care of him during treatment. But there was no way I was going to let her around him after what she did to him and after what she said to me."

Fuck, I love this girl.

"You're good down to your core, Hal. You know that?"

"So are you, baby." She wraps her arms over my shoulders. "Now let's stop wasting energy on her. I can tell you're worked up right now, but she's not worth it."

There's that soft, contented smile again and I decide to focus on that. Focus on her and us and what's ahead instead of what's in the past. It was six years ago, and she's clearly moved on.

"Call me 'baby' again."

Chuckling, she drops a kiss on my lips before turning to head for my room, but once again, I stop her.

"Thank you." The words come out like a breath of relief because that's exactly how it feels. "Thank you for coming to talk to her, Hallie. You have no idea how much that means to me."

Or rather she does know and that's why she did it.

Hallie's expression softens as she puts a hand on either side of my face, thumbs running gentle strokes against my skin. "I'd do anything for you, Rio." Her eyes bounce between mine. "Anything."

"I think you meant to say, 'I'd do anything for you, *baby*.'"

She playfully rolls her eyes as I take the last two steps to meet her. Picking her up, I carry her the rest of the way to my childhood bedroom where I don't put her back on her feet until we're inside, with the door closed behind us.

Hallie immediately takes herself on a tour, as if she hasn't been in here a million times before. It hasn't changed since I last lived here in high school. My walls are still covered in Boston Bobcats memorabilia. My closet is still filled with clothes I haven't fit into since I was a teenager.

She rifles through the closet before finding one of my old team hoodies, slipping it off the hanger and pulling it over her body.

Leaning back on my door, I watch her.

It feels like déjà vu without one specific memory to tie it to. Her in my childhood room, wearing my high school team sweatshirt. Shit, just her being in Boston again feels nostalgic.

Where it all started.

I spent six years missing a huge piece of who I am because that's how integral she is in my life. That's how embedded she is in the fabric that makes me *me*. I've heard the claim that you don't know what you've got until you've lost it, but I knew what I had. It made losing us that much more unbearable.

Those six years were their own kind of torture, and it would've made it a hell of a lot easier to go through if I knew this was the outcome. Me and her, for good.

I'd rewind and relive every goddamn moment.

Hallie continues her tour of my childhood bedroom while I cross to the window to check the roof. As I had hoped, it's clear.

"It's almost midnight," I remind her, sliding it open.

She looks at me over her shoulder. "Are you trying to say it's almost my birthday?"

"Meet me on the roof?"

Her smile is soft as she crosses the room to me, carefully climbing out the window. Once I'm sure she's steady on her feet, I grab a blanket off my old bed and follow her out.

It's a crescent moon tonight, but it's big and bright, and feels impossibly close. It always had a way of showing off on these nights, lighting the roof enough that we could see one another. It does the same tonight as we move to the center point of the roof on instinct, regardless that Hallie no longer lives in the house that connects to this one.

I follow her gaze when her attention snags on the window of her old bedroom.

"Does it feel strange to be back here?" I ask her gently.

She shakes her head. "It feels good. A little sad because I miss that time in my life, but these nights were always my favorite memories."

"Want to make another one?"

With my hand that's not holding the blanket, I offer to help her sit, but when she slips her hand into mine, she takes a step closer to me, staying on her feet.

Looking up, her eyes bounce between mine before she exhales the words as if desperately needing to get them off her chest. "I told your mom that I love you."

I can't help the smile that slowly slides across my lips, or the way the skin around my eyes creases at the corners.

Fuck, that feels good to hear.

Of course, I already knew that Hallie loved me, but the words sound like music to my ears after not having the privilege of hearing them for six years. Like a form of music that I wish actually *was* a song, just so I could add it to our playlist.

I slide my hand along her lower back, pulling her into me. "You don't think you should've told me before you told my mom?"

Hallie chuckles, picking up on the connection to the first time we said those words to each other, when I told Luke that I loved his sister before I told her.

"I thought it was another one of those unspoken things." Reaching up, she wraps her arms around my neck. "But it shouldn't be. It should be said as much as possible. Because I love you, Rio. I have loved you since we were children, and I will love you until we're old and gray. But if you didn't already know that, then I've been doing something wrong."

My smile only expands. "I know you love me, baby, and you know I love you. I haven't *stopped* loving you."

"Not once," she agrees.

It's the most peace I've ever felt, Hallie coming back into my life. To know that I'm loved, long before hearing the words again. To feel it in every fiber of my being. To see it in the way she looks

415

at me. To hear it in the way she speaks to and about me.

We are rare. What we have is rare and I'm going to spend the rest of my life protecting it.

"I love you, Hallie Hart. Spoken or unspoken, I've always loved you."

Leaning down, I kiss her. Soft and slow, but for a long while. So long, I eventually have to pull back because I know it's after midnight now. "Happy birthday."

She smiles against my lips, pressing up to give me one more kiss before we take our seats on the roof.

With my legs spread wide, she sits between them, leaning back against my chest. I wrap the blanket around us, crossing my arms in front of her.

Hallie sighs this content sound, and I understand that calm, that peacefulness. It feels like we've come full circle, sitting in the same place on the same date where I once sat with the girl next door on her thirteenth birthday.

But there's one thing that this birthday is missing.

Digging into my pocket, I pull out my wireless earbuds, handing her one and putting the other in my own ear.

"What's this for?" she asks.

On my phone, I tap on the music app and scroll to the playlist I've been putting together since October.

"Every birthday, I used to love listening to you tell me about all your important moments from the year, so I was hoping on this birthday, I could tell you about mine."

She turns back to look at me. "Really?"

With a nervous smile on my lips, I nod.

"Yes. Please. I'd love that, Rio." She drops her head back to rest on my shoulder. "I'd really love that."

"I couldn't exactly make you a mixtape like you always did for me, so this modern version will have to do."

I press play on the first song on the playlist.

As it starts filtering into the earbuds, she closes her eyes and listens. "What important thing happened with this song?" she asks.

I rest my head against hers. "This is the song I was listening to in the locker room right before I went out to play the game where I saw you for the first time again."

She quickly turns, her eyes shooting to mine.

Without letting the whole thing play through, I skip to the next song because I'm not going to be able to wait the entirety of this playlist to tell her what I need to say.

She swallows hard. "And this one?"

"This is the song I played in my house that first day you came over for a design meeting. It was the first time you ever stepped foot inside that house, actually."

Her brows crease as she begins to catch on to what's happening.

I skip to the next. "This is the song you fell asleep to in my car the first night I drove you home from work."

Her hazel eyes begin to gloss over, but then the next song plays, and she laughs, though it's a bit watery. "*Moana*?"

"The night you came over to help me babysit," I explain. "The first night it felt like maybe we could be us again."

Next.

"The song that was playing the night you asked me to keep driving. It was the night we kissed for the first time again."

Next.

"This is the song you played over the speaker system in the house. It was the first time I heard you voluntarily play music for yourself again."

Her soft expression shifts, lifting a brow. "You mean the day I walked in on you in the shower."

"Yeah, that may have happened that day too."

She laughs, head falling back to my chest as I hold her tight and skip to the next song.

"This is the song we danced to in the kitchen when we decided to give us another chance."

As it plays in the earbuds, Hallie shakes her head in disbelief. "They're all *our* important moments."

I press pause.

"Hallie, do you remember the very first day we met, and you were listening to music? You had to finish the song before you could talk to me."

She smiles to herself. "Of course."

"Do you remember why you said you kept track of those songs?"

"Something about when I want to relive a moment, I can rewind it back and start from the beginning."

"Exactly. I want to rewind all of it, Hallie. I want to remember everything. You made sure we could remember our first years together, so I made sure we would remember this one."

She's looking out over the neighborhood with her head leaning back on me, but I can still see her attempt to discreetly wipe at her cheek. "Are they *all* moments we shared?"

"Actually." I hover my thumb over the last song on the list. "You weren't there for this one."

Pressing play, I let the music come through the earbuds. I let her listen for a while. I let her be the one to ask.

She looks up at me. "What happened while you were listening to this song?"

I smile at her softly. "This is the song I was listening to when I signed my contract extension with the Chicago Raptors."

Those hazel eyes go wide as she abruptly sits up. "What?"

I just chuckle at her reaction because I know she heard me.

Turning, she straddles my lap, knees bent on either side of me with a mix of panic and confusion etched on her face. "But...but I heard you. After family dinner, talking to Indy. You said you were signing."

I search for the memory of what she's referring to until it clicks. "Yeah. I was referring to signing with Chicago."

"You said, and I quote, 'How is she supposed to come visit?'

and 'I don't know how I'm going to tell her.'"

I can't help but laugh. "So nosey, baby."

"Rio. You were talking about me visiting you in Boston."

"No, Hal. I was talking about my mom. I didn't know how I was going to tell *her*," I explain. "She's been planning on me moving back here for years now. And I didn't know how it'd work with her visiting Chicago because she wouldn't be allowed to stay with us if she continued to have an issue with our relationship."

I watch as the realization settles in.

"You're serious."

"I asked team management to not make the announcement until next week. I've been planning to tell you like this. Listening to our important moments together. On your birthday. On the roof. Only, I didn't know it'd work out so perfectly that we'd end up back on *this* roof."

She puts her hands on either side of my face, holding my attention as if it weren't already on her.

"Rio, playing for Boston is your childhood dream."

I shake my head. "*You're* my childhood dream."

Her lips part without words.

"Some dreams have changed, but others have remained the same." I brush her hair behind her ear. "I love the city we live in. I love my team. I love my friends. And I love you. We lost six years, Hallie, and I'm not missing another day of you again."

Her brows crease with worry. "If it's about me staying in Chicago, I don't have to. I can come with you. I don't want you to give up the chance to play for your hometown team for me."

"Playing for Chicago feels like I'm playing for my hometown because it *is* my home now. *You're* my home. Being loved by you for the rest of my life is the only dream of mine that's never wavered. There's no doubt in my mind that I'm already exactly where I want to be."

She lets the idea settle in before the beaming smile slowly lifts on her lips. "You're staying."

"I'm staying, baby. But I've got to say, if we ever do decide to move, we need to pick a warmer place to live if we're going to keep sitting on the roof in fucking March. It's freezing right now, and I know the roof of our home in Chicago is just as cold."

She laughs, her head falling back, until my words sink in, and her eyes cautiously make their way back to mine. "*Our* home?"

"Our home." Sliding my palms up her thighs, I pull her tighter against me. "I thought you would've realized it the first time you came over. Hallie, the irony of hiring you to design the house, is that you're the person I bought it for."

Those eyes start to gloss over again, and she shakes her head. "I thought there was no way, at first. I noticed the white walls and the four bedrooms. The proximity to the city while still being in a neighborhood, but I thought there was no way you would have remembered that."

"I remember everything about us."

"When I learned you still had the mixtapes and I saw the tattoo, I thought maybe it could be."

"The house has always been yours, Hallie. *Ours.* It was just waiting for you to come make it a home."

She laughs this small disbelieving sound, but still, she's emotional. It's sweet and beautiful and vulnerable. So much more vulnerable than she was when we first ran into each other again a handful of months ago. It's my soft girl I grew up falling in love with.

Watching her allow herself to feel what she needs to feel, seems so much bigger than her simply shedding a few tears.

Hallie leans in and kisses me, whispering against my lips, "How lucky am I to have been loved by you for fifteen years now?"

"What do you say we get to work on making that number so high we start losing track?"

She smiles against my mouth. "I think we can do that."

"Happy birthday, baby."

"Thank you for making it my favorite one yet."

EPILOGUE

Rio

TWO MONTHS LATER

"Hey, guys. Come on in." Opening the front door, I let a group of my teammates into my house to join the party. "Food is in the kitchen and drinks are in the coolers out back. Help yourselves."

As I greet each of them, they look around the place. Other than Zanders, none of my teammates have been here since renovations began and this new home has become unrecognizable from the hockey frat house they're used to.

Every time someone new walks in the door, I get to enjoy watching their reactions to my girl's work. Hallie turned blank white walls into the most beautiful home I've ever seen. It's warm, inviting, and comfortable. It's a family home now, as it was always meant to be.

Before I leave the entryway, I grab a planter from the front porch to use as a door stop because I've answered the door too many times today. And this housewarming party is more of an open-door, everyone-is-welcome kind of thing anyway.

The house is packed, and the backyard is full of our friends, my teammates, and a few neighbors. The renovation got wrapped up about two weeks ago, but between our playoff schedule, Ryan's playoff schedule, and the Rhodes brothers being in the middle of baseball season, whether they're playing or coaching, it took some time to land on a date that worked for everyone.

But the house...*fuck*, the house is stunning.

The renovations were supposed to be done a few weeks earlier, but once we got home from Boston, Hallie and I had some honest conversations about the future we saw in this house. There were no more attempts at roundabout ways to make sure Hallie was designing her dream home. It was straightforward conversations about the kids we hope to have one day, what would work best for us when our families wanted to visit, and what we as a couple wanted our home to be.

The house was already headed into the family-friendly territory with the renovations anyway, but we took a few more weeks to make sure it was right for *our* future family.

On my way to the backyard, I find Hallie in the kitchen with a few of the other players' wives and girlfriends, showing them all the features she packed into it.

Leaning my shoulder against the wall, I watch her.

She's wearing this stunning smile as she gives them a tour of the cabinetry she chose, the new appliances, fixtures, and hardware. When they ask, she tells them all about the countertops and backsplash. About the lighting and the floors. She even shows them the coffee corner but gives me full credit for that.

She's fucking beaming and I love that. I love that she's proud of herself, and I love that this house is everything she wanted it to be.

I also love that it's hers.

She catches me watching out of her periphery and those freckled cheeks turn a sweet shade of rose. Slipping away from the group, she finds her way to me.

"I'm showing off your kitchen."

I wrap an arm around her waist, pulling her into me. "*Our* kitchen, you mean."

Hallie finally moved in with me after construction wrapped up, and it's been like a dream waking up with her each day.

It *is* a dream, I suppose. The one we dreamt of six years ago that's finally come to fruition.

"*Our* kitchen." She tilts her head back, chin on my chest. "Have you talked to your mom yet?"

There's nothing weary in Hallie's gaze when she mentions my mom, only pure excitement and love. They've been so good since that visit to Boston. My mom treats her as her own, just as she used to, and with Hallie's own mother no longer in the picture, I can see how much it means to her to have that type of relationship back in her life.

I think the two of them talk on the phone more often than my mom and I do, and when she came to visit last month, my mom spent most of that time with my girlfriend instead of me.

It's been a massive relief to see the two most important women in my life heal their relationship with each other and get to the place they're at now. The same place they were six years ago.

"I haven't talked to her yet," I tell Hallie, running my hand down her spine. "I'm going to go do that now."

"Do you want me to come with you?"

"Do you want to come with me?"

She shakes her head no. "I think that conversation should be between you two, but I want to make sure she knows I'm on board for it."

My smile blooms as I look down at her. I truly could not love this woman more than I already do.

But I thought that yesterday and the day before. Shit, I thought that a decade ago, and daily, I'm proven wrong. Because each new day, I fall for her a little more.

"I'll make sure she knows." Leaning down, I kiss her, right

there in our kitchen. In our home. "I love you, baby. Keep showing off the house."

"I love you too." With one more quick kiss, Hallie slips out of my hold and rejoins the group.

Music is playing as I walk outside, but it's not so loud that you can't have a conversation. I find my mom and my uncle Mikey talking with Ryan, Indy, and their kids.

I sling my arm over my mom's shoulders as I join, but Navy immediately hurls herself off her dad's body at me.

She drops her head against my shoulder as Indy and my mom continue their conversation.

"If the taste isn't coming through, it's most likely too thin. You need to reduce to a simmer and thicken that up to concentrate the flavor."

"I think I need to video call you next time," Indy decides.

"Or you could just ask me," I cut in. "I've perfected my mom's Bolognese."

Indy's eyes shoot to mine. "And why haven't you volunteered that information before?"

I shrug playfully. "It was kind of nice that you all took care of me all these years. I liked it. But yeah, I'm not bad in the kitchen."

My mom chuckles. "He's *great* in the kitchen, actually."

"Rio DeLuca," Indy says with accusation while Ryan just laughs next to her. "You're going to start cooking for family dinner."

"I can get on board for that." I turn to my mom. "Can we talk for a second?"

"Of course."

Ryan takes his daughter back while the two of us head to a quieter corner of the new back deck.

After Hallie and I got off the roof back in Boston, I went downstairs to talk to my mom. She apologized, and we talked through most everything. She was busy beating herself up over the way she handled my dad's affair, especially using her hurt to manipulate my feelings.

That was her choice of words, not mine. I never felt manipulated by her. I simply wanted to protect her. I still want to protect her, which is why I was nervous to break the news that I re-signed with Chicago for another six years.

She took it far better than I expected, and didn't seem all that surprised. But me deciding to stay, didn't mean I was no longer worried about her being alone all the way in Boston.

We lean against the deck railing, facing each other.

"Is everything okay, honey?"

"Yeah, I'm great," I tell her honestly.

A pleased smile lifts on her lips as she watches me. She knows I'm good, but I want to make sure *she* is.

"Hallie and I have been talking, and we were wondering what you thought about possibly moving here. To Chicago. I'd be happy to buy you a place, and we'd both love to have you closer."

My mom's eyes go impossibly wide, and I think for the first time in her life, this loud woman is speechless.

"I hate that you're all alone in that house," I continue. "I hate that you're alone, period."

"But I'm not alone."

Confusion cinches my forehead.

"I have a whole community there. I stay busy, Rio. You don't need to worry about me. Those families in the neighborhood are like my extended family. You know that."

"But the house. It's a lot of upkeep and I worry about that as you get older."

"Excuse me?"

"I mean, as you stay the exact same age of twenty-nine, just as you have been for my entire life."

"Thank you." A smile cracks on her lips before she pulls her eye contact away. "Your uncle Mikey helps me around that house."

"I know, but it's not like he's there all the time."

She tosses her head from side to side. "He's there most of the time."

"What do you mean?"

For a woman who has never been shy a day in her life, my mom is acting real coy right about now. "He and I..."

"You and him, what?"

"He and I"—she straightens her spine, meeting my eye—"have been seeing each other."

"Mikey?" My voice raises, pointing a finger in his general direction. "You're referring to my uncle Mikey. As in, my dad's brother?"

"Oh, don't sound so appalled." She brushes me off. "It's not like I met some random guy and brought him home. I've known him practically my whole life. In fact, I met him before I ever met your father. We've been friends for a long time, and last year, when he started coming around more...I don't know. Things changed."

I let that information sink in. My uncle and my dad haven't had the closest relationship, so Mikey wasn't around unless it was a holiday or a birthday. But he's a good man. For most of my life I wondered why the two of them didn't get along until I learned that my dad *wasn't* a good man.

"You're dating Mikey," I state in disbelief, leaning back on the fence. "Is it serious?"

"No, Rio, we're just talking." Her tone is laced with sarcasm. "I don't know how to answer that. Yes? It's not like we're going to run off and get married tomorrow, but we enjoy each other's company. At my ripe age of twenty-nine, that's all that matters. That's why it's so important that the person you're with is your friend."

"What happened to believing that childhood relationships don't work out because you grow up and grow apart? You've known him since you were a kid. How's that any different?"

Her expression softens. "Sometimes people can grow together. I was recently reminded of that by my son."

"Geez." I cross over my chest. "Mikey?"

I look in that direction to find him still chatting it up with Ryan and Indy. Don't get me wrong, I've always liked him. He's honest and kind, and I guess that's all you can really ask for in someone who's dating your mother.

I exhale a long breath. "Well, does he make you happy?"

A genuine smile curves on her lips, and I note the sparkle in her green eyes. It seems almost foreign because I haven't seen her look this elated in over six years.

She glances over her shoulder, and when she does, he catches her eye and grins softly at her.

"He does make me happy."

"He better."

Chuckling, my mom playfully smacks me in the arm.

"So, I take it that means you're not moving here."

She shakes her head no. "Maybe one day, but not right now. Boston is my home, just like Chicago is yours. Regardless of what happened in that house, it is still *my* house. I grew up there and your nonna grew up there. I want to keep it in our family, and even though you and Hallie don't see yourselves living there again, that house will be yours one day. I hope you take my grandbabies back there to show them where their parents first fell in love."

Slipping my arm over her shoulders, I pull her into my side. "We definitely will. That house will always stay in the family, so don't ever worry about that."

She pats my back. "But if you really wanted to find a way to get me to move here, you and Hallie girl could get to work on those grandbabies."

Laughing, I pull her in closer. "We will. Not yet, but one day, we will."

"Love you, Rio."

"I love you too, Ma."

Hallie and Wren exit the house through the back door, arms linked together as they chat about something. Wren's older brother, Cruz, follows behind, talking to Zee and Stevie.

"Go ahead. We'll catch up later." My mom pats my back before taking off to go find my uncle.

Still not fully wrapping my head around the idea of her dating again, I cross the yard to join my friends at the firepit. Ryan and Indy join too, where Kai, Miller, Isaiah, and Kennedy are already hanging out.

"Hey, Cruz." I put my hand in his. "Good to see you. Glad you could make it."

I give his sister a hug before standing behind Hallie, crossing my arms over the front of her shoulders and pulling her back to me. The twelve of us circle the firepit, some sitting and some of us standing.

"The house looks amazing," Cruz says. "But I've got to be honest, I am so thankful you didn't try to sell at the same time as me."

"Hey!" Hallie playfully cuts in.

"Don't get me wrong. My house is beautiful and sold for way over the asking price, but this place? You outdid yourself, Hallie."

She smiles proudly. "Well, thank you very much."

"When do you hand over the keys?" I ask Wren.

"Tomorrow." There's an edge of sadness in her tone, but I know most of her is looking forward to moving home. "Cruz is in town to help me finish packing up the moving truck, and we'll start the cross-country drive in the morning."

"I'm going to miss you," my girl says.

Wren's expression turns a bit sorrowful as she looks at her former roommate. "I'm going to miss you too. You'll come visit though, right?"

"Definitely. Rio and I are already looking for a good time that'll work with his hockey schedule."

"You're welcome anytime," Cruz cuts in. "You're never going to get bad weather, regardless of the time of year. And our family's property is pretty spacious. There's plenty of room for you to stay."

"You mean, for *all* of us to stay?" Ryan asks.

There's a collective laugh among the group, though Cruz and

Wren don't pick up on it. And why would they? Who would expect Ryan fucking Shay to be a fanboy, but we've quickly come to learn that he's a huge fan of the Wilder brothers.

"Absolutely," Cruz says. "I'm pretty sure my brothers would freak the fuck out if Ryan Shay came to visit."

"Let alone the whole town," Wren adds.

Kennedy cuts in. "How close are you to San Francisco?"

"Not too far, but far enough that it doesn't feel anything like a big city," Wren explains.

"We live in a pretty small town," Cruz adds. "But our family's land is large enough that we each have our own slice of it. Soon, all four of us have our own homes there, but my brothers and I each have our own place in the city too so we don't have to commute every day while we're in season."

"That sounds amazing," Stevie says. "You all kind of live together, but separately."

"Exactly." Wren grins, turning to Hallie. "My house is the last to get built, so anytime you want to come decorate for me, you're welcome."

"I'd love that."

"Do you need help getting anything into the moving truck?" Zee offers.

"Actually, yeah. That'd be great." Cruz throws a thumb over his shoulder. "There are a few big items we could use some help lifting."

All the guys move to head next door, but when I do the same, Ryan stops me. "Rio, it's cool. You're hosting a party. We'll be right back."

I narrow my eyes suspiciously. "Don't do anything embarrassing, Shay. Wren is my friend. Please don't go asking her a million questions about her brothers."

He has the least innocent smile on his face. "I have no idea what you're talking about."

Ryan jogs off to join the rest of the group, and I turn to find

Indy who can't stop laughing. "He sounds exactly like you when you're busy fanboying over him."

When the rest of the girls disperse, some chasing after their kids and others going for a drink refill, I take a seat, pulling Hallie onto my lap as the fire roars in front of us. The sun is starting to go down and the hanging bistro lights have just flipped on. It's perfect.

"How'd it go with your mom?" she asks.

"Oh my God, Hal. You're never going to believe this, but she and my uncle Mikey are together."

"Well, of course they are, baby." Hallie laughs, gesturing in their direction. "Look at them. Look at the way he looks at her. He's totally in love with your mom."

I wince before I school my expression, simply because it's strange to think about my mother with someone. But then I note exactly what Hallie is talking about when I see the way Mikey looks over at her, watching her speak to someone. He watches her like she sets the sun.

He watches her like I watch this girl in my lap.

"He is, isn't he?"

"Kind of makes you wonder," Hallie says. "He never married. He never brought anyone around in all the years I knew him. Maybe he's always felt that way about your mom."

"What are you saying?" I ask with a laugh. "That my dad just got there first?"

"I could see it. He and your dad never got along. It's not that farfetched to think he may have been pining for her all this time."

"Okay, let's stop romanticizing my mom's love life. And God..." I grimace. "Don't ever let me use the words 'love life' and 'my mom' in the same sentence ever again."

Hallie chuckles against me, her head resting on my shoulder.

We sit there a while, silently observing the party around us. Everyone is having a good time, flowing in and out of the house.

Our house.

"We did good, Hallie Hart."

Her smile tilts. "We did do good. This is the first of many."

This house will host future birthday parties and celebrations, maybe even a few family dinners. We'll have our friends over. One day, our kids will have their friends over, and I'm looking forward to giving our future family the same sense of home and community that Hallie and I were raised with back in our old neighborhood.

Hallie slips an arm over my shoulders as she sits in my lap, and as she watches the party happen around us, I can practically see the same picture being painted in her head of our future here.

"I love you, Hal."

She turns back, smiling at me. "I love you, Rio. Always have. Always will."

Hallie leans her head against mine as I hold her.

Before, when we were kids, I felt lucky. Love fell into our hands. We were neighbors turned friends who eventually fell in love. But this time, it feels like we earned it. We get to be in love because we worked for it. We decided to forgive and understand one another.

This second chance doesn't feel like luck. It feels like a reward.

"Look who made it," I say as Hallie's dad and brother walk out into the backyard.

I go to stand, but Hallie doesn't move from my lap.

"He looks good, right?" From this distance, she watches him.

He does look good. He looks healthy and sturdier than the last time we saw him. There's more color in his skin. He's gained a bit of weight.

"He looks really good."

A relieved smile ghosts her lips, and when I go to stand, she stops me again. "Wait. Rio, look."

I follow her line of sight to watch as my mom and her dad make eye contact from across the yard. Mr. Hart freezes in place, as does my mom.

As far as I know, they haven't seen or spoken to each other since the day they both found out about their spouses, regardless that they were great friends prior. I didn't exactly think this through when I invited them both here.

It sounds like the music has cut out. It feels like the yard has emptied. All I can do is focus on the two of them and pray that this goes okay.

Mr. Hart's face lights up with a smile, and I watch a mirrored one lift on my mom's lips before she quickly crosses the yard to meet him.

They hug. They hug the way you do when you see a long-lost friend again, because that's exactly what they are.

Fuck, that kind of makes me want to cry. It makes me feel more emotional than I assumed it would. Checking on Hallie, I can tell she feels the same way with her pink nose and sheen-coated eyes.

After so many years, this portion of the DeLuca and Hart families is okay again.

"Let's go say hi," I suggest, and this time when I go to stand, Hallie stands with me.

Holding hands, we make our way to our families, but once we're close, Hallie lets go of me and quickly wraps her dad in a hug.

"Hallie girl." Closing his eyes, he holds his daughter tightly. "Missed you."

"I missed you too, Dad."

With the renovation and my hockey schedule, we haven't been able to make a trip back to Minnesota since we were there in the hospital. But we have a week-long trip planned to stay at Luke's place in mid-June and they're all headed back here for the Fourth of July.

Speaking of Luke, after he hugs my mom, he turns to me.

"Hey, man," I say with a smile.

"The house is sick."

"That was all your sister."

Stepping forward, he opens his arms, and we quickly embrace.

We've talked a few times and it's been nice, shooting the shit and catching up. I missed my old friend and I'm glad to have him back in my life.

I hug his wife too then bend down to the little guy holding on to his dad's leg.

"This is Hudson," Luke says, hand on his head. "Hudson, this is our friend, Rio."

"Hey, little man." I hold my fist out and after a beat, Hudson smiles at it and slams his own fist as hard as he can against it. "Oh, dang!" I shake out my hand. "You're super strong."

Hudson giggles and holds out his fist to do it again. He keeps pounding his against mine until he spots Hallie and instead moves to his aunt to say hello.

I stand and find her dad.

"Hey, Mr. Hart." As I hug him, he pats my back a couple of times. "I'm so glad you guys could make it."

"Thank you for the invite. I'm looking forward to checking out the house."

"Hal, you should take them on a tour. Show them everything you've done."

She smiles excitedly and though I'd love to go with her, I know she wants to show off for her dad. And in equal measure, I know he wants to witness her living out her dreams, especially after she put them on hold for so long.

In fact, just last week, he and I discussed that on the phone. Well, the purpose of that phone call was for an entirely different reason that's currently hidden in my pocket, but I also made sure he knew I was taking care of his daughter like he asked me to. I made sure he knew that Hallie was happy because at the end of the day, that's all he wants for her.

Hallie's energy is palpable as she guides her family back into the house, explaining everything that's been changed. I can't help the stupid fucking smile on my face as I watch her in her element. It's permanent these days, I swear.

Back at the firepit, I find the guys have returned from Wren's house, so I take a seat with the four of them as Isaiah hands me a beer.

Leaning forward, we all clink our bottles in a cheers.

"So." Zee takes a swig of his drink. "You've got the house. You've got the girl. What's next?"

Looking over my shoulder to make sure no one is looking, especially Hallie, I pull the ring out of my pocket. "Need to ask her for forever."

Checking their surroundings too like some kind of secret boys' club, they all lean forward. Zee takes the ring first before passing it around so they can all examine it.

"Hell yeah, Rio." Kai clinks his bottle with mine.

"It turned out amazing." Ryan turns the ring over in his fingers, looking over it from every angle. "Indy told me about it, but it's so much better than I could've imagined."

The engagement ring isn't a family heirloom or anything like that. We don't exactly have the greatest track record with marriages in our family, so this is brand new and all Hallie's. And yeah, one day it'll become something we'll be able to pass down, but she'll be the first to wear it.

Indy came with me to my initial appointment with the jeweler, but once we were there, I realized I didn't need as much help as I thought I would. There's no one who knows my future wife better than me.

The mix of white and yellow gold in the band screams Hallie Hart and I can't wait to see it on her hand. Which is fitting that it's going to happen tonight, seeing as she just got her nails done and painted each finger a different color.

The ring makes it back to me and I carefully tuck it back into my pocket.

"Do you think she'll say yes?" Isaiah asks.

We all whip our heads in his direction.

He holds his hands up. "What? It's a valid question."

Kai smacks his brother on the shoulder. "I guess he could always take her to Vegas and get her drunk to make sure she agrees to marry him."

A sneaky smile lifts on his lips. "That did work well for me."

Chuckling, I shake my head. "She's going to say yes. We've been talking about getting married since...*fuck*, I can't even remember. Feels like we've always known we'd marry each other."

"When are you going to do it?" Zee asks.

"Tonight, after you all leave."

Ryan takes a swig of his drink. "And how?"

"I'm going to take her on the roof of the house and do it there."

All four of them look at me like I've lost my goddamn mind, but I swear, if I would've told their wives my plan instead of them, I'd be rewarded with resounding approval from all four of those women.

And they wonder why I like attending girls' night.

But I don't feel the need to explain the significance of that proposal location to anyone else. She'll understand it. Hallie and I fell in love on the roof that connected our parents' homes. I'm going to ask her to spend forever with me on the roof of ours.

Max Rhodes comes padding over to his dad, huffing and puffing from all his running around. He chugs from a straw of a water bottle that Kai holds out for him, and without saying a word, turns and runs back to continue playing with the other kids.

Four of them—Max, Taylor, Navy, and Iverson are running around chasing one another, but Emmy is upstairs sleeping in one of the spare rooms. Kai's phone is sitting on the armrest of his chair with the baby monitor connected and displayed on the screen.

"Are you and Hallie going to add to that crew?" Ryan asks, nodding towards the kids.

"Hopefully, one day. But she's spent so long taking care of someone else, I want to make sure Hallie gets to do everything she wants to do before we start trying. But yes, eventually, we want to."

Zee clinks his bottle with mine. "Good man."

The girls are gathered on the back deck, talking and laughing with each other. Hallie joins the other four after taking her family on a house tour, and as soon as she does, Miller wraps her arm over her shoulders and pulls her into the conversation as if she's been a part of it the whole time.

She looks so at ease, like she's known them for so much longer than she has.

Hallie just fits, but that's no surprise. She's always been outgoing and friendly, and now, I'm even more thankful she is who she is. Jumping into a very well-established group of nine friends would've been intimidating for just about anyone else, but not her. We were always meant to find our way back to each other, and she was always meant to be a part of this group.

There's not a world in which I could imagine anything different.

I watch as each of my friends catch their partner's attention from across the yard. I've witnessed this happening for years. This silent check-in in a crowded room. A soft smile before continuing their conversation. A discreet wink. A little smirk.

I've constantly felt like the third wheel catching a private moment I wasn't supposed to be a part of, but at the same time, it was something I longed for in my own life.

I've always wanted what my friends had.

I always wanted what *I* once had.

With my attention locked on the group of women, Hallie is mid-conversation when those hazel eyes find mine from across the yard. She holds eye contact for a long while, still talking, still fully engaged and when the smile lifts on my mouth, it reflects on hers.

She's everything I've ever wanted, everything I've been looking for. Everything I was so desperate to find because I had already found her once and knew she was missing from my life.

The five of them migrate our way, and though they could not be more different from one another, they get along so well.

Hallie slides onto my lap, while the others find their way to their person.

Then it's the ten of us. How it was always supposed to be.

The sun has set, but there's still enough of a glow to see the contented smile on Hallie's lips. "I could get used to this life," she says quietly.

"It looks good on you."

Her hazels sparkle. "I love you."

I chuckle because damn, I'm never going to get over hearing her say that to me. "Hallie baby, I love you."

"Rio," Indy calls from across the firepit, sitting on her husband's lap. "Ryan has something he wants to tell you."

We all shift our attention his way.

"Uh..." he stumbles, and Indy gives him an encouraging nod. "I just wanted you to know that..." He clears his throat. "I love you, man."

My eyes go comically wide while everyone else stays perfectly silent.

I've been waiting to hear him say that for years.

"I don't know, Ryan." I toss my head from side to side, studying him from across the firepit. "It just didn't hit the way I always imagined it would."

"Oh, get fucked!"

Laughter bounces off everyone in the group.

Miller chuckles. "It doesn't help that Hallie told him she loved him about two seconds before Ryan did. Not sure how you're supposed to top that."

"Yeah, well..." Ryan huffs. "I used to be the love of his life."

Hallie smiles at him. "Sorry about that, Ryan."

"Who would've thought," Indy says. "Rio found someone he loves more than my husband."

I press a kiss to Hallie's shoulder before wrapping my arms around her middle. "Ryan, I love you too, man. Less than her, but I still love you. I love all of you." I look around at the entire group.

"Friends are the family you choose, and I've got to say, I've got the best family a guy could ask for."

"Absolutely."

"Hell yeah."

"That's right," is echoed around me as everyone leans forward to connect whatever they're drinking in a cheers.

We all take a drink before Hallie leans back against my chest, and conversation continues as it always does. Laughing with each other, a bit of shit-talking, and of course the real stuff too.

I just sit back and watch nine of the most important people in my life.

I'm the luckiest man alive, I swear.

When I was younger, I remember how much I wished I had a sibling. Someone to play hockey with. Someone to talk to. Someone who understood me.

Little did I know, as a grown man, I'd end up with eight of them.

These girls are practically my sisters, and there's no question that these guys have become my brothers.

I spent years complaining about being the single one of the group, the odd man out. But even though I was the last one, how lucky am I that I got a front-row seat to watch each of my best friends fall in love?

I watched Zanders strip the façade he wore for so long to allow the flight attendant on his team's plane to see the real him.

I watched Stevie learn to love herself the way the arrogant hockey player who followed her everywhere loves her. The way we all do.

I watched Indy come out of a relationship she wasn't meant for and learn to be loved in a new, quieter way.

I watched Ryan allow someone into his home and his heart after shutting everyone else out for so long, only for the brightest ray of sunshine to move in and light every dark space she could touch.

I watched Kai learn to ask for help, only for that help to come in the form of a firecracker pastry chef who taught him how to have fun again.

I watched Miller stop running and grow deeper roots than she ever thought she could by falling in love with a single dad and his little boy.

I watched Kennedy learn how to love and be loved thanks to her husband who refused to go a day without showering her with it.

I watched Isaiah persist in showing his wife exactly who he was behind the smile, all while keeping his heart open for the only woman he wanted to have it.

I watched Hallie, with so much goddamn pride, as her heart softened again. She forgave me while also continuing to stand up for herself along the way.

And I...well, I found love because it was always out there, waiting for me, even when I questioned its existence. In fact, I found it right next door—where it had always been.

I feel so incredibly blessed that I get to go through life with these nine people.

Besides Indy, we're all a bunch of transplants from other places who found a home in the windy city...and with each other.

I'll speak for all ten of us when I say, there's nowhere else we'd rather be.

THE END

You didn't think I forgot about Monty, did you?!

Turn the page for a sneak peek of my next book!

1

EMMETT MONTGOMERY

I s this the beginning of the end?

It feels like the beginning of the end.

At what point do I *know* this is my fate? That this is my last first day here. My last first staff meeting. My last first 'hello' to the coworkers I haven't seen in months.

An off-season has never felt shorter.

Typically, I'm itching for baseball to return, counting down the days until winter is over, but not this year. This year, I've dreaded the idea of returning to my office at the field, knowing my every move is going to be analyzed.

Because this season, I have a brand-new boss—one who no longer sees me as the right fit to be the field manager for Chicago's MLB team, even though I've held the position for seven years now.

This morning, the film room is buzzing with noise. Every person who works for the Windy City Warriors, outside of the players, is packed in the stadium-style seats. This is the room we use to go over game film to prepare for an upcoming opponent, or when a one-on-one session is needed to make corrections.

Today though, we're sandwiched in here for our first meeting with the new team owner.

Reese Remington.

The thirty-five-year-old is the granddaughter of the previous owner, a guy who held the title almost as long as I've been alive, an owner who allowed me to run my team the way I saw fit.

His granddaughter, however, judging by our interactions last season, when she was simply training to take over, will be anything but hands-off.

Kai nudges my elbow with his from his seat next to mine. "What time do you want to meet tomorrow to go over the pitching lineup?"

"Let's say 11:30."

"I might have Max with me. I hope that's okay."

I give my future son-in-law a deadpanned glare. "Of course that's okay, Ace."

He chuckles. "I don't think you can keep calling me Ace. You're going to have a new Ace pitcher this season. We just need to figure out who that is."

I brush him off. "You're always going to be Ace. Good luck to the next guy."

Kai, or Ace as we call him, was the Windy City Warriors Ace pitcher ever since he came to the team four years ago. That is, until he retired at the end of last season, leaving me without my go-to guy on the mound.

But as much as I'm going to miss being able to count on him every few starts, I'm even more proud of him for making the decision that was best for his family. Especially because that family now includes my daughter.

A couple of years ago, the two of them met when Miller spent the summer nannying for Kai's son and the rest is history. I couldn't imagine a better man for my girl, and now seeing Miller so calm and at peace here in Chicago with him and Max, it's hard to remember the wild child I raised who once never felt settled in one place.

As proud of Kai as I am for calling it quits when the timing felt right, he was missing the game before spring training even ended.

So, though I may not have him on my roster anymore, I now have him on my coaching staff.

Perks of being the field manager of a Major League baseball team. I get to hire my own staff and there's no one more qualified to be my new pitching coach than Kai Rhodes.

The door to the packed and rowdy room opens and my body instantly tenses, expecting *her*, but when a short redhead with a bouncing ponytail and three coffees balanced in her hands ambles through the entry, I relax back into my chair.

"Did I miss anything?" Kennedy asks, taking the empty seat on my other side before passing Kai and me each one of the coffees.

"Not yet." I hold my cup up. "Thank you for this."

"Anytime, Monty."

"Happy first day, Dr. Rhodes."

My words cause Kai to beam from the seat next to me, looking over at his sister-in-law.

A heat creeps up her cheeks. "Thank you."

Kennedy is not only the new team doctor, but also married to one of the players— Kai's little brother, Isaiah.

The Rhodes brothers have become a part of my family since we all landed in Chicago. There are times I take on a more fatherly role for them when they need it. There's not a huge age difference between us, just over a decade, so other times, I'm simply their friend.

Yes, they've both been my players and me their coach, but our bond is a whole lot tighter than that. It just so happens that Kai is marrying my daughter soon and Isaiah married the team doctor who I work with closely, so it's one big clusterfuck of non-blood related family.

"We'll see you guys for dinner tonight?" Kai asks.

She nods. "We'll be there."

"Same," I confirm.

Even though the film room is loud, I can hear the squeak of the door perfectly clear, and the sound has tension rippling through every one of my muscles.

Reese is the last to arrive and as soon as one high heel is past the threshold, my attention is immediately on her.

Short blonde hair cuts sharply below her jaw. A charcoal-gray pencil skirt paints her curves. Navy-blue eyes that are impossible to read, cooly assess the room.

And when they slice to me, they silently scream how much she doesn't like me.

Well, I take it back. I guess she's pretty fucking easy to read when it comes to me.

The unimpressed stare lasts only a second before she pulls her attention away and continues to the podium at the front of the room.

I don't know what it is about me that bothers her so much, that's caused such a bad taste in her mouth, but I feel the same way towards her.

However, I have my reasons.

First of all, the woman spent the entirety of last season reminding me that her first year as the official team owner is the same year I'm up for a new contract. Like she needed to verbally remind me that the fate of my career lies in the palm of her hands this season.

Secondly, she's already been on my ass about schedules, budgets, and reallocating funds, as if *I'm* the reason certain departments of the organization are operating in the red and not because her grandfather didn't have the energy to keep up. Truthfully, there's not an ounce of me that wants anything to do with the backend of how the club is run as long as my players are taken care of. I just want to coach baseball.

And lastly, her biggest fault of all...she looks like *that*.

My new boss is not only a pain in my ass, but she's also fucking *stunning* and the first woman my body has decided to pay attention to in God knows how long.

Eventually the rest of me will get the memo that we don't like her, it just might not be until I'm packing up my desk at the end of the season because my new boss refuses to extend my coaching contract.

"You good?" Kai nudges my arm.

I clear my throat. "Yeah, of course."

"Okay." The word is laced with this annoyingly knowing tone that doesn't go unnoticed when he leans over to Kennedy and the two of them share a look.

"I saw that," I mutter.

"We weren't trying to hide it," Kennedy laughs.

Standing in the front of the room, Reese says something to the audience, but the crowd is so rowdy, everyone so excited to see their coworkers after the off-season that no one pays attention or tries to hear her.

I watch as her throat works its way through a swallow, like she's pushing down the nerves, hands tightly fisted to the podium. And I get it. Not only is she the first female team owner that the MLB has ever seen, but she's also the youngest.

But Reese is a boss. Not just *my* boss, but a gets-things-done, doesn't-take-shit-from-anyone *boss*. I saw it last year while she was training for this new role. She's the reason Kennedy is here and taking over the position she should've had years ago. Reese saw what her grandfather didn't—that the previous team doctor was a sexist piece of shit—and handled it. She fired him and gave Kennedy his job, making her the first female team doctor in the league.

As much as I don't personally love the idea of working for someone who doesn't want me here, Reese will be a breath of fresh air for this organization. But first, she needs to get through this staff meeting.

She opens her mouth to speak again, but no words come out, nerves holding her back, the room too preoccupied with their own chatter to realize she's here and asking for their attention. Her knuckles go white from her firm grip around the podium, her knees slightly shaking which I can only see because I'm sitting in the front row.

The laughter and chat behind me is pissing me off for her.

Fuck. I internally berate myself for what I'm about to do. Blame it on my daughter. She's the reason I'm so damn soft.

"Hey!" I stand up, turning to face the room from my seat, and all eyes immediately fall to me. "Let's have a little fucking respect, why don't we?"

The room goes silent at my tone.

"Fuck's sake," I mutter under my breath.

Sure, I come off like a grumpy bastard most of the time, a little intimidating with my build and tattoos, but anyone who knows me knows I'm a nice fucking guy until you piss me off. And this is pissing me off.

I retake my seat, feeling Reese's eyes on me and it takes a moment for me to return the eye contact and look up at her.

She gives me a curt nod, her tone all professional when she says, "Thank you for that, Emmett."

And then there's that... *Emmett.*

She's the only person in all of Chicago who uses my first name when everyone else calls me by my nickname. And I know she does it on purpose, like she's refusing to allow any sort of comfortability between us. It's as if she's once again reminding me that she's my boss, I'm her employee, and regardless of how much time we're about to spend together this season, we aren't friends and we're never going to be.

It'll make it that much easier for her to fire me at the end of the year.

Fucking great.

"For those of you who don't know me, I'm Reese Remington." With the room silent, she confidently begins her first staff meeting. "The new owner of the Windy City Warriors."

ACKNOWLEDGMENTS

This is probably going to be a bit long-winded, but I write 400+ page books, so are we really all that surprised? Grab a snack and take a seat. I just finished my very first series (that's so wild to type out) so I'm going to take my time with this one.

First, as always, I need to thank you all—the readers. If it weren't for your love and excitement for my books, I wouldn't have the chance to tell stories for a living. When I first started this series, I was a flight attendant for a hockey team (hello, MILE HIGH plotline), and I kept that job until I finished PLAY ALONG. Writing REWIND IT BACK was the first time I wrote a book as a full-time author. Even though I've been writing for years now, when people asked me what I did for work, I would always tell them that I was a flight attendant. Mostly, because saying that I was an author seemed unrealistic and a bit of a pipe dream. The other day, I was in my local coffee shop finishing the last few chapters of this book and the barista asked what I did for work. It was the first time I can remember saying, "I'm an author" out loud and it was this wild moment of realization—that I get to tell stories, live in my imagination, share my love of romance, and call it my job, all because of your guys' love for this series. So, THANK YOU for making my dreams come true. I am truly so grateful for you.

This part is a bit heavier, but it's such an integral part of how this book came to be. When I plotted this book out, especially Hallie's storyline, I thought it was going to be therapeutic for me to write about the feelings surrounding having a sick parent at such a young age. I also spent most of my twenties and early thirties worried over a sick parent, but luckily for me, unlike Hallie, I had a very involved brother who always shared that responsibility. The week I started writing this book, my mom went into the hospital. For the entirety of the three months it took me to write this book, she stayed in the hospital, and suddenly those old feelings I thought would feel therapeutic to get down on paper, were my current reality again. There were times I wanted to reconsider Hallie's storyline because my real life was heavy enough, but then she became this safe place to spill exactly how I was feeling at the time. It *was* therapeutic to write, but in a different sense than I originally believed. Hallie became exactly what I needed at exactly the right time.

All that being said, the second person I need to thank is my brother, Andrew. If it wasn't for him stepping up and taking on my mom's needs so I could put my head down and write, I never would've finished this book on time.

To Allyson, who has been here since the beginning. Well, you've been here since I first told you I wrote a book (which was about a year after I had written it because I kept that secret from all my friends and family for as long as possible). So you've *basically* been with me from the beginning, and I'm so grateful for you! I can't believe we've been talking about you coming to work with me for years now, and it has finally happened! I'm so lucky to have you as one of my best friends and it's a dream to have you a part of my team now.

To Sierra and Chas. Thank you for everything you do! Whether that be creating content, hyping me up during my first draft, or sending me crying selfies. Love you both.

To Sam, my PA, who has been since shortly after I published MILE HIGH, I'm so grateful to have you on my team and appreciate you.

To Acacia, thank you for creating the stunning skyline covers that have become such a recognizable brand for this series. I am so grateful for your creativity and what it has done for my books.

To Erica, I can't believe we just finished a whole series together! I am so grateful for you and your friendship. Your insight is always so valuable to me, and I feel so lucky to have you in my corner.

To Jess and the SDLA team, because of you, I now get to see my books in stores! Thank you so much for all the work you put in behind the scenes to make my books successful and more accessible to readers.

To Lucy and the Hodder team & Jessica T and the Entangled team, thank you for taking a chance on me and this series. It's been incredible to not only have the opportunity to have my books in stores, but to also have the support of all of you behind me.

And to Marc—five for five, my friend. TTP, you know what I mean??

Don't miss the exciting new books
Entangled has to offer.

Follow us!

@EntangledPublishing

@Entangled_Publishing

@EntangledPub